GENTLE ARROGANCE

FRANK HELLER

Black Rose Writing | Texas

ISBN: 978-1-68513-450-1
PUBLISHED BY BLACK ROSE WRITING
www.blackrosewriting.com

Printed in the United States of America
Suggested Retail Price (SRP) $24.95

Gentle Arrogance is printed in Book Antiqua

*As a planet-friendly publisher, Black Rose Writing does its best to eliminate unnecessary waste to reduce paper usage and energy costs, while never compromising the reading experience. As a result, the final word count vs. page count may not meet common expectations.

Praise for
Gentle Arrogance

2024 Maxy Award for General Fiction

Gentle Arrogance

Jamie Williams, a brown-eyed boy of fourteen, thought the Spring of 1965 had been remarkably turbulent, but not in a meteorological way. In late March, when his father announced—pontifically, Jamie thought—that he had been called to pastor a church in Louisiana, thunder rolled, and lightning flashed. High-strung and hot-tempered, Jamie considered pitching a walleyed fit, but pitching a fit, he knew, would accomplish nothing. His father was a church-freak, full of Christian crap, and to Calvin Williams what God wanted took precedence over everything, including family.

Jamie admitted there had been times when leaving Hot Springs would have been a godsend. In the seventh grade, for example, he had to fight Jeffrey Davis, a big redhead, to get him off his back. Then, in the eighth grade, Dalton Hilliard, a prominent attorney's son, tried to make his life miserable when Jamie earned the starting quarterback position on the Central Junior High School football team. Dalton, however, did not have the balls to fight him, and the stuck-up blueblood had backed down, proving he was all bluster but an enemy worth watching.

Tall for his age, lithe and graceful, and already a basketball phenom, Jamie played football simply because the Hot Springs School District required its athletes to take part in every sport.

Forcing basketball players to wear pads and knock the hell out of each other was, in Jamie's opinion, like training chihuahuas to be guard dogs; their attitudes were fine, but their bark and bite did not generate fear in burglars and thieves. Truth be known, Jamie's passion had been, and always would be, basketball, since the first time he popped the net when his older brother tried to break his nose by throwing a basketball at him hard, fast, and head-high.

Leaving Hot Springs was, in Jamie's opinion, a dumb thing to do. But in early June, after an incredibly stormy spring, he wandered through the vacant parsonage that had been his home for fourteen years and felt as empty as the house. But what could he do? He was fourteen years old, shackled to the whims of his parents, moving to Louisiana, and there was not a damned thing he could do about it.

•   •   •

The disgusting smell of rotten eggs oozed thickly up Jamie's nostrils when Calvin Williams drove the rented U-Haul across the Pearl River into Bogalusa, Louisiana. Why his father wanted to live in a septic tank that smelled worse than a dead skunk was a mystery to Jamie, but he was old enough to know that life is full of mysteries, accepted the inevitable, and stared out the window at the smog filled town that was now his home.

Fifteen minutes later, after several crooks and turns down unfamiliar streets, Calvin Williams backed the U-Haul into the driveway of a small, gray house dotted with pine trees. Several men from Trinity Baptist church were waiting on the front porch to help the new pastor unload the truck and set up the parsonage.

Gene Forester, a gray-headed man sporting a crew cut, beamed, and extended his hand with a wide swoop. "I reckon y'all didn't have any trouble getting here, did you, Preacher?"

"No, Gene, we didn't."

Forrester glanced at Jamie and smiled. "And who is this young man?"

"My youngest son Jamie."

"It's good to meet you, boy. What do you think of our little town?"

"It smells bad enough to gag a maggot."

Calvin Williams rolled his eyes.

Gene Forester leaned his head back and guffawed. "You'll get used to it, boy. That's bacon and eggs you smell."

"Bacon and eggs?" Jamie asked incredulously.

"I mean," Forester replied with the deepest drawl Jamie had ever heard, "that's money you smell, boy, it puts food on the table, and it won't be long till that ole paper mill smells as good to you as it does to everyone else in this here town."

Jamie listened to Gene Forester's lecture on bacon and eggs—politely, of course—then turned and scanned the neighborhood. The parsonage was small, well-kept, and the yard was big. He found a large pine tree to hang his basketball goal on and noticed there was not a garage to park the car in. A narrow creek bordered the backyard—he thought that might be fun in time—and there were plenty of houses in the neighborhood, which meant there should be kids his age to hang around with.

For a moment, Jamie thought Bogalusa might not be so bad after all, but then he heard thunder in the distance and decided that he should not count his chickens before they hatched.

CHAPTER 1

Volatile winds of change were stirring up dust, water, and the souls of men in Bogalusa, Louisiana. Integration, an old word used in a new way, had caused the tempest, as if a late summer hurricane had moved inland, breaking hearts instead of buildings.

Two words, "civil rights," — the people who believed in them and the people who did not — generated the storm that had transformed Columbia Road, Bogalusa's main street, into a bizarre carnival, where blacks, carrying signs of protest, boycotted white merchants, while the Ku Klux Klan kept a wary eye on its invisible domain.

The issue was State's Rights, the battle-cry of the Old South. Bogalusa's white population did not believe the Federal Government had the authority to force integration on autonomous communities and had, therefore, become more than a little suspicious of outsiders, regarding them as Northern Instigators, freethinking liberals who had moved south to help people of color attain equal rights. Sadly, the once open society closed, and the residents began shunning new arrivals, often verbally abusing them. Jamie Williams found himself caught in the maelstrom.

At first, Jamie tried to like his new home. His peers — on the surface — seemed friendly, but they never allowed him to get close. In fact, every time he approached a potential friend, there was an aloofness, a coolness, an invisible wall with no gates. For the first time in his life, Jamie felt like an outsider, someone to look through and ignore.

To Jamie's surprise, fitting in had not been a problem for his older brother. Bud had met a girl, Judith Webb. She had introduced him to several kids his age, and his transition had been smooth. Once school started, Jamie hoped he would find his niche, but to his chagrin, storm clouds gathered, thunder rolled, and lightning flashed the first day he walked through the doors of Bogalusa Junior High School.

•   •   •

Rick Cullin nodded at the new kid walking down the hall and said to his friends, "Watch this." They laughed, knowing the new kid's welcome would be more than a little interesting. Lanky, and curly-headed, Rick believed Nathan Bedford Forrest had called him from the grave to show new students—who were probably Northern Instigators anyway—their subservient position at Bogalusa Junior High School.

Smiling arrogantly, Rick grabbed Jamie's arm when he approached his first-period classroom. Jamie ignored the fingernails digging holes in his left arm.

"Who the hell are you, new-boy?"

"I'm Jamie Williams."

"Where you from, Jamie Williams?"

"Hot Springs, Arkansas."

"I'll be damned, boys, we got us a hillbilly." Rick snorted and squeezed Jamie's arm tighter. "And look at them shiny new shoes. Is that your first pair? I hear you hillbillies run around barefoot all the time."

Jamie considered coldcocking the asshole with the sharp fingernails. It was important, he believed, to let potential adversaries know he would not take their garbage. Jerking his arm free, he gave the asshole an icy stare, then walked into the classroom and sat down at an empty desk.

Dumbfounded, Rick could not believe he had not intimidated the new kid. New kids usually broke out in a cold sweat when he welcomed them to school, but Jamie Williams had not broken out in a cold sweat. He had, Rick noticed, mean eyes, and had given him a go-to-hell look that had made his spine tingle.

Rick could not let that stand.

If anyone, especially an outsider, found a crack in his armor, his reign of terror would come to a screeching halt. Knowing he had to assert his dominance, Rick followed Jamie into the classroom, leaned against the teacher's desk, crossed his arms, and cleared his throat loudly.

Catching up after summer break, the students turned and faced the front of the room. Rick was not popular, or even well-liked, but his off-the-wall antics, especially with new students, were often amusing, and usually worth watching.

"I hate to tell y'all this, but a new Instigator just checked into our school."

He pointed at Jamie.

"And this one's a hillbilly from Arkansas."

Several students giggled.

"I want y'all to notice his new shoes."

Loud whistles echoed off the wall.

"Being a hillbilly, y'all know he's never worn shoes before."

More laughter.

A girl sitting behind Jamie patted his shoulder, an obvious sign of sympathy, but he did not have time to think about that. The curly-headed jerk needed his ass kicked, and Jamie had decided that he was more than capable of filling that need. Before he could slip out of his desk and take care of business, however, the teacher walked into the classroom and unwittingly prevented the confrontation.

Pleased that he had shown the cocky outsider who was King of the Hill, Rick sauntered to his desk, blissfully ignorant of the fact that he had just scheduled an appointment with disaster. Jamie Williams did not take garbage from anyone, especially curly-headed cretins who made new students feel like stinking sacks of week-old garbage.

Jamie moved from class to class as the morning progressed and quickly concluded that Bogalusa Junior High School was a powder keg waiting for a spark; whites associated with whites, blacks with blacks, and no one crossed the invisible barrier. In fact, Ole Jim Crow ruled the place with an iron fist, even the restrooms, where black students and Yankee Instigators were not welcome. The one time Jamie went to take a leak, a pack of irate punks pushed him from wall to wall and threatened to drown him in a urinal filled with disgusting yellow water. Jamie's temper flared, but he bit his tongue and escaped out the door unscathed.

Jamie looked out the window during third period and saw the morning PE class playing flag football. Whooping and hollering, the boys were obviously enjoying themselves. A little physical activity, Jamie hoped, might improve his less than favorable impression of Bogalusa Junior High School. Surely, there had to be someone—maybe in PE?—who was not a condescending asshole. Two hours later, that hope quickly faded when he walked into Rebel Field House for the first time.

Jamie noticed he had to walk through a poorly lit tunnel beneath the bleachers to reach the dressing-room. When he reached the middle of the tunnel, four boys stepped out from behind a boiler, grabbed him by the neck, and pulled him to the floor. Warily—the hillbilly had mean eyes—Rick Cullin pressed a knee against Jamie's chest and hissed, "We're watching you,

Yankee. If you do one little thing we don't like, and that's all it'll take, one little thing, we'll be on you like stink on a skunk."

Jamie wanted to gag. Rick's breath was foul and sickening. The knee inched higher near his throat, almost choking him. "Do you understand me, Yankee?" Rick asked again, and louder.

Jamie did not consider himself overly endowed with courage, but experience had taught him that if he took garbage now, the harassment would never end, his life would be miserable, and there was no way in hell he was going to let that happen.

"I am *not* a Yankee," he answered coldly.

"I didn't ask if you was a Yankee, Yankee. I asked if you understood."

Rick slapped Jamie's face, stunning him. A stinging left cheek told him a red handprint would soon replace the ringing in his ears. Pinned to the floor, outnumbered and defenseless, Jamie saw the writing on the wall and grudgingly mumbled, "I understand."

Pleased that he had tamed a feisty stray dog, Rick ran down the tunnel laughing with his friends. Jamie picked himself up off the floor, steadied himself, took a deep breath, and then stormed into the dressing-room. Leaning against the wall, Rick crossed his arms sullenly, while fifteen faces, itching for a fight, glared at Jamie with burning eyes.

Before his powder keg temper led him into a fight he could not win, a tall, gray-headed coach walked into the dressing-room and immediately knew there was a problem. A new kid stood on one side of the room, arrow straight and alone. Fifteen scowling faces stood on the other side of the room glaring at the new kid, obviously intending to pound his face into the concrete floor. Coach Sam Lequieu noticed a handprint on the new kid's face and shook his head with disgust. Fitting in at a new school was always difficult. Fitting in during a time of social unrest had to be unbearable.

"Are you Jamie Williams?"

"Yes, sir."

"I'm Coach Lequieu. When you change clothes, come to my office—it's on the left when you come out of the tunnel—I want to talk to you for a few minutes."

"Yes, sir."

Jamie flopped down on the nearest bench, glared at the curly-headed asshole, pulled off his shoes, and wondered what he had done to ruffle the feathers of the gruff-sounding old coach. The last thing he needed was a grumpy coach breathing down his neck.

•   •   •

Sam Lequieu was, by nature, gruff, but he was not at all disgruntled. He was, in fact, excited, because if Jamie Williams was half the basketball player his Arkansas coach said he was, the Bogalusa Junior High School basketball team had increased its chances of winning dramatically. His established players would resent it when he placed Jamie Williams on the team— that would be a problem—but who played, or did not play, for the Rebels was his decision, not theirs, and like it or not, they were about to get a new teammate. Winning was more important than the bruised feelings of fourteen-year-old boys.

•   •   •

Coach Lequieu looked up and pointed at a folding metal chair when Jamie walked into his office. After several seconds—it seemed much longer to Jamie—he closed a manilla folder and mumbled, "You're bigger than I thought you would be."

"How do you know me, Coach?"

"Your coach in Hot Springs placed a letter in your transcript."

Coach Lequieu leaned back in his chair, crossed his arms, and stared into Jamie's eyes. Rattled by a shaky start in a new school, Jamie wanted to break eye contact and stare at the floor, but he could not do that. His father had taught him, and he believed it was true, that a man looks another man in the eyes.

"What kind of basketball did you play in Hot Springs, Williams?"

"I don't know what you mean, Coach."

"Were you just a shooter, or did you pass, penetrate the lane, and take the ball inside?"

"I was the Point-Guard, Coach. I did a little bit of everything."

"Your coach in Arkansas says you seldom miss a shot. Tell me how you do that."

Jamie smiled drolly. "I just shoot the ball and most of the time it goes in the hole."

He's cocky. Maybe a little too cocky? But that's okay. He'll have to be cocky to play for the Rebels. The hometown boys aren't open to outsiders, and they'll be mad as old wet hens when I put Jamie Williams on the team, even if he is, as his Arkansas coach stated, destined for greatness.

"Do you want to play for the Rebels?"

"Sure, Coach. Teach me your game and I'll play it."

●   ●   ●

Jamie did not think his new teammates would be overly excited about a new puppy hiking its leg on territory they had already marked. In fact, he thought he would soon stand at the foot of Mt. Everest with no guide, no equipment, and no hope. But when he opened the door and stepped inside the weight-room, the familiar smell of sweat and dirty socks graced his nostrils, and Jamie knew he was home.

The young coach, supervising the workout, stared at Jamie irritably. Obviously, he considered the weight-room hallowed ground, and interlopers were not welcome.

"What the hell are you doing in here?"

"I'm Jamie Williams. Coach Lequieu told me to work out with the basketball team."

"I thought you were from the PE class. Sorry about the welcome. I'm Coach Westerman."

Jamie nodded and glanced at his new teammates.

They were glaring at him.

He understood their resentment and thought he would probably feel the same way if some new guy weaseled in and tried to win his position. He hoped, in time, the ice would melt, but when Coach Westerman put him to work lifting weights and the hostile stares continued, Jamie knew the situation would get a lot worse before it got any better.

CHAPTER 2

Rick Cullin stared at what he considered easy prey walking across the Bogalusa Junior High School campus. Unbeknownst to Rick, Jamie Williams did not consider himself easy prey—he never had, and he never would. In fact, when Jamie stepped off the bus and saw Rick staring at him, he decided that if the curly-headed jerk wanted his ass whipped, he would be more than happy to oblige him. It was no big deal. He had handled bullies before, and he would handle this one too.

"I see you found your way back to school, Hillbilly."

"It's a big building. I couldn't miss it."

"I hear you're trying to make the basketball team."

"Trying isn't the right word. I'm already on the team."

"I don't believe that. No Yankee has ever played for the Rebels."

"Well, as the old saying goes, there's a first time for everything."

Rick grabbed Jamie's arm when he stepped toward the doorway. Jamie glanced at Rick's hand, looked him in the eyes, then coldly asked, "What's your name?"

"Rick Cullin."

"Let me give you some advice, Rick Cullin."

"Speak your mind, Yankee."

"Let go of my arm."

"And if I don't?"

"I'll whip your ass from one side of this school to the other."

"What makes you think you can whip my ass, Hillbilly?"

"Because I don't take shit off anyone. I'm bigger than you, and you're alone."

Jamie jerked his arm free.

Rick cringed, stepped back, and bolted like a scared rabbit.

Jamie chuckled, shook his head, and walked into the building.

The only early arrival was a girl with auburn hair and deep brown eyes. Jamie vaguely remembered that she had patted his shoulder during Rick Cullin's embarrassing tirade the previous day. He mumbled, "Hi" and sat down at his desk.

"Everyone's treating you awful, aren't they?"

Surprised by a friendly voice, Jamie replied, "New guy harassment. You know how it is."

"You think we're terrible, don't you?"

"No," Jamie lied, "just different."

The girl smiled. "What's your first name? I know your last name is Williams."

Jamie shook his head and chuckled. "Occasionally, Hillbilly. Asshole is popular. Now and then, Instigator. Personally, I prefer Jamie."

The girl laughed, and he liked that.

"Everyone isn't like Rick Cullin, Jamie."

"I hope you're right."

"Rumor has it you're going to play basketball."

"Well." He paused, then asked, "What's your name?"

"Michelle Martin."

"I'm on the team, Michelle, but no one seems too excited about it."

Brimming with new confidence, Rick Cullin, surrounded by friends, walked in the room, slowly moved his head from side to side, and growled, "You can't talk to *our* women, Williams."

Enough, Jamie decided, was enough. He had taken all the garbage he was going to take. It was time to make a statement and make it forcefully. He scooted out of his desk, stood, stared darts into Rick's eyes, grabbed his shirt, and pulled him close.

"Who I talk to is none of your business, Cullin."

Jamie tightened his grip on Rick's shirt.

"I do what I want to do when I want to do it, and I won't answer to you or your asshole-friends."

Rick's face paled. "I'll take care of you after school, Williams."

"No! Take care of me now."

Jamie released Rick's shirt, shoved him hard with both hands, and watched him stumble against the teacher's desk. "Hey, man," Rick whined, "you better cut it out."

"You haven't cut it out with me."

Rick looked into Jamie's eyes and did not like what he saw. He lowered his head, slithered back to his seat, and sulked. Jamie, his anger raging, turned and faced the class.

"What I said to Cullin goes for all of you. If you want to pick on the new guy, do it now."

No one said a word.

"Just as I expected. When you catch someone by surprise, or by himself, you're big and brave, but one-on-one, you're nothing but a bunch of stinking cowards."

Jamie sat down, steaming.

His classmates did not say a word.

•   •   •

It was obvious to Sam Lequieu that the hometown boys could not stand being on the court with Jamie Williams. They were, in fact, expressing their discontent by excluding Jamie from the action. A few years ago, the same boys would have welcomed Jamie with open arms, but that changed when the trouble came. Now there was distrust and secret covenants that excluded anyone who was different. Coach Lequieu often wondered when, or if, the insanity would end. He was southern born and southern raised, a native of Southeast Louisiana, but he was an educated man and did not think anyone, including the Ku Klux Klan, had the right to disrespect a person because of where he came from or the color of his skin.

The previous day, after the school principal had walked into his office and handed him the letter attached to Jamie William's transcript, Coach Lequieu decided, because of the social climate in Bogalusa, he would have to be patient with his team. But as he watched the boys practice and saw Don Franklin, for the third time, refuse to pass Jamie the ball, he realized being patient was a pipedream.

Red-faced, Coach Lequieu blew his whistle, stormed the court, grabbed Don by the jersey, and nearly lifted him off the floor. "What the hell are you doing, Don? Williams was wide open, and you passed the ball to Allan. That kind of stupidity will cost us two points in a game. Do you want to sit on the bench? Or do you want to play basketball?"

Don did not know what to say. Coach Sam demanded that his players follow his instructions to the letter. The team had agreed, however, not to let Jamie Williams touch the ball, and the last thing Don wanted to do was break a sacred trust.

"Do you want to sit on the bench or play basketball?" Coach Lequieu asked again, and louder.

"I want to play basketball, Coach."

"Then stop thinking with your ass and play the way I taught you."

Jamie caught the in-bounded pass, dribbled to the top of the key, and passed the ball to Jack Perone. With no open shot, Jack flipped the ball back to Jamie. He dribbled left, split two defenders, jumped, shot the ball, and hit nothing but net.

Stunned, the hometown boys stopped dead in their Converse All Stars. Jamie Williams had just made a shot that most high school players could not make. Obviously, he was an outstanding basketball player. But what difference did that make? He was a Yankee, and Yankees were not supposed to play for the Rebels. But what could they do? Coach Lequieu was a mean old fart, and he wanted Jamie Williams on the team.

Ten minutes later, Jamie charged the board and rebounded a missed shot. Jack Perone grabbed the ball, elbowed Jamie in the face, a hard blow, and knocked him to the floor. Allan Ramsey kicked him in the ribs, then fell to the floor, holding his arm, faking an injury. Jamie jumped up quickly, but blood dripping from his nose proved Allan and Jack had made their point: Yankees were not supposed to play for the Rebels.

•   •   •

Jamie sensed he was about to be kicked off the team, and that, he believed, was wrong. It was not his fault Jack Perone and Allan Ramsey had bloodied his nose, and he did not think it was right that *he* had to pay the price for what *they* had done. But Coach Lequieu had been cussing-mad when he stormed the court, ended practice, and brusquely told him he wanted to see him in his office.

Jamie understood Coach Lequieu's dilemma—the man was between a rock and a hard place—but there was no way in hell he would go down without a fight. Jamie quickly realized that he had jumped to conclusions when Coach Lequieu leaned back in his chair and said, "You're a hell of a basketball player, Williams, and I want you on my team, but you don't have to put up with the bullshit. If you walk out of Rebel Field House and never look back, I won't hold it against you."

"Quitting won't change anything, Coach. This is heaven compared to the rest of my day."

Coach Lequieu narrowed his eyes. Deep wrinkles creased his forehead. "Are you serious?"

"Yesterday I was called an Instigator, whatever that means, and today I was told that I can't talk to the girls in this school."

"This is a bad time in Bogalusa, Jamie. I don't know when things will improve, but for what it's worth, I think the situation will work itself out."

"What gives you that idea?"

"You're a winner, and winning changes everything, even reluctant teammates."

Coach Lequieu glanced over Jamie's shoulder and smiled drolly. "Your new friends, it seems, have finished their showers. Do you think you can make it to the dressing-room without getting your ass whipped?"

Jamie chuckled, walked out of Coach Lequieu's office, and knew he had a decision to make. Two doors led into the gymnasium. If he walked through the door on the right, he could avoid his teammates. If he walked through the door on the left, he would have to face them.

Jamie chose the door on the left.

"Did you get us in trouble for roughing you up, Williams?"

"No, Jack, I didn't," Jamie replied.

"We figured you'd try to put us in Coach Sam's doghouse."

"What happened is part of the game. I have to admit, though, you damn near broke my nose."

The boys laughed and Jamie felt a glimmer of hope, but he did not linger or press the issue. He gave Jack Perone a thumbs-up and walked into the darkened gym, thinking a bloody nose and a smartass remark may have opened the gate of acceptance.

Allan Ramsey rubbed his chin thoughtfully. "Maybe Williams isn't so bad after all?"

"He's still an outsider," Don Franklin observed. "Maybe we should back off a little, but not get too close."

Jack Perone shook his head, obviously disgusted. "The damn fool challenged the English class to a fight this morning. You've got to admire him. He has guts. If we judged him too fast, he's one of us, and if he's one of us, we'll have to back him to the hilt."

"Yeah," Fred Pendleton agreed. "A little bird told me Jamie Williams, whoever he is, may need some help to get on the bus. Y'all want to pull some guard duty?"

The boys nodded their heads in agreement.

Jack Perone chuckled. "I never thought I'd be taking up for a Damn Yankee. Williams rides bus number two. Let's make sure he gets on it without a problem."

•   •   •

Jamie slipped on his street-shoes, ran through the gym, and hit full stride when he reached the sidewalk. The last thing he wanted to do was to miss the bus and have to walk home. When he approached the loading zone, he slowed to a walk; then rolled his eyes and groaned. Rick Cullin and friends were standing near the bus he intended to board.

That's a welcoming committee meant for me. Oh, well, Bud has always said that someday I'd let my big mouth overload my butthole, and it looks like today is the day.

Rick Cullin stepped out of the surly pack.

"Let's see if you're man enough to back up your big words, Williams."

"I always mean what I say, Cullin."

"Well, let's get it on," Rick replied tauntingly.

With a quick, powerful move he had learned playing football, Jamie knocked Rick flat on his back, pinned his shoulders to the ground, and calmly said, "If you'll leave me alone, I'll let you up. All I want to do is catch that bus and go home."

Rick filled his mouth with saliva and spit in Jamie's face; the foul-smelling slime oozed down his forehead toward his left eye. Jamie raised his fist—Rick's friends, as one, stepped toward him—but Jack Perone, Don Franklin, Alan Ramsey, and Fred Pendleton stepped forward and stopped them dead in their tracks.

"Let me up, Williams," Rick whined. "I'll leave you alone. Honest."

Commonsense said, "Let the obnoxious asshole up, get on the bus, and go home," and Jamie almost followed its advice...until he remembered the tunnel. Throwing common sense to the wind, Jamie raised his hand, slapped Rick's face, then stood and faced his teammates.

"Thanks for the help."

Rick, like a cur-dog, scurried away with his tail tucked between his legs.

Jack Perone, hands on hips, looked Jamie in the eyes, and said, "The verdict is still out on you, Williams, but we take care of our own down here."

Jamie nodded, climbed on the bus, took a seat near the back, and thought—for a few seconds—that his situation might have improved slightly, but decided counting his chickens before they hatched was a dumb thing to do. His teammates *had* taken up for him, but less than an hour before they had bloodied his nose in Rebel Field House.

Jamie smiled smugly. He had marked Rick Cullin the way Rick Cullin had marked him—he liked that—and despite repercussions, he regretted nothing.

CHAPTER 3

Jamie rolled his eyes when the telephone rang. Some church members thought they had to call every time they had a snotty nose. Jamie often wondered why his father had to hear about everyone's ailments. In fact, he asked him why church members felt they had to call him when they were sick. Calvin Williams tried to put off the question, saying that it was just part of his job. Jamie, however, was not satisfied, and continued pressing him for an answer. Calvin Williams finally told him, "If you want to know the truth, son, it's about attention. It is surprising how little attention most people get. I take time to listen, and they're always willing to tell me their problems." The explanation made sense, but Jamie thought it was dumb, and usually had a catty remark prepared whenever the phone rang.

"I'll get it, Mom. Someone's probably constipated again."

Louise William leaned through the kitchen door, smiling. Her baby boy was special. He had a warped sense of humor, was often crude, destined for greatness, and she loved him deeply. Jamie winked and then answered the phone with a sugary hello.

"Jamie?"

"You've got him."

"This is Michelle Martin."

"Hi, Michelle."

"I heard about your fight after school. Are you okay?

"I'm fine. It really wasn't much of a fight." Jamie glanced uncomfortably at his mother, eased into the hallway, and continued the conversation. "Thanks for calling, though."

"Rick Cullin is a jerk. I hope you flattened him."

"What's his problem? Is it me, or what?"

"I don't know. I haven't paid that much attention before."

"Maybe he'll get the message and leave me alone. If he doesn't, it's no big deal. I've handled jerks before, and I'll handle Rick too. I'm glad you called, though."

"I just wanted to see if you were okay. I guess I'll let you go."

Jamie did not intend to keep Michelle talking if she wanted to get off the phone, but after three lonely months, having someone his age to talk to felt good. "Okay, I'll see you in the morning."

"Maybe we can have lunch together?"

"That sounds great."

When Jamie hung up the phone, his mother teasingly asked, "Michelle?"

"She's the only person who talks to me at school."

The cheerfulness left Louise Williams' voice. "No one talks to you, Jamie?"

"Just Michelle. Bogalusa's a strange place, Mom."

"I agree."

"Thank God! I thought it was just me."

"It isn't you, Jamie. People here are…different, but we'll have to keep that less than flattering opinion to ourselves. Your father and brother like this smelly little town."

"You can't tell me they haven't noticed how weird these people are. You'd think we had the plague or something."

"Is it that bad, Jamie?"

"It's terrible. I even had a fight after school today. If my teammates hadn't taken up for me, four or five boys would have whipped my ass." Louise Williams rolled her eyes and ignored Jamie's less than flattering reference to his gluteus maximus. "To tell you the truth, I don't understand why they took up for me. Less than an hour before, two of them roughed me up on the basketball court. Honestly, the only person who talks to me at school is Michelle. Is it bad? You bet it is."

"I knew something was bothering you."

"Jack Perone, a guy on the basketball team, said the verdict was still out on me. Who knows? The jury may decide I'm okay. And there's Michelle."

"Is there anything I can do?"

"How about convincing Dad to move back to Arkansas?"

"I wish I could, but until that day comes — and I don't think it will — you and I will have to make the best of an unpleasant situation." Louise Williams sighed and nodded toward Jamie's bedroom. "You'd better get your homework done. Supper will be ready in about an hour."

•   •   •

Calvin Williams dropped his coat on the living room sofa, pulled off his tie, and chuckled when he heard his free-spirited wife singing along with a gravelly voiced band about something called a wooly bully. Obviously, Louise did not consider rock and roll the devil's music. He eased into the kitchen, placed his arms around her waist, and kissed her neck. She moaned, pressed against him — rather seductively, he thought — then elbowed him in the stomach and said, "You're late."

"What's a wooly bully?"

"I have no idea."

"If it's what I think it is, there's a wooly bully I'd be interested in tonight."

Louise Williams rolled her eyes. "What did you do? Take a stroll down Bourbon Street?"

"Actually, I did."

Louise stared at her husband wide-eyed.

"In fact, a bartender asked me if I knew a redhead who needed a job. I told him there's a sexy pastor's wife in Bogalusa who covers her wooly bully with a G-string and hangs tassels on her boobs."

"You're insane, Cal."

"I'm late, wife of mine, because traffic going in and out of New Orleans is terrible, and I had a hard time finding Charity Hospital. But the drive across Lake Pontchartrain was spectacular. You cross a bridge nearly thirty miles long over open water."

"You'll have to take me to see it."

"If your wooly bully works its magic tonight, I'll plan a trip to New Orleans."

"It seems to me, after twenty years of marriage, you would know that my wooly bully, with very little encouragement, works quite well. Now, be a good boy and set the table."

•   •   •

After supper, Jamie picked up a little red football and threw it toward the ceiling. He enjoyed throwing little red footballs at ceilings and had been doing it for years for no reason other than the nonsensical habit relaxed him. After several minutes, he misjudged the distance; the ball hit the ceiling, left a red mark, and bounced weirdly across the floor.

"If Mom catches you doing that, she'll call down the wrath of God."

"Not on me." Bud chuckled. Jamie, the baby of the family, got away with things he and his older sister, Sherry, never got away with. "Judith can't talk tonight?"

"No. She's doing homework."

"I have a question, Bud."

"Okay."

"Why do you like Bogalusa?"

"I like Judith, not the town.

"I hate it."

"Why? You have everything going for you. You're the right size and you're an outstanding athlete. There's no reason for you to be unhappy. What's your problem, man?"

"Nobody likes me, even the guys on the basketball team. After school today, four or five punks were about to lay into me when I jumped on their buddy."

"You've already had a fight?"

"Not really. I tackled this guy, pinned him to the ground, and could have whipped his ass if I'd wanted to. His friends didn't like it much and were about to lay into me when my teammates stepped in and stopped them."

"I thought you said your teammates didn't like you."

"They don't. But they took up for me this afternoon. It's hard to understand. They bloodied my nose during practice, then thirty minutes later, they came to my rescue."

"Maybe they've decided you're okay."

"They have a strange way of showing it."

Bud grabbed Jamie's arm and pulled him to the dresser they shared and pointed at the mirror. "Look at yourself, Jamie. You're not much smaller than me now."

"So what?"

"If I was your age, I'd think twice before I tangled with you."

"So, you think the jerks will leave me alone?"

"If you don't take garbage off them, they'll eventually get the message." Bud took his eyes off the mirror and stared at Jamie. "Have you made any friends?"

"Only one. She called this afternoon to see if I was okay after the fight."

"Are you telling me that the single-minded Jamie Williams, who doesn't have time for anything but working out and shooting basketballs, has a girlfriend?"

"Maybe. I'm not sure."

"What's her name?"

"Michelle."

"My advice, Little Brother, is don't take garbage and spend time with Michelle."

"So, Judith is the reason you like Bogalusa?"

"Absolutely."

"Well, that answers my question about you fitting in down here."

"I figured out a long time ago, Little Brother, that if God gave the world an enema, He would insert the syringe in Bogalusa, because Bogalusa is the asshole of the world."

Jamie felt better. If Bud, who focused on grades and scholarships and rarely used profanity, thought Bogalusa was the asshole of the world, he was confident that he was man enough to chase away the hounds of hell that were nipping at *his* tail.

Chapter 4

Jamie stepped off the bus, scanned the campus, and thought the place looked like a war zone. Olive-green Army trucks parked on the street, and National Guardsmen, in starched fatigues, stood as sentries near the school's doorway. A nervous-looking guardsman impatiently motioned Jamie toward the building.

The problem, Jamie surmised, had to be racial. Michelle confirmed his suspicions when he walked into his first-period classroom and asked, "What's going on?"

"Someone has threatened the black students. The National Guard is here to protect them."

"What's wrong with this town, Michelle?"

"I don't know. It's a strange time in Bogalusa, Jamie."

"I've noticed. Are we still meeting for lunch?"

"Yes, if we stay that long."

"What do you mean?"

"My Dad said that school will probably be dismissed."

At first, the day seemed normal, until a group of black students approached the concession area during morning recess. Like loyal sons of the Confederacy, several white boys blocked the vending machines and started whistling *Dixie*. Within seconds, the whistling became the dominant sound in the schoolyard.

Before the situation spiraled out of control, leather pounding gravel echoed off the buildings and National Guardsmen marched across the schoolyard—a line of green—protecting black and white from ignorance, prejudice, and misdirected southern pride. Finally, an officer stepped forward, raised a megaphone to his mouth, and firmly said, "Recess is over. Go back to class."

Thirty minutes later, the intercom squeaked shrilly as the principal's voice echoed throughout the building: "The school board has dismissed School for the rest of the week. We have notified parents and buses are waiting in the loading zone. Don't loiter in the hallway or on the school grounds. Go directly to your means of transportation."

Red and blue lights were flashing on state and local police cars when Jamie exited Bogalusa Junior High School. Camera crews from New Orleans were filming the crisis, and reporters, microphones in hand, were interviewing those in charge of the debacle. Looking more than a little uncomfortable, National Guardsmen held their positions.

•   •   •

Louise Williams had heard on the local radio station that racial tensions had erupted at Bogalusa Junior High School and was waiting outside when Jamie stepped off the bus and crossed West 12th Street. "What happened?" she asked, as he stepped up onto the porch.

"A near riot?"

"Was anyone hurt?"

"I don't think so. Did anything like this go on in Arkansas?"

"Yes, Jamie, it did, and worse. In 1957, thousands of people lined the streets of Little Rock to prevent black students from attending Central High School. It was disgusting. Arkansans looked like cretins in the newspapers and on national television. Things have settled down, but the South is still the South, and Arkansas *is* a southern State.

"I haven't noticed anything like this before."

"That's because you're white, Jamie. You've always been so inquisitive I'm surprised that you never asked about the 'White Only' water fountains in Hot Springs."

"Why don't I hate black people?"

"Your father and I believe God created all men equal. We're not bigots and we didn't raise our children to be bigots. As you learned today, we're in the minority."

"Shouldn't we do something?"

"In this environment, that would be dangerous."

"So, we sit back and do nothing?"

"Eventually, we'll have to speak our minds, but speaking our minds would put our lives in danger. Several years ago, someone murdered and buried civil rights workers and college students near a lake in Mississippi simply because they helped black people register to vote, and Mississippi is just across the Pearl River. As a human, I hate prejudice, but as a mother, the last thing I want is for you to get hurt."

CHAPTER 5

The phone rang, startling Jamie. The distraction, however, was not unwelcome. His first day out of school had been boring, and he appreciated anything that would break the monotony. Sitting around doing nothing was worse than hearing about someone being constipated or having a case of the runs.

"Hello."

"Jamie?"

"Hi, Michelle."

"I'm glad you survived, as they're calling it on television, 'the near riot' yesterday."

"What a crazy day! Has anything like that happened before?"

"Not that I remember. But as you know…"

"Things have been weird in Bogalusa lately."

Michelle laughed. "I guess it's time to retire that explanation."

"Probably. What are you doing for the rest of the week?"

"I suppose I'll sit home and watch the Soaps. How about you?"

"I have basketball practice in the morning. Nothing, even a 'near riot' can stop Coach Sam from working our butts off. I'm glad, though. I hate sitting around doing nothing."

"Why don't you drop by my house tomorrow after practice? Mom and Dad won't mind."

"Where do you live?"

"West 13th Street."

"We're practically neighbors. I live on West 12th Street."

"Then why don't you come over now?"

"Sounds good to me."

Jamie hung up the phone and scurried across the living room. Louise Williams closed the book she was reading—something about women and the Bible—and grabbed Jamie's arm as he reached for the door.

"Where are you going?"

"To Michelle's house. She only lives a block over."

Louise Williams held back a smile. Jamie having a girlfriend was something new and unexpected. "Be back by six o'clock. Supper should be ready by then."

As he walked toward West 13th Street, Jamie tried to enjoy the early September weather, which was not as cool as it would have been in Arkansas. The trees were not changing colors, but since the pines outnumbered the hardwoods, the change, Jamie knew, would not be as colorful or dramatic. And the humidity, which would have tapered off in Hot Springs, though less oppressive, was still hanging on in Bogalusa.

Despite constant harassment at school, Jamie felt better. Spending time with Michelle was an unexpected and positive development. In fact, his heart skipped a beat when she waved at him from the porch of a modest blond-brick house. He smiled, ran up the stairs, two at a time, and sat next to her in a green porch swing.

"You must live close. It didn't take you long to get here."

"It's rock throwing distance. Thanks for inviting me. I was bored to tears."

Michelle smiled. "What have you been doing all day?"

"Not much. I tried to play basketball with some guys in the neighborhood. They wouldn't let me, though. Said they didn't want a Yankee hanging around."

"Who said that?"

"Brett Smithers and several others."

"You didn't miss much. Brett and his friends are jerks."

"So far, everyone I've met, except you, has been a jerk."

At school, Jamie's classmates ignored him—unless they were making a snide remark—and he thought it was more than a little strange that Michelle was the only person who talked to him. He did not want to be overly cautious—he liked Michelle, and he wanted her to like him—but a gnawing question kept popping into his mind: why was she the only person who talked to him at school? The last thing he needed was for Michelle to be a player in a cruel joke concocted by assholes. Before he lowered the bridge and let her cross the moat, he wanted to clear the air.

"You know how it is for me at school. Why don't you treat me like everybody else?"

"I decide who is or who isn't going to be my friend. I really don't care what people think."

Jamie wanted to high-five God. Michelle was not a conspirator in an elaborate hoax. She liked him, and he liked her, the way she looked, the way she talked, even the way she smelled.

"To be honest, I don't care who does or doesn't talk to me, as long as you do."

"You don't let people push you around, Jamie. You have courage. I like that."

"Courage, hell! Ninety-nine percent of the kids at Bogalusa Junior High School would like nothing better than to see me get my ass whipped. Half the time I'm scared shitless."

"Do all preacher's kids cuss like sailors?"

"How should I know? I like to cuss. It's a part of who I am."

Michelle smiled drolly and said, "Actually, I don't give a shit." Jamie smiled and chuckled. "Whether you'll admit or not, it took courage to challenge the English class to a fight."

"Stupid is a better word. I always go a little crazy when I get mad. My coach back home calls it my dark side. If everyone took me seriously, this may be a long year."

Pamela Martin stepped out onto the porch and placed two glasses of iced tea on a small, white wrought-iron table. She thought Jamie Williams was sitting too close to Michelle and noticed that he was much bigger than she thought he would be.

"So, you're Jamie."

"Yes, ma'am."

"I understand your father is a Baptist minister."

"Yes, ma'am. He pastors Trinity Baptist Church."

"How do you enjoy living in Bogalusa?"

"We're adjusting, Mrs. Martin," Jamie replied, trying to be diplomatic.

Pamela Martin smiled and walked back into the house.

"Your Mom seems nice."

"She's just being nosey."

"All mothers are nosey, Michelle."

"Ever since I outgrew my training bra, she won't let me out of her sight."

Jamie instinctively glanced at Michelle's chest.

"I knew you were going to do that."

"Do what?"

"Look at me."

"You're crazy, Michelle."

"Why? I like it when you look at me."

"Where does your dad work?" Jamie asked, quickly changing the subject.

"Guess."

"He's not a preacher, is he?"

Michelle snickered. "No, dad isn't a preacher."

"Then what does he do?"

"He's the head basketball coach for the Bogalusa High School Lumberjacks."

"You're kidding!"

"Nope. The two of you should get along just fine."

In Arkansas, Jamie had been a gym-rat, basketball had been his number-one priority, and he did not think he had time for girls. That, he now believed, had been a mistake, because Michelle made him feel like he had never felt before: happy, excited, and full of life. He slipped his arm over her shoulders and laughed when she said, "You better not touch anything. Mom is probably peeking through the curtains."

CHAPTER 6

The day was cloudless, still very warm, but not as humid, as Jamie stood on the sidewalk in front of the Martin's house admiring the view. Michelle, wearing cutoff jeans and a T-shirt, was busy raking pine straw. Lost in her work, she bent over and at the precise moment Jamie decided basketball would never again be his number-one priority.

"Working hard?"

Michelle dropped the rake and grabbed her chest. "You nearly gave me a heart attack, Jamie."

"Sorry."

"How long have you been standing there looking at my butt?"

"Not long enough."

Michelle rolled her eyes. "Well, I hope you enjoyed the view."

Jamie chuckled. "I did."

"Dad's home this afternoon. Do you want to meet him?"

Jamie's brain started ticking. If Coach Martin did not like him, Michelle would be off-limits. If Michelle was off-limits, basketball would have to be his number-one priority again, and he did not like that at all; basketballs were hard and round, not soft and shapely like Michelle.

"Sure. Why not?"

Howard Martin, wearing gray slacks and a black pullover shirt, was tall and athletic looking. The shirt, Jamie noticed, had "Lumberjacks" written in gold on the left side.

"Dad, this is Jamie Williams."

Howard Martin extended his hand. His grip was firm. In fact, Jamie thought it was downright painful. Under normal circumstances, he would have jerked his hand back and asked, "What are you trying to do, Hercules, crush a rock?" But since he thought it was important to make a good first impression, he endured the bone-crushing grip until Howard Martin finally released his injured paw.

"Glad to meet you, Jamie."

"It's good to meet you, too, Coach Martin."

"Thanks."

"Michelle told me you coach the Lumberjacks."

"Yes, I do."

Thick silence flooded the room. Jamie felt as if he had not measured up to some mystical standard, or that he had taken a simple test and had unexpectedly failed. Michelle, however, thought her father's lukewarm reception was hilarious. She was not a rebellious girl, but she liked Jamie, and really did not care what her father thought.

"We're going for a walk, Dad. Is that okay?"

If first impressions meant anything, Jamie Williams seemed like a good kid, but he was pursuing Michelle, and Howard Martin did not like that at all. Until Michelle started talking about Jamie — incessantly — she had been untouchable, as far as boys were concerned. But what could he do? Pretty girls attracted hairy-legged boys.

"Sure."

Jamie followed Michelle outside and mumbled, "I don't think your dad likes me."

"He doesn't know you yet."

"He was really distant, Michelle."

"Give him time, Jamie."

•   •   •

"Well, look at the lovebirds."

The sullen look on Brett Smithers' face told Jamie and Michelle that he did not think it was appropriate for a Bogalusa native to be holding hands with a Damn Yankee.

"How's it going, Brett?" Jamie asked dryly.

"Not bad, once the Klan finally puts an end to this integration bullshit."

"Well, at least school starts back on Monday," Jamie replied, remembering the conversation he had had with his mother, wanting to say something—anything—but knowing whatever he said would not change Brett Smithers, or the world.

"Yeah, and things will get back to normal, won't they, Yankee?"

Jamie's short fuse sparked and ignited his powder keg temper. "Do you really think I give a shit?"

With his jaws clinched and his eyes spitting fire, Jamie stepped toward Brett. Michelle quickly grabbed his arm and pulled him toward the street. Wide-eyed, Brett took a deep breath and exhaled when Jamie turned away and followed Michelle down the street.

"Temper, temper."

"I don't like that asshole."

"I don't either."

"Why?"

"He has a big mouth and runs it all the time."

"Talk is cheap, Michelle."

"None of the girls at school like him. He talks dirty about them. You know what I mean?"

"Oh," Jamie replied, then quickly added, "If he says anything about you, I'll whip his ass."

Michelle stopped, stood on her tiptoes, and kissed Jamie on the lips. The kiss surprised him, and he was even more surprised when she said, "That settles it."

"Settles what?"

"That we're meant for each other."

"What?"

"Don't act so surprised, Jamie."

•   •   •

Howard Martin was not a patient man. Instead of waiting in the house for Michelle and Jamie to return, he walked outside and started shooting a basketball at a goal he had installed above the garage for Michelle—at least that was the reason he had given Pamela—when he bought the house five years before.

He glanced at his watch. Michelle and Jamie had been gone for over an hour and he thought it might be a good idea to go looking for them. Then he saw the disgusting lovebirds walking down West 13th street holding hands, and he wanted to gag.

When the disgusting lovebirds turned into the driveway, Howard Martin flipped the ball to Jamie, which caused the young, enraptured male of the species to release Michelle's hand. The young, enraptured male of the species caught the ball, dribbled toward the goal, sank a fifteen-foot jump shot, crossed his arms, and smiled arrogantly.

Obviously, the young, enraptured male of the species was cocky and wanted to strut his stuff. Coach Martin, an established alpha-male of the species, obliged him. Fifteen minutes later, after a heated and physical game of one-on-one—alpha-males never give up without a fight—Howard

Martin grabbed the ball and sat down on the grass near the concrete driveway, sweating profusely, and breathing hard.

"Don't let it go to your head, Jamie, but you have potential."

"I'm learning, Coach Martin."

"You could play for the Lumberjacks right now."

"Do you boys want a glass of tea?" Michelle asked in a sarcastic and motherly tone. "You've been playing awfully hard." Jamie and Coach Martin nodded their heads and watched from different perspectives as Michelle walked across the yard and into the house.

"Michelle told me you're having a hard time at school."

"I'm having a hard time everywhere, Coach Martin."

"Don't let a few ignorant punks get you down, Jamie. You have a bright future ahead of you. You may not realize it, but you've got something a coach seldom sees: an uncanny ability to put the ball in the hole. No one can coach that. It's a gift."

"Believe it or not, my brother told me the same thing."

"Your hand-eye coordination is remarkable. If you keep working on your game—your moves, your defense, and your passing—when you graduate from high school, you'll have your choice of scholarships."

Michelle returned carrying three plastic cups, handed one to Jamie and one to her father, then sat down, crossed her legs, and sipped her tea. After several quiet moments, Howard Martin drained his cup and asked Jamie, "So, your father is a Baptist minister?"

"Yes, sir."

"Maybe we'll come and hear him preach one of these days."

"You'll be welcome, Coach. Dad, I know, will be glad to meet you."

Howard Martin smiled, said, "I guess I'll leave you kids alone," then pushed himself off the ground, grunted, walked up the steps to the porch, and went inside the house.

Michelle smiled triumphantly. "Well, you impressed my dad."

"Yeah, but does he like me or my athletic ability?"

"Who cares? Just so he likes you."

CHAPTER 7

Calvin Williams was up and ready for church long before the rest of his family ventured out of bed. He had always been an early riser and idly wondered why; the sun was not noisy when it rose, and there was no reason to get up with the chickens.

He poured a cup of coffee, sat down at the dining room table, and stared at the trophy Jamie had brought home from Baton Rouge:

JAMIE WILLIAMS
MOST VALUABLE PLAYER
JUNIOR HIGH DIVISION
TIGER STATE BASKETBALL JAMBOREE

My son is the best junior high basketball school player in Louisiana, and I've never watched him play. What kind of father does that make me? Obviously, not a very good one.

Calvin Williams did not attend Bud and Jamie's baseball and basketball games, and he had never watched Sherry cheer in front of a crowd at football games, but that did not mean he was not interested in his children. He was, in fact, interested in everything they did, but he had strong convictions about high school athletics. It was Calvin Williams' opinion that coaches, grown men who should know better, took advantage of kids, sometimes maiming them, and for what reason? None that he could see. When he had picked Jamie up at two o'clock in the morning, the boy had been so tired that he could barely keep his eyes open. And what had he received from all his hard work and effort? A gold-plated trophy.

On a positive note, Calvin Williams admitted that basketball had helped Jamie adapt to his new home. He touched the trophy with the tip of his fingers, sighed, placed the empty cup in the kitchen sink, and walked out the door.

Since I make time for everything else, I suppose I should make time for Jamie, too. Who knows? I might enjoy watching him run up and down a basketball court.

Time, unfortunately, had become a problem for Calvin Williams. His church had grown, a new building was under construction, and his personal work—evangelism, visiting nursing homes and hospitals—kept him busy day and night. Every week he usually spoke at a service club, and he preached revivals—Monday through Saturday—for weeks at a time, which compounded his problem with time.

Calvin Williams was a busy man. He loved it, but his body reminded him daily that he needed to slow down. He was only forty years old, yet he was having mysterious pains in his chest. At first, he passed the symptoms off as indigestion, but when they continued for several weeks, he sensed that something might be wrong.

Several of his friends, fellow pastors, had died of heart attacks in their late thirties and early forties. Calvin Williams did not want to die young, and he had scheduled an appointment with Doctor Matthew Pennington, a member of Trinity Baptist Church. He believed it was time to find out if he was seriously ill or if he had a minor problem that could be easily corrected. He would know Monday morning. Today, however, was Sunday, and problems—physical and mental—had to be set aside so that he could preach the Word of God.

When Calvin Williams pulled into the church parking lot ten minutes later, he thought that the contractor Horace Webb, a foul-mouthed ogre with an eye for the ladies, was right. The new building would be completed within two months. He gazed at the steeple and his heart brimmed with pride. He was a busy man, probably too busy, but he had never been happier or more excited in his life.

*   *   *

Jamie was not like his father.

After a late night, he would have skipped church and slept late without batting an eye, but he could not do that because his father was a church-freak and had told him many times, "As long as you put your feet under my table, you'll go to church every Sunday.

Church, to Jamie, was boring.

Calvin Williams put a great deal of time and preparation into his sermons—Jamie knew that—and he usually listened to what dear-old-dad had to say, even when he ranted about long hair, short skirts, rock music, and anything else he did not like. Jamie loved his father, admired him in fact, but he thought browbeating people about hair, clothes and music probably turned them off to God and church. Jamie, in fact, liked long hair, girls in short skirts, and he believed John Lennon and Mick Jagger could teach church musicians how to liven up morning worship.

Louise Williams thought of Jamie as her strange child because he was different—nothing like Sherry or Cal Junior—and his opinions often contradicted his Christian-raising. That, she believed, was her fault, because after Jamie finished the *Dick and Jane* books in the first grade, she encouraged him to read anything and everything. They had, in fact, spent countless hours in the Garland County Library. Jamie, therefore, became an avid reader and an excellent student. Louise Williams, of course, would never admit that she loved Jamie more than her older children. She did, however, favor him, because he was creative, witty, sarcastic, often crude, a freethinker, and the joy of her life. Although she did not put on public displays protesting archaic Christian rules, Louise Williams, like her youngest son, was a freethinker, and she had not swallowed all her husband's legalistic mumbo-jumbo.

Two minutes after the Sunday School Superintendent began his monotone devotional—Jamie thought it was boring—the doors to the sanctuary opened. Although his father had told him repeatedly that staring at guests made them feel uncomfortable, Jamie glanced toward the foyer and saw Howard, Pamela and Michelle Martin looking for a place to sit.

Finally—it seemed like hours—the Superintendent ended his long-winded monologue and Jamie led Michelle downstairs to a basement classroom. He never heard a word the teacher said, just gave him an occasional glance. His mind was on more important things, like the feel of Michelle's hand clasped warmly in his lap.

•   •   •

Trinity Baptist Church was stunningly quiet when Calvin Williams stepped away from the pulpit. Jamie glanced at the Martins, knew they were impressed, and felt that it would be just a matter of time until Michelle sat next to him every Sunday.

In the foyer, Howard Martin, smiling broadly, clasped Calvin Williams' hand and said, "Pastor, that was a powerful sermon, very convicting. I've been out of church for several years, but I want you to know that I'm going to change that."

He glanced at his wife. "I know this is short notice, but Pam always cooks more than we can eat on Sunday. Would you and your family like to join us for dinner?"

"Wouldn't that be too much trouble, Coach Martin?"

"No, Brother Williams, it wouldn't," Pamela Martin interjected. "All I have to do is set a few extra plates."

"Then we'd love too."

Howard Martin smiled wryly. "I'm sure Jamie can show you the way."

CHAPTER 8

"I would think that you're one proud father, Cal."

"Yes, I'm proud of my children, Howard."

"I'm talking about Jamie."

Calvin Williams slowly rubbed his temples, which bothered Howard Martin; in his opinion, men who rubbed their temples were indecisive and usually hiding something.

"I'm sure Jamie's an excellent athlete—he was the most valuable player at the Jamboree—but to be honest, I've let my boys play ball simply because they wanted to. Personally, I've never been interested in athletics."

Calvin Williams chose his words carefully. "I don't want to offend you, Howard, but it has always been my opinion that coaches work young athletes too hard. I've seen Bud and Jamie come home from football, basketball, and baseball practice red-faced and sick. To be honest, I tried to make them give up athletics." Calvin Williams frowned, and then mumbled, "To be even more honest, I've never watched Jamie play."

Howard Martin was stunned. How could any father, regardless of the sport, never watch his son play? Then, like Calvin Williams, he chose his words carefully. "I know there are people who feel the way you do, Cal, and I don't want to offend you either, but they, and you, are wrong. I'll admit we work the boys hard, and some coaches may work them too hard, but most of us don't. I do, however, think you should watch Jamie play. He's a special young man."

"This morning I stared at Jamie's trophy and felt guilty. I'm his father, and shouldn't a father attend his son's basketball games? When we moved to Bogalusa, Jamie wasn't adjusting well. If it hadn't been for basketball, I don't think he would have adjusted at all. Anything that turns a miserable kid's life around can't be all bad." Calvin Williams smiled drolly. "And a pretty girl named Michelle has helped a lot, too."

Howard Martin chuckled. "Basketball—any sport really—helps a boy fit in. And to tell you the truth, I'm pleased that Jamie and Michelle have hit it off. It's reassuring to know that my daughter has good taste. If I had a son, I'd want him to be like Jamie. Feisty, but not mean. Talented, but not bigheaded. Just an all-around good kid."

"Most of the time Jamie is a good kid, but he has his moments. To be honest with you, I don't know where he got his talent. Bud, my older son, calls it a gift. You're a coach, Howard. What's your professional opinion of my baby-boy?"

"Jamie may be the best I've ever seen. And yes, Bud is right, Jamie has a gift, and he is an outstanding shooter, but that's only part of his game. Sam Lequieu, the junior high school coach, says Jamie is smart, that he has tremendous court awareness, and that he can play inside the lane and outside. You may not realize it, Cal, but if Jamie continues to grow and improve, he can attend any college he wants when he graduates from high school. And I'm talking about big-time schools like LSU, Kentucky, and North Carolina."

"Are you saying that Jamie may receive an athletic scholarship?"

"Yes, I am."

"That surprises me."

Now and then a kid comes along who has a special knack for some sport. Jamie is one of them. Call it a gift, a talent, call it what you want. Jamie's the best I've seen in twenty years of coaching.

As Calvin Williams listened to Coach Martin speak glowingly about his son, he was proud, but somewhat troubled. How would Jamie handle the pressure and the attention? Would his high school experience be normal? Already, in Calvin Williams' opinion, Jamie was too mature for his age. Was pressure and high expectations making him grow up too fast? Unlike his father, however, disturbing questions were not clouding Jamie's mind as he sat next to Michelle on her bed.

"I bought you something."

Michelle handed him an unopened LP.

"Bob Dylan! Thanks, Michelle."

"Since you're a big fan, I thought you might enjoy it."

As Jamie examined the album, Michelle placed both hands behind his neck, pulled him close, and kissed him for a long time. Uncomfortable with their parents in the adjacent room, Jamie broke the embrace and glanced toward the door.

Michelle smiled slyly. "Don't worry. It's locked."

CHAPTER 9

When Calvin Williams checked in at the Bogalusa Family Medical Clinic, he expected a lengthy wait. To his surprise, just five minutes later, the receptionist called his name and guided him down a well-lit hall to an unusually small examining room. A few minutes later, Dr. Pennington stepped in and stared inquisitively at his pastor.

"Since you made an appointment to see me, I won't ask how you're feeling."

Calvin Williams chuckled. "I've been having chest pains for several weeks, Matt. Nothing severe, but when they hit, they get my attention."

"Have you had any shortness of breath?"

"No."

"Do you have them when you preach?"

"No."

"Do you have them after you eat?"

"Yes. Especially after I've put in a long day. Like when I spend the morning at the office, drive to the hospital in New Orleans, and make a few calls when I get back to Bogalusa. After supper—sometimes after I go to bed—they start. I hate to admit it, but they frighten me."

"I'll see a couple of patients while my nurse takes an X-ray and runs an EKG. When she's finished, I'll look at her handiwork and come back and talk to you."

Doctor Pennington squeezed Calvin Williams' shoulder and left the room. Five minutes later, a white-clad nurse led him to a dimly lit room, took an X-ray of his chest, and then led him to another room where she hooked him to a gray machine that plotted his heart-rhythm. Several minutes later, she tore the graph from the machine, unhooked the wires, and led him back to the first examining room.

•   •   •

"Your chest X-ray is clear, and your EKG doesn't show any abnormalities." Dr. Pennington flipped through Calvin Williams' chart for nearly a minute, collected his thoughts, and then asked, "How many hours do you work each day, Cal?"

"Twelve. Sometimes more if I make a trip to New Orleans."

"Do you take any days off?"

"An occasional Saturday."

"How about hobbies? Do you have one?"

"No. My life is my ministry."

Dr. Pennington frowned. "A man can't function without rest, Cal. What your body is doing is warning you, telling you to slow down or something bad may happen. Take its advice."

"I have a church to pastor, Matt. How can I get things done and slow down, too?"

"No one will complain if you take time off, Cal. Pick up a hobby. Better yet, you have a son who plays basketball. Follow the team! Take your wife to the games and relax."

"Maybe you're right."

"Maybe I'm right? Some people have spastic colons because of stress, others shake, and others have heart attacks and die. You're wound up like an eight-day clock. I'm going to prescribe a mild tranquilizer and recommend a two-week vacation."

"Can the vacation wait until after Christmas?"

"Sure, if you'll take time off each week."

Dr. Pennington glanced at the chart, then placed it on the counter. "You may not realize it, Cal, but you're the best thing that's happened to Trinity Baptist Church in twenty years. I want to keep you around for a while. Take my advice. You'll last longer."

"I've always thought it was better to burn out than to rust out, but either way I'm out, and I don't think God wants that right now."

"Absolutely not! You have a lot of work left in you, just less in a day."

Dr. Pennington smiled and patted Calvin Williams' shoulder. "You'll be fine, Cal. I do, however, want you to come back in a month for another EKG. If you have any problems, day or night, call me."

"Thank you, Matt. I'll see you on Sunday."

•   •   •

Calvin Williams marveled at the bright sun when he walked out of the crowded clinic and met the cool, late November day. He glanced at a cloudless sky, took a deep breath, and thought, *It's time this old dog learned some new tricks. I have a wonderful family, a fantastic church, and good friends. It's time to stop and smell the coffee.*

Instead of heading for his office, he drove home, walked into the parsonage, pulled off his tie, loosened the top button of his white Oxford shirt, smiled at his wife, and asked, "Do you want to go to New Orleans and tour the French Quarter?"

"What about the boys?"

"Leave them a note, a twenty-dollar bill, and tell them to go out for pizza."

Louise Williams was not a fool. She had been married to Calvin Williams for twenty years and intuitively knew that a day trip to New Orleans was not a spur-of-the-moment decision. "Is something wrong?" she asked, looking him in the eyes.

"Nothing's wrong, Lou. I've simply decided that all work and no play…"

"Makes Jack a dull boy. Have you finally discovered, *Brother* Williams, that you have a life of your own?"

"I believe I have, Lou."

"Well, it's about time."

CHAPTER 10

Sherry Williams stepped out of the bus station, tightened the red scarf around her neck, and boarded a Trailways bus for the ten-hour trip to Bogalusa, Louisiana. The weather was cold in Arkadelphia, Arkansas, and the sky, silver-gray, spat occasional snowflakes. Sherry was more than a little depressed.

Randy Jackson, her steady boyfriend for three years, had broken up with her two nights before. Sherry, of course, had been stunned when Randy gave his canned speech, turned, walked away, and left her crying in the doorway of the Pines Dormitory.

The next day, she found Randy in the Student Union with Kimberly Westfall, a free-spirited girl bent on working her way through every boy on campus. Sherry did not consider herself a prude, but when she saw Kim sitting on Randy's lap kissing him, she felt nauseous. Then, when they finally came up for air, Kim glanced at Sherry and giggled. Humiliated, Sherry walked out of the Student Union without looking back.

When the bus pulled away from the station, Sherry sat silently all day, not cognizant of time, holding back tears, and hurting. Ten hours later, the Silver Eagle pulled into Bogalusa's small but crowded terminal. Tears flooded Sherry's eyes when she saw her parents anxiously scanning the bus. She grabbed her purse, exited the bus, then ran across the asphalt parking lot and fell into the welcoming arms of her mother.

Uncomfortable with tearful reunions, Calvin Williams walked toward the terminal to pick up his daughter's luggage, while Sherry, wiping away tears, asked her mother, "Where are the boys?"

"Bud's working and Jamie has a ballgame."

Five minutes later, Calvin Williams placed Sherry's luggage in the trunk, slid beneath the steering wheel, and cheerfully asked, "Are you girls ready to go home?"

"You wouldn't believe how ready I am to be home," Sherry replied, her voice signaling to her mother that all was not right in her world. Calvin Williams, blissfully ignorant of the subtle feminine caveat, pulled away from the terminal.

"How are the boys doing, Mom?"

"Bud's working at the A & P store. He has a girlfriend, Judith Webb, and seems happy. Jamie had a few problems at first, but when basketball season started, things got better in a hurry. And believe it or not, he has a girlfriend."

"Are you telling me the single-minded Jamie Williams, who never has time for anything but running, lifting weights and shooting basketballs, has a girlfriend?"

"Yes, and I worry about it, too. Jamie's too young to be carrying on the way he does with Michelle."

Calvin Williams knew his wife had aimed her last remark at him. "Don't start, Lou! Jamie and Michelle are good kids. There's nothing wrong with the way they act."

"Wow!" Sherry exclaimed, seeing fiery darts flashing from her parents' eyes. "It seems my baby brother has stirred up a stink in the Williams' house."

"Oh, and that's not all. Your father has a new attitude. He takes time off now. Can you believe it? He even attends Jamie's basketball games." Louise Williams glanced at her husband, and then tempered her criticism. "But that's long overdue."

"Changing the subject, how's Bud doing in school? Is he still the family scholar?"

"He's maintaining a 4.00 GPA and will probably receive a substantial scholarship when he graduates in May." There was more than a little pride in Calvin Williams' voice.

"Mom, what's wrong with Jamie having a girlfriend?"

"Nothing. I just think he's too young to be carrying on the way he is."

"What do you mean?"

"If they're not holding hands, Jamie has his arm around her. I even saw him kiss her on the sofa while I was preparing supper the other night. That is ridiculous for a fourteen-year-old. And your father! He's compounding the problem."

"How?"

"He bought Jamie a motorcycle for Christmas."

"It's just a Honda 150, Lou. Good Lord, you make it sound like I bought the boy a Harley."

"But," she persisted, "it's big enough for him to get killed on, and besides that, it'll give Jamie and Michelle too much freedom. There's no telling where they'll go, or what they'll do."

"Michelle's a good girl, Lou. Howard and Pam—they're her parents, Sis—are our closest friends. You're making a mountain out of a molehill."

"You've mellowed, Dad. When I was living at home, you weren't at all trusting with me. In fact, you always said, 'Be home by ten and don't be late.'"

"See, Cal. Even your daughter thinks you've changed."

Calvin Williams turned onto West 12th Street, pulled into his driveway, and winked mischievously at Sherry. "A leopard can change its spots, Sis," then he stepped out of the car and opened the trunk.

"What's happened to him?"

"I don't know. One day he's the same old business-as-usual Brother Williams. The next day, he's a changed man. That's odd, don't you think?"

Louise Williams reached for the doorhandle, hesitated, then asked, "Is something bothering you, Sherry? At the bus station, you seemed upset."

"Randy and I broke up. I'll be fine. I just don't want to talk about it tonight."

CHAPTER 11

Judith Webb did not like pastors and considered them judgmental Bible-thumpers who pointed self-righteous fingers at normal people in a normal world. In fact, Judith did not think anyone, especially holier-than-thou preachers, knew what normal really was. Calvin Williams — thankfully — did not impose his moral agenda on Judith, but he made her feel uncomfortable, as if he knew that beneath her short skirt and bikini panties, she was ripe for the picking. Also, she resented it when Calvin Williams invited her to church. If she wanted to go to church, she would go to church, and since she did not want to go to church, Calvin Williams, in her opinion, should shut his holier-than-thou mouth and drop the subject…forever.

Complicating the situation, Judith believed Jamie was Calvin Williams' favorite son. When he started attending Jamie's basketball games, Bud casually mentioned that his father had never watched him play. Judith, of course, considered that little nugget gross neglect. Judith, therefore, considered Calvin Willias a neglectful ogre, and there was nothing Bud could do or say to change her mind. Although he had never been jealous of Jamie, Judith kept pointing out inconsistencies. The constant onslaught was having an effect, and for the first time in his life, Bud doubted the depth of his parents' love.

When Bud told her that his father had bought Jamie a motorcycle for Christmas, that, for Judith, was the straw that broke the camel's back. "That's horrible," she observed archly. "They're spoiling Jamie rotten just because he's good at basketball. What are they getting you for Christmas? A pair of socks? A shirt maybe? They may even throw in a tie for good measure. I don't see how you put up with it, Bud."

"It's not that bad, Judith."

"Did they ever buy you a motorcycle?"

"No."

"Then I rest my case."

Knowing how Judith felt about his family, Bud dreaded dropping the bomb he thought would more than likely blow up in his face. Two days after Sherry arrived in Bogalusa, he tentatively asked her, "Jude, will you do me a favor?"

"That," she replied cautiously, "depends on what you want me to do."

"My sister, Sherry, is in town for the holidays. I want you to meet her. Since Jamie plays ball tonight, we're attending the game as a family. Would you consider going with us?"

"You want *me* to watch your arrogant little brother strut his stuff? You've got to be kidding."

An unexpected anger surfaced and surprised Bud with its ferocity. After months of listening to Judith badmouthing his family, he was tired of her incessant criticism and constant whining. "All I'm asking is a couple of hours of your precious time. It wouldn't kill you."

Judith scooted to the far side of the car and coldly said, "Take me home, please."

"I'll be happy to."

Five minutes later, Bud pulled into Judith's driveway, crossed his arms, and waited for her to open the door. Judith knew she had pushed Bud too hard. Driving her home, he had not said a word, and he usually stepped out of the car and opened the door for her.

"What does this mean?" she asked, her voice less demanding.

"Whatever you want it to mean," Bud answered coldly.

"Are you coming back?"

"I don't know."

"I thought you wanted me to meet your sister."

"Why? You won't like her, anyway."

"You're angry with me, aren't you, Bud?"

"Have I ever said anything bad about your parents?"

"Why didn't you say something before?" Judith asked meekly.

Bud hesitated, and then blurted, "I was afraid I'd lose you."

Judith scooted across the seat and kissed him, her hand creeping up his leg. He responded positively—she knew he would—and then she whispered, "I'll go to the stupid ballgame."

CHAPTER 12

More than a little pleased with himself, Calvin Williams walked in the living room dangling a set of keys. For several days, he had been dickering with the Ford dealership, trying to work out a deal on a new Mustang as a Christmas and graduation present for Bud. Finally, he decided the price was right, made the down-payment, signed the contract, and drove the car home. When he walked in the house, Louise shook her head and asked, "Have you lost your mind?" Calvin did not know if she was disgusted, or if she thought he was crazy.

"I wanted to do something special for Bud. Negative comments are not solicited."

"Are you sure you're okay? First you buy Jamie a motorcycle, and now you buy Bud a car. It seems to me you're putting us in debt for the rest of our lives."

He grabbed her arm and pulled her outside. "It's a Ford Mustang. It has a V-8 engine and a four-speed transmission. Let's take it for a ride before Bud gets home."

"Why not?"

He backed out of the driveway, took the Mustang through its gears, and reached sixty miles per hour in a matter of seconds. "Don't you think this car is too powerful for Bud?"

"Absolutely not! Every young man should have a sports car at least once in his life."

"You paid a fortune for it, didn't you?"

"Not really. In fact, I got a good deal. But it doesn't matter. Bud is a good kid, his grades are excellent, and with all the attention Jamie's been getting lately, I thought it was a good idea to let him know that we're proud of him, too."

"Your logic, as usual, Brother Williams, is impeccable. Where are you going to hide it tonight?"

"I don't think Bud will believe Santa Claus carried a black Mustang to Bogalusa in his sleigh, but to satisfy you, Howard said I could park it in his garage and that he would sneak it down later. I'll leave a set of keys with him, then wrap this one and put it under the Christmas tree. Don't you think Bud will be surprised?"

Louise Williams leaned against the seat and enjoyed the smell and smoothness of the car. "Surprised? You'll probably give the poor kid a heart attack."

•   •   •

Colored lights, large red bells hanging from power-lines, storefronts adorned with Santa Claus, Rudolf the red-nose reindeer, and cotton posing as snow had transformed Columbia Road into a holiday wonderland. Last-minute shoppers, who clearly were not used to the unusually cold weather, hurried in and out of stores.

"What do you have in mind?" Sherry asked. Leaning against the jewelry counter inside Bogalusa's most popular department store, Jamie looked lost and confused.

"I don't know. Something nice, though."

"How much money are you going to spend?"

"I have twenty-five dollars."

"That's a lot of money to spend on a friend."

"Michelle's more than a friend," Jamie replied with fire in his eyes.

"Well, excuse me! Do you want my help or not?"

"Sorry, Sis. I've always had a short fuse and you know it."

"The gift has to be special, huh?"

"Yeah. Do you have any ideas? I'm lost when it comes to buying presents."

"ID bracelets are popular."

"May I help you?" an attractive saleslady asked.

"Yes, ma'am," Jamie replied. "Do you have ID bracelets?"

The saleslady opened a sliding glass door and displayed several white and yellow gold bracelets.

"Which one do you like, Sis?"

Sherry pointed at a white-gold bracelet, dainty, but not too plain.

"How much does this one cost?"

"18.95."

"I'll take it."

"Do you want it engraved?"

"Yes, ma'am." Jamie glanced uncomfortably at Sherry. She took the hint, rolled her eyes, and walked to the front of the store. "I want 'Michelle' on the front and 'with love, Jamie' on the back."

The saleslady took the bracelet and disappeared through a swinging metal door. Feeling more than a little pleased with himself, Jamie looked nonchalantly around the crowded store. Fifteen minutes later, the saleslady returned and handed him the bracelet.

"It looks great. Thank you very much."

"The total price is $19:40, tax included."

Jamie handed her a twenty-dollar bill. She placed the money in the cash register and handed him the change. He thanked her again, walked through the clothing department, and found Sherry admiring purses displayed on a table near the front of the store.

"You ready to go, Sis?"

"Did you get your business taken care of?"

Jamie smiled smugly. "I did."

They exited the store and scurried down the sidewalk to the Impala. Sherry unlocked the door and scooted beneath the steering wheel, glad to be out of the wind. "What will Mom and Dad say about you spending so much money on Michelle?"

"What they don't know won't hurt them."

"They'll find out, Jamie. They always do."

CHAPTER 13

Judith Webb repeatedly told Bud that the middle child is always neglected. On Christmas morning, it looked as if she may be right. His Levi's and Madras shirts were stylish, and he looked forward to wearing them, but he had received nothing that compared to Jamie's motorcycle, or Sherry's jewelry and electric typewriter.

"Have you opened all your presents, Bud?"

Calvin Williams seemed shocked by his older son's small take.

"Yes, sir, I think so."

"I thought you had another present under the tree. Where is it, Lou?"

Louise Williams pulled a tiny package from behind her back and handed it to Bud. Confused by the excitement caused by such a small gift, he opened the box and stared at a set of keys.

"What do I do with these?"

"You drive with them." Calvin Williams chuckled. "Let's go outside and see what they fit."

Bud stared wide-eyed at the glistening black Mustang. "You bought this for me?"

"Merry Christmas, Son."

Speechless, Bud wrapped his arms around Calvin Williams and gave him a bearhug. When Jamie saw tears streaming down Bud's face, he rolled his eyes and walked back into the house, disgusted by his brother's less than manly display of emotion.

"How can I ever thank you, Dad?"

"I received all the thanks I needed when I saw the look on your face. The Mustang is a two-fold present, by the way."

"What do you mean?"

"It's a Christmas *and* a graduation present. I bought it now so that you could enjoy driving it during your last semester in high school."

"You won't have to buy me another present for the rest of my life, Dad. Nothing, and I mean nothing, will ever top this."

Calvin Williams smiled, hugged his son, and knew he had done well.

•   •   •

The aroma of baked ham filled the house as Louise Williams prepared Christmas dinner in the kitchen. She was happy because her family had had an abundant Christmas but depressed because they were not home for the holidays. In Arkansas, she did not prepare Christmas dinner—this was Granny Williams' annual chore—and the thought of missing the family gathering brought tears to her eyes.

"Why the tears, Lou? We've made three kids happy today."

"It's just the onions, Cal."

"You miss the family, don't you?" Louise nodded. "We'll be home in a couple of days."

"But it won't be Christmas," she replied, more harshly than she intended. Calvin Williams lowered his head and closed his eyes. "I'm sorry, Cal. I'm happy *we're* together, but since we're not with family — yours and mine — Christmas doesn't seem like Christmas."

"We'll see them next week. That's the best I can do under the circumstances."

"Hey, Mom! Can I ride over to the Martins? I want to give Michelle her present."

Louise Williams smiled. "Nothing's bothering Jamie. I don't think he's ever been happier."

"Mom?"

"Go ahead, Jamie, but be back in an hour. Dinner will be ready by then."

•   •   •

Howard Martin answered the door, glanced toward the sidewalk, frowned, and sternly said, "If I was your coach, you wouldn't be riding a motorcycle." Dumfounded, Jamie did not know what to say. "But since I'm *not* your coach, can I take it for a ride?"

"Sure. Anytime, Coach."

"How did Bud like his car?"

"I figure he'll pack up his clothes and live in it until he graduates."

Howard Martin laughed and turned toward the kitchen. "Michelle, Jamie's here!"

The small, colorfully wrapped package suddenly seemed huge and gaudy. Sensing Jamie's discomfort, Coach Martin decided he should help Pamela in the kitchen.

Jamie handed the gift to Michelle.

She unwrapped the box and read the inscription on the bracelet, then walked into her bedroom, returned, and handed Jamie his gift. He unwrapped the box — clumsily — and then stared at an ID bracelet much like the one he had given her, just more masculine. His had his name written on the front, and on the back the inscription: "I'll love you always, Michelle."

They clasped the bracelets around their wrists and felt as if something binding had taken place. Michelle reached for Jamie's hands, looked into his eyes, and softly murmured, "Let's make a promise."

"What kind of promise?"

"That no matter what happens, no matter where we go, no matter how much time passes, we'll look at these bracelets and know that we belong together."

Jamie glanced at the chain clasped to his wrist and mumbled, "I promise."

●   ●   ●

"You seem happier than you did a few days ago."

"Being with family is a great healer, Mom."

"What went on between you and Randy?"

"He traded me in for a—how do I put it?—a lady of the evening?"

"I'd say he's not worth having."

"I know you're right, Mom, but I thought I loved him, and I thought he loved me. One day, he was fine. The next day he tells me we should date other people. Then, twelve hours later, he's making out with a girl bent on working her way through every boy on campus." Louise William said nothing, just kept her eyes on her daughter and listened. "Mom, I don't want to go back."

"You can't drop out of school, Sherry. You've always wanted to be a teacher."

"I could transfer to Southeast Louisiana University."

Louise Williams liked the idea of having her daughter close, but thought transferring schools so quickly would be difficult.

"I don't think you'll have time for that. It would be foolish to lose a semester."

Ignoring her mother's logic, Sherry replied, "I'll check it out next week. The second semester doesn't start until the middle of January. If I can get a copy of my transcript from Henderson, I'll have a week to enroll at SLU when we get back to Bogalusa."

"Don't make a rash decision, Sherry. Look before you leap. Okay?"

"I won't, but to tell you the truth, Mom, I like Bogalusa."

•   •   •

"Did your dad really buy you this car?" Judith asked incredulously.

"It's not the gift a father buys a son he doesn't love, is it?" Judith took a deep breath, closed her eyes, and quietly exhaled. "I'm sorry, I shouldn't have said that."

"I deserved it, and I was wrong when I badmouthed your parents."

"Forget about it. Let's go for a ride."

Judith leaned back in her seat and giggled.

"What's so funny?"

"We'll have to work around these birth control seats when we go parking."

Bud blushed. "Maybe not."

Judith smiled. *I know not.*

•   •   •

Lying next to her husband, Louise Williams was restless and could not sleep. Questions kept churning in her mind: Would Sherry stay at Henderson? Would Bud drive too fast and wrap his Mustang around a tree? Would Jamie get run over by a tractor-trailer rig riding his motorcycle? And why on earth did Cal go to such extremes this Christmas?

"What's your problem, Lou?"

"You are."

"Me? What have I done?"

"Nothing. But I have a question that's bothering me."

"Well, spit it out so we can get some sleep."

"Why did you go overboard this year? You know? Bud's car and Jamie's motorcycle?"

Calvin William turned and faced his wife. "Remember the first day I took off work in November?"

"Yes."

"I'd been to the doctor."

"Why?"

"I had been having chest pains for several weeks, so I had them checked out."

"Don't tell me this is your way of leaving everybody with a special gift."

"No, you won't be collecting my life insurance soon, Lou. Doctor Pennington told me to take more time off. That's what I've been doing, following doctor's orders."

"Then it wasn't serious?"

"Fortunately, no, but stress and indigestion taught me a valuable lesson, a lesson I wish I had learned years ago: to slow down, enjoy life, and to not be in such a hurry all the time." He paused and fluffed his pillow. "Lou, I wish I'd spent more time with you and the kids. I've missed too much the past ten or fifteen years." He took a deep breath and exhaled loudly. "Do you want to hear something that hit me in the face recently?"

"I suppose so, Cal."

"I've spent more time with church kids than I have with my own kids. But from now on, things are going to be different. It may be too late for Sherry and Bud, but Jamie's just in the ninth grade, and he's going to know that he has a father."

"You know Bud and Sherry love you."

"Yes. But do they know I love them?"

Louise giggled, scooted close, and hugged him tightly. "After today, they should."

Calvin Williams grunted and turned to his side. "Now that I've answered your question, Madam Interrogator, may I go to sleep?" Louise Williams lay still for several seconds, then methodically, almost painfully, tapped Calvin's shoulder.

"Now, what do you want?"

"If you ever get sick again without telling me, Calvin Williams, I'll divorce you. And, as you know, divorce sticks out like a sore thumb on a pastor's resume."

CHAPTER 14

Sherry Williams left Hot Springs and crossed Lake Hamilton on State Highway 7, a crooked and steep road that meandered between mountains, through the village of Bismarck, over the Caddo River, and up a deceptively steep grade to Arkadelphia. Despite her mother's advice, Sherry intended to withdraw from Henderson State Teacher's College and enroll at Southeast Louisiana University. College was college, and with Randy Jackson out of the picture, why go to school in Arkansas?

Just as she had expected, receiving a copy of her transcript was not a problem, and within minutes, she was standing outside the Administration Building, holding a large yellow envelope. She glanced at her blue Volkswagen, decided she wanted a Coke, walked across the parking lot to the Student Union, and saw Randy Jackson sitting at a table alone. She inserted two quarters into the Coke machine, opened the can, hesitated, then walked to Randy's table and sat down.

"I thought you were in Louisiana," Randy said, testing the water.

"I was. Mom and Dad came home for a few days. What are you doing here?"

"I'm protecting Henderson from left-wing radicals bent on blowing up the place."

Sherry laughed. "ROTC?"

"Since I live less than an hour away, the Colonel put my name on the duty roster. My uniform is in the car. I'll change in the armory. What brings you to Arkadelphia?"

Sherry nodded at the envelope. "I'm transferring to a school in Louisiana."

"I'm sorry to hear that."

"Where's your friend?"

"I don't know?"

"Oh?"

"We had a temporary fling, Sherry. Nothing serious."

"Well, I hope you enjoyed it."

Randy's eyes hardened, then he smiled and said, "To tell you the truth, I did."

"So, the cowboy has another notch on his gun?"

"Get off your high-horse, Sherry! The only time you objected to my hand being under your panties was when I unzipped my jeans and tried to do what we both wanted to do."

Randy was right. He had taken her to the limit frequently — in his car and in her dorm — but each time she had pushed him away. Sherry knew she had frustrated him, especially when he started calling her a tease. A short time later, he broke up with her, and she saw him making out with Kimberly Westfall in the Student Union.

"I can't believe you'd mention that."

"No one will ever know."

"Thank you."

"I'm sorry I hurt you, Sherry."

"I'm sorry you think I'm a tease, Randy."

The brisk December air was not invigorating — it was just cold — when Sherry walked across the parking lot and scooted beneath the Volkswagen's steering wheel. She drove off campus and glanced at her watch. It had only taken two hours to start her new beginning and free herself from the strings that tied her to her home state.

Sherry sighed, turned on the radio, and listened to *California Dreaming* by the *Mamas and the Papas*. The blue sky and yellow sun shining over the mountains briefly rejuvenated her. She rolled down the window, but the wind slapped her hair rudely against her face. She rolled the window back up, thought about her conversation with Randy, and wondered if she had made a mistake leaving Henderson.

•   •   •

For a moment, Duane Smith thought he had convinced the good-looking carhop to go for a ride when she got off work at ten o'clock. She hesitated briefly, considered the offer, then shook her head no, and strutted across the parking lot swishing her tail. More than a little disappointed, Duane sipped his root beer and glanced at the black Mustang parked next to his pickup truck, an older GMC, dark blue, with mag wheels.

"I'll be damned if ain't Bud Williams! When did you get back?"

"Last night."

"You just visiting?"

"Yeah."

"When did you get the wheels?"

"Would you believe it's a Christmas present from my dad?"

"I wish my old man would buy me a new car. I'm lucky if I get a pair of socks."

"You want to go for a ride?"

"Hell, yeah! We'll run over to the Burger Chef and see if we can pick up some girls. We shouldn't have any trouble in this rig. Mustangs are panty droppers."

As Bud negotiated the hilly backstreets of South Hot Springs, Duane leaned his head against the seat and asked, "Have you been getting any lately?"

"I'm going steady."

"That wasn't what I asked you."

"My answer is, it's none of your business."

Duane rubbed his chin thoughtfully. "Do you want to sample a little Arkansas hospitality before you head back to Louisiana? There's this girl I know—actually, she's a married woman—who likes to fool around with high school boys. I'll set her up for you tomorrow night."

"You don't have to do that, Duane."

"What are friends for? Be at my house at seven o'clock tomorrow night. We'll take my truck. I don't want to get your new car dirty. She lives a long way out of town, down a dirt road and everything, but I think you'll find that she's worth the trip."

Bud wanted to tell Duane no—his father had raised him to be a Christian gentleman—but his mind went blank, and he could not think of a legitimate excuse not to meet his friend for a rendezvous with a married woman who liked, quoting Duane, to fool around with high school boys. Against his better judgment, Bud accepted Duane's invitation and wondered what fine mess he had gotten himself into. Taking Judith parking was one thing. Going to bed with a married woman was another.

• • •

When Bud pulled into Duane Smith's driveway, his stomach was in knots. Twenty minutes later, a short distance past the Bull Bayou Bridge, Duane turned down a gravel road canopied with trees and dense vegetation, drove three miles, turned left, then left again up a narrow lane, and stopped in front of a white-framed farmhouse bordered by a rusty wire fence. Smiling from ear to ear, Duane said, "Welcome to Paradise, Bud," and then stepped out of the truck and walked toward the house.

The porch light flickered on, then the front door opened and slammed against the wall. A burly, hairy-chested man stepped out of the house carrying a double-barreled shotgun.

"Are you the boys who've been messing with my wife?"

The man pointed the gun menacingly.

"We didn't know she was married, Mister," Duane replied meekly.

"You admit it, then?"

The man waved his gun from side to side. Bud's heart beat wildly, and his hands trembled. The man was extremely angry, and Duane had lost his cocky attitude.

"What are you going to do, Mister?" Duane whined.

"I'm sending you boys to meet your Maker. Heaven or Hell. It don't matter to me."

The man squeezed the trigger, the gun roared, and light flashed against the darkness. Duane grabbed his chest, hit the ground, groaned, and went limp.

Bud bolted, but the man pointed his gun and stopped him dead in his tracks. "How about you, boy? Have you been messing with my wife?" Bud tried to speak but couldn't. "Cat got your tongue, boy? I asked you a question. Have you been messing with my wife?"

A woman, dressed in a plain, short nightgown, stepped out of the house. "Harvey, what are you doing?" She saw Duane lying on the ground and screamed, "Oh my God!"

Bud turned and ran when the man glanced at his wife. He knew the diversion would be brief. Too quickly, the man yelled, "Come back here, boy!"

Harvey pulled the trigger.

The crack of the gun boosted Bud's adrenaline. He approached the wire fence, jumped it like a deer, and ran through the briars and sagebrush. When he reached the road, he continued to run, going back the way he had come, thanking God he was still alive.

Gritting his teeth when he heard Duane's truck start, Bud glanced over his shoulder and saw two narrow beams of light moving down the driveway. Terrified, he jumped the ditch, crawled into the underbrush, and lay flat on the ground until the truck passed by.

His spine tingling, Bud crawled back to the road and ran, suspended in time, no sounds, just heavy breathing, his lungs working hard, inhaling and exhaling the chilly night air. Finally, he saw Highway 270 in the distance, but his heart sank when he looked over his shoulder and saw Duane's truck approaching from the rear.

Whoever was in the truck—probably Harvey—had to have seen him, but Bud knew Harvey would have a hard time finding him once he left the road. He jumped the ditch and ran deep into the underbrush, his heart beating so hard that when the truck stopped and a door slammed, Bud felt as if it was lifting him off the ground with each beat.

"Come on out, Bud! It's me, Duane! It's all a joke, man." Bud did not move or say a word. "The guy back at the house is my cousin. His name is Harvey Mills. Come on out. It's okay."

Bud crawled out from under the fat cedar tree, scrambled to his feet, and saw Duane, alive and in one piece, standing in front of his truck. Torn between anger and relief, Bud stumbled toward the road and jumped the ditch. Duane backed away cautiously. He was not sure how his old friend would react after running three miles on a chilly night.

"I see you don't have a hole in your chest."

The ice in Bud's voice told Duane that he did not appreciate the prank. Expecting a fist to his face or gut, Duane chuckled nervously, backed away, and leaned against his truck.

"Harvey was pretty convincing, wasn't he?"

"He scared the crap out of me."

"What about my Oscar-winning death scene?"

"All I saw was a hairy chest and a shotgun."

"I didn't expect you to take off running—and I'm sorry about that—but when I saw you running down the road pumping your arms, a question popped into my mind."

"Apology not accepted. What's your question?"

"Have you ever thought about trying out for the Olympics?"

"No. Why do you ask?"

"You're one hell of a runner."

Bud shook his head and chuckled. "I can't believe I fell for this setup hook, line and sinker."

"Does that mean all is forgiven?"

"No. You're still on thin ice, Duane."

"I guess that means you want to call it a night."

"What do you think? I'm worn to a frazzle."

CHAPTER 15

When practice ended, Coach Lequieu—in his usual gruff manner—told Jamie that he wanted to see him in his office. Jamie, naturally, wondered why. He had, in fact, worked his butt off. His uniform was soaked with sweat, and he could think of nothing that he had done wrong. Fifteen minutes later, he knocked on Coach Lequieu's door, stepped into his office, and asked, "You wanted to see me, Coach?"

Coach Lequieu pointed toward an empty chair.

Jamie sat down.

"Has anyone talked to you about playing basketball with mortals?"

More than a little uncomfortable, Jamie did not respond.

"Have you ever wondered why you're such an outstanding basketball player?"

Jamie shrugged his shoulders.

"Other players can't do what you do because they're not as talented—No! As gifted—as you are. You already have what most young men work years to achieve. Coaching only makes you better. Think about it, Jamie. When you walked into my office three months ago, you didn't know beans from bologna about my coaching philosophy. But was it hard for you to learn? Or to do? No! You picked up on it right away, because you're blessed with the skills it takes to play the game."

"I don't want you to think I'm bragging, Coach, but the first time my brother put a basketball in my hand..." Jamie laughed, and said, "What he really tried to do was break my nose—I knew I could be an outstanding basketball player."

"Knowing you're good isn't bragging, Jamie. In fact, knowing *and* doing is the difference between mediocrity and excellence. You have a swagger about you. I like that. When you step onto a basketball court, you believe you're the best player on the floor. That's okay, if you have the talent to back it up, and you have the talent.

"Having talent and using it is important. Think about it, Jamie. The world would be a lesser place if Beethoven and Bach hadn't given the world their music, and the world would be a lesser place if Henry David Thoreau, Ernest Hemingway, John Steinbeck and a thousand others hadn't given the world their writing. The Sistine Chapel would be nothing more than cold stone walls without the paintings of Michelangelo. And the world would be a lesser place if athletes didn't use their talents. Consider what Jesse Owens, a black man, accomplished. He rubbed mud in the face of Adolf Hitler and his so-called master race. Talk about poetic justice!

"So, your feelings and expectations aren't strange, Jamie. They're something you must live up to. You're a gifted artist marching to the beat of his own special drum."

"I've never thought about it like that, Coach."

"Have you ever considered the dark side of being an artist?"

"I don't know what you mean, Coach."

"Some people are gifted and normal, while others are gifted and abnormal. History is full of people who, because of prominence, skill, or intellect, took advantage of those who weren't prominent, skilled, or intellectual. They were talented, yet abnormal, because they considered themselves better than common people.

"Jesus, for example, was the most gifted man who ever lived. And what was his philosophy? Treat people the way you want to be treated."

Coach Lequieu stared into Jamie's eyes for several seconds, then asked, "You know why I'm telling you these things, don't you?"

"You don't want me to get the big head."

"That's right, so let me give you some advice about playing basketball with mortals. Consider every player an equal, Jamie. When you do, he'll fight and die for you. When you don't, he'll kick your ass when you're down. Also, get your points every time you take the court—you deserve it, and the fans deserve it—but look out for the other guy, help him score, and he'll love you for it.

"Don't get the wrong idea! I'm not telling you to hold back, or to lower yourself by being less than artistic with what you do. What I'm saying is, bring your teammates up to your level. It's surprising how well an average player can play when he knows an above average player has confidence in him.

"I'm sixty-two years old, Jamie. I have been coaching for forty years. In all those years, I've never coached a player like you. I think you're the best I'll ever see, so I want to be truthful with you and share some thoughts that may help you in the future."

"Okay, Coach."

"Sooner than you think, an education will mean more to you than basketball."

A trace of doubt surfaced in Jamie's eyes.

"Don't look so damned shocked! What you learn in high school and college will determine what you become in life. You're almost fifteen years old, Jamie. Do you realize your playing career is probably half over? How many thirty-year-old basketball players do you see?"

"Except for the pros, not very many."

"After age thirty, even pros go downhill. My point, however, is this: Because of your talent, you can probably slide through school. But don't slide! Apply yourself! Be smart! Be articulate! Prepare yourself for something besides basketball! The day is coming sooner than you think, when your body won't allow you to run up and down a basketball court. Age catches up with everyone, Jamie, even the gifted."

"I guess you're right, Coach."

"I *know* I'm right."

"Yes, sir."

"There is one more thing I feel obligated to tell you, Jamie: your talents belong on a basketball court. If you play football or even baseball, you'll triple your chance of injury. Don't do that! If coaches can't see where your talents lie, they're nothing but damned fools, anyway."

Coach Lequieu leaned back in his chair, stretched, and grunted. The conversation was over. Jamie stood, said, "Thanks for the advice, Coach," and then walked out of the office more than a little perplexed. Jamie knew he was a talented basketball player, and he had never been stuck up—being a snob was not his style—but being the best basketball player Coach Sam had ever seen was a little too hard to believe. He shrugged his shoulder, walked out of Rebel Field House, and thought, as he straddled his Honda, that he had had a pretty good day.

CHAPTER 16

It did not take Calvin Williams long to become bored with television, naps, and long walks. The cabin on Lake Hamilton was rustic and comfortable, and the view — mountains and blue water — was spectacular, but it was too cold to swim, the fish were not biting, his daughter adamantly refused to attend college in Arkansas, his oldest son was restless, and his wife was worried about Jamie. Doctor's orders or not, it was time to go home.

After dinner, he followed Louise into the bedroom and grabbed her arm. She smiled drolly. "What do *you* want?" Calvin had been more than a little frisky for several weeks.

"I want to go home."

"Are you serious?"

"We can drive all night, rest when we get home, and watch Jamie play ball tomorrow evening."

"Are you sure, Cal?"

"Absolutely. I've never been good at vacations, anyway."

•   •   •

An hour later, Calvin Williams shifted the Volkswagen into fourth gear as Malvern Avenue narrowed and became Highway 270 East. He glanced at his wife and smiled. "Why don't you get some sleep? It's going to be a long night." Louise Williams sighed, leaned her head against the seat, and looked out the window.

"Is something bothering you, Lou?"

"I was thinking that it would be nice to live in Hot Springs again."

"You don't like Bogalusa, do you?"

"I like some people, especially the Martins, but it's not home."

Although she had a daughter in college and a son who would soon graduate from high school, Louise Williams still had the same girlish figure that had attracted Calvin when they were students at Hot Springs High School.

"If you want me to, I'll resign and move back to Hot Springs. You know I'll do anything for you."

She leaned across the gearshift and kissed his cheek. "No. I'll continue making my contribution to the Ruth Paradigm, going where you go and lodging where you lodge."

Bud shook his head like a disgruntled parent.

"Look at those two. Married twenty years and they still act like a couple of honeymooners."

"I hope someday I can be as happy as they are."

"Yeah, me too."

"I guess it's an understatement to say that you'll be glad to get home."

"Yeah, this has been a long week."

"We'll probably break Jamie's heart by coming home early."

Bud chuckled. "Staying with the Martins is probably a dream come true for him."

"Mom thinks Jamie and Michelle are too young to be carrying on the way they do."

"He's just taking his big brother's advice."

"What do you mean?"

"Four months ago, Jamie was miserable. He didn't have a friend to his name, and he was being picked on at school. When Michelle entered the picture, it was instant happiness."

"Jamie's so arrogant and hot-tempered, how could anyone pick on him and get away with it?"

"He fought them tooth and toenail. As you know, Jamie doesn't take garbage from anyone. Anyway, he was miserable. But when he started running around with Michelle, everything changed. I told him she'd make his life more enjoyable, like Judith has for me. He took my advice. And I was right. Michelle's good for Jamie."

"You told him that?"

"You have a problem with it?"

"No, not at all. I never realized you were so smart."

"It's about time you saw the virtues of your slightly younger brother."

"I've always seen your virtues. You wouldn't believe how many of my girlfriends wanted me to fix them up with you."

"Why didn't you?"

"Meanness, I guess. Speaking of girlfriends, tell me about Judith."

"You met her, Sis."

"I know, but *really* tell me about her."

"Judith is different from the girls I dated in Hot Springs. They played silly games, and I never knew where I stood with them. Judith doesn't play games or keep me guessing."

"Can I tell you something that will probably make you mad?"

"Nothing's stopped you before."

"Silly games are a nuisance, but they serve a purpose, like preventing babies."

"What makes you think we're about to go all the way?"

"Your statement about 'silly games' clued me in." Sherry paused and weighed her words carefully. "If you both want it, there's not much anyone can do to stop it. All I'm saying is a little hanky-panky can cause big-time problems."

"What happened between you and Randy?"

Sherry giggled and leaned against the seat. "He wanted to, and I didn't."

Bud glanced at his sister and saw no regrets.

"If you found a guy you really liked, I mean *really* liked, would you go all the way with him?"

"That's a little too personal, Bud."

"What's good for the goose is good for the gander."

"I *really* liked Randy, and I didn't go all the way with him. I guess I have too much of my daddy in me. I'm not a prude—at least I don't think I am—but I'd rather wait until I'm married."

Sherry giggled.

"What are you laughing at?"

She pointed at the Volkswagen. "Mom and Dad would have a conniption fit if they knew what we're talking about."

"I don't think they, especially Dad, understand the sixties."

•   •   •

Bored by long miles on a dark highway, both couples fell silent. Louise Williams and Sherry mostly slept, only awakened when they passed through small towns, blinking traffic signals, and the drone of diesel engines shifting gears down empty streets.

Calvin Williams, deep in thought, felt troubled as he considered starting a new year in a world gone crazy. Everything was changing. The values he had preached his entire adult life were being washed away by a radically different generation. Young people were no longer content with the intrinsic values of their parents. In fact, Calvin Williams had concluded that if values made little sense to the new generation—regardless of how sacrosanct they were—the new generation simply ignored them. An unpopular war was being fought on the other side of the world in a place called Vietnam—he watched it escalate every day on the evening news—and from Los Angeles, to Detroit, to Selma, African Americans would never again allow bigots force them to sit on the backseat of a bus.

My God! We're in the middle of a revolution! A lesser people would take to the streets, fighting to maintain their aging precepts. But not us. We watch, listen, and bury our heads in the sand, pretending everything is the same, when nothing will ever be the same.

Calvin Williams adjusted his seat. His left hip was aching, and his legs were numb. He glanced at his sleeping wife and thought about his children and their future.

I wonder how the changes will affect those I love most?

CHAPTER 17

Parents and students packed Rebel Field House to watch the undefeated Rebels play their first game of the new year. Pamela Martin and Louise Williams sat together, as usual, awaiting the opening tip. Michelle, sitting next to her mother, watched Jamie go through his pregame ritual, moving methodically around the court, taking warmup shots from varying distances.

Once the game started, Hammond, the evening's opponent, fell behind quickly. Jamie's outside jumpers, and Jack's aggressive play in the middle, gave the Rebels an early lead they never relinquished.

When the teams headed for their dressing rooms at halftime, Michelle left her seat and walked to the smoky foyer to buy a Coke and a bag of popcorn. As she stood in line at the concession, a hand lightly tapped her shoulder. Michelle turned and faced Alice Jackson, a classmate who was not a close friend.

"Your boyfriend is really good."

"Thanks, Alice. I'll tell him you said that."

"Rick Cullin told my boyfriend when school starts that he and his friends are going to corner Jamie in the restroom and beat him up so that he can't play basketball."

"Is your boyfriend involved?"

"No. He can't stand Rick."

"Did Rick say why he wants to hurt Jamie?"

"Jamie embarrassed him last year, and he wants to get even."

"That's stupid."

"I know. Tell Jamie. I don't want him caught by surprise."

"I'll tell him, Alice."

Michelle returned to her seat, seething. Pamela Martin, noticing her daughter's sour demeanor, asked, "What's wrong? You're sulled up like an old bullfrog?"

"Alice Jackson just told me that when school starts, some boys are going to corner Jamie in the restroom and beat him up so that he can't play basketball."

"Do you think they're serious?" Louise Williams asked.

"Jamie's had problems with them before. They want to get even."

Jamie had mentioned several times that he had had a hard fitting in at Bogalusa Junior High School and had said frequently that most of his classmates did not like him. Thinking her baby boy was about to stand in harm's way, Louise Williams told Pamela Martin, "Come over to the house for coffee after the game. We'll talk to Howard and Cal about the threat and decide how we'll handle it."

•   •   •

"What do you think about Rick Cullin's threat, son?"

Jamie laughed. "There's nothing to worry about, Mom. I'll pee before I leave home and won't drink anything all day. That should take care of the problem."

"I'm serious, Jamie. What if Rick Cullin follows through with his threat?"

"If the rabbit hadn't stopped to take a leak, mom, the turtle wouldn't have won the race."

Calvin Williams chuckled. "What should we do, Howard?"

"I'll talk to Coach Lequieu and have him explain the situation to the school principal. That will probably take care of the problem. Who knows? The kid may be blowing smoke."

Despite his wife's objections, Calvin Williams agreed. Why make a mountain out of a molehill? Mothers are, and always have been, overly protective creatures.

•   •   •

Precocious and spoiled, Judith Webb usually got what she wanted: new cars, new clothes, and...boyfriends. When she crawled into bed and turned out the light, Judith knew she had gotten exactly what she had wanted in the back seat of Bud's pretty, black Mustang. She was her father's child, and Horace Webb had often told her he would walk barefoot through hell to get what *he* wanted.

When Judith started dating a Bible-thumper, Horace Web was not at all thrilled, simply because he never had been, and never would be, a religious man. Regardless of what Bible-thumpers proclaimed, Horace Webb believed there were certain sacred cows a man should never give up: a cold beer after work, profanity with a touch of art, and an occasional mistress.

Despite his hoity-toity background, Bud Williams seemed like a pretty good kid, polite and smart, but Horace was not at all comfortable around him. How could he be? Bible-thumpers were snobs that looked down on people who cussed, told dirty jokes, drank beer, and cheated on their wives. To his credit, Bud Williams, Horace noticed, did not act like a Christian Storm Trooper, and he told Judith, "At least he's not a holier-than-thou asshole. I'd shit and fall back in it if you dated a Bible-toting fanatic."

Judith fluffed her pillow and stared at the ceiling. She had been the first girl Bud had taken all the way—that was obvious—but she could not make the same boast. She had, in fact, lost her virginity two years before when the son of one of her father's business associates took her flirting a little too seriously, pushed down her panties, and took what she obviously was so proud of on a swampy back road close to Thibodaux. Although the experience was unexpected—Judith could not have stopped Tommy Rucker even if she had wanted to—shock gave way to pleasure, and she learned a fascinating lesson: sex was not a mystical union shrouded in the sanctity of marriage, but a physical experience, like running and jumping, that should be enjoyed. And she *did* enjoy it, but discreetly, usually with boys she met when she vacationed with her parents on the Gulf Coast.

In her hometown, Judith remained remarkably chaste, simply because the right boy and the right circumstances had not presented themselves. Those she accepted socially considered themselves southern gentlemen and handled her like a fragile China doll. Others she considered beneath her dignity and would never stoop that low. With his ingrained morality, Bud, of course, fell into the southern gentleman category, but after he had tasted the forbidden fruit—he could not keep his hands off her when he kissed her goodnight—Judith knew she could look forward to many exciting trips down secluded logging roads in the backseat of Bud's pretty, black Mustang.

CHAPTER 18

Jamie opened his eyes, stared sleepily out the window, and sighed. The weatherman had been right, a torrential rain was falling, and he could not ride his motorcycle to school. He slid out of bed, pulled on his jeans, and headed for the bathroom, thankful that Sherry had heard the weather forecast on the ten o'clock news and had volunteered to drive him to school and pick him up after basketball practice.

An hour later, Sherry backed her cold-natured Volkswagen, spitting and sputtering, out of the driveway. Jamie, she thought, had been unusually quiet all morning.

"Aren't you excited about going back to school?"

"Not really."

"Why? I thought you were a popular jock."

Jamie laughed cynically, Sherry thought. "I'm the best player on the team, but the hounds of hell are nipping at my tail."

"The *best* player?"

"Yep."

"You're too cocky, Jamie."

"I couldn't survive at Bogalusa Junior High School if I wasn't cocky. If someone thinks I'm weak, he'll try to whip my Yankee ass from one side of Bogalusa to the other."

"That's hard to believe."

"Believe what you want."

"You've changed, Jamie."

"How have I changed?"

"You're foulmouthed and more aggressive than you used to be."

"I've always been foulmouthed and I'm aggressive because I have to be."

"Why?"

"The kids at school—probably because I'm new—think I'm a Northern Instigator. You know? Someone who has moved south and sided with black people. If I don't take up for myself, someone will whip my ass the first time I let my guard down."

"You're kidding, of course."

"Nope."

Ten minutes later, Sherry pulled next to the curb fronting Bogalusa Junior High School and said, a little too sarcastically, Jamie thought, "If you survive the day, what time do you want me to pick you up?"

Jamie chuckled and opened the door. "Practice usually ends around five o'clock."

•   •   •

Sherry Williams, unaware that visitors were not allowed in Rebel Field House during practice, slipped into the gymnasium and sat in the bleachers. Coach Lequieu had learned the hard way that visitors—especially strong-minded parents—and practice were like fire and gasoline, an explosive and volatile combination.

"Who's that, Phil?" Coach Sam asked, nodding at the young woman sitting in the bleachers.

"I don't know, but I'm going to find out."

Phil walked across the court, stood in front of the young woman, put both hands on his hips, and asked, a little too sternly, Sherry thought, "May I help you?"

"No," she replied, and motioned him out of the way.

"You're not supposed to be in the gym during practice."

"What do you want me to do, wait out in the rain?"

"Yes, as a matter of fact, I do."

"Are you serious?"

"Do I look serious?"

Red-faced, Sherry reached for her purse.

"Keep your seat. It will be at least fifteen minutes."

"Thank you *very* much," she replied sarcastically.

"You're *very* welcome," Phil replied, mocking her. "Who are you anyway?"

"I'm Sherry Williams, Jamie's sister."

"I didn't know Jamie had a sister."

"I just moved to Bogalusa. I've been attending college in Arkansas."

Phil climbed onto the bleachers and sat down. "Your brother's a good kid."

"Are we talking about the same person?" Phil chuckled, and Sherry liked that. "Jamie is, and always has been, ill-tempered and arrogant."

Phil glanced at the scrimmaging players, then said, "Jamie *is* arrogant, but in a gentle sort of way."

"Gentle Arrogance?"

"Yeah. Gentle Arrogance. That describes Jamie well."

"Sounds like a contradiction in terms to me."

"Maybe it is. Changing the subject, what college are you going to attend?"

"I've enrolled at Southeast Louisiana University."

"SLU is a good school. Are you going to live on campus?"

"No. I'm going to commute, at least for this semester."

Phil had graduated from SLU the previous May, landed the job at Bogalusa Junior High School, and had spent too much time alone in a city where he knew very few people. Sherry Williams did not know him from Adam, but he could not think of one good reason to shy away from a girl who was drop-dead gorgeous and probably unattached.

"A new restaurant, the Duck Inn, opened a few weeks ago. It serves excellent shrimp and catfish. Would you like to have dinner with me tonight?"

Sherry almost turned down the invitation, then looked, for the first time, at the brash, young coach who had asked her out. He was handsome, in a rugged sort of way, and she liked his confidence. Most guys did not anger her and then ask for a date five minutes later.

"What time do you want to pick me up?"

"How about seven o'clock?"

"It's a date." Phil smiled and stepped off the bleachers. As he walked toward the old guy standing near mid-court, Sherry raised her voice and said, "Hey, wait a minute!" Phil turned back and faced her. "Since we're going to be buddies, I think I should know your name."

"I'm Phil Westerman."

"I'll see you at seven, Phil."

He nodded and took his usual place next to Coach Lequieu.

"Well, who is she?"

"Jamie Williams' sister."

"I didn't know Jamie had a sister."

"I didn't either. She's pretty, isn't she?"

"Very."

"I'm having dinner with her tonight."

Coach Lequieu rolled his eyes and shook his head. "You just met the girl, and you already have a date? That's incredible, Phil. I'm either old-fashioned, or just old."

Sam Lequieu was a fine man, a southern gentleman, in fact, but Phil lived in the sixties, and a guy did not have to ask daddy's permission to date his daughter in the sixties.

CHAPTER 19

Calvin Williams' new office and attractive secretary made him more than a little uncomfortable. He was proud of what he had accomplished at Trinity Baptist Church and believed he deserved the plush office and its amenities. However, he saw himself as a man of the people, not as a king sitting in an ostentatious throne room.

With his church and family doing well, and no storm clouds on the horizon, Calvin Williams felt optimistic about the foreseeable future. Lou was involved in women's ministries, and Sherry—this surprised him—was dating one of Jamie's coaches. With the season completed, except for the State Tournament in Baton Rouge, Jamie and the Rebels were undefeated, and Bud, except for an unusual reticence, seemed pleased with the scholarship he had received from Baylor University.

The intercom buzzed.

"Brother Williams, Howard Martin would like to see you."

"Send him in, Wanda."

Howard Martin walked into the office, slouched comfortably in a plush leather chair, and glanced around the room. "I believe you've made the big time, Cal."

"A little too fancy, huh?"

"No, I like it."

"What's on your mind, Howard?"

"I need some advice."

"Oh?"

"I've been offered the head coaching job at Southeast Louisiana University and I'm having a hard time deciding whether I should take it. You know how it is. Bogalusa is our home, and our church and friends are here. There's a lot to consider."

Calvin Williams searched Howard Martin's eyes, looking for a hint of what the man wanted to do. He saw nothing and asked, "Do you want to coach on the college level, Howard?"

"Coaching college ball has always been my dream. In fact, I'm afraid if I turn the job down, there might not be another opportunity. I'm not getting any younger."

"Tell me about it. I'm just a couple of months older than you are."

"Have you ever sold out to follow your dream, Cal?"

Calvin Williams chuckled. "Less than a year ago. I had a comfortable ministry in Hot Springs. I had been at my church a long time—I liked the people, and they liked me—but I had a sneaking-desire to come down here, so I resigned and moved to Bogalusa. So far, it has worked out. The Lord has blessed, and my family is doing well."

"What made you do it?"

"Maybe I needed a change? Maybe I just wanted to try something different? Maybe I was having a mid-life crisis? Basically, I thought I could do a good work in Bogalusa."

"So, you're saying go for it."

"No! I *am* saying, however, that if a man can follow his dream, he may regret it if he doesn't give it a shot." Calvin Williams let his words sink in, then asked, "Are you absolutely sure that you want to coach on the college level, Howard?"

"It's what I've worked for my entire adult life."

"You have already made your decision, then."

"You're right, of course. It's simply a matter of admitting it."

"I'm proud for you, Howard, but I hate losing my best friend."

"Hammond isn't far away. We can visit back and forth easily."

"You're right, and we will. When will you be moving?"

"I'll take over immediately, but I won't move to Hammond for several months. Howard Martin stood, reached across the desk, and clasped Calvin Williams' hand. "I haven't known you long, Cal, but I want you to know that your friendship means the world to me. I've never had a friend who cares, really cares, about me and my family."

Howard Martin released Calvin Williams' hand, turned, walked across the room, and quietly shut the door. Tears welled in Calvin Williams' eyes. Coach Martin's compliment had touched his heart. Uncharacteristically, the intercom buzzed again.

"Yes, Wanda."

"Brother Williams, your son would like to see you."

"Which one?"

"Bud."

"Send him in."

Bud seemed unusually nervous. Calvin Williams thought he had probably had a fender-bender in the Mustang, which was no big deal; bent fenders could be repaired.

"What's wrong, son?" Bud opened his mouth, tried to speak, and then burst into tears. "Son, what's wrong?" Calvin Williams asked again, intuitively knowing that the light at the end of the tunnel was now a fast-moving train.

"I don't know how to say it," Bud answered between sobs.

"Just say it, good or bad, and we'll deal with it. Now, what's wrong, Son?"

"It's Judith."

"What's wrong with Judith?"

"She's pregnant, Dad."

The color left Calvin Williams' face. "Are you sure?"

"Yes, sir. Doctor Pennington confirmed it today." Bud nervously ran his fingers through his thick brown hair. "Her dad is so mad he says he going to kill me."

"When people are angry, son, they say things, make threats, they don't intend to keep. We'll work the problem out."

The intercom buzzed again.

"Brother Williams, Mr. Webb would like to see you."

Horace Webb stormed into the office, slammed the door, grabbed Bud by the shirt, and jerked him out of his chair. Calvin Williams jumped up, circled his desk, grabbed Horace Webb's arms, and coldly said, "Take your hands off my son."

The ice in Calvin Williams' voice surprised Horace Webb — a preacher was supposed to be cheek-turning pussy, not a hard-talking man with cold eyes — but to make a point, he hesitated briefly, and then slowly removed his hands from Bud's shirt."

"Please, sit down, Mr. Webb. Let's handle this like gentlemen."

"Gentlemen, hell! Your son knocked-up my daughter and I'm out for blood."

"There will be no bloodshed, Mr. Webb."

"What makes you so sure?"

"Simply this: If you lay a hand on my son, I'll break it. I'm a patient man, Mr. Webb, but when someone strikes out at my children, I lose control."

"You're a preacher. You can't do a thing."

Calvin Williams pinned Horace Webb's arms to his sides, pushed him to the chair next to Bud, and, with a voice cold as steel, said, "Mr. Webb, don't force me to do something I will regret later. Are we going to talk or fight? It really doesn't matter to me. My patience has worn thin, and I'd just as soon do one as the other."

For several seconds, the two men stared darts into one another's eyes. Bud had never seen his father look so formidable, and he had never respected him more in his life. Horace Webb grunted, shook his head from side to side, and gave in.

"Let's talk."

"I think that's a wise decision." Calvin Williams leaned against his desk and crossed his arms. "Now, what do you suggest we do about the situation, Mr. Webb?"

"I've got an eighteen-year-old daughter—a little girl, for crying out loud—who's pregnant as a nanny-goat. The damage is already done. I don't know what the hell we're going to do."

"Mr. Webb, my son is the father of the child your daughter is carrying. He's a good boy. He's smart. He has a scholarship to Baylor University. I think he loves your daughter. People make mistakes. Perhaps our children should get married."

"Judith and I have already decided to get married, if it's okay with y'all."

"Now's a hell of a time to ask," Horace Webb replied sarcastically. Calvin Williams chuckled. Horace Webb's eyes turned to ice. "What's so damned funny, Preacher?"

"Certainly not our situation, Mr. Webb. Your sarcasm amuses me."

Webb smiled lightly. "Since we're going to be in-laws, why don't you call me Horace?"

Calvin Williams extended his hand. "Why don't you call me Calvin?"

Horace Webb shook Calvin Williams' hand, then turned to Bud and asked, "When do you and Judith plan on getting married?"

"When school's out, Mr. Webb. After that, we'll take a trip to Waco and find a place to live."

"You're moving my daughter to Texas?"

"Yes, sir. That's where I have my scholarship."

"What's wrong with a Louisiana school?"

"Nothing, Mr. Webb. But my scholarship is at Baylor."

Horace Webb took a deep breath and swallowed hard. "I won't object to your plans, but there's something that bothering me." Calvin Williams rolled his eyes, wondering what the next bombshell would be. "It doesn't seem right for Judith, being pregnant and all, to go two months without a husband."

"Couldn't we keep it a secret?" Bud asked.

"I'm sure," Calvin Williams replied, "that everyone in town will think Judith has been overeating. No, we can't keep Judith's pregnancy a secret. One thing, however, must be considered above everything else."

Horace Webb and Bud leaned forward and listened intently. "I don't think married students can attend high school. If that's the case, the wedding is off until Bud and Judith graduate."

Sensing the finality in Calvin Williams' voice, Horace Webb kept his mouth shut. "Now, gentlemen," he said, picking up his suit coat, "it's time for the hard part."

"What's that, Dad?"

"Telling your mother."

CHAPTER 20

Calvin Williams walked into his office, sat down at his desk, and pondered the curveball he had been thrown the day before. He felt as if he had fallen off a mountain, landed in a flooded river, and the devil was pulling at his heels. An old rule, written in stone, was still in effect: when a pastor or a member of his family messes up, the pastor does not get a second chance. Calvin Williams knew, regardless of how much good he had accomplished, that he would suffer the consequences for his son's behavior.

Although he knew the pulse of his church—most of his parishioners would want him to stay—he also knew that a vociferous minority would never tolerate a pastor whose son had impregnated a young woman before marriage. Twenty years of ministry told him that a self-righteous few would soon unite and make his life a living hell.

How many families have I helped with the same dilemma? Dozens! But that doesn't matter. People expect pastors to set a proper example and don't give them a second chance.

Calvin Williams sighed, leaned back in his chair, and considered his options.

The thing to do is keep the church united, help Bud and Judith start a life together, then resign and move back to Hot Springs. I don't like it, but when the news about Bud and Judith surfaces, and it will surface, I'll have to spend most of my time putting out fires, and once the fires are extinguished, it will be time to move on.

It's inevitable. The pressure will come, especially when the self-righteous few learn that Bud and Judith aren't getting married until after they graduate in May. But I won't nullify Bud's scholarship by marrying him to Judith now. He has worked too long and too hard. They'll stay in school, graduate, and go to college together.

Calvin Williams decided that sitting around worrying about what might or might not happen was a waste of time. He opened his Bible, reached for his pen and legal pad, and then started jotting down thoughts for his Sunday Sermon. An hour later, the intercom buzzed.

"Yes, Wanda?"

"Brother Williams, Mrs. Ardmore would like to see you."

"Send her in, Wanda."

Calvin Williams took a deep breath, knowing disaster was about to walk through the door. Edna Ardmore, the ruling-matriarch of Trinity Baptist Church, was a gossiping old bitty who spread bad news like a twenty-four-hour virus. She took great pride in being the pastor's critic, and although Calvin Williams had escaped her scathing tongue so far, when Sweet Miss Edna stepped into his office, he saw the pious smirk on her face, and knew that she was relishing his predicament.

"Brother Williams, I've heard some disturbing news that I want to discuss with you."

"I know what you're going to say, Mrs. Ardmore."

"Then it's true? Your son has gotten that poor little Webb girl in trouble?"

"Yes, ma'am."

"And what are you going to do about it?" she asked indignantly.

"I plan to marry them in May."

Miss Edna tilted her head and stared down her nose at Calvin Williams.

"Why not immediately?"

"If Bud and Judith marry now, they can't graduate in May."

"Waiting is despicable, Brother Williams. You *will* marry them now."

Calvin Williams did not want to lose his temper—there would be far-reaching repercussions if he did—but the past twenty-four hours had been difficult, and he was approaching the point of no return.

"Mrs. Ardmore, that's out of the question. An education is important to young people, even when they're pregnant. Whether you like it or not, my son *will* graduate from high school."

"Right is right, Brother Williams, and if that means your son and his pregnant girlfriend can't graduate, so be it. The situation sets a poor example. An apology to the church and an immediate wedding is the only course of action."

Stress and tension finally took their toll.

Calvin Williams lost his temper.

"Mrs. Ardmore, please leave before I say something I may regret."

"I won't leave until I'm satisfied that you're going to do something about this disgusting situation. There is sin in the camp and the church will suffer if you don't do something about it now."

Calvin Williams pushed the button on the intercom. "Wanda, if Mrs. Ardmore doesn't pass your desk in one minute, will you please call the police?"

"Yes, Brother Williams."

Wanda glanced at the clock and stared at the door. Sweet Miss Edna smirked, raised her nose into the air, and stubbornly kept her seat. "You wouldn't dare."

"You've wasted approximately fifteen seconds, Mrs. Ardmore, which means you have forty-five seconds to pass

Wanda's desk. Keep your seat and you'll find out how serious I am."

Calvin Williams walked to the door and opened it. Sweet Miss Edna, defying him, hesitated, then abruptly stood, and walked out of his office. "You'll hear more about this, Brother Williams."

"I'm sure I will, Mrs. Ardmore."

Calvin Williams watched the self-righteous old bitty pass Wanda's desk with her nose in the air. Commonsense said, "Let her go," but commonsense did not prevail.

"Mrs. Ardmore!" Sweet Miss Edna turned and faced her rude, immoral, and ill-mannered pastor. "It's raining outside. If you don't lower your nose, you might drown, and that would be unfortunate, don't you think?"

"Well," she exclaimed, and then rushed out the door. Calvin Williams shook his head and returned to his office. Two minutes later, Wanda knocked on his door.

"What's going on, Brother Williams?"

"I thought you probably put two and two together when Horace Webb stormed into my office yesterday. It seems, Wanda, my son has impregnated Judith Webb without the benefit of marriage. Mrs. Ardmore felt obliged to give me her matriarchal advice. I didn't take it well, as you obviously noticed."

"She deserved everything she got, Brother Williams, and more. Someone should have put Edna Ardmore in her place a long time ago. What do you plan to do?

"I'll pastor the church until June, then I'll resign and move back to Arkansas."

"That's not fair."

"It goes with the territory, Wanda. I'm not the first pastor who has faced a situation like this, and I certainly won't be the last."

Tears surfaced in Wanda's eyes.

"Hey, don't cry. Things will work out. They always do."

He patted Wanda's shoulder, said, "I'm taking the day off," and then walked through the new, glistening foyer to face the rain. Thunder rolled when he opened the door, and a furious downpour mussed his freshly cleaned suit. Calvin Williams did not care.

CHAPTER 21

The Rebels made it to the finals of the State Tournament and would play the Shreveport Bears on Saturday afternoon for the Louisiana Junior High State Basketball Championship. A lot had happened during the week, most of it had been bad, and there was much Calvin and Louise Williams had to discuss on the two-hour trip to Baton Rouge.

Hammering Edna Ardmore had felt good, but she had rallied several supporters who were hell bent on removing Calvin Williams as the pastor of Trinity Baptist Church. Sweet Miss Edna did not have the votes to accomplish her goal, but her clamorous followers, with their snide remarks and cold shoulders, made him feel tainted and cheap.

"You know, Lou, if it wasn't for Bud and Judith, I'd resign Sunday and move back to Arkansas."

"Aren't you being a little hasty? We've had more supportive calls than hateful ones."

"You're right, of course. It's just that I'm feeling a little down right now. I've worked hard for this church. Then something happens that's beyond my control and the hounds of hell stalk me and try to nail my hide to the wall. It just isn't fair."

"Why, Calvin Williams, I believe you're feeling sorry for yourself."

His wife's words stung him like an angry wasp.

"Am I exempt from self-pity simply because I'm a pastor?"

"No, Cal," she answered flatly. "It's just not like you, that's all."

They rode in thick silence for several miles. Finally at Denham Springs, Calvin braked the car, and pulled onto the parking lot of a crowded café.

"I need a cup of coffee. Do you want one?"

Louise nodded her head and opened the door. Calvin walked around the car, reached for her hand, and then led her to a corner booth inside the restaurant.

"You're right, Lou."

"What do you mean?"

"I *am* feeling sorry for myself." He sipped his coffee. "We've made it through hard times before and we'll make it through this bump in the road, too." She smiled and nodded her head in agreement. "You realize, don't you, that I can't stay at Trinity?"

"I know when the handwriting is on the wall, Cal. It's just a matter of time." She poured creamer into her cup and slowly stirred the coffee. "It'll be nice living in Hot Springs again."

"I've been thinking for the last couple of days."

"About what?"

"What I'm going to do when we move home. We've been able to save some money the last couple of years, so I'm considering taking a smaller church, one that's not so demanding, and working on my doctorate."

"Now that sounds like the man I married and have loved for twenty years, a man who takes adversity and turns into something positive. I think working on your doctorate is a great idea."

•   •   •

Shreveport could not buy a basket in the third quarter. The Bear's Center was exhausted—Jack Perone had leaned on him the entire game—and frustrated Guards kept taking desperation shots from downtown Baton Rouge and missing badly. The Rebels held a 46 to 38 lead going into the fourth quarter.

"Will they crack, Howard?"

"I don't think so, Cal. Shreveport is tired, down, and doubting."

The Rebels did not crack, the Bears hibernated, and Coach Sam Lequieu won his first State Championship. It was, he thought, surreal, dreamlike. He had coached several outstanding teams, deserving teams, that had fallen short of a championship. As he watched his Rebels celebrate at mid-court, Coach Lequieu knew—there was not a doubt in his mind—that he had won his first State Championship because a cocky, fifteen-year-old boy had willed it.

Calvin, Louise, and Sherry Williams worked their way through the celebratory melee and found Jamie at mid-court hugging his big brother. Savoring the moment, Calvin Williams realized—at that precise instant—that the simple pleasure of seeing his sons, tall, strong, and handsome, made his sun come up every morning. He took his girls by the hand and approached his boys, beaming with pride.

"I thought you had to work, Bud."

"I couldn't miss seeing my little brother win a State Championship, Dad."

"I'm glad you came," Jamie said. "You taught me how to shoot a basketball."

"All I did was try to break your nose."

"What if I had missed that shot in the backyard?"

"You didn't miss," Bud replied. "You never miss, Jamie."

CHAPTER 22

"I resign my office as pastor, effective June first."

Calvin Williams had thought about the decision, agonized over it in fact, and had concluded resigning was the right thing to do. His supporters would be disillusioned for a while, but he knew, in time, that would pass. He intended to pull the church together, and then leave, avoiding an inevitable church fight. Although his ministry was ending much too soon, he was proud of the fact that Trinity Baptist Church was better off now than it had been when he took over as pastor.

Michelle squeezed Jamie's hand, aching inside for Calvin Williams. She would move to Hammond in August, but Hammond was only an hour away, and Jamie had a motorcycle, so they would see each other often. But Hot Springs was three-hundred miles away—Jamie would live on the moon—and that disturbing reality tied her stomach in knots.

Sherry, caught in the crossfire, considered herself collateral damage. A week before Bud broke the news that Judith was pregnant, Phil had asked her to marry him, and she had said yes, thinking her family would live in Bogalusa indefinitely. Now, because of her father's resignation, she would have to move back to Arkansas with her parents or marry Phil and remain in Louisiana.

Sherry was and always had been, closer to her father than Bud and Jamie. She understood—truly understood—how excited he had been about his church and how deeply it hurt him to give it up. Seeing him handle church members—supporters and non-supporters—with dignity and grace had broken her heart. With her blood boiling, Sherry glanced at Sweet Miss Edna and decided that she would not darken the doors of another church. If church people were the best God had to offer, God, Sherry believed, was in deep trouble.

•　•　•

Sunday afternoon, a soothing calm swept over Calvin and Louise Williams. Alone and relaxed, they were discussing the move to Hot Springs when, uncharacteristically, Sherry and Phil walked in the parsonage several hours earlier than usual and sat down on the sofa.

Calvin Williams stared at his daughter suspiciously and he felt his stomach pang as he analyzed the situation. *They want to get married. Why didn't I see this coming?*

"Dad, Phil has something he wants to discuss with you."

Sherry smiled and walked out of the living room with her mother. When his girls had settled in the dining room, Calvin Williams asked, "What's on your mind, Phil?"

"Sherry and I want to get married, Brother Williams.

"When?"

"On May fifteenth," he replied, and then hurriedly explained: "We didn't intend to get married this quickly, but with you moving back to Arkansas, we had to move it up."

Calvin Williams leaned forward and looked hard into Phil's eyes. "What if I don't give my consent?"

Phil sat up straight and coldly replied, "I'll marry her anyway, sir."

"Then why are you asking me?"

"I'm asking because it's the right thing to do."

"Very well. You have my consent."

"I'll be good to her, Brother Williams."

"I believe you, Phil. Congratulations."

"Thank you, sir."

"Your life may be very interesting."

"What does *that* mean, Brother Williams?"

"Sherry is a lot like her mother."

Phil chuckled. "That doesn't seem like a terrible prospect to me."

"You've got a lot to learn, Phil."

Calvin Williams, rather smugly, offered no explanation.

CHAPTER 23

"So, you're moving back to Hot Springs?"

"Yes, sir."

"Don't forget the advice I gave you."

Jamie tapped his head and smiled drolly. "I won't get the bighead, I won't be a ball hog, I won't play football, and I'll make good grades."

"Maybe you *do* listen now and then."

"Only to people I respect, Coach."

Sam Lequieu rolled his eyes and handed Jamie a manila envelope. "For what it's worth, this"—he nodded at the envelope—"lists your accomplishments at Bogalusa Junior High School and my recommendations for you as a player. Give it to your coach in Hot Springs. It may keep you from breaking your leg on a football field."

"Thank you, Coach."

"Before you leave, Jamie, I want you to do me a favor?"

"Anything, Coach?"

"A few years down the road when you and your beloved Razorbacks reach the finals in the NCAA Tournament, send me a ticket. It will be fun watching you win a national championship."

• • •

Rick Cullin elbowed his friends when Jamie Williams and Michelle Martin walked into the theater. Except for Michelle Martin, Jamie Williams was alone. It had been a long time coming, but revenge, Rick believed, was going to be sweet.

Five minutes later, Jamie told Michelle that he needed to go to the restroom. With nothing on his mind but the latest James Bond movie—No one had harassed Jamie in months—he walked in the men's room, took a leak, zipped his pants, and stepped away from the urinal. When he leaned over the vanity to wash his hands, the restroom door opened, and he saw Rick Cullin glaring at him in the mirror. Vulnerable and alone, Jamie knew he was in deep trouble.

"Well, look who's all by himself."

Rick's friends, like a pack of wolves, circled Jamie, grabbed him by the neck, secured his arms, then pulled him to the wet, grimy floor. Rick waited until he was sure that Jamie could not fight back, then mounted his chest and snarled, "If I remember correctly, Yankee, this is the exact position you had me in last year."

"There is one difference," Jamie replied.

"Oh?"

"I didn't need any help."

Rick's fist seemed huge as he pounded Jamie's face and nose, the pain almost unbearable. Jamie took his beating silently and did not give Rick and his friends the satisfaction of hearing him cry out in pain. Finally, it grew dark, and Jamie was glad.

Michelle had become edgy. Jamie had been gone ten minutes, and the movie was starting. Then she vaguely remembered seeing Rick Cullin and his friends sitting at the back of the theater. She turned and searched the back row. It was empty.

The threat! They wouldn't!

Jamie opened his eyes and remembered. The pain in his head and side would not allow him to sit up. He placed a hand to his nose—thick blood covered his fingers.

The door squeaked open. Sickened by Jamie's bloody face and swollen eyes, the manager ran and kneeled beside him. "Who did this to you?" he asked, concern and anger in his voice.

•   •   •

Dr. Matthew Pennington walked into the waiting room and reached for Calvin and Louise Williams' hands. "Jamie will be fine. His ribs are bruised—that will be painful for several days—but thank God there is no damage to his eyes."

Dr. Pennington slammed a fist into his open left hand. "Cal, he wouldn't tell me who did it. He wants to take care of it himself. That, and I am sure you agree, isn't going to happen. Whoever did this to Jamie needs to be in jail."

Michelle had said very little since she arrived at the Emergency Room with her parents, but when she heard Dr. Pennington describe Jamie's injuries, she could not allow foolish male-pride to keep Rick Cullin from getting what he deserved.

"Rick Cullin and his friends were in the theater when Jamie went to the restroom. Their seats were empty when he didn't come back. It had to be them. They threatened Jamie in January."

Howard Martin walked to the pay phone, inserted a dime, and dialed the Bogalusa Police Department. "This is Coach Howard Martin. I want to report an assault."

•   •   •

Leaving Michelle bruised Jamie's heart worse than Rick Cullin had bruised his body. The external bruises were no big deal—they had faded in less than two weeks—but when he crawled into the backseat of his father's Impala, Jamie was not sure if the internal bruises would ever heal.

Living in Bogalusa had not been easy, especially at first, but with Michelle as a constant companion, Jamie could not remember ever being happier. When Calvin Williams backed onto West 12th Street for the last time, he mumbled, "I'm never getting close to anyone again."

"Don't say that, Jamie," Louise Williams replied. "You know you don't mean it."

"Yes, I do. It hurts too much to say goodbye."

Having spoken his mind, Jamie closed his eyes and went to sleep.

CHAPTER 24

The Williams new home, a modest stucco structure on Bower Street, was, in Jamie's opinion, a great place to live. Several of his classmates from Central Junior High School, including his closest friend Bill Mitchell, lived nearby—he liked that—but regardless of what he did or where he went, Michelle was always on his mind.

Bill quickly noticed that Jamie was not the same fun-loving guy he had grown up with. In fact, Bill did not like the new Jamie. He wanted the old Jamie back, and had decided—one way or another—to help his friend get over ole What's-Her-Name in Louisiana. In Bill's opinion, it was stupid to moon over a girl who lived three-hundred miles away when there were plenty of well-stacked girls in skimpy bathing suits strutting their stuff on the lakes surrounding Hot Springs.

"You want to ride out to Spillway Landing and check out the scenery?"

"Sure," Jamie replied with very little enthusiasm.

Bill rolled his eyes, more than a little disgusted. If Jamie was half a man, he would be excited about riding out to Spillway Landing, a popular recreational area west of Mountain Pine frequented by teenagers during the summer. Bill, in fact, had conspired to set Jamie up with his cousin Vicki Hems, who was waiting at Spillway Landing with his girlfriend Nancy Fuller. If

Vicki and Jamie hit it off, he would get over ole What's-Her-Name in Louisiana, and of course, Bill could spend the day with Nancy.

Thirty minutes later, they pulled off their T-shirts and left their motorcycles on the sealed parking lot near the boat ramp. Tanned and muscular—only their youthful faces betrayed their manhood—they strutted to the edge of the water, dove in, and swam fifty yards, stroke for stroke, to a floating dock secured to the bottom of Lake Ouachita by metal cables. They slithered up on the dock, shook the water from their hair, lay on their stomachs, and stared at skiers in the distance.

"Hi, Jamie."

The girl was lying on her side in a pink, two-piece swimsuit. Her blonde hair, shoulder-length, was wet and clinging to her shoulders. She was pretty and vaguely familiar.

"Hi," he mumbled.

"You don't remember me, do you?" Jamie shrugged his shoulders indifferently. "In the eighth grade, I sat across from you in every class." Nothing clicked. Jamie rested his head on his arm and closed his eyes. Vicki glanced at Bill, shrugged her shoulders, and pressed on. "I thought you moved to Louisiana."

"Things didn't work out, so I'm back home."

"And you'll be going to Hot Springs High School?"

"Yes."

"Are you going to play football and basketball again?"

"No." Vicki was disappointed, then pleased when Jamie said, "Just basketball. If everything works out, I'll be running and shooting, not blocking and tackling."

"Jamie was an MVP in Louisiana last year, Vicki."

"You don't say," she replied, seemingly unimpressed. "Maybe I can cheer you on?"

"Vicki's a cheerleader," Bill explained.

"You don't say," Jamie replied, mocking her; and then rested his head on his arm and looked the other way.

Vicki glanced at Bill and frowned. What could he say? It was not his fault that Jamie was acting like a lovesick fool. He sat up, shrugged his shoulders, and dipped his feet in the water.

"Nancy Fuller is in the camper with mom. I'm sure you remember Nancy, Jamie. Why don't we swim to the bank, get something to drink, and listen to the radio?"

"Sounds good to me," Bill replied.

Jamie threw Bill an icy stare, stood, and dove into the water.

"He's not a happy camper," Vicki observed matter-of-factly.

"Give him time and he'll crawl out of his shell."

Vicki watched Jamie swimming toward shore and thought of the many times she had caught the eyes of some girl's boyfriend. She walked to the edge of the dock, hesitated, then turned to Bill and said, "Let's see if I can make him forget Louisiana."

•   •   •

Jamie was more than a little suspicious when Bill and Nancy clasped hands and walked down the narrow road winding through the recreational area. *That,* he quickly decided, was not a coincidence, or a chance encounter, and it pissed him off.

"You and Bill set me up, didn't you, Vicki?"

"What do you mean?" He pointed at Bill and Nancy—angrily, Vicki thought—and walked stiffly toward the parking lot. "Where're you going?"

"Home."

"Why?"

"I don't like being set up."

"I wanted to get acquainted with you," Vicki said as Jamie pulled on his T-shirt and straddled his motorcycle. "What else could I do? You ignored me when I walked up and down the sidewalk in front of your house, so I asked Bill..."

"Wait a minute. Bill is..."

"My cousin. He owed me a favor. I introduced him to Nancy. If I had known you were going to act like this, I wouldn't have asked Bill to bring you here."

Vicki turned and walked across the parking lot. Her swimsuit, Jamie noticed, had inched upward, exposing an extremely white cheek. She reached behind her back, adjusted the swimsuit, and the white cheek, to Jamie's chagrin, disappeared.

He started the Honda, but when the engine settled to a smooth, resonant idle, he shut it down, followed Vicki back to the campsite, and slouched in a folding lawn chair.

"I thought you were leaving."

"Since you went to all the trouble, I might as well stay."

"Don't flatter yourself, Jamie."

"Actually, it was your butt."

"What?"

"I liked it when you covered your pretty, white cheek."

"That was totally..."

"I'm just picking on you, Vicki."

"All I wanted to do was get to know you, Jamie."

"Then get to know me."

He smiled, and for the first time noticed how pretty she was: deep-blue eyes, blonde hair, which was rather wild looking because of the wind and water, and a summer tan.

"I'm glad you two are finally talking to one another," Nancy Fuller observed as she walked across the campsite, holding Bill's hand. "Do you remember me, Jamie?"

"Sure, Nancy. How are you?"

"I'm good. Just ask Bill. Welcome home."

Jamie chuckled.

"Do y'all want to stay for supper?" Vicki asked. "We're roasting hotdogs."

Bill glanced at Jamie, expecting the lovesick fool to decline the invitation. When Jamie nodded his head yes, Bill wanted to high-five God. Hotdogs for supper and Nancy Fuller for dessert. Life, in Bill's opinion, did not get much better than that.

•   •   •

Jamie and Vicki swam to the floating dock as the sun dropped below the mountains sheltering Lake Ouachita, the wake from passing boats rocking them as they lay side by side under a darkening sky. Vicki kissed Jamie, then laughed when they came up for air. He looked like a mischievous little boy caught with his hand in a cookie jar.

"What's so funny?"

"You are."

"I don't understand."

"You look guilty." Jamie took a deep breath and exhaled. "I know you have a girlfriend in Louisiana. Bill told me. I also know you're about to start high school. What are you going to do? Stay home with mommy and daddy while your friends are out having fun?"

"I don't know."

"I could really like you, Jamie, but if you're going to sit around and mope over a girl you never see, I don't want to. Is there something wrong with me? What does she have that I don't have?"

"There's nothing wrong with you, Vicki."

"The girl, whatever her name is, will never know."

"Her name is Michelle, and we're going steady."

"How can you go steady with someone who lives in another state?"

"Good question."

"You can see me anytime you want, Jamie."

He smiled drolly. "I like what I'm seeing now."

"What do you mean?"

"Your boob is showing."

Vicki glanced at her chest, saw that her top had shifted and that she was giving Jamie a pinup view of her left breast. She adjusted the top. "I didn't intend for you to see that much of me."

"I think it's time to have fun again."

Vicki noticed a change in Jamie's eyes when he kissed her and did not object when he pulled down her top. She glanced at the sky—it was dark and there was no moon—then she glanced toward the shore and saw vague shapes sitting around the campfire. Confident that her mother could not see what she was doing, Vicki kissed Jamie eagerly until his hand slid down her stomach and inched beneath her swimsuit. She stiffened, removed his hand, and mumbled, "Not that much fun."

CHAPTER 25

Jamie pulled his T-shirt over his head, lay face down on a quilt he had spread in the backyard earlier in the day, and closed his eyes. Twenty minutes later, Vicki Helms nudged him with her foot and said, "I think you're addicted to the sun, Jamie."

"Why don't you pull off your blouse and join me?"

"This isn't Spillway Landing."

Vicki sat on the quilt and crossed her legs.

Jamie smiled drolly. "I'd rather look at your panties, anyway."

"You're disgusting."

Vicki straightened her shorts, but she was smiling.

Jamie pulled on his T-shirt, grabbed Vicki's hand, helped her up, and led her toward the house. "We'll make out for a while and then take a walk through the neighborhood."

"What about your parents?"

"They'll be gone all day."

For two weeks, Vicki and Jamie had been bold explorers and their adventures had been more than a little exciting. After Spillway Landing, she usually let Jamie push down her bra—that was no big deal—but she had limits. When he became too adventurous and tried to slide his hand beneath her panties, she always removed it and told him no. Some of her girlfriends had let their boyfriends take them all the way, but Vicki had not decided about that. Jamie wanted to do more, but a panty massage was enough for her, and that was as far as she would go — for now.

Twenty minutes later, she pushed his hand away, adjusted her shorts, said, "I think it's time for our walk," and then pulled him outside. They meandered through the neighborhood for several minutes, walked up a steep hill, and entered a different world covered with affluent homes and large, meticulously maintained lawns. One natural-stone house — it looked like a mansion to Jamie — caught his eye.

More than a little bored, Dalton Hilliard turned off the television, glanced out the window, and saw Jamie Williams and Vicki Helms standing on the sidewalk in front of his house. Dalton did not like Jamie, wondered if he had moved back to Hot Springs, hoped he had not, and decided now was as good a time as any to find out. He stepped out on the front porch, walked across the lawn, forced a smile when he approached the gate, and sarcastically asked, "What are y'all gawking at?"

"We're just killing time," Vicki replied, feeling the electricity sparking between the two boys like corpses in an old Frankenstein movie. "You remember Jamie, don't you?"

Determined not to blink or look away, the two boys stared at one another. After several seconds, Dalton finally said, "Yeah, I remember Jamie. How's it going, man?"

"Not bad. Yourself?"

"Kind of bored. You know. Nothing's going on."

"I know what you mean. I'll be glad when school starts."

"Are you just visiting, or have you moved back to Hot Springs?"

"I moved back. Things didn't work out in Louisiana. You know?"

"Yeah, I guess," Dalton replied, not caring one way or the other, and showing it.

The tension, veiled with small-talk, fascinated Vicki. She quickly noticed that she had become a non-person, as Jamie and Dalton, like two Tomcats, hissed and sized each other up.

Questions were churning in Dalton's head, and he decided that offering a peasant something to drink would be a small price to pay to satisfy his curiosity. "Do y'all want a Coke?"

"Sure," Vicki answered.

Dalton opened the gate and led them to a spacious patio surrounded by hedges and then walked into the house to fetch the Cokes. Jamie threw Vicki an icy stare. She smiled, ever so sweetly, and said, "I thought the two of you might want to get reacquainted."

"Are you crazy? Dalton got me kicked off the football team when we were in the eighth grade. We can't stand each other."

"I didn't know that."

"Let's make this fast. As you can see, we're both uncomfortable."

Dalton handed Jamie and Vicki their Cokes, then walked across the patio, slouched in a padded lawn chair, crossed his legs, popped the tab, and stared over the can at his guests. Jamie thought Dalton looked like the comic book character Richie Rich.

"Are you going to play football this year, Jamie?"

"No. I'm going to concentrate on basketball."

"What about the rules?"

"Rules are made to be broken, Dalton."

Dalton chuckled. "So, what are you going to do?"

"I'm going to tell Coach Johnson that I'll play basketball, not football."

"And if that doesn't work?"

"I'll have my dad talk to him."

"And if that doesn't work?"

"I guess I'll play football."

Both boys laughed, and an unexpected rapport surfaced.

"I don't want to play football either. Why don't we talk to Coach Johnson together?"

"Sounds good to me."

"You want to shoot a few hoops to get ready for the season?"

"Why not?"

"When do you want to start?"

"How about today?" Jamie asked, extending his hand.

"Sounds great," Dalton answered, grasping it. "I don't like you, but I need the practice."

Jamie laughed. "Do you think I give a shit?"

"You never have, Jamie."

CHAPTER 26

Standing outside the Hot Springs High School Athletic Complex, Jamie and Dalton were more than a little nervous about confronting Coach Johnson. Rules were rules, but when rules did not make sense, someone — it might as well be them — had to change the system that made them.

Stan Smith, the Trojan's head football coach, was leaning against the counter separating the offices from the foyer when Jamie and Dalton walked into the building. Tired of dealing with confused students and their stupid questions, Coach Smith asked, "What do you boys want?" His brusque voice told Jamie and Dalton that the best thing they could do was yelp, tuck their tails between their legs, and run.

"We want to talk to Coach Johnson," Jamie replied.

"Why?"

"It's kind of personal, Coach."

"If you have a personal problem, go see the guidance counselor."

"We don't need a guidance counselor," Jamie persisted.

"I don't have time for Mickey Mouse games. Get the hell out of here."

Coach Johnson stepped out of his office, immediately recognized Dalton, and after a moment, recognized Jamie as the kid who could not miss two years ago. The first thought that popped into his mind was with Terrance Brooks, Dalton Hilliard and Jamie Williams, the Trojans were going to be one hell of a basketball team.

"What do you boys want?"

Jamie said, "If you have time, Coach Johnson, we'd like to talk to you…alone."

Coach Smith glared at Jamie and Dalton, lifted the hinged-counter, and stepped out of the way. Coach Johnson, somewhat amused—no one bucked Coach Smith and got away with it—walked back into his office and sat behind his desk. Without saying a word, Jamie Williams handed him a legal-sized envelope. Coach Johnson opened the envelope, scanned the contents, and then placed it on his desk.

"You've done well, Jamie. I'm proud of you."

"Thank you, Coach."

"Now, what's this visit about?"

"As you just read, Coach, I've been advised to concentrate on basketball."

"I believe that's sound advice."

"Dalton and I don't want to play football this year."

Coach Johnson shook his head emphatically. "Both of you know that when you're in athletics, you play football and basketball and that you run track."

"Why?" Jamie asked.

"I don't know, and I don't care. That's the rule."

Jamie glanced at Dalton. "Well, I guess that settles it."

They turned and walked toward the door.

"Settles what?" Coach Johnson asked, stopping them.

"That we won't be playing for the Trojans this year."

"Are you telling me you won't play football *and* basketball?"

"That's right, Coach," Jamie replied.

Dalton nodded his head in agreement and reached for the door handle. Coach Johnson stared darts at the two boys, trying to intimidate them. "I don't like being threatened."

"We're not threatening you, Coach," Jamie replied matter-of-factly. "Basketball is rough enough. If we play football, we're doubling our chance for injury."

Coach Johnson tapped his fingers on the desk, one after the other, and weighed Jamie and Dalton's argument. "I'll ask you one more time: If you have to play football, you won't play basketball?"

"That's right, Coach," Jamie replied.

"I talked to my dad about it," Dalton added. "He said that I shouldn't waste my time with football when it's obvious basketball's my game. He's backing me to the hilt."

Coach Johnson leafed through Jamie's papers. "Two MVP awards and a State Championship in the same season?"

"Yes, sir."

"And you'd give up a game you obviously excel at over a technicality?"

"Yes, sir."

"You're crazy."

"Yes, sir."

Coach Johnson searched his brain, trying to remember why the rule had been implemented, and decided that Jamie Williams' coach in Louisiana was right: the rule was dumb, counterproductive, and paper-pushing bureaucrats, who did not know their asses from a hole in the ground, should not force basketball players to play football.

"I won't make any promises, but I'll see what I can do."

•   •   •

"What did they want, Jim?"

"Would you believe that I've been threatened with a strike?"

"A strike? What do you mean?"

"Dalton and Jamie say they're basketball players and refuse to play football."

"To hell with them! We don't need them, anyway."

"I'm not so sure about that."

He handed Coach Smith Jamie's folder. Two minutes later, Coach Smith shook his head and said, "It seems your eighth-grade prodigy has turned into a genuine blue-chipper. But that doesn't give him the right to march in here and make demands."

"Jamie simply did what his Louisiana coach told him to do. You read the packet, Stan. The question is, what are *we* going to do?"

"Did they get smart with you?"

"No."

"Do you think they're serious?"

"Very."

"Then change the rules and make everybody happy."

"Okay."

"What's the world coming to, Jim? Fifteen-year-old boys are packaging their goods like professionals. The next thing you know, they'll want us to pay them for playing."

Coach Smith chuckled. "You have to admit Jamie and Dalton have guts."

"Or gall." Coach Smith looked up at the ceiling and rubbed his chin. "This doesn't make sense, Jim."

"What do you mean?"

"Jamie Williams and Dalton Hilliard being friends."

"I don't understand."

"You know? Like father, like son? I went to school with Calvin Williams *and* William Hilliard. William came from a well-to-do family. Calvin didn't have a pot to pee in or a window to throw it out of. William would always pick on Calvin, and Calvin would always fight him. Just like Jamie, Calvin didn't take garbage from anyone. The funny thing is, Calvin always won the fight. But William never gave up and always came back for more. After each whipping, Calvin would say, 'Willy'—and William hated it when someone called him Willy—'anytime you think you can take me, come on back, I'll be waiting.' William would lick his wounds for a while, and then, in time, come back and start another fight.

"Think about it, Jim! Two years ago, Jamie and Dalton *were* their father's sons. They hated each other. I kicked Jamie off the junior high football team because he lost his temper and popped Dalton on the head with his helmet. Now they're friends? It doesn't make sense."

"Well, Stan, as Bob Dylan says, 'the times they are a changing.'"

CHAPTER 27

Vicki had not talked to Jamie all day. He had paired off with Dalton Hilliard that morning and they had walked—purposefully, she thought—toward Trojan Field House. She was curious about what they had been up to and had decided it had something to do with basketball. Jamie and Dalton were obsessed with basketball.

Surprised that he had not noticed her when he passed her in the crowded hallway—Jamie's mind was a thousand miles away—Vicki watched him stuff his books in his locker, then walked up behind him and squeezed his arm. Startled, he jumped, looked at her, and smiled. "Where have you been hiding out?" she asked. "I haven't seen you all day."

"Dalton and I have been talking to Coach Johnson."

"Do you want to run over to Pappas Brothers for some chili?"

"Let's walk instead."

Vicki giggled, liking Jamie's good mood.

"How's your first day back at dear old Hot Springs High?"

"Like I never left."

Jamie reached for Vicki's hand and then led her outdoors and off campus. Ten minutes later, they crossed Central Avenue and stepped inside the Pappas Brothers Restaurant. Although the place was jampacked, the waiters, accustomed to rowdy teenagers, took their order, and within minutes, Jamie and Vicki were sitting in a high-backed booth, sprinkling oyster crackers on steaming bowls of chili and cheese.

"Well, look who's back."

Jamie looked over his shoulder and saw a familiar freckled face. Two years before, Jeffery Davis had picked on him constantly. Jamie had finally gotten a belly full, caught Jeff by surprise, and fought him on the sidewalk in front of Central Junior High School.

"Revenge is going to be sweet, Williams."

"You couldn't handle me two years ago, Jeff. What makes you think you can handle me now?"

"You won't catch me by surprise again. This time, I decide when and where."

Seemingly unfazed by a pending fight and the blustering idiot sitting in the booth behind him, Jamie turned to his lunch. "You're not going to fight him, are you?" Vicki asked apprehensively.

"I haven't decided yet. It's no big deal."

Vicki knew Jamie was angry; his eyes had narrowed, and he had stopped talking. She had dated Jamie long enough to know that when someone pissed him off, he usually clammed up. They ate their lunch without talking, left a small tip on the table, and then walked outside the restaurant. Jamie hesitated and leaned against the building. Seeing fire in his eyes, Vicki grabbed his arm and pulled him toward the street.

"You have nothing to prove, Jamie."

"I'm not going to prove anything. Just prevent a problem before it starts."

The restaurant door opened.

Jamie stepped between Jeffery Davis and Ouachita Avenue.

By the look on his face, Jeff did not expect the confrontation.

"Are you ready for your revenge, Jeff?"

"Not today. It has to be on my terms."

Jamie grabbed Jeff's shirt and pushed him against the building. "I'm not going to take your shit, Jeff, not for one second." He pulled Jeff's shirt tight. A button popped off, fell on the sidewalk, and rolled toward the street. Vicki backed away, shocked by Jamie's menacing demeanor and the fear in Jeff's eyes. "Right now, in front of God and Vicki, put up or shut up, Jeff." Jamie backed away and placed both hands on his hips. "Are you going to leave me alone? Or do I have to whip your ass?"

"I'll leave you alone."

Jamie chuckled as Jeff scurried down the sidewalk. It was all the big redhead could do to keep from running. He reached for Vicki's hand and headed back to school.

"You're insane, Jamie."

"No, I'm not."

"If you had ignored him, Jeff would have left you alone."

"Jeff is a bully, Vicki. Give him an inch and he'll take a mile. Things would have only gotten worse. It's better to face a problem head on and settle it, once and for all."

"But what if Jeff had fought you and won?"

"I've never lost a fight or a basketball game."

"There's always a first time."

"It hasn't happened yet."

Vicki did not know if Jamie was brilliant or insane. He *had* bluffed Jeff effectively, but what if Jeff had called his bluff? She admired Jamie's confidence, but that confidence bordered on arrogance. She had just witnessed a side of him she had not seen before, a darker side — it was swift, angry, and decisive — and she did not want to see it again.

•   •   •

Jamie geared down his Honda and pulled into a parking slot in front of Sterling's Department Store on Ouachita Avenue. His

English teacher's lecture on literature and writing had awakened something new in him. Miss Lowe was young, articulate, and pretty. Jamie had decided during her lecture that he needed an outlet, a means of verbalizing his feelings, and had concluded that the outlet would be the written word.

He walked to the office supplies at the back of the store, picked up a small, hardbacked Record Book, and flipped through the lined pages, pleased that he would fill them with his deepest thoughts. He paid for the book and drove home.

His mother did not greet him when he opened the front door and stepped into the living room. She had accepted a position at a local insurance agency and would not be home until after five o'clock. His father had been called to pastor a small church near Kirby and spent two or three evenings a week working among the people. The empty house, however, did not bother Jamie at all. In fact, he enjoyed the solitude and usually spent the time listening to the radio, doing homework, or just thinking.

He walked outside to the mailbox and found a letter from Michelle. She missed him, could not wait to see him, and sounded depressed. He placed the letter on the nightstand next to his bed, stared at Michelle's picture for a long time, saw the same fixed smile, the same clothes, the same eyes, and the same hair. Nothing had changed. Nothing would ever change. It was just a picture. He picked it up and placed it in the drawer. Why not? He could not touch or kiss dry paper and cold glass.

He thought about his confrontation with Jeffery Davis, and his stomach tightened instinctively. The difference in emotions—Jeff and Michelle—fascinated him, and then he remembered Miss Lowe's lecture. "A writer," she had said, "verbalizes, puts into words, what he feels. Perhaps it comes from the solar plexus, or the heart, maybe even the liver. But wherever it comes from, writing is the result of some emotional spur." Jamie reached for his Record Book and wrote:

An emotion flutters by like a bird in the sky,
Spreading its wings to the wind.
Is it joy with lightness of heart?
Or is it anger, with drums pounding in my ears?
It could be a mixed emotion caught between two fires.
Or hate with its bitter taste.
Or love, light as a feather, but painful to the heart.
Or the biting grasp of fear tempting me to run.
Emotions constantly change.
I wish I could understand them.

Jamie scanned the words he had written, shook his head, dropped the Record Book on the bed, picked up his transistor radio, walked outside, and sat down on the front porch. An unusually strong cold front had changed the dog days of September to a refreshing October-like feel. He glanced up Bower Street and saw Vicki, wearing jeans and a bulky Hot Springs Trojan sweatshirt, walking down the sidewalk.

"Aren't you rushing the season?" he asked when she sat down beside him.

"No, Jamie," she replied defensively. "I thought it was dumb to be cold when I could wear a sweatshirt and be warm. You're such a jerk. I don't know why I put up with you."

"Sorry. The sweatshirt looks great. It's the jeans I don't like."

When Vicki wore shorts—especially athletic shorts with elastic waistbands—she was more adventurous. She had a rule—no skin beneath the waist—and Jamie respected that, but when she wore jeans, her sense of adventure vanished; she always pushed his hand away, and Jamie thought that was more than a little odd.

"I can't believe you would even hint about something like that."

"Thank God it will be eighty-five degrees tomorrow."

Vicki's eyes narrowed. "I let you do more than most girls would."

"And I appreciate it." Jamie smiled facetiously. "Do you want to go inside and fool around?"

"I'm wearing jeans, remember?"

"No problem. All it takes is one little snap."

Vicki laughed and followed him into the house.

CHAPTER 28

Piney Baptist Church was small, struggling, and nothing like Trinity Baptist Church in Bogalusa. The building, a white-framed structure with a dirt and gravel parking lot, did not have lined parking spaces; cars parked where there was room between pine trees.

The seminary crowd, men who in fact and deed charted the direction of the International Baptist Convention, thought Calvin Williams' call to and acceptance of Piney Baptist Church was a humiliating demotion. Gone was the plush office, attractive secretary, and new auditorium filled with affluent and prominent people. Despite the contrast—or demotion, depending on one's perspective—Calvin Williams loved Piney Baptist Church and the farmers and timber workers who attended it.

To Piney Baptist Church, as with every Baptist church, calling a new pastor was a special occasion. And when the new pastor accepted the call, Piney Baptist Church, like every Baptist church, hosted a Sunday afternoon fellowship to welcome the new pastor and his family.

In Bogalusa, Jamie stood in a receiving line for two hours while church members shook hands and introduced themselves. He hated every minute, but that was a year ago, and he had changed. Jamie now considered the receiving line an opportunity to meet new girls. Since it made little sense to drive home after morning worship—Kirby was forty miles from Hot Springs—church members invited the pastor and his family to their homes for Sunday dinner. Since he would be stuck in the boondocks every Sunday, Jamie thought he should find a girl to make Sunday afternoons interesting. He found her while standing in the receiving line.

She was tall and athletic looking. Her brown hair was short, her eyes were brown, almost oriental, and they sparkled when she talked to someone she obviously liked. They did not sparkle, however, when she took Jamie's hand and said, "I'm Marian Wood."

"I'm Jamie," he replied. "You know my last name."

He struck her as arrogant, and when he stared into her eyes, she flushed and felt uncomfortable. If she had liked him, pleasant would have described her feelings more accurately. Several boys, with roaming hands and probing fingers, had tried to make her feel this way. In fact, she had let Steven Parker, a senior and captain of the basketball team, take her all the way. Steven seemed to know what he was doing and had pushed the right buttons when he slid his hand beneath her skirt, but when she gave him what he obviously wanted, after a few seconds he filled her with slime, pulled up his jeans, and drove her home without saying a word. They broke up the next week—by mutual consent—and three months later he left for college.

Marian's blatant attraction to Jamie Williams surprised and annoyed her. Her first experience had been disappointing, and despite occasional damp panties, she had concluded that God had placed sex in the context of marriage, not in the cramped backseat of a Mustang GT. She had decided not to let another boy stick his pecker in her—she had worried about being pregnant for a month—and quickly decided that distance was the best strategy for this tall, good-looking, and arrogant preacher's son.

She released Jamie's hand, poured a glass of iced tea, sat down, crossed her legs, and occasionally glanced at him. The way he flirted with the girls was disgusting. She closed her eyes and wondered what it would be like to kiss him. Surprised by the moist longing between her legs, she sipped her tea and stared at Jamie until he met her eyes and smiled.

Marian quickly turned her head.

•   •   •

Three weeks after the new pastor's reception, the Woods invited the Williams home for Sunday dinner. Although Marian had been ignoring him, Jamie was looking forward to the day, thinking that in a one-on-one situation, he could win her over.

Marian, however, did not seem at all interested. Several times during morning worship he had caught her eye, but each time, expressionless, she had looked the other way. After the final amen, she glanced at Jamie—he knew she would—and when she saw he had been expecting the glance, she blushed, and rushed out the door.

The Woods lived a mile and a half down the road from the church in an old but well-kept home. A large porch with a wooden swing covered the front of the house, and smoke, Jamie noticed, was billowing from the chimney into the clear October sky. Inside, the house smelled of fried chicken and burning wood, a pleasant smell, a homey smell. Jamie sat down, liking the place, and slouched in a large brown chair with wide arms.

Playing the role of an obedient daughter, Marian helped her mother and Louise Williams set the table. To Jamie's delight, she dropped a potholder on the floor and bent over to pick it up. The view, he thought, was more than a little pleasing, but when she looked over her shoulder and glared at him, he decided that God had equipped girls with backward-seeking radar. Obviously disgusted, Marian frowned, filled several glasses with iced tea, then sat down at the dining table with her mother and Louise Williams.

The meal—fried chicken, creamed potatoes, corn on the cob and fried okra—was excellent, but with Marian treating him as a non-person, and tired of acting like an obedient preacher's son, Jamie refused dessert, excused himself—politely, of course—walked outside to the porch swing, sat down, and slowly rocked back and forth.

Five minutes later, the door opened.

Marian glared at him, sat on the steps, and cuttingly said, "The only reason I'm out here is because my mother told me I shouldn't let you sit out here by yourself."

"You can go back in the house for all I care."

Tired of icy stares and failed attempts at conversation, Jamie had had enough. Marian, he decided, slept under the porch, scratched fleas, and only came out when a strange car pulled in the driveway, barking, bristling fur, with dog snot dripping from her fangs.

"You seemed interested a few minutes ago."

"I like long-legged girls."

Marian stared straight ahead and said nothing.

"That was supposed to be a joke."

"So, you don't like my legs?"

"You have great legs. I meant…"

"I know what you meant."

"May I ask you a question?"

"It's a free country. Why not?"

"What have I done to piss you off?"

Marian stared coldly into his eyes. "It's not what you've done, it's who you are."

"I don't understand."

"You think you're better than the *hicks* who live in Kirby."

"You're crazy as hell."

"You think you can look up my skirt and check out the merchandise because you live in Hot Springs and go to a big school. Well, I have news for you, Jamie Williams: I won't fawn over you like a bitch in heat. Just because you come to Kirby and slum it on weekends doesn't mean I'll giggle and swoon like the rest of the girls at church."

"You have nothing to worry about."

"Oh, really?"

"I don't go where I'm not wanted."

"That's a relief."

Jamie's eyes narrowed and his temper flared.

"You're a pretty girl, Marian, probably the prettiest girl I've ever seen, but I won't put up with your bullshit, even if you have long legs and a sweet ass. Why don't you go back into the house with your momma? I don't want to offend you with my superiority and big city ways."

Marian's mouth flew open, and she turned her head as if he had slapped her. Jamie did not know if she was going to explode or cry. She looked as if she was about to say something, then she jumped up, ran into the house, and left him on the porch.

Five minutes later, she returned.

"I'm going to get a Coke. Do you want to go?"

"Is it your idea, or your mother's?"

"Both."

"Okay, I'll go."

Marian scooted behind the steering-wheel of her father's green pickup truck—an old Chevy—started the engine, and then pulled onto the gravel road. "I hope you have a driver's license," Jamie observed dryly.

"Of course, I have a driver's license. Don't you?"

"Only for a motorcycle. I won't be sixteen until February."

Marian clutched the truck and pulled onto Highway 70. Her skirt, Jamie noticed, had inched upward. He stared at her legs because he knew she wanted him to.

"You're peeking again."

"I like the view."

Marian laughed and did not straighten her skirt.

•   •   •

Doc's Drive-In, a white concrete block building, smelled of French Fries and onion rings. A black and white menu hung on the wall behind the counter. Jamie and Marian ordered Cokes, and then walked to a table where three girls were sitting.

The girls thought it interesting that Marian was with a boy. Marian, they knew, had not dated since Steven Parker left for college. One girl, curious, asked, "Who's your friend?"

"Jamie Williams, our new pastor's son."

"Has he moved to Kirby?"

"No," Marian replied. "He lives in Hot Springs."

Jamie raised his hand. The girls, including Marian, stared at him quizzically. "Believe it or not, ladies, I learned to talk a long time ago." He pointed at each girl and asked their names. Lisa Anderson and Susan Jackson, like Marian, were in the eleventh grade. Joyce Atkins, like Jamie, was in the tenth grade.

Susan asked, "Since you can talk, city boy, how do you like Kirby?"

Jamie smiled drolly. "So far I haven't been impressed."

Marian's eyes narrowed. "Don't say a word, Jamie."

"I believe," Lisa observed, "that Jamie tried to hit a home run with Marian and didn't make it to first base."

"Bingo!" Jamie replied. "Not even a kiss."

"If you want a kiss, I'll give you one."

Joyce Atkins pushed back her chair, walked around the table, sat on Jamie's lap, and kissed him. A little too deeply, Marian thought. After several seconds, she broke the embrace, stared into Jamie's eyes, and returned to her chair, fanning her face.

Marian did not like that at all.

Jamie should have been kissing her, and he would have been, if she had not acted like a frigid old maid. She wanted him the first day he walked in Piney Baptist Church, but instead of feeding his ego like the other girls at church, she ignored him, pretending she was not attracted to the new preacher's arrogant but good-looking son. That, she now realized, had been a mistake. She wanted Jamie when he held her hand in the receiving line. She wanted him now, and there was no reason to pretend she did not.

A burst of laughter brought Marian back to the present. Jamie had made some catty, off-the-wall remark. She reached across the table and grabbed his arm. "Sorry, Casanova, it's time to take you home before your momma gets worried."

"Yes, ma'am," he replied, and obediently followed Marian to the door.

"Jamie!"

He stopped, turned back, and faced Joyce Atkins.

"Let's do it again when you have more time."

"How about next Sunday, if the Ice Princess will bring me back?"

It pleased him to see the girls laughing when Marian pulled him out the door. Smiling broadly, he walked toward the truck and noticed that Marian had not let go of his hand.

"I think I'm going to like Kirby."

She scooted beneath the steering-wheel and started the engine.

"Are you always this outgoing?"

"I have my quiet moments."

"What do you do then?"

"I write poems."

"You don't seem like the poem-writing type."

"I'm a man of many talents, Miss Wood." Marian rolled her eyes. "If you'll bring me back to Doc's next week, I'll bring some of my poems and let you read them."

"So you can make out with Joyce again?"

"I'd rather make out with you."

For a moment, Jamie thought he had pissed her off again, but changed his mind when she turned down a narrow lane sheltered by trees and tall brush, stopped the truck, and killed the engine. When she scooted across the seat, slid onto his lap, and kissed him, Jamie knew he was free to do anything he wanted to do. He slid his beneath her skirt, fondled her panties, and then pushed them down. Marian moaned and kissed him passionately. Several minutes later, before she lost control, Marian scooted off his lap, faced the front of the truck, and pulled up her panties. She stared into Jamie's eyes, smiled smugly, and asked, "Do you still think I'm an Ice Princess?"

"Hell, no!"

"Am I a better kisser than Joyce?"

"Hell, yes!"

"I shouldn't have let you do that."

"We'll finish next Sunday."

"What makes you think I'll let you finish?"

"You like it."

"I should slap your face."

"But you won't."

"Don't look so smug, Jamie."

CHAPTER 29

Graham Wallace, Sports Editor for the Hot Springs Sentinel Record, was more than a little pleased when Coach Johnson told him that Jamie Williams had moved back to Hot Springs and would play for the Trojans. Wallace had taken an interest in Jamie two years before when he started his basketball career at Central Junior High School. Wallace remembered — there are some things you never forget — a conversation he had had with Coach Johnson and an interview he had had with Jamie Williams following Central's conference championship in 1965. After the post-game ceremony — Jamie had not missed a shot during the game — Wallace walked into Coach Johnson's office and bluntly said, "Tell me about Jamie Williams."

Coach Johnson replied — suspiciously, Wallace thought — "We just won a conference championship and all you want to talk about is Jamie?"

"Don't play games with me, Jim. I know, and you know, that neither of us has ever witnessed a display of shooting like we saw today. Tell me about Jamie Williams."

"I can't describe it, Graham. You saw him. He's good. No! He's better than good. There are times, it seems, when Jamie can't miss. What else can I say?"

"When did it start?"

"He could fill the hoop the day I met him. It's almost eerie, isn't it, Graham?

"Does he ever talk about it?"

"No, he doesn't. I did, however, talk to his older brother about it. He said—and don't quote me on this, Graham—that Jamie has a gift and just can't miss."

"Do you believe him?"

"No, of course not! I'm an educated man, and I don't believe in fairytales, but I have to admit, I've never seen anyone shoot a basketball like Jamie Williams."

"What about his stats for the season? Has Jamie missed many shots?"

"Some, but not many."

"So, you have a player who rarely misses, and you've never mentioned it?"

"How can I tell the world about a kid I don't understand? So, yes, I've kept him under wraps, even held him back a little. To tell you the truth, Graham, I'm afraid someone will pinch me and say, 'Wake up, it's only a dream.'"

Wallace chuckled and rubbed the back of his neck. "You believe his brother's hocus-pocus, don't you, Jim? You believe that Jamie Williams has a special gift."

"You know the situation now. Explain it to me."

"I wouldn't touch that with a ten-foot pole." Wallace glanced at his yellow legal pad, then asked, "Can I talk to him?"

"Sure...if you won't say anything about a gift in your article."

"Don't you think it would make a good human interest story? I can see it now: A BOY AND HIS GIFT LEADS HOT SPRINGS CENTRAL TO A CONFERENCE CHAMPIONSHIP." Coach Johnson cringed. "Don't worry, Jim. Your secret's safe with me. I would like to see Jamie's field goal and free-throw percentages, though."

"I'll give them to you before you leave."

That night, questions kept churning in Graham Wallace's mind. How could Jamie Williams, a likable, outgoing preacher's son, shoot a basketball from just about anywhere on the court and rarely miss?

Is it his vision? Does he have special hand-eye coordination?

As Wallace recalled the interview, he could not help but think how normal Jamie Williams looked. With street clothes on, he was just another brown-haired, brown-eyed kid, no different from any boy his age. But on a basketball court, he was Superman.

Wallace eased out of bed, lumbered to his study, put on his half-framed glasses, lit his pipe, and slowly scanned the statistics Coach Johnson had given him. They *were* intriguing. Not, however, what he had expected. Jamie Williams was human, and he missed occasionally.

Where's my great story?

Coach Johnson said that he had held Jamie back; with a player like Terrance Brooks on his team, that was understandable, but Wallace had expected Jamie's stats to be more impressive. His field goal and free-throw percentages, however, would be remarkable for any level of competition.

How does he do it?

Wallace scanned his notes, recalled how quickly Jamie had overcome his initial nervousness, and how he answered each question like a seasoned professional. And Wallace recalled how patient *he* had been, asking all the obvious questions, leading up to the ultimate: "Jamie, how do you shoot the ball so well?"

"I don't know, Mr. Wallace. I just shoot it and it goes in."

A simple, straightforward answer. Obviously, the kid hasn't been tutored by anyone. Coach Johnson said his brother calls it a gift. Is there such a thing? Does God look down from Heaven and say, "Here's a good kid. I'll give him the gift of shooting a basketball, go out and get 'em, son?" No! God has more important things on His mind than basketball.

Wallace leaned back in his chair and rubbed his eyes, acutely aware of the position he held as the Sports Editor for the Sentinel Record. He had covered the city's athletic programs for fifteen years. He had seen a few good years, but to the community's shame, there had been too many bad ones. Since his articles often took on a critical format, Graham Wallace had become an institution, a voice that commended the good and condemned the bad.

Once in the early sixties, he received a great deal of criticism because of an article he had written about the Trojan basketball team. Pointing out the political aspect of the city's athletic programs, Wallace challenged the Trojan varsity to a game with a local church team. He wrote the Trojans would be led as sheep to the slaughter, meaning there was more talent in the church leagues than on the court in Trojan Field House. His question: Why aren't these obviously talented young men playing for their alma mater? His answer: they would if they could; they can't so they're not.

Graham Wallace wrote things as he saw them. His critics thought he was too blunt and accused him of not liking young people or athletics, which was not true. Wallace honestly liked kids and never focused his wrath on them, but on coaches, or the powers-that-be. However, if a young man was playing a position, and it was blatantly obvious he did not belong there, Wallace felt obliged to speak out. Like the year the Trojans started a fat, two-hundred-and-thirty-pound quarterback, who was, Wallace wrote, "about as agile as an armadillo crossing the road on a foggy night, trying desperately to make it to the shoulder before an approaching car turned it into some odious thing with four stiff legs pointing at the afternoon sun."

On another occasion, Wallace nominated the Hot Springs High School football coach as coach of the year following a disastrous 3 and 7 campaign. His reasoning: "Any man who can endure the outside pressure he has and still field a semi-competitive football team with a backfield weighing over five-hundred pounds and an offensive line weighing four-hundred pounds, must have something on the ball." He closed the article by saying, "For crying out loud, folks, when is it going to end? When will the administration, the school board, and influential parents allow coaches to play young athletes where their diverse talents dictate, regardless of race, wealth, or social standing?"

In the Spring of 1965, when Jamie Williams, a white preacher's son, and Terrance Brooks, a black attorney's son, led Central Junior High School to a conference championship, Graham Wallace used them as a case-in-point on the value of diversity in athletics. His article sent shockwaves through the city of Hot Springs:

ARE THE GOOD OLD DAYS FINALLY OVER?

Graham Wallace
Sports Editor, Hot Springs Sentinel Record

Can the citizens of Hot Springs say the good old days are finally over? Can they say that the days of impotent athletic teams playing with dreams of pseudo-grandeur are finally a thing of the past? If the recent success of the Central Junior High School Spartans in basketball is an indicator — and I believe it is — success for Spartan/Trojan athletics is just around the corner.

Without the help of the city fathers, Coach Jim Johnson has built a team that knows how to win. To this writer, Hot Springs finally has a coach who makes decisions on competitive-merit instead of inherited-privilege and should be the obvious replacement for the retiring Trojan mentor.

Imagine the 1967 Trojan basketball team coached by Jim Johnson! Imagine Terrance "Tree" Brooks and Jamie "Can't Miss" Williams gracing Trojan Field House with power, soft touch, and savvy.

Both young men are exceptional. Terrance, a ninth grader, led the Spartans in scoring. Jamie, an eighth grader, set a school record for field goal and free-throw percentages.

To this reporter, Coach Johnson and his charges can lead the Trojan basketball program out of its doldrums into a fair and competitive system that gives every young man an opportunity to play, regardless of race, wealth, and social standing.

Are the good old days finally over?

If they are, it's about time.

CHAPTER 30

The weather had warmed considerably during the week. In Arkansas, afternoon temperatures often reached the eighties in late October. Since it was a warm day, Marian had convinced Jamie, with a little sarcastic persuasion, to go horseback riding. Jamie stared at the horse quizzically and quickly realized he was not in his element.

"How do I get on this thing?"

"You've never ridden a horse before?"

"Nope."

Marian helped Jamie put his foot in the stirrup, laughed as he landed precariously in the saddle, then easily mounted her own horse, and said, "Let's go."

"That's easy for you to say."

"Just press her sides with your heels."

Jamie nudged the buckskin and grabbed the saddle-horn when the horse lunged forward.

"How do I drive this thing?"

"Pull the reins right or left. It's easy."

As Marian led him across brown pastures and past murky-green ponds, Jamie decided in time—lots of time—he might learn to enjoy horseback riding. Five minutes later, when he decided he could ride and talk without falling off the horse and breaking his neck, he asked Marian, "Where are you taking me?"

"To my favorite place."

Ten minutes later, they crossed a fast-moving creek, stepped off their horses, and tied them to a low-hanging limb. Marian gazed at the isolated landscape and said, almost reverently, "I love this place. Sometimes I feel I'm the only person who comes here."

Jamie picked up a rock and threw it in the creek. Marian rolled her eyes and smiled drolly. "I can't help it," he explained. "I like to throw rocks and little red footballs."

"Tell me about yourself, Jamie. I hardly know you."

"There's not much to tell."

"What do you do when you're not writing poetry?"

"I play basketball."

"I do too. For the Kirby Trojans. Are you pretty good?"

"My coach says I am."

"He should know. Do you have a girlfriend?"

"Sort of."

"What does that mean?"

"I'm dating a girl in Hot Springs and going steady with a girl in Louisiana."

"That's a rotten thing to do."

"The girl in Hot Springs—her name is Vicki—is cute but bitchy. The girl in Louisiana—her name is Michelle—is special; she was a friend when I really needed one."

"So, Michelle in Louisiana is the love of your life?"

"I guess you could say that."

"I don't believe you,"

"Why?"

"Because you're a flirt."

Jamie chuckled. "You're right. I like girls. You found that out last week."

"About last Sunday, Jamie. I shouldn't have let you…"

"Why? We both enjoyed it."

Marian blushed. "You pushed down my panties."

"And you moaned when I..."

"I can't believe you'd bring *that* up."

"Why not? I thought about it all week."

"I'm not sure I want you to think of me like that."

Jamie leaned against a fat oak tree and folded his arms. "You've made your point. Are you ready to head back? The Dallas Cowboys are on television this afternoon."

The last thing Marian wanted was to go home and watch the Dallas Cowboys. What she really wanted was for Jamie stick his pecker in her. She had led him to her favorite place so that he could finish what he had started the previous week. He was supposed to make a bold move, and she was supposed to play hard to get—that is how you play the game—but Jamie had given up quickly and easily. Whatever happened next, Marian knew, was up to her, and she gave in quickly.

"I'm a little disappointed that you gave up without a fight."

"Marian, do you want to fool around or not?"

"Yes, Jamie, I do."

There was, he noticed, a quiver in her voice.

•   •   •

"Do I look okay?"

"You look great."

"I mean, is it obvious what we've been doing?"

"No, you look fine."

Marian mounted her horse. "We should head back. Our parents may be suspicious."

Jamie mounted his horse...awkwardly. "They think we're ten-year-old kids playing cowboys and Indians, not You-Show-Me-Yours-And-I'll-Show-You-Mine."

Marian giggled. "The first day I saw you, I wanted you."

"I know."

Marian rolled her eyes. "Has anyone ever told you that you're too arrogant?"

Jamie laughed. "I can't help it if I'm exceptionally good at everything I do."

CHAPTER 31

Casandra Lowe read Jamie's poem and liked it. The assignment for the tenth-grade English class had been to write a poem about a place the students had seen or visited. Most were quite average, but Jamie Williams' was different, almost haunting. He named it "Rosboro" after a once prosperous village that had been abandoned because its lone source of wealth, a sawmill, had shut down. She read it again:

Rosboro

It has been a long time since I have seen the old town,
The buildings have fallen, and the boards are rotten.
But I recall a thriving place
That most people have forgotten.
The old church is still standing,
With windows broken, paint weathered and worn.
The organ never plays, and the choir never sings
On the holy Sabbath morn.
The old sawmill is still standing,
A ghost of bygone times.
The smokestack rises to the sky,
As if to show a sign.
It once had been the life of the town,

But closed and became its death.
When its boilers cooled, the people fled,
So they could pay their debts.
The old town has changed,
Changed with the winds of time.
And sometimes when a cold wind blows,
The old church bell still chimes.

Miss Lowe laid the poem on her desk. Jamie Williams was an outgoing young man, a basketball player, and well liked. Not the type, she thought, who wrote poetry. On her desk, however, was a poem he had written, simple words that painted a mental picture of a dead community destroyed by time and a changing world.

When the bell rang, ending her sophomore English class, Miss Lowe told Jamie that she wanted to talk to him. He nodded and took a seat in a desk on the front row. Miss Lowe crossed her arms, leaned against her desk, and said, "I like your poem. Where did you get the idea?"

"From a town I pass through on the way to church."

"Is it accurate? A true story?"

"I asked several people why Rosboro is a ghost town. They told me about the sawmill closing, but I've never heard the church bell ring, if that's what you mean."

Casandra Lowe smiled lightly. "When did you begin writing?"

"On the first day of school, when you told us to write what we feel. Now, when a feeling hits me, I write about it."

"Do you have to work at it?"

"No, ma'am. Most of the time, the words just flow."

"You have potential as a writer, Jamie."

"Thank you, Miss Lowe."

"If you have no objections, I would like to enter Rosboro in the Arkansas State High School Writing Contest."

"That's fine with me, Miss Lowe."

"Have you written other poems?"

"Yes, ma'am."

"If you don't mind, I would like to read some of them."

Jamie wondered what poems he would let Miss Lowe read. His writing was personal, an outlet, and a well-kept secret. Other than Marian, no one knew he penned his thoughts and kept them in a ledger. He quickly decided why not? If he let Miss Lowe read some of his poems, he might pull an "A" in English.

*   *   *

Jamie stretched out in his father's recliner, glad the day was over. He was tired—Coach Johnson had worked his butt off—and impressed, now that he had had time to think about it, that Miss Lowe liked his poem. He considered what poems he would let her read—some were just too personal—and then, as usual, his thoughts turned to Michelle.

Sometimes it seems as if I never lived in Bogalusa, or that I ever knew Michelle. The only proof I have is a picture with the same fixed smile. I stopped wearing the bracelet she gave me a long time ago. I wonder if she is still wearing hers?

Jamie had changed a lot in six months. Michelle Martin, once the dominant factor in his life, did not seem real anymore. Vicki Helms, to his chagrin, had morphed into a crab; she nagged him constantly about breaking up with Michelle, and her preoccupation with the subject grated on his nerves. Marian Wood, however, was an exciting surprise—they talked about everything—and she rarely objected to fooling around.

Even his attitude about Hot Springs had changed. Lately, his father had hinted about moving to Kirby. At first, Jamie did not know how he felt about that. Playing basketball for Hot Springs, a larger school, would enhance his resume and help him earn a scholarship when he graduated from high school. If he moved to Kirby, however, he would be closer to Marian, and *that* did not seem like a terrible idea.

Jamie's positive attitude toward Kirby amazed Calvin Williams. Compared to Hot Springs, there was absolutely nothing to do, except to meet at Doc's Drive-In, listen to the jukebox, and play the pinball machines. Calvin Williams, of course, did not know that Jamie and Marian were more than just friends. To Calvin Williams, sixteen-year-olds held hands, and did not go parking down secluded country roads.

Although Jamie was just a weekend visitor, Marian's friends had welcomed him into their clique, and basketball had nothing to do with his acceptance. When he sat at a table in Doc's Drive-In, his new friends — most of them girls — liked him because he was fun and made them laugh, not because he played basketball.

Kirby was a different world, relaxed, slower, and easy to like. Each week when he cruised the Burger Chef and A & W Drive-Ins, hassled with Vicki over Michelle, or looked out the windows at school and saw the Ouachita Hospital and other large buildings in downtown Hot Springs, Jamie thought about winding dirt roads, pastures dotted with black Angus cattle, chicken houses, and Marian slithering out of her jeans.

Jamie knew it was only a matter of time until his father became tired of driving back and forth and that dear old dad would be surprised when he did not pitch a wall-eyed fit about leaving Hot Springs and transferring to a new school.

CHAPTER 32

With two games a week and trips to Kirby on weekends, 1966 quickly became 1967. Bud and Judith became the proud parents of an eight-pound boy—they named him Calvin Williams III—and Sherry and Phil surprised Jamie when they moved to Arkansas. During their Thanksgiving visit, Phil had been hired as the head basketball coach at Benton High School. Jamie thought it was odd that his brother-in-law would coach a conference rival, but his parents liked the idea of Sherry living close, and he decided beating Phil and the Panthers would be a lot of fun. And, of course, the Hot Springs Trojans, led by Terrance Brooks, Jamie Williams, and Dalton Hilliard, completed an undefeated season, and won the State Championship.

Jamie had done well athletically and scholastically. His achievements on the court brought rave reviews in the State newspapers, and his report cards, as usual, were covered with "As." Miss Lowe's interest in his writing had motivated him and he found that his interest in English and Literature had spilled over to other subjects as well, even Math, which he hated.

During the spring awards assembly, Jamie received plaques from Miss Lowe and Coach Johnson. Rosboro had placed number-one at the State Writing Contest, and state coaches and the media had selected Jamie as Newcomer of the Year, an award given to Arkansas' most outstanding sophomore basketball player.

The only problem was his motorcycle. He had grown and thought his Honda 150 was too small. He had, in fact, persuaded his father to go with him to the Honda dealership to look at a red and white 350. The previous owner had neglected the engine, but the dealership had overhauled it and put in oversized racing pistons, which boosted the machine's horsepower. Jamie wanted the bike, and his father did not disappoint him. The bank approved the loan within an hour.

•   •   •

The new bike sounded different, powerful, yet mellow, like a huge, resonant bee, as Jamie inched the machine out of the Honda dealership, turned left on Ouachita Avenue, and drove home. Five minutes later, Calvin Williams parked his Impala in the carport, pulled up a chair, and sat next to Jamie on the front porch.

"Your mother is going to pitch a fit when she sees that thing."

"Should we have asked her first?"

"I learned a long time ago, son, that it's easier to ask forgiveness than permission."

Jamie laughed and Calvin Williams smiled smugly; they had had a lot of fun sneaking around and buying the bike without Louise Williams knowing about it.

"You'll have to be careful riding that thing, Jamie. I didn't realize the dealership had souped it up."

"It's just what I need until I graduate."

"That's hard for me to believe."

"What's hard for you to believe, Dad?"

"That in two years, you'll graduate from high school." Calvin Williams shook his head and grunted. "I guess I'm getting old."

"All grandfathers are old, aren't they?"

Calvin Williams groaned. "You're as old as you feel, and I still feel eighteen."

Jamie chuckled, stepped off the porch, walked across the yard, and pulled a stack of advertisements and a letter from Michelle out of the mailbox. After he read the letter, he dropped it on the porch and stared at his father. "The Martins are coming to Hot Springs next month."

"That's good news."

"Good news? How am I going to explain Vicki?"

"I suppose, Casanova, the same way you're going to explain Marian."

"You're a big help."

"How long are the Martins going to stay?"

"A week. They want us to spend a few days with them in Eureka Springs."

"I think we can manage that. It will be good seeing the Martins again."

Calvin Williams watched a paperboy riding a Cushman Scooter throw a newspaper in the neighbor's yard. He took a deep breath, then tentatively said, "We need to talk, Jamie."

"About what?"

"Piney has picked up dramatically since I became the pastor."

"That's what you do, build churches."

"Piney wants to raise my salary," —He paused and looked Jamie in the eyes—"which means we'll have to move to Kirby. If you don't want me to accept the offer, I'll tell them no. The last thing I want is for you to have another Bogalusa experience."

"I have friends in Kirby. It won't be like Bogalusa."

"What about basketball?"

"I'm a Triple-A player. Kirby is a Class B school. No problem."

Jamie laughed.

"What's so funny?"

"Kirby High School is so small that it doesn't have a football team, so I won't have to worry about playing two sports. Kirby doesn't even have a band."

"Then you wouldn't object?"

"No, sir. Do you want me to start packing?"

"Not yet, son." Calvin Williams squeezed Jamie's knee. "Despite being a two-timing jerk, you're a pretty good kid."

"Pretty good? According to the Republic, which, as you know, is the largest newspaper in Arkansas, I'm the best sophomore basketball player in the State."

Jamie ignored his father's remark about him being a two-timing jerk.

CHAPTER 33

Jamie woke up startled until he remembered he had camped out in the mountains north of Hot Springs with Bill Mitchell and Dalton Hilliard. He glanced at his watch—he should have been home two hours ago—then packed his knapsack, strapped it to his motorcycle, and left Bill and Dalton to break camp later in the day.

The Honda responded strongly as he pushed it through its gears on Highway 7 North. The machine's power, as always, thrilled him. He gripped the handlebars tightly and twisted the throttle. The Honda responded and literally jumped to eighty-five miles an hour. As he approached the city limits, he slowed down, obeyed the speed limit on Park Avenue, turned right on Bower Street, and thirty seconds later, pulled under the carport.

"You're late," Louise Williams said when he walked into the kitchen.

"Sorry, Mom. I overslept."

Pamela Martin, sitting at the kitchen table, smiled and said, "Hello, Jamie."

"Hi, Mrs. Martin."

"I believe you've grown a foot."

"Not that much." He glanced toward the living room. "Where's Michelle?"

"She went to the store with Howard and your father."

Jamie walked outside and sat on the front porch, dreading his reunion with Michelle. Ten minutes later, the Martin's Oldsmobile Ninety-Eight parked next to the curb. Howard Martin, Calvin Williams, and Michelle stepped out of the car and walked across the yard. Michelle did not look happy. Coach Martin gave Jamie a bearhug, asked several questions about his basketball season, and then walked into the house with Calvin Williams.

Michelle did not give Jamie a hug or a warm greeting. She had, in fact, been livid when she walked into the Williams' living room and saw Jamie was not there to greet her. That, she thought, had been insulting, and a slap in the face. And what was he doing now? Staring across the street at a middle-aged neighbor playing with his dog. She had not ridden ten hours in the backseat of a car to be cordially ignored and treated like an overbearing stepsister coming home for a weekend visit.

"Unless I misread your letters, Jamie, I expected a warmer welcome. What am I supposed to do? Bend over and show you my butt?"

Jamie was stunned by the fire in Michelle's eyes and the anger in her voice.

"A year's a long time."

"Yes, it is, but common courtesy says, when you know someone is coming, you should be there to greet them. I felt like a fool when I walked in your house and your mom told me you were playing boy scout with your little buddies."

Jamie's eyes widened. He had not expected a tongue-lashing.

"You're right, and I'm sorry."

"You should be."

Jamie glanced at her arm. "I see you're still wearing the bracelet."

"But you're not wearing yours."

"Bogalusa seems like a long time ago."

"Not to me."

"So, you still feel the same?"

"You don't, do you, Jamie?"

It surprised him when the same old feelings surfaced.

"Some things never change, Michelle."

Michelle smiled wanly, relieved that the fire, although dimmer, was still burning. At first, she had had her doubts, because Jamie had seemed so distant, but when she saw the ice melting so quickly, she knew all the fire needed was a little kindling.

•   •   •

Crooked and steep, Highway 7 from Dover to Jasper offered colorful vistas overlooking steep hills and deep valleys. Jamie had driven through the mountains of North Arkansas many times with his parents, but with Michelle by his side, he felt as if he was on an exotic journey in a foreign land, instead of the Ozark National Forest.

Eureka Springs, a city filled with craft shops, hotels, miniature golf courses and country music shows, gave Jamie and Michelle ample time to be alone and to rekindle the fire he had nearly extinguished with Vicki Helms and Marian Wood. They did not discuss their year apart, just enjoyed the time they spent together, rising early, and going to bed late, knowing in a few short days the reunion would be over.

On Friday, they headed back to Hot Springs, drove south and west to Fayetteville, where they stopped and toured the University of Arkansas. As Jamie walked past Old Main, Razorback Stadium, and Barnhill Field House, he felt euphoric knowing that in two years he would fulfill his dream and play for the Razorbacks.

Too soon, in Jamie and Michelle's opinion, the summer visit ended. Jamie knew, even then, that he would not keep the promise he had made to Michelle. Regardless of how faithful he intended to be, the next time he went to Kirby, Marian would take him to the barn, where they would feed and water the horses, and she would douse the fire Michelle had worked so hard to rekindle.

Two weeks later, he received a letter freeing him from a promise he never intended to keep.

Jamie,

When I got back to Hammond, I received a letter from a girl by the name of Vicki Helms. She told me you started dating her two weeks after you moved back to Hot Springs.

I can't say that I wasn't hurt, but now that I've had a few days to think about it, I've decided it's crazy to carry a torch when there is so much distance between us — more than I ever expected.

I took your bracelet off and put it in a drawer.

I don't care what you do with yours.

Michelle

CHAPTER 34

Vicki Helms apologized when Jamie confronted her about writing to Michelle, but he did not give a rat's ass about Vicki or her stinking apology. The further away from her, the better. And when his father confirmed they were moving to Kirby, Jamie welcomed the move. In fact, he liked his new home, a white-framed house on a narrow, tree-lined lane.

After Jamie helped his father and Horace Wood unload the furniture and appliances, the endless task of storing towels and condiments bored him. Since Marian was helping with *that* monotonous chore, he walked outside, started his motorcycle, pulled onto an adjacent pasture, and started jumping terraces.

Ten minutes later, after landing the Honda—not too gracefully—on its rear wheel, he saw Marian standing on the front porch with both hands on her hips, a disapproving, motherly posture. He popped a wheelie, accelerated across the pasture, and slid to a stop near the front steps.

"Show out."

"You want to go for a ride?"

"I can't. Mom has me on a short leash today." Jamie killed the engine and pushed the Honda onto its stand. "How about tomorrow? We'll have more time."

"Okay."

Jamie's reply, Marian noticed, was not at all enthusiastic.

"What's wrong with you? Three weeks ago, being alone with me would have turned you on."

"I've been sort of down lately."

"Why?"

"All the changes, I guess."

"There's more to it than that, Jamie."

"Remember when you told me that dating Vicki and going steady with Michelle was a rotten thing to do?"

Marian knew Jamie dated Vicki Helms, and she knew he had strong feelings for Michelle Martin, but she honestly believed *she* had taken Vicki and Michelle's place. Other than calling Vicki a pain in the ass, he had not mentioned either girl in months.

"I remember."

"Vicki wrote Michelle and told her we have been dating for a year."

"What did Michelle do?"

"She dumped me."

"Do you want her back?"

"No. I'm not good at carrying on a long-distance romance."

"That's good news."

"What do you mean?"

"You've been avoiding me for three weeks."

"No, I haven't."

"You have, Jamie."

"Dad was on vacation for two weeks. The third week, we packed up our house in Hot Springs. This is the first time we've been together in a month."

"The Sunday before you went on vacation, you didn't come see me."

"Dad made me go to a family reunion at Caddo Gap."

"That night after church, you hardly talked to me."

"Dad was in a hurry to get home."

"I thought you were trying to dump me."

"Why would I do that?"

"That's what I've been trying to figure out."

"I'm not dumping you, Marian."

"Then act like it, Jamie. I need reassurance."

•   •   •

Marian squeezed her legs together, pushed Jamie's hand away, straightened her shorts, and stared at the closed door. "In case you haven't noticed, our parents are in the next room."

"You don't think they'd understand our unique relationship?"

Marian giggled. "Unique relationship?"

"How about our 'illicit sexual relationship?' That's what Dad calls it when teenagers fool around."

Marian blushed. "Let's change the subject. Was it hard for you to leave Hot Springs?"

"I'll miss my friends, but I think I'll like Kirby High School. I know you and a few others, so I won't be facing a bunch of strangers. And, of course, there's basketball."

"I don't want to rain on your parade, Jamie, but you may have a hard time making the team. The senior boys have played together since the seventh grade."

He opened a cardboard box and placed it on the bed.

"You want to help me put these up?"

Marian examined Jamie's trophies and skimmed through his scrapbook.

"Why didn't you tell me you were the Newcomer of the Year?"

"I told you I played for Hot Springs High School and that we won the State Championship."

"You were only a sophomore. I thought you sat on the bench."

"Don't you read The Republic?"

"All we get is the local Glenwood paper. You should have told me, Jamie."

"You already think I'm too arrogant."

"I would have been proud of you. What do you think I am? A witch?"

"I think you're beautiful and the best thing that's ever happened to me."

"Marian smiled and scooted off the bed.

"Where're you going?"

"To feed and water the horses. I'm ready to continue our unique relationship."

"You mean our…"

"Shut up, Jamie!"

• • •

Marian could not sleep.

She kept thinking about Jamie.

After Steven Parker left for college, grades, basketball, and potential scholarships had kept her mind occupied. In fact, after a disappointing first experience with Steven, Marian decided she did not want another boy scratching on her panties. But when Jamie marched into her life, everything changed, and it only took two Sundays.

At school, she was untouchable, virginal. Their quick coupling had embarrassed Steven, and he had remained discreet. Being untouchable, however, meant she did not have to worry about getting pregnant.

But that was before Jamie.

And that's how she looked at things now.

Before Jamie, she never had to worry about periods; they came and went like clockwork. Now she had to worry every month. So far, she had been lucky; her periods had come and gone without delay, but now that Jamie only lived five miles away, she knew the odds of her becoming pregnant had skyrocketed.

She cuddled her pillow and thought about her afternoon with Jamie in the barn. The first time they made love in the hay, the straw had scratched her butt; she had had whelps for three days and was afraid her mother would notice them. But the barn was a good place, a private place, and her parents were not at all suspicious when she and Jamie fed and watered the horses. After the straw had scratched her butt, she had taken a quilt from her bedroom closet and left it in the barn permanently. That, she now believed, had been one of her wiser moves.

Sometimes Marian felt guilty about her relationship with Jamie—she was a Christian and believed God had placed sex in the context of marriage—but she enjoyed having sex with Jamie, a little too much she often thought, and she did not want to stop 'putting out,' as her classmates so crudely called it. But now that Jamie lived so close, and with opportunities occurring more than a couple of weekends a month, she knew the time for carelessness had passed.

Birth control pills were out of the question; no doctor would prescribe them to an unmarried seventeen-year-old girl. But in every gas station restroom there were machines hanging on the wall and for a quarter Jamie could take care of the problem. And that, she decided, was the answer. She would make him ride his pretty, red motorcycle to the nearest gas station, fill up his tank, go to the restroom, and buy condoms.

With that problem settled, Marian closed her eyes and went to sleep.

CHAPTER 35

Jamie was not nervous when he rode his motorcycle onto the Kirby High School campus. What was there to be nervous about? He had been running around with Marian and her friends for months. But his stomach tightened when he realized, other than Joyce Atkins, he did not know any of the kids in the junior class.

Feeling less confident, he parked his motorcycle and walked into the one-story red-brick building. The floors sparkled with fresh varnish and wax, and the staged auditorium, which served as a study hall during the week, was filled with desks and students waiting for their teacher. The school, Jamie thought, had a homey atmosphere, and was nothing like Hot Springs High School, a massive four-story building.

Curious eyes stared at him when he walked into his first-period classroom. The teacher, Mrs. Wyatt—her name was on the chalkboard—had smiling eyes, and Jamie liked her immediately. He walked to the back of the room and sat down at an empty desk. His classmates seemed interested, but not hostile.

A student office-worker walked into the room and handed Mrs. Wyatt a note. She smiled warmly, thanked the girl, and told the class she would return shortly. The atmosphere changed quickly when a black-headed boy doubled his fist, placed it against his forehead, and pointed at Jamie. Within seconds, every boy in the room had placed a fist against his forehead.

Jamie thought that was more than a little weird and decided that his welcome had been testy, not warm. Five minutes later, Mrs. Wyatt returned, smiled at the class, and Jamie discovered that English grammar was no easier at Kirby High School than it had been at Hot Springs High School.

During the lunch break, he grabbed a tray of food and scanned the cafeteria. Marian, he saw, had saved him a place. He pulled out a chair and sat down.

"How's it going?" she asked.

There was concern in her voice. Jamie was not his usual cocky self.

"I may have been overconfident. Other than Joyce Atkins, I don't know anybody in the junior class." He smiled uncomfortably. "They don't know me from Adam."

"They're not being mean, are they?"

"No. Just standoffish."

"What do you have next period?"

"My schedule says, 'Gym, Coach Benson.'"

"That's basketball, Jamie. The team practices after lunch."

"Well," he replied, turning to his food. "It's time to see if I'm good enough to be a Kirby Trojan."

•　　•　　•

David Thompson had seen Jamie off and on at Doc's Drive-In playing pinball with Marian Wood, and that had surprised him. Marian had not dated since Steven Parker left for college, but he could not help but notice that she hung all over Jamie Williams like a bitch in heat. David did not like that at all. Steven was a nice guy, a hell of a basketball player, and a stuck-up city-slicker who made girls giggle and swoon, in David's opinion, did not belong in the Trojans dressing room.

"You're not supposed to be in here, Williams."

"Why not?"

"The dressing-room is for basketball players."

Jamie narrowed his eyes and asked, "Who made you the keeper of the portals?"

"What are you talking about?"

"That's a book by V. S. Nelson. You should read it."

Jamie Williams was cocky, and David did not like that either. What he really wanted to do was slap the grin off Jamie's face and see how he liked them apples.

"Your name isn't on the team roster."

"It soon will be."

"What gives you that idea?"

"You'll find out in about ten minutes."

Jamie hung up his jeans and slipped on the shorts he had worn at Hot Springs High School. The shorts were light gold and David thought they were more than a little feminine looking.

"Those are some ugly shorts."

Jamie smiled drolly. "What's your name?"

"David Thompson."

"These are championship shorts, David Thompson."

"Are you telling me you played for the Hot Springs Trojans?"

"You'll find out in about ten minutes."

Jamie bent over, tied his shoes, glanced at David, then asked, "What did it mean this morning when you put a fist on your forehead?"

"When one of us farts, we put a fist on our forehead. Anyone who doesn't put a fist on his forehead has to eat it, which means you ate at least five farts this morning."

Jamie rolled his eyes, said, "Thanks for the warm welcome, David Thompson," and then walked out of the dressing-room. David bent over, tied his shoes, and decided that he would teach the smart-ass preacher's kid a lesson on humility...in about ten minutes.

•   •   •

Coach Benson decided he would not take the traditional path up the coaching ladder. In fact, being an assistant coach at a larger school, where he would spend several years learning from an established master, did not appeal to him at all because he had unorthodox ideas about high school basketball. He was not a fool—the game was not for midgets—but he believed speed, quickness and stamina were just as important as size. After he graduated from Henderson State Teacher's College, he applied for the head coaching position at Kirby, a Class B school, and landed the job. Coach Benson did not enjoy living in the boondocks—he had been born and raised in Little Rock—but he did like being the boss.

Coach Benson was a realist, and he did not think a Class B school would ever win a State Championship. Class B schools simply did not have enough athletes to compete against the larger classifications. He did, however, intend to win his District and at least make it into the State Tournament, where, despite being stuck in Class B, he could make a name for himself and hopefully land a better job at a larger school.

According to his predecessor, he had quality talent for a small school. Unfortunately, most of his players were young, only sophomores and juniors. There was, however, one bright spot: David Thompson had been All Conference as a sophomore and should, with aggressive coaching, become more accomplished as a junior. Coach Benson believed he could build a winning team around one exceptional player.

The Trojans had very little height, but height, in Coach Benson's opinion, was over-hyped anyway. Sound players with quick feet could outmaneuver slow-footed giants and win games with speed, quickness, and determination.

He glanced at his watch — practice would not begin for another ten minutes — took a seat in the bleachers and watched his team warming up on the court. The sound of squeaking tennis shoes was music to his ears. He was twenty-three years old, the head coach of a high school basketball team, and life did not get much better than that.

•   •   •

Jamie hated his gold shorts.

Several students had whistled insultingly when he walked out of the dressing room onto the court. Even Coach Benson, slouching in the bleachers, laughed at the oddball wearing girly-shorts, and would have dismissed him, but there was something about the kid that demanded attention. Whoever he was, he thought he was something special. There was nothing concrete that told Coach Benson the oddball was a self-centered jerk, but the confident way he carried himself screamed, "Girly-shorts or not, I'm the best player on the court."

David Thompson, more than a little curious about the smartass in the ugly shorts, passed him a basketball. Jamie caught the ball, dribbled once, shot, and hit nothing but net.

Thinking the kid in the girly-shorts had a smooth, quick release, Coach Benson blew his whistle, gathered his team around him, put ten players on the court, and started practice with a scrimmage. The best way to judge a team's talent, Coach Benson believed, was to watch them play the game.

Embarrassed by his gold shorts and eager to silence the catcalls, Jamie could not wait to get the ball. Finally, from the top of the key, he faked a shot, left David Thompson grasping air, then drove the lane and made an acrobatic shot over a stout but chubby Center.

The catcalls ceased.

David Thompson, wide-eyed, stared at Jamie.

Stunned, Coach Benson blew his whistle, gathered his players at mid-court, stared at the new kid, and sarcastically asked, "What's your name, Goldie-Lox?"

"I'm Jamie Williams."

"Where'd you learn to play ball?"

"In Hot Springs and in Louisiana, Coach?"

"You're *that* Jamie Williams."

"Yes, sir."

Coach Benson held back a smile. He had an AAA player with exceptional skills at his disposal. With David Thompson and Jamie Williams, the Trojans would win, and win big.

David Thompson was awed.

•　　•　　•

The bright afternoon sun temporarily blinded Jamie as he walked across the parking lot. Joyce Atkins, the girl he had kissed at Doc's Drive-In, was leaning against his Honda.

"Hi, Jamie."

"Did you miss the bus?"

"I did. Can you give me a ride home?"

"Sure."

Joyce was wearing an extremely short skirt and Jamie wondered if she could climb on his motorcycle without exposing herself. She looked him in the eyes, smiled, then lifted her skirt, straddled the Honda, placed her mouth close to his ear, and purred, "Turn left when you pull off the parking lot. I live about five miles down the road.

As Jamie took the Honda through its gears, Joyce wrapped her arms around his waist. Her fingers, spider-like, inched below his belt. Five minutes later, she pointed at a redbrick house. Jamie geared down, pulled into the driveway, and waited for Joyce to step off his bike.

"Do you want a Coke?" she asked, straightening her skirt.

"Sure."

Joyce grabbed Jamie's hand and led him into the house. She pointed at a large sofa, said, "I'll be right back," and then walked into the kitchen. Jamie slouched comfortably until she returned, handed him a glass, and sat next to him on the sofa.

"How do you like Kirby High School?"

"School is school."

"You never mentioned playing basketball when I'd see you at Doc's."

He placed the glass on the coffee table. "It didn't seem important."

"But you're All-State."

"Maybe I can help the Trojans win a few games…if they'll have me. I don't think my gold shorts impressed anyone. I didn't realize how ridiculous they were until today."

Joyce giggled. "They were kind of…" She paused, searching for the right word. "Different."

"At least you could have said pretty, just the wrong color."

"Gold?" she asked, holding back a laugh.

"They *are* ugly. Coach Benson said he'd get me a maroon pair. I hope he doesn't forget."

Joyce placed her glass on the coffee table, turned to Jamie, and kissed him. Her short skirt inched upward when she crawled onto his lap, and she moaned when his hand inched beneath her panties. Three minutes later Joyce purred, "I'm ready for you, Jamie. Let's go to my bedroom. My parents won't be home for two hours."

Why not? I am, after all, All-State.

Jamie removed his hand.

"I can't."

"Why not? You felt me, and I feel you."

"I told my mom I would help her move furniture this afternoon."

"Call and tell her you'll be late."

"I want to, Joyce, but I can't."

Joyce eased off his lap and straightened her panties. "Marian Wood is your girlfriend, isn't she?"

"Yes."

"What Marian doesn't know won't hurt her, Jamie. I'm good at keeping secrets."

"Maybe we can get together later."

"You know where I live, Jamie. I'll always be ready for you."

•   •   •

"You were supposed to be home early."

"Sorry, Mom. I drove a friend home after school."

"Nelda and Marian have been waiting for over an hour."

Jamie did not like his mother's strict-parent-obedient-child display of parental authority. In fact, he despised strict parent-obedient-child displays of parental authority, especially from his mother. She was not and never had been a disciplinarian.

"Did someone pee in your Rice Krispies this morning?"

"What?" she asked incredulously.

"Since you're so snippy, I figured someone must have peed in your Rice Krispies."

Marian covered her mouth and giggled.

Louise Williams considered bringing down the wrath of God, but when she glanced at Nelda Wood and saw her staring at her feet holding back a laugh, she shook her head and said, "Jamie, you have a smart mouth." Then, she forced him to move furniture around the living room until she was satisfied the sofa, chairs, and end-tables had been arranged according to Better Homes and Gardens.

When he completed the boring job—without complaint, of course—Jamie glanced at Marian, walked outside, crossed the yard, and leaned against Horace Wood's pickup truck.

"Okay, why were you late?"

Telling the truth, the whole truth, and nothing but the truth, Jamie thought, would be a dumb thing to do. If he mentioned Joyce coming on to him, Marian would press him for details, and he was not an innocent victim. He kissed Joyce, and he pushed down her panties, but he did not take the plunge, which, in his opinion, did not make him a two-timing jerk. Joyce was right. What Marian did not know would not hurt her.

"Joyce Atkins missed the bus and asked me to give her a ride home. When I pulled into her driveway, she invited me in for a Coke. We talked for a while. It was no big deal."

"I don't think I like that."

Jamie changed the subject.

"Several kids at school asked if you're my girlfriend."

"What did you tell them?"

"I told them yes."

"I guess everyone has put two and two together."

"I don't care."

"Me either."

"Do you want to go steady?"

"That's sort of like the groom asking the bride to marry him after she's had the baby." Jamie's eyes widened. Even after a year, Marian's natural bluntness still surprised him. "And if you haven't figured it out by now, Jamie Williams, I *am* your girlfriend, which means, if you give another girl a ride home after school, it'll be a cold day in hell before you feed and water the horses in *my* barn."

CHAPTER 36

After twenty years of covering athletics in Hot Springs, Graham Wallace left the staff of the Sentinel Record to become the Sports Editor for The Republic, Arkansas' largest newspaper, headquartered in Little Rock. His articles now received a statewide following, which made him the de facto voice for athletics in Arkansas.

As he prepared an article on the upcoming high school basketball season, Wallace thought the defending State Champions would probably repeat. Who could stop them? Terrance Brooks, Jamie Williams, Dalton Hilliard, and a loaded supporting cast had finished the previous season with an unblemished record and had won the Overall State Championship. Since the coach of the defending State Champions was an old friend, and no one, in Wallace's opinion, knew more about high school basketball than Jim Johnson, he picked up his telephone, placed a call to Hot Springs High School, and waited while the receptionist transferred the call.

"Coach Johnson."

"Graham Wallace, Jim."

"So, the big city sportswriter still remembers the little people?"

Wallace chuckled. "Haven't you heard? Mingling with peasants is part of my job description. But since I *am* writing an article on the top teams in the State, and since Hot Springs is the defending champion, peasant or not, I thought I should call you."

"With Terrance Brooks and Dalton Hilliard, we should make the finals."

"What about Jamie Williams?"

"Jamie moved again."

"Out of State?"

"No. To a Class B school. Kirby, I think."

"Are you telling me that Jamie Williams will play for a Class B school?"

"Unfortunately, yes, I am."

"Well, there goes his second State Championship."

"I'm not so sure about that, Graham. Any team with Jamie Williams on it can't be bad."

Wallace laughed. "Maybe I should place Kirby in the preseason Top Ten?"

"That may not be a bad idea. Changing the subject, how do you like your new job?"

"It keeps me busy and pays the bills. Next week I'll attend the Southwest Conference Basketball Media Day in Dallas, which will be interesting."

"How do the Razorbacks look this year?"

"Not too good. Thanks for the heads up on Jamie. I'll talk to you later, Jim."

Wallace hung up the phone, rummaged through his desk, pulled out a state map, and located Kirby. He stared at the map for several seconds, reached for his tweed sports coat, and then walked out of his office. "Where are you going, Mr. Wallace?" his secretary asked.

"Kirby."

"Where?"

It was abundantly clear that his ever efficient and somewhat controlling secretary had never heard of the place. "Kirby. If anyone calls, tell them I'll be back in the morning.

•   •   •

Coach Benson was, in the opinion of his players, an intense and demanding young man. He made them run laps to begin and end each practice and pushed them to the limit on the basics. An errant pass resulted in more laps. A mishandled reception meant the bumbler had to stand in front of a concrete block wall and throw a basketball against it until he caught fifty ricochets without a fumble. Then there were the repetitive agility drills, which, he said, developed quick hands and feet.

The more Coach Benson worked with his team, the more positive he became about the season. Jamie Williams was amazing; his outside shots were unbelievable, his inside play uncanny, and his enthusiasm contagious. There was, Coach Benson thought, something about Jamie that made his teammates better. Although he rarely said anything—Jamie talked with his eyes—there was not a doubt in Coach Benson's mind that Jamie raised his teammates to a higher level, and he did it without being a condescending jerk.

David Thompson had picked up on Jamie's style of play and would have an outstanding year. If Randy Murray became a little more aggressive, he would probably start at Forward. Jim Lawrence, Coach Benson had decided, *would* start at Forward. Jim was not an offensive threat, but his defense was phenomenal. B. J. Heller, the tallest man on the team—six feet five inches tall—was not a typical Center. B. J. was deceptively chubby, but Coach Benson liked him because he was sneaky, had a mean streak, and could score with defensive players hanging all over him.

Coach Benson glanced toward the foyer when he heard the front door to Trojan Field House opening. He ruled his fiefdom with an iron fist and resented anyone who invaded his territory uninvited. He frowned when a well-dressed man carrying a black-leather portfolio walked into the gym, took a seat in the bleachers, observed the team, and made occasional notes. Stone-faced, Coach Benson walked to where the man sat, placed both hands on his hips, and asked, rather sharply, "May I help you?"

The man extended his hand. "I'm Graham Wallace."

Coach Benson shook the extended hand and wondered why The Republic's Sports Editor was visiting a small school like Kirby. Little Rock, Hot Springs, Pine Bluff, Texarkana, or Fort Smith? Sure! But Kirby? No way! Graham Wallace had to be crazy or lost.

"Your team looks good."

"Thank you."

"You're Coach Benson, aren't you?"

"I apologize for not introducing myself, Mr. Wallace, but I was trying to figure out why the Sports Editor for The Republic drove a hundred miles to scout a Class B team with a first-year coach."

Graham Wallace chuckled. "I won't keep any secrets from you." He watched Jamie fake a drive and put up a twenty-foot jumper. "It's Jamie Williams. I like the kid and think he may be the best I've ever seen. I'm sentimental, and I want to see for myself that Jamie is doing well at his new school."

"Really?"

"Sportswriters are human too, Coach Benson."

"I'm sorry, Mr. Wallace. I didn't mean that the way it sounded."

"I know you didn't. Your name is Chuck, isn't it?"

"Yes, sir."

"Call me Graham. I have a feeling we'll be talking often."

"Because of Jamie?"

"Uh-huh. You know about his past accomplishments?"

"Every coach in Arkansas knows about Jamie Williams."

"If Jamie had remained in Hot Springs, he would have been All-State again. From what I've seen today, I think he'll still make it. Your team looks good."

"I think so, but I'm not very objective about these guys."

"Jamie isn't your only talented player. You'll go a long way."

"Depth will be a problem."

"Obviously, you'll do well in your District, but in the State Tournament, numbers will take a toll. They always do. Regardless of how good your starting five is, if you don't have players to give them a breather, they'll wear down in the fourth quarter."

"I believe we'll surprise some people, though."

"That's why I drove down here. I'll mention your Trojans as a possible dark horse in the high school preview. If you win some games out of the starting gate, I'll give you a lot of attention."

"Do you think we're *that* good?"

"Well, as one coach told me earlier today: 'Any team with Jamie Williams on it can't be bad.'"

Wallace reached into his pocket, pulled out a business card, and handed it to Coach Benson. "My office and home phone numbers are on that card. Keep in touch and let me know how many points Jamie scores in each game. People need to know about your team."

Graham Wallace tapped Coach Benson's shoulder and walked out of Trojan Field House, knowing the larger schools with their numerical edge and superior talent would not overshadow Jamie Williams and the Kirby Trojans. His future articles would make waves in the predictable sea of high school basketball, but come hell or high water, Jamie Williams would not be ignored. He, Graham Wallace, would see to it.

CHAPTER 37

Jamie hated algebra and needed help. Since Marian was the brightest person he knew, and since she had aced Algebra the year before, he rode his motorcycle to her house, looking for a little help, and anything else she might give him.

When he stepped off his Honda, it surprised him to see Horace Wood sitting on the porch. Marian's grumpy father was obviously waiting for him, and Horace Wood confirmed Jamie's suspicions when he motioned for him to sit down.

The conversation, Jamie decided, would not be pleasant when Horace Wood looked him in the eye and said, "I decided a long time ago to have a little talk with any hairy-legged boy Marian dragged home. Since you live in Kirby now, and since she spends so much time with you, it's time for you to hear the speech, Jamie."

"Okay, Mr. Wood."

"Marian's pretty, isn't she?"

"Yes, sir."

"And that's the problem. Do you understand what I'm saying?"

"Yes, sir."

"Marian's a beautiful girl, and I'm proud that she's a beautiful girl, but being a beautiful girl makes a boy want to do things that might get him in a whole peck of trouble."

Jamie suddenly found his feet very interesting. Horace Wood hardened his voice and said, "Don't drop your head when I talk to you. Look me in the eye like a man."

Jamie lifted his head and stared darts into the older man's eyes. Horace Wood saw anger—Jamie, no doubt, had a temper—and he had not noticed that before. He smiled, insincerely, Jamie thought, and then pointedly continued: "I like you, Jamie, I truly do, and I don't mind you going out with Marian, but when a boy and a girl spend a lot of time together, they're tempted to do things that are reserved for married folks."

Horace Wood narrowed his eyes and hardened his voice. "I don't want Marian pregnant before she graduates from high school, Jamie. She's smart and deserves more out of life than wiping butts and changing diapers. She wants to go to college, and I don't intend for you, or any boy, to mess that up. Do you understand me?"

"I'd be a fool if I didn't."

Horace Wood chuckled. "You and Marian have fun, Jamie—I mean that—but if things get too hot to handle, I want you to remember this conversation. I won't be easy on you, or any boy, who gets in my daughter's pants and messes up her future."

Horace Wood slapped Jamie on the knee good-naturedly. Relieved the lecture was over, Jamie walked stiffly into the house. When he stepped into Marian's bedroom, she was sitting cross-legged on the bed wearing the same short skirt and sweater she had worn at school earlier in the day. Although the view was spectacular, and he thought it was a fine time to feed and water the horses, Jamie decided that the smart thing to do was study algebra.

•   •   •

Trojan Field House was jampacked and smelled of popcorn. The crowd applauded when the senior boys stood and sauntered toward the dressing room midway through the fourth quarter of the senior girl's game. For several weeks, they had been hearing rumors about their beloved Trojans. In fact, there had been a rumor going around that a sportswriter from Little Rock had interviewed Coach Benson. Trojan loyalists found that hard to believe—Class B schools were always an afterthought to the State newspapers—but when an article appeared in The Republic touting the Trojans as a dark horse with championship potential, hopes and expectations soared.

To most Trojan fans, Coach Benson's blue, pen-striped suit and red tie seemed out of place in a gymnasium filled with faded jeans, flannel shirts, and overalls. In fact, most fans thought the new coach looked stilted, not at all relaxed, and had serious doubts about his coaching ability. The junior and senior high girls had won their games convincingly, but the junior high boys had lost by a substantial margin, and that had been hard to stomach. If the senior boys were not as good as the Little Rock reporter had written, Mr. Fancy Pants would have a brief stay at Kirby High School.

The Amity Rams controlled the opening tip, but before the visitors could set up on offense, Randy Murray stole the ball and threw it to Jamie, who streaked down court and laid it in the hoop for an easy two. From that moment on, crisp ball movement, pinpoint passing, selective shooting, and hard-nosed defense overwhelmed the visitors from Amity. Kirby led 20 to 6 at the end of the first quarter.

As the game progressed, Coach Benson loosened his tie, slouched—almost arrogantly—in his chair, and watched his Trojans annihilate the Amity Rams. The team's quickness amazed the crowd as David Thompson and Jamie Williams anticipated each other's moves and left their defenders grasping at air. When the rout ended, Kirby fans, loving their young coach—he was, after all, a brilliant tactician and a great motivator—gathered in the foyer and celebrated the overwhelming victory.

Why were the Trojans so good? Was it the new coach? Was it the preacher's son? Was it team chemistry? Or was it a combination of the three? What difference did it make? The Trojans were a great team, and a State Championship—something they had never considered—now seemed a distinct possibility.

CHAPTER 38

CAN CLASS B SCHOOLS COMPETE?

Graham Wallace
Sports Editor

Several weeks ago, I wrote an article picking Kirby, a Class B school, as a possible dark horse in the Overall State Championship picture. Because of that article, I have received calls and letters disagreeing with my prediction. But since I wrote the article, the Kirby Trojans have won ten games without a loss, and to this point in the season, have not been challenged. However, out of respect for my critics, I will answer the question: Can Class B schools compete on the State level?

Class B is the State's largest classification and its smallest. Class B comprises approximately 140 teams, which makes it Arkansas' largest school grouping. Class B, however, also comprises the smallest schools in the State, usually having less than one hundred students in the top three grades.

In Class B, basketball is king. Most of the schools do not field a football team — there simply are not enough students — yet spirit and enthusiasm are not lacking. Each week fans fill local gymnasiums to support their home team. Interestingly, Class B schools are well into their season by the time their larger counterparts begin competition, and by the end of the year have played close to thirty-five games, forty if they make the playoffs.

Usually, in terms of quality and numbers, Class B schools do not have the athletes to compete with the higher classifications. Class B, however, counters this with tradition and mastering the fundamentals of basketball. Notice I did not say "always" but "usually" Class B schools do not have quality athletes and numbers. It is this distinction that makes the Kirby Trojans an exception. They have two excellent athletes, Jamie Williams and David Thompson, with a stable and consistent supporting cast.

It is true the higher classifications have the talent and athletes to be dominant, but a fundamentally sound Class B school with one or two exceptional players, plus a roster filled with above average players, can make waves on the State scene, and play with anyone.

The Kirby Trojans are such a team.

No Class B school has ever won the Overall State Championship, but by season's end, do not be surprised to see the Kirby Trojans in the thick of things. And, if they take home all the marbles, let Graham Wallace be the first to say, "I told you so."

Oh, and to answer the question. Yes, Class B schools can compete on the State level.

•   •   •

Jamie tightened the strap on his safety helmet, revved the Honda's engine, and glanced at the black Chevelle Malibu SS roaring next to him. David Thompson's older brother, Harold, owned the car, and had challenged Jamie to a drag race, confident a two-cylinder motorcycle could not outrun his Chevelle SS 396.

Both machines accelerated, the Honda's front wheel leaping off the asphalt as Jamie power-shifted the transmission. With smoke boiling from its tires, the black Chevy swerved from side to side as Harold popped the clutch and took it through all four gears.

It was no contest.

Disgusted, Marian slammed her father's pickup truck into low gear and headed for school, ill as a hornet. The race, Marian thought, had been stupid, the smoke and noise nothing more than the abuse of machines by boys pretending to be men. And the way the Honda's front wheel had jumped off the ground each time Jamie shifted gears was absurd; if he had lost control, the county coroner would have had to scrape the pieces of his mangled body off the highway and dump them in a black, rubber bag.

"How fast did you make it through the quarter?" David asked, rubbing his hands, warming them against the unusually chilly December morning.

"I didn't look until I was past you. I was going over a hundred then."

Harold handed Jamie a ten-dollar bill. "That thing is wicked. I didn't think anything in Southwest Arkansas could outrun my Chevelle."

Jamie folded the ten-spot and placed it in his pocket. "Thanks, Harold. This will come in handy when I take Marian to the Drive-In Saturday night."

"You'll probably have to go by yourself," David observed matter-of-factly. "Marian looked pissed off when she headed back to school a few minutes ago."

Jamie shrugged his shoulders indifferently. "She'll get over it."

A guy, Jamie believed, had to do what a guy had to do. Marian did not understand that racing Harold had been a matter of face, and that if he had backed down, he would look like a yellow-belly chicken. In fact, he had told Marian—rather smugly—to build a bridge and get over it.

•   •   •

There was not a doubt in Jamie's mind that he loved Kirby High School. His classmates liked his outgoing, often crazy, personality, and his academics impressed his teachers. Happier than he could ever remember being, Jamie was in a jubilant mood when he sat down next to Marian during lunch.

He noticed her cool reception and thought it would pass—Marian never stayed mad it him for long—but when she did not respond to his attempts at small talk, he pushed back his chair, picked up his tray, and hissed, "I don't have to put up with your bullshit."

Stunned, Marian dropped her fork. The silent treatment had not worked—Jamie was madder than an old wet hen—and that was the last thing she wanted.

"Where are you going?"

"To find someone who won't give me the cold shoulder."

"Wait a min…"

Jamie stormed out of the cafeteria without looking back.

•   •   •

The argument with Marian bothered Jamie. He tried to put it out of his mind by throwing a little red football and watching it spin very near the ceiling of his bedroom. Some things, he thought, never change. He was seventeen years old and still throwing a little red football at the ceiling, just as he had when he was ten.

He wanted to call Marian but could not make himself do it. He had, in fact, reached for the phone several times, but stubborn pride clouded his thinking and kept him from making the call.

The red football bounced off the ceiling, fell on the floor, and rolled beneath the nightstand next to his bed. He reached for the ball, but opened the nightstand drawer instead, and picked up his picture of Michelle. Maybe it was because he had had a fight with Marian? Jamie really didn't know. But for some unexplainable reason, he felt the need to communicate and picked up a pen and paper:

Michelle,

I know it has been a long time since you wrote to me, and this letter is probably the last thing you want, but I think, after all these months, that I should apologize for being a two-timing jerk.

Yes, I did date Vicki when I moved to Hot Springs. I never intended to, but it happened. That was a mistake. I should have been honest with you, but I didn't want to hurt you, and most of all, I didn't want to lose you. All I can say is I'm sorry.

Enough about that.

We've moved to Kirby now — it's a small place a little over forty miles from Hot Springs — and I love it. I'm still playing basketball, of course, and we're undefeated after twelve games. Also, I'm dating a girl. Her name is Marian Wood. The reason I'm telling you this is, if you decide to write me back, you'll know I'm not hiding anything from you.

Overall, I guess I'm happy, but tonight I realized I needed to make things right with you. I'm sorry I hurt you, and I'm sorry Vicki wrote that stupid letter. If I could go back in time, I would handle everything differently. Oh, well, as Dad always says, "Hindsight is twenty-twenty."

You were a friend when I needed one, Michelle, and I will never forget you.

Love,

Jamie

P.S. Maybe it's wishful thinking, but I hope someday we can talk and be friends again.

He reread the letter, placed it in an envelope, and decided to mail it from the Kirby Post Office on Monday morning. He stretched, then pulled back the comforter, eased into bed, and thought, *Is it possible to love two girls at the same time? Oh, well, Mom has always said that I'm her strange child.* Jamie fluffed his pillow, closed his eyes, decided to make up with Marian, and thought that he probably should have called her.

•   •   •

Piney Baptist Church was singing the opening hymn when Jamie walked into the building. Calvin Williams stared at him, a disapproving frown on his face. Jamie shrugged his shoulders, mimed "I'm sorry," then took his usual seat on the back pew.

Marian cut her eyes toward him and then buried her face in a hymnal. Jamie stared at her and waited for the next furtive glance—he knew it would come. As he expected, she cut her eyes toward him again, then quickly turned her attention back to the hymnal. Finally, she cut her eyes toward him a third time and did not look away. Jamie smiled and mimed, "I love you." Marian turned her attention to the Sunday School Superintendent's boring devotional, then looked back at Jamie and smiled.

The battle was over.

• • •

After lunch, Jamie and Marian saddled their horses and rode to the secluded creek where they went to be alone. He picked up a rock, skipped it across the water, and mumbled, "I've decided to sell my Honda and buy a car."

"Because of me?" Marian asked incredulously.

"I would be lying if I told you no, but the main reason is, if someone wants to race, I won't turn him down. And you're right, Marian, if I keep it up, someday I'll crash. There are two kinds of motorcycle riders: those who *have* crashed and those who *will* crash. The obvious answer is to sell my bike and buy something a little tamer."

"I feel like I'm forcing you to do something you don't want to do."

"You're not. The more I think about it, the more I want a car."

"I like the idea."

"It can't be just any car. It'll have to have style. The best Point Guard in the State of Arkansas has to look good when he drives."

Marian rolled her eyes. "I hope you get stuck with an old, beat up, four-door Plymouth."

"Wouldn't you be embarrassed to ride in it?"

"If I'm with you, I don't care what you drive."

CHAPTER 39

Most followers of high school basketball thought Graham Wallace had lost his mind when he touted the Kirby Trojans as dark-horse contenders for the State Championship. The media—men who followed and wrote about the sport—knew that there was no way a Class B school could compete with Little Rock, Hot Springs, Fort Smith, and Texarkana. The experts admitted that the Kirby Trojans were a great Class B team—they *had* finished the season with thirty-two victories and *were* their district's champion—but Graham Wallace, they believed, had been around long enough to know that Class B schools always folded their tents when they faced the higher classifications in the Overall State Tournament.

The Hot Springs Trojans, like the media, took umbrage at Graham Wallace's outrageous opinion. There was not a Center in Arkansas that could hold his own against Terrance Brooks— Terrance was bigger, tougher, and smarter than all of them— and major colleges nationwide were recruiting him. They may have lost the anointed one, Jamie Williams, who was now playing for Kirby, but Dalton Hilliard was not a slouch, he was a great defensive player, and the Trojans had won every game without the anointed one's pinpoint passes and deadly outside shots.

The brackets had been drawn, and the battle-lines formed. Each District had its champion and local newspapers were asking, "Will our boys go all the way?" Beneath the friendly banter, however, lay the insulting implication that smaller schools could not compete against, much less defeat, the larger schools. For a half? Maybe! But for four quarters? No way!

Many outstanding Class B schools had played in the Overall State Tournament, but when they faced the higher classifications—usually in the first two rounds—they succumbed to the pressure and depth of the larger schools. This was the norm, the history of the tournament, and the Kirby Trojans, even with Jamie Williams, could not stop numbers and superior talent in the fourth quarter.

•   •   •

Jamie and Calvin Williams found the perfect car at the Chevrolet Dealership in Hot Springs: a maroon, 1964 Nova Super Sport with a white leatherette interior. The car had a 283 V-8 engine and a four-speed transmission. Although it was four years old, the Nova had very few miles on it and the previous owner had maintained the car well. Calvin Williams made the deal quickly, handed Jamie a set of keys, and watched him scoot beneath the steering-wheel of his first car.

The dual exhausts sounded mellow as Jamie drove down Ouachita Avenue, gearing down and releasing the clutch when he approached a traffic signal so that he could hear the dual exhausts rumble and pop. The Nova had power and style, a combination Jamie loved, and driving it removed any doubt he had had about selling his Honda.

•   •   •

"What's cooking, Good-Looking?"

"I've been waiting for you to call."

"Planet of the Apes is playing in Hot Springs. Do you want to go?"

"Sure."

"The movie starts at seven. I'll pick you up at five-thirty."

"I'll be ready."

Jamie chuckled. "Ready?"

Marian blushed, glanced at her parents, and mumbled, "Yes."

"I'll pick you up in about an hour."

•   •   •

Jamie parked the Nova in a metered area behind the Malco Theater, bought tickets for the movie, and then walked into the lobby holding hands with Marian. She stepped to the side when he headed for the refreshment counter to buy popcorn and Cokes.

As he stood in line, a finger tapped repeatedly between his should blades. Jamie winced and turned around, fully intending to break the rude digit digging a hole in his back, but the digit belonged to a friend, Dalton Hilliard, who smiled broadly and said, "So, you finally crawled out of the sticks and came back to bright lights and civilization?"

Jamie laughed. "Kirby doesn't have a theater, and I wanted to see Planet of the Apes."

"Are you by yourself?"

"My girlfriend is with me."

Jamie nodded at Marian.

"Wow! She's pretty."

"I think so."

"Why don't y'all sit with us? All our friends are here."

"Wouldn't we be intruding?"

"Jamie Williams intruding? Are you kidding me?"

•   •   •

"Look what the cat drug up, boys and girls: the pride of Arkansas basketball." Dalton couldn't resist the sarcasm. He was, by nature, a sarcastic young man.

"Why didn't you call and tell me you were coming?" Bill Mitchell asked.

"I didn't know I was until a couple of hours ago."

Vicki Helms glanced at Jamie and smiled, but he did not notice, did not care, or was simply ignoring her. Jamie, Vicki knew, was an expert at ignoring anyone who had pissed him off.

"I traded my Honda for a car today, Bill."

"Really?"

"A '64 Nova Super Sport."

"I'll check it out after the movie."

Dalton did not care about Jamie's motorcycle or his new car. He did, however, care about the State Basketball Tournament, and did not hide the fact that he thought it was absurd that Jamie Williams, a native of Hot Springs, would play against his alma mater and former teammates.

"Are the *dark-horse* Trojans ready for some big-time basketball?"

"Yes, we are."

"According to the brackets, Hot Springs and Kirby won't play unless we both make the finals."

"Kirby will make the finals, Dalton."

"So, Jamie Williams is going to play against his alma mater?"

"Yes, he is, and he'll do what he always does: win."

Obviously disgusted, Dalton gritted his teeth, shook his head, and said, "You realize we'll be guarding each other, don't you?"

"Maybe you'll sprain an ankle. I really don't want to embarrass you, Dalton."

Marian, Jamie noticed, was uncharacteristically quiet. He leaned over and whispered, "If you're uncomfortable, we can sit someplace else. I want to be with you, not them."

She squeezed his hand. "I'm fine, Jamie. Let's watch the movie."

•   •   •

Marian seemed more than a little distant after the movie. Jamie thought that was odd. The only time she was cool or distant was when he did something stupid, like racing his motorcycle. He replayed the evening in his mind and could think of nothing he had done to upset her. After several minutes of silence, he drove past the Hot Springs Municipal Airport and opened the mysterious can of worms.

"Okay, what's bothering you?"

"I realized tonight what you gave up when you moved to Kirby."

"I didn't give up anything."

"That's not true. You have friends, close friends, in Hot Springs."

"I grew up with the kids you met tonight."

"Vicki is beautiful. I can't believe you don't like her."

"I told you what she did."

"She still likes you."

"I don't care."

"Did you notice how she stared darts at me?"

"She's a bitch, Marian." Jamie dimmed his lights for an oncoming car. "If I had known taking you to Hot Springs was going to upset you, we wouldn't have come."

"What did you expect, Jamie? Before tonight, I never paid a lot of attention to your life in Hot Springs. I'd hear you talk about friends, but when they developed faces, pretty faces, it was kind of shocking. You were a big part of their lives, and still are."

"They're friends, Marian. That's all. Given the choice between Kirby and Hot Springs, I'd choose Kirby. And if I had to choose between you and Vicki, I'd choose you every time."

"There's no way I can compare to Miss-Blond-And-Beautiful.

"Bullshit! You're smarter than Vicki, you're prettier than Vicki, and you're a hell of a lot nicer than Vicki. I'd rather be with you than anyone in the world."

"Are you trying to sweep me off my feet?"

"I did that a long time ago."

"Jerk!"

"Do you want to go parking before I take you home?"

"I'm always *ready* for that, Jamie."

CHAPTER 40

As improbable as it seemed to followers of high school basketball in Arkansas, the Kirby Trojans, a Class B school, had fought its way into the finals of the Arkansas State High School Basketball Tournament and had earned the right to play the Hot Springs Trojans for the Overall State Title in Little Rock's T. H. Barton Coliseum.

The Hot Springs Trojans and the Kirby Trojans were teams with contrasting styles. In each game, Kirby built a substantial lead, and then, because of a lack of depth, had to defend its lead in the fourth quarter. Hot Springs, however, dominated from start to finish and had walked away from each game with a ten to fifteen-point win.

Most sportswriters thought the Kirby Trojans had lucked their way into the championship round. Several top teams had been upset by lesser teams, and the lesser teams—naturally— lost their edge when they played a lowly Class B school. They did not say it in their articles—they *were* writing about teenaged boys—but most sportswriters thought it would take a miracle from God and an Act of Congress for Kirby to beat Hot Springs. History had proved—repeatedly—that Class B schools, regardless of the hype, were nervous and intimidated when they played the higher classifications in the State Tournament. Why should 1968 be any different?

•   •   •

"Number 13, Terrance Brooks, is the key to this game," Coach Benson said, as he began his pre-game preparations. "B. J., you know how to play him. He *will* score. Don't worry about it. Just make it as hard as you can for him to get the ball.

"Jamie, I want you and David taking the ball inside. Brooks has never faced a Guard tandem like you. If you get him in foul trouble, the game is ours. Terrance Brooks is the only player Hot Springs has that can stay on the floor with you guys."

Coach Benson knew his team, except for Jamie Williams, was nervous—nothing, he had learned, ever made Jamie nervous—and he knew the odds were against his Trojans making it back to the State finals. Reaching the championship game once was hard enough, reaching it twice, as Hot Springs had done, was nearly impossible, especially for a Class B school.

The door to the dressing room opened.

Calvin Williams, wearing jeans, tennis shoes, and a Kirby Trojan T-shirt, walked to the front of the room carrying a Bible. Coach Benson said, "Guys, I've asked Brother Williams to talk to you about fallen champions," then he stepped back and leaned against the wall.

Looking solemn, Calvin Williams opened his Bible.

"There went out a champion from the camp of the Philistines named Goliath."

He snapped the Bible shut and stared at the boys.

"Goliath was huge, probably nine feet tall, and there wasn't a man alive who wanted to fight him. If anyone had enough courage to confront him, Goliath said things like, 'When I'm through with you, I'll feed your mangled body to the birds.' Israel's army, of course, believed Goliath. Soldiers cowered in fear when he spoke, and they ran like whipped puppies when he approached them, because they didn't want to be Goliath's next victim.

"Why did soldiers, men of war, cower in fear? And why did they run?

"They ran because they *thought* Goliath was unbeatable.

"Enter David, a teenager, a young man about your age.

"With five smooth stones and a shepherd's sling, David challenged the Philistine. And what did Goliath do? He disdained David and treated him like an unworthy opponent.

"David, however, reached for a stone, put it in his sling, swung the sling, released it, and buried the stone in Goliath's head. The big man fell face first to the ground. With Goliath out cold — I don't know if he was dead or alive — David reached for a sword, cut off the Philistine's head, and in a split second there was a new champion: David!

"Was David as big as Goliath? No! Was he as talented? No! Was he as experienced? No! But with guts, a big heart, and a lot of faith, David defeated the undefeated, and *he* became the champion.

"There is a moral to this story, boys: the bigger they are, the harder they fall."

Calvin Williams paused, glanced at Coach Benson, then roared, "Goliath's head is going to roll tonight!"

Cheers echoed off the walls.

Laughing, Coach Benson stepped forward. "Guys, you've come farther than any Class B school in history. What you've accomplished probably won't be repeated. Now, I've read in the newspapers that we're a little bitty David and that we don't stand a chance against big ole Goliath. Two weeks ago, the same papers said the same thing, but here we are playing for the State Championship. To be honest, I believe we're the better team, and I believe we're going to win. We've got five smooth stones. So, let's go out on that court in front of a hostile crowd and make Goliath's head roll."

The Hot Springs Pep Band was playing the Trojan fight song when the Kirby Trojans entered T. H. Barton Coliseum. Jamie took several warm-up shots, scanned the large arena, then confidently walked to mid-court where his old friends and former teammates were standing. Dalton Hilliard shook his head, obviously disgusted.

"That's one ugly uniform, Jamie."

"If you'll study history, Dalton, you'll learn that ancient Trojans wore maroon and white, not black and gold."

"You've always been a fountain of useless bullshit, Jamie."

Terrance Brooks laughed. "I don't know if you pulled that ancient Trojan story out of your ass, Jamie, but Dalton is right. That's an ugly uniform."

"You guys are just jealous."

Terrance and Dalton rolled their eyes and walked toward their bench. Jamie stared at his former teammates and thought—nostalgically—of the many games they had played and won together. Then he walked to the sideline and sat down.

"What was that about?"

"Just checking out the competition, David. You ready to kick some ass?"

"Yep."

"Then let's do it."

•   •   •

Terrance Brooks out-jumped B. J. Heller and hit Dalton Hilliard for an easy bucket. After the made basket, Kirby hustled down court and ran their motion offense. Randy Murray set a quick screen and Jamie tied the game in a heartbeat.

Coach Benson knew adrenaline was high and that his Trojans were showing Hot Springs they were not intimidated, but he did not like the fast-paced beginning; running and gunning was exactly what the Hot Springs wanted them to do. After several swapped baskets—enough time to let the adrenaline settle—Coach Benson lifted his hands, formed a "T," and called a timeout.

"Okay, you proved you can run with them, but slow it down. You're playing their game, not ours. Take the ball inside and get Brooks in foul trouble. That's the plan. You got it?"

Jamie and David met each other's eyes, broke the huddle on Coach Benson's signal, and stepped back onto the court. On the next possession, Randy Murray grabbed a rebound and passed the ball to David. With no open shot, David passed the ball to Jamie. Jamie faked left, dribbled right, penetrated the lane, was fouled by Terrance Brooks, then walked to the charity stripe and completed the three-point play.

Kirby, as planned, played a tight zone, boxing in Terrance Brooks beneath the goal. With the lanes closed, David intercepted an errant pass and took it the length of the court for an easy lay-up, giving Kirby a five-point lead. After another quick turnover, Jamie received a pinpoint pass from David and attacked the rim. Terrance fouled him on the way up, Jamie made the shot, and once again went to the charity stripe and took care of business, giving Kirby an eight-point lead.

Dalton Hilliard was not having his usual stellar game. When he played Jamie close, he passed the ball to David Thompson for a short jumper. When he played him soft, Jamie sank a long-range bomb. Frustrated, and more than a little embarrassed, Dalton held the ball, looked toward Coach Johnson, and called timeout.

Midway through the second quarter, Jamie flipped the ball to David under the basket. Out of position, Terrance knocked David to the floor, but the shot fell, and the referee called another foul. As the two teams lined up for the free-throw, Terrance Brooks walked to the bench. From that point on, the first half belonged to Kirby. The Class B Trojans poured it on and held an impressive sixteen-point lead at halftime.

Hot Springs, however, had too much talent, pride, and depth to fold. Terrance Brooks and Dalton Hilliard adjusted, asserted themselves, and the Kirby Trojans began to tire. Terrance—on a mission—repeatedly opened the back door and manhandled B. J. Heller.

With the third quarter winding down, and Hot Springs methodically chipping away at Kirby's lead, David sneaked up the baseline and hit Jamie with a quick, no-look pass. Terrance tried to block the shot, bumped Jamie from behind, and knocked him to the floor. Both boys stared at the referee, who was blowing his whistle and pointing at Terrance. Jamie hit both free-throws and gave Kirby an eight-point lead, while Terrance Brooks, with four fouls, took a seat on the bench next to Coach Johnson.

The fourth quarter was a war, as Hot Springs continued its tide of fresh players. Finally, with four minutes left in the game, Coach Johnson made his move: Terrance Brooks, with fire in his eyes, came off the bench and back into the game.

Sore, battered, and exhausted, B. J. Heller knew he could not handle Terrance Brooks. In fact, B. J. thought he would be bruised for weeks—Terrance was that physical—but when he saw Dalton Hilliard pick up a loose ball, B. J. established position near the goal and drew a charge as Terrance attacked the rim and knocked him to the floor. Afraid that he was going to puke, B. J. wanted to fall to his knees and thank God when he saw Goliath walking toward the Hot Springs Trojan bench.

Game over!

Coach Benson kept the ball in Jamie's hands during the foul-fest and Jamie did not miss a free-throw. Three minutes later, Kirby became the first Class B school to win the Overall State Championship.

Jamie knew he had shattered one dream and fulfilled another. Terrance and Dalton had fallen short of their dream, and he had fulfilled his by winning a second State Championship. As he watched his friends sitting on their bench twisting towels in frustration, winning the Overall State Championship, although spectacular, seemed tarnished.

The crowd grew quiet as the Public-Address Announcer began the post-game ceremonies: "Ladies and gentlemen, the President of the Arkansas Athletic Association will now present the Overall State Championship Trophy to Kirby High School and Coach Chuck Benson, who is the first coach to lead a Class B school to the Overall Title."

The crowd applauded politely as Coach Benson, surrounded by his team, accepted the trophy. When the applause subsided, the Public-Address Announcer continued: "The Most Valuable Player in this year's tournament, a young man who has averaged twenty-seven points per game, is Jamie Williams, from Kirby High School."

The crowd applauded as Jamie walked to mid-court and accepted the trophy. He briefly held it above his head and then joined his teammates for the traditional net-cutting ceremony.

Graham Wallace realized that winning consecutive state championships would have been a monumental accomplishment for Coach Johnson, and he felt sorry for his friend, but seeing a small school, an underdog, defeat a school ten times its size was gratifying *and* historic. He was proud of Jamie Williams, the Kirby Trojans, and Coach Benson, a cocky young man who had just experienced what most coaches work years to achieve and never see.

•   •   •

Jamie climbed on the bus and literally fell into his seat. Winning five games in the State Tournament had taken a toll, and he was mentally and physically exhausted. Although he had won two MVPs in Louisiana and had been named Newcomer of the Year in 1967, nothing compared to the attention he received in Little Rock. Several coaches from major universities had attended the game scouting Terrance Brooks, but they could not ignore Jamie Williams, the Tournament's Most Valuable Player. He was only a Junior, and they could not recruit him, but their warm handshakes told him that next year he would be the object of their attention. Although the coaches treated him with respect, strangely, Jamie felt weird, like a mutation, or a freak of nature, something to be used and discarded. For a moment, he understood why his father, in the past, had disliked high school and college athletics.

Jamie rested his head against the seat as the bus pulled onto Roosevelt Road. The starting and stopping finally ceased when the driver negotiated the last traffic signal and merged onto Interstate 30. Jamie closed his eyes and went to sleep, too tired to celebrate the glory the night had provided.

Marian sighed as she contemplated the news she would soon share with Jamie: Texas Tech University had offered her a full ride. She did not want to accept the scholarship—applying had been a shot in the dark—but her father had scraped for years so that she could attend college, and the scholarship would save him most of his nest-egg. Accepting it was the right thing to do, but it depressed her…because of Jamie. Time, she believed, would temper their parting, and she, like others, would be lost in his past.

Marian stared into Jamie's peaceful face and whispered, "I love you."

"What?" he asked, almost incoherently.

"Go back to sleep, Jamie. I was just talking to myself."

CHAPTER 41

Calvin Williams leaned back in his chair, stared out the window at a deserted country road, and came to the unsettling conclusion that he was wasting his time pastoring a church that was what it always would be. Not that he did not like Piney Baptist Church. He did—the people were kind and loving—but a rising star in the International Baptist Convention pastored large churches, trendsetting churches, influential churches. Now that he had completed his doctoral thesis, opportunities had opened, and Calvin Williams—when he was honest with himself—believed it was time to move on.

He had impressed the faculty at Mid-South Seminary as a doctoral candidate, and they had asked him to move to Little Rock to head the Evangelism Department. The students enjoyed his lectures when he substituted for their retiring professor, and since he was a proven church-builder, the search committee had asked him to join the faculty in the Fall. There was, however, a problem: he had promised Jamie that he would not have to move again, and that he would graduate from Kirby High School.

The phone rang, interrupting his thoughts.

"Piney Baptist Church."

"Cal. Howard Martin. You busy?"

"Actually, I'm not."

"Since I'm in Texarkana recruiting the next Pistol Pete Maravich, I looked at the map, saw that Kirby wasn't far away, and thought we could meet for lunch."

Calvin Williams glanced at his watch. "I'll meet you at Brice's Cafeteria in downtown Texarkana."

"I could meet you halfway."

"Not unless you want to eat at the Dew Drop Inn." Howard Martin chuckled. "I want to get away for a while, anyway. I'll see you in a couple of hours."

Calvin Williams hung up the phone, glanced at his doctoral thesis, and then walked out the door. Painful decisions and new storms, he believed, were on the horizon.

•   •   •

Calvin Williams walked into the foyer at Brice's Cafeteria and saw Howard Martin rising to greet him. They shook hands warmly, worked their way through the serving line, found an empty table, and made small talk as they ate their lunch.

"How's your family, Howard?"

"Michelle is doing fine — she's making straight 'As' — and Pam is teaching fifth grade at an elementary school in Hammond. How are Lou and Jamie?"

"Lou, a leader of leaders among women..." Howard Martin chuckled... "is President of the convention's Ladies Artillery — Excuse me. I mean Ladies Auxiliary. Jamie, of course, never changes. It's basketball, basketball, and more basketball. In fact, Kirby played giant-killer this year and won the Overall State Championship. No Class B school has ever done that. It was an unbelievable experience."

"And, of course, Jamie played a major role?"

"He was the tournament MVP, which is unheard of for a kid from a Class B school."

"Jamie's one of a kind, Cal."

Calvin Williams sipped his coffee, looked over the cup at Howard Martin, smiled drolly, and asked, "How is Michelle doing since my baby boy isn't writing her letters?"

"He did write once."

"I didn't know that. Jamie never mentioned it."

"Michelle played Miss-High-And-Mighty and didn't write him back. I think she still likes him, though, because she hasn't dated any of the boys in Hammond. Says she wants to be a lawyer and spends most of her time studying. With her grades and attitude, I believe she'll make it."

"What's wrong with her attitude?"

"She's too serious-minded. I tell her to go out and have some fun. Aren't high school kids supposed to have fun, Cal? But she gives me the old it's-none-of-your-business stare and does her own thing. Changing the subject, what going on in your life?"

"My church is doing well, but I may have a problem."

"What kind of problem?"

"Mid-South Seminary wants me to take over the Evangelism Department."

"Isn't that good news?"

"Yes, unless you're seventeen years old and extremely happy in your present circumstances."

"Jamie doesn't want to leave Kirby."

"I promised him he wouldn't have to transfer schools again."

"What are you going to do?"

"Try to persuade Mid-South to let me commute for a year."

"What if the administration won't allow you to do that?"

"Hopefully, they will. I really want this position, Howard. Teaching evangelism is something I would be good at. I know how to build a church and sharing my experience with young preachers will, I believe, have a positive effect on the work."

Howard Martin rubbed the back of his neck. "It seems we have similar problems."

"What do you mean?"

"I have a tempting job offer."

"Where?"

"The University of Arkansas."

"Really? Is the Arkansas job a good one?"

"It will be a challenge—The U of A is a football school—but on a positive note, the athletic director assured me I'll have a green light to build a program from the ground up. He'll give me time to recruit quality athletes—black *and* white, which, as you know, is important to me—and to install my system."

"Sounds like a good deal."

"I know, but how do I sell the idea to my wife and kid?"

"Don't ask me. I have my problems of my own."

•   •   •

A relaxing spring evening on the Williams' front porch took an unexpected turn when Marian said, "Jamie, I have to tell you something."

"Okay."

"Texas Tech University offered me a scholarship."

"Texas Tech?" Jamie asked incredulously.

"Yes. Texas Tech. Taking the scholarship will save my dad a lot of money. It wouldn't be fair to him if I turned it down. We're talking tuition, books, housing, and an on-campus job. No Arkansas school has even come close."

"Damn!"

Marian glanced toward the pasture and watched a herd of Black Angus cattle lumbering toward a moss-covered pond. "My parents don't have a lot of money, Jamie—Dad has worked in the logwoods all his life—it wouldn't be fair for me to stay in Arkansas just to be near you."

Jamie grunted, stared at the ceiling, and replied, "You know, when you leave, nothing will be the same." Marian glanced at Jamie suspiciously. "Not that we won't try, but time and distance will destroy us. I know. I've been through this shit before."

"What are you telling me, Jamie?"

"That when you leave in August, we'll hang on for six months, maybe a year, but sooner or later, you'll find some there, and I'll find someone here."

Tears flooded Marian's eyes. "You're wrong, Jamie! You're the only boy I'll ever love. I'll do anything for you, and you know it." She turned away from him, then quickly turned back. Tears were streaming down her face. "I'll wait for you until hell freezes over. You're just leaving yourself a way out so you can date other girls when I'm gone."

Marian's words stung like an angry, red wasp, and Jamie's temper flared...until he realized she was right. "I shouldn't have said that, Marian. I'm sorry." He placed his arm around her waist and pulled her close. Marian laid her head against his shoulder. "You have to admit, though, I have lousy luck with women."

CHAPTER 42

The University of Arkansas flew Howard Martin and his family to Fayetteville and made its offer. The decision was now in his hands. Pam, he knew, had been impressed, but Michelle seemed ambivalent and had said very little about the potential move. Howard Martin, of course, was concerned—any father would be—about his daughter's ambivalence toward living in a new city and state. Time and Jamie Williams, he decided, would eventually settle the issue for Michelle...one way or another.

He leaned back in his chair and thought about the positive and negative aspects of becoming the head coach at the University of Arkansas. It *would* be a challenge. The Razorbacks had finished the season in the Southwest Conference cellar and fan support had dropped significantly. If he took the job, Howard Martin knew he would face the biggest challenge of his coaching career. But it was inevitable. When he visited the hilly, picturesque campus, he knew he had found the place where he would make his mark. With his mind settled, Howard Martin placed a call to the Athletic Director in Fayetteville, accepted the job, and then typed a letter of resignation to the Athletic Director at Southeast Louisiana

University. Finally, he called his wife and told her they were moving to Arkansas.

• • •

Moving to Fayetteville was not a big deal to Michelle; she had always been apathetic toward Hammond, anyway. Unfortunately, the person who caused her apathy also squelched her enthusiasm about moving to Arkansas. His name was Jamie Williams.

Michelle stared at the bracelet Jamie had given her and frowned.

You've made my life miserable for two years. One missing you, the other hating you. Now we'll live in the same state and probably go to the same college.

She threw the bracelet on the dresser. The noise, louder than she expected, startled her. She reached for the last letter Jamie had written, read it again, and threw it down.

Who does he think he is? Apologizing six months after I wrote to him.

On the summer trip she had taken to Northwest Arkansas with Jamie, Michelle had been impressed with Fayetteville and the University of Arkansas. On her recent visit, however, she had felt nothing as she walked the campus with her mother.

And tomorrow I have to face the two-timing jerk. Dad wouldn't think of taking a trip to Arkansas without spending the night with his good friend Calvin Williams. If I'm lucky, Jamie will be gone, chasing some girl he has waiting in the shadows.

• • •

Jamie followed his parents outside to the front porch when the Martin's Oldsmobile pulled up the lane and stopped in the driveway. He watched Howard, Pamela, and Michelle Martin step out of the car, glanced at Michelle, and then focused on the adults and the front yard reunion. He did not want Michelle to think he was gawking.

When the reunion moved to the front porch, Jamie smiled and said, "Hi, Michelle." Without making eye-contact, she mumbled, "Hello, Jamie" and then followed her parents into the house. He had expected the cold reception—Michelle had chewed his ass out when he had not been home to greet her when she arrived in Hot Springs—hid a smile, walked into the kitchen, and opened the refrigerator.

"Mom, we're out of Cokes. Do you want me to go to the store and get some?"

"Good idea, Jamie. Your father is grilling hamburgers. We'll need some Cokes."

"Would you like to go, Michelle?"

"No. I'll stay here with Mom."

"Go with him, Michelle. You've been stuck with me all day."

Michelle threw Jamie an icy stare, followed him outside, scooted into his car, sat—emphatically close—to the passenger's door, and cuttingly said, "I really don't want to go anywhere with you."

"Then get out."

"That wouldn't please my mother."

"It wouldn't please me either."

Jamie started the Nova and drove down the lane.

"What will your girlfriend think?"

"I told her I was spending the day with you."

"Well, aren't you courteous?"

"I'm trying to be."

"Don't patronize me, Jamie. Let's endure the day and move on."

"You're too pretty to be acting like a horse's ass, Michelle."

"What?"

"You heard me. The big-bad-bitch routine doesn't work for you. You're not the type and you know it."

"Maybe I've changed."

"I don't think so."

Michelle was not a happy camper—any one-eyed, half blind fool could see that she was one pissed off girl—but Jamie thought Michelle's pissed off act was hilarious and wanted to laugh. Commonsense, however, told him laughing would only add wood to the fire, so he slammed on the brakes instead. Michelle, wide-eyed, grabbed the dashboard as the tires screamed in protest and the Nova came to a screeching halt.

"Are you crazy?"

"I've always been crazy, Michelle."

"Turn this stupid car around and take me home."

"To Louisiana?"

"No, you idiot. To your house."

"I will, if you'll look me in the eye and tell me you don't like me." Michelle stared stubbornly at the floorboard. Jamie put his hand under her chin, raised her head, and stared into her eyes. "Come on, Michelle, tell me you don't like me." She pursed her lips and said nothing. Jamie chuckled, shifted into first gear, pulled back on the highway, and confidently said, "Just as I thought. You still like me."

Michelle remained in the car—she *was* more than a little stubborn—when Jamie parked the Nova and walked into Ernie Dunlap's store. She shook her head when she saw him flirting with the cashier, an attractive woman in her thirties, noticed that when he spoke to the gas attendant, an older man who needed a shave, that the man guffawed and patted him on the back, and then rolled her eyes when Jamie raised his arms in triumph as a car passed by and honked its horn. Accepting the inevitable, Michelle dropped the silent treatment when Jamie scooted into the car and closed the door.

"Are you some kind of god around here?"

"Nope! Just a hero of mystical proportions."

Michelle giggled. She could not help it. Jamie always made her laugh, one of the many reasons she loved him. "Since it is rude to ignore a god, I suppose I have to talk to you."

"What do you want to talk about?"

"How about Vicki Helms?"

"What do you want to know?"

"Why you started dating her two weeks after you moved back to Hot Springs."

"I decided Ben Franklin was wrong."

"Okay, I'll bite. Ben Franklin was wrong about what?"

"That absence makes the heart grow fonder."

"Two stinking weeks, Jamie? Obviously, you weren't very fond of me."

"I was, and I am."

"But two weeks?"

"We were fourteen years old when we met, Michelle. We had one good year together. Hammond is a long way from Hot Springs, and I'm not good at playing the waiting-game."

"But I'm moving to Fayetteville."

"Which is two-hundred miles from Kirby. I'm done with promises, Michelle. It's a long way to Fayetteville. I can visit now and then, and that's all."

"Then what are we going to do?"

"Enjoy each other when we have the chance."

"Would it bother you if I started dating?"

"Eventually, it's going to happen. I'm surprised it hasn't already."

"But would it bother you?

"Sure."

"Good," she replied. "That makes me feel better."

"So, you feel good when I feel bad?"

"Yep."

"You're crazy, Michelle."

"You're the one who slammed on the brakes and nearly killed us."

• • •

It was obvious to Howard Martin and Calvin Williams that Jamie and Michelle had settled their differences when they stepped out of Jamie's Nova, ignored them, and walked across the yard laughing. Howard Martin smiled and shook his head. "All is right with the world, Cal. Jamie, as usual, has put a smile on Michelle's face."

"It's too bad that circumstances seem to work against them."

"When Jamie plays for the Razorbacks, they'll have their chance."

Enjoying the shade of a sprawling oak tree, Calvin Williams and Howard Martin stretched, leaned back in their lawn-chairs, and took in the sounds of rural Arkansas: cattle braying in the distance, crickets chirping in the underbrush, and the intermittent croak of a grumpy bullfrog complaining about the fickle warmth of Spring.

• • •

A damp but gentle south wind greeted Jamie and Michelle when they stepped out of the house and sat down in folding lawn chairs in the front yard. The moon was full and hidden at times by low-flying clouds. Jamie was tempted by Michelle's welcoming glances and a warm spring night to rekindle old fires…until she stopped talking about the move to Fayetteville and said, "Tell me about Marian."

"What do you want to know?"

"Anything. Just tell me about her."

"She's pretty." Jamie smiled smugly. "You know I have good tastes."

Michelle stared darts into his eyes. Jamie cleared his throat. "Sorry. You asked about Marian. She's pretty, she's smart, she's tall, she's nine months older than me, and she'll start college this fall."

"Really?"

"In August she'll leave for Texas Tech University."

"And that, of course, doesn't set well with you."

"It's the story of my life."

"Mine, too." Michelle glanced at the moon, then softly asked, "Do you think there's hope for us?"

"I don't know."

"That was a simple question, Jamie."

"I don't have a simple answer, Michelle."

"Just be honest with me."

"You want honesty? I'll give you honesty. If love is possible for a fourteen-year-old kid, I fell in love with you the first day you talked to me at Bogalusa Junior High School. But like I said before, absence doesn't make the heart grow fonder." Michelle leaned forward and listened intently. "You may find it hard to believe, especially after the way I treated you, but I don't like hurting people. It would be cruel to dump Marian just because you marched into my life for twenty-four hours, when it will probably be six months or a year before I see you again."

"So, you're telling me to forget you and find somebody else?"

"I'm not telling you a damned thing, Michelle."

Jamie shook the cobwebs from his head, walked to the driveway, and leaned against his Nova, knowing just as thunderstorms would erupt when the next cold front collided with the sultry, Spring air, that he was about to be up to his neck in alligators. The last thing he wanted was to get hung up on Michelle Martin again.

"You're not being honest with me, Jamie."

"I won't hurt Marian."

"I haven't asked you to."

"Then what do you want me to do?"

"I want you to kiss me."

Michelle wrapped her arms around Jamie's neck and pulled him close. Passion, long suppressed, overwhelmed them. Jamie finally broke the embrace, leaned against the Nova, and mumbled, "I hate what you do to me, Michelle."

"No, you don't. You want me just like I want you." Michelle pressed against Jamie, and then leaned back and stared into his eyes. "I love you, Jamie, I've always loved you. We're meant for one another, and someday we'll be together."

He turned his head from side to side, trying to relax the tension in his neck. "If we're meant for one another, why have there been so damned many bumps in the road?"

"I don't know, and I don't care, but we'll finish what we started in Bogalusa. Our time will come, Jamie."

He looked into Michelle's eyes, and, for a moment, he almost believed her.

CHAPTER 43

The summer of 1968 was a confusing time for Jamie. His feelings for Marian never wavered—he loved every minute he spent with her—but occasional letters from Michelle kept him off balance. Marian, however, unwittingly counterbalanced the confusion. When a letter from Michelle signed, "I love you," made Jamie wonder if *he* loved *her*, he would drive to Marian's house, she would take him to the barn, they would feed and water the horses, and within minutes he would forget about Michelle.

As July gave way to August, instead of obsessing about a pending goodbye, Jamie and Marian spent their days waterskiing on Lake Greeson behind David Thompson's boat. Always ready for a fast pull, Jamie adjusted his ski as David eased the throttle forward and tightened the rope. Jamie raised his hand, David pushed the throttle forward, and accelerated quickly. When he approached the middle of the lake, David turned sharply left. Jamie jumped the wake and nearly passed the boat.

"Aren't you going too fast?" Marian asked, trying to be heard over the wind and motor. David shook his head no and carefully guided the boat, watching for traffic and downed skiers.

Two minutes later, Jamie released the handle with his right hand and reached behind his back. He had recently learned to ski backward, but rarely made the transition, and usually lost his balance and fell hard—but harmlessly—on his back. On this attempt, however, something went wrong: his weight shifted oddly. The ski dipped beneath the water, Jamie flipped end-over-end for several yards, and then came to rest in one big splash.

David immediately turned the boat, circled Jamie, idled the engine, and dove into the water. Jamie was out cold, and a large purple knot had risen above his left eye. Momentarily panicked, Marian wanted to scream as David pulled Jamie toward the boat, but she forced herself to remain calm, knowing Jamie *and* David needed her help.

"Is he breathing?" she asked, trying to maintain her composure.

"I think so. Can you help me?"

"Yes."

They pulled Jamie into the boat. Marian placed his head in her lap and noticed the purple knot above his left eye. David pushed the throttle forward and raced back to Daisy State Park. Five minutes later, Jamie opened his eyes, realized he was in pain, and gritted his teeth. Marian pushed the hair out of his eyes and tried to reassure him.

David backed down the concrete loading ramp, pulled the boat out of the water, drove back up the ramp, stopped in the parking area, and ran back to the boat.

"Has he come to yet?"

"Yes."

David glanced at the knot on Jamie's forehead. "Can you walk to the truck?"

"No. My knee is killing me."

The knot had looked so ominous that David and Marian had not examined the rest of Jamie's body. They both were sickened when they saw his twisted and swollen left knee. David lowered his head and moaned, knowing what the injury meant: Jamie Williams, the most heralded Point Guard in Arkansas, would miss his final year of high school eligibility, and possibly, from the looks of his ugly knee, never play again.

•   •   •

"Mrs. Williams, will you accept a collect call from Marian Wood?"

"Yes, I will."

Fighting tears, Marian told Louise Williams that Jamie had taken a fall waterskiing, that his life was not in danger, that his knee looked bad, and that he was at the Ouachita Hospital in Hot Springs.

"Okay, Marian. Stay calm. We're leaving now."

Stunned, Louise Williams hung up the phone, then turned and faced her husband.

"What's wrong, Lou? You look like you've seen a ghost."

"Jamie hurt his knee. Marian says it looks bad. He's at the Ouachita Hospital in Hot Springs."

Calvin Williams closed his eyes, moaned, then reached for his wife's hand and led her outside to the Impala, feeling ominous. An injured knee was hard on any man, but for an athlete like Jamie, the ramifications were too great to fathom.

•   •   •

Howard Martin had just lowered his recliner when the telephone rang. He glanced at his watch. It was 9:30 PM. Pamela handed him the phone. "It's Calvin Williams. He sounds worried."

"Cal, is something wrong?"

"Jamie's had a skiing accident. He has a concussion, which he'll get over, but he also injured his left knee."

"How bad is it, Cal?"

"The X-rays show cartilage and ligament damage."

"What can I do to help?"

"I want to know what surgeon the university uses, Howard. Jamie is an athlete. I want to do everything I can to help him, and that includes choosing the right doctor. You know as well as I do if Jamie can't play basketball, it will devastate him."

"Hold on a minute."

Calvin Williams gritted his teeth, ignoring the pain in his tightly clenched jaws, until Coach Martin finally returned to the phone and said, "Cal, it's Doctor Franklin Clark in Little Rock. Where are you now?"

"The Ouachita Hospital in Hot Springs."

"I'll contact Doctor Clark. He'll call the hospital and have Jamie transferred to Little Rock. You take care of Jamie. I'll handle the details from here."

"Thank you, Howard. I thought you would know the right doctor for this sort of thing."

"It's the least I could do, Cal. I'll see you in a few hours."

"There's no need for you…"

"Don't even say it, Cal."

Coach Marin hung up the phone.

"What happened to Jamie?"

"A skiing accident. He injured his left knee. Cal wanted the name of a doctor, one who works with athletes. He wants to give Jamie his best shot at a full recovery."

Michelle walked into the den. "Jamie's been hurt?"

"He messed up a knee, honey. We'll be leaving for Little Rock in a few minutes."

•   •   •

The surgery waiting room in the Baptist Hospital was filled with people milling in and out, drinking coffee, anxiously awaiting news from their doctors. Calvin Williams had been in the place many times as a comforter and a source of strength to his parishioners. Today, however, was different: his youngest son was in surgery, having his knee repaired, giving him—hopefully—another opportunity to play the game he loved.

Calvin Williams was more than a little amazed by Jamie's popularity. Coach Martin, Coach Benson, and Coach Johnson were sitting together, looking glum. Graham Wallace, The Republic's sports editor, rather rumpled looking, was slouching in a chair next to the coaches. David Thompson, Bill Mitchell, Dalton Hilliard, and Terrance Brooks, obviously awed by Howard Martin, were sitting together supporting their fallen comrade. Louise Williams, Pamela Martin, Marian Wood, and Michelle Martin were also sitting together. Calvin Williams thought Marian looked uncomfortable, out of her element, and ready to bolt.

He sighed, leaned his head against the wall, and thought about the last substantive conversation he had had with Jamie when he broke the news that he was moving the family to Benton. He recalled pushing aside his plate, pouring a cup of coffee, and tentatively saying, "Son, Emmanuel Baptist Church in Benton has called me as pastor." Since that night, Jamie had been in a sullen mood and rarely talked to him.

"Is it time to pack my bags?" Jamie asked sarcastically.

"Possibly."

"You promised me I would graduate from Kirby High School."

"I know, Son, but Benton is closer to Mid-South Seminary, and I won't have to drive so far."

Feeling betrayed, biting words filled Jamie's mouth, and he could not hold them back. "The truth is, Dad, you're not *Brother*

Williams anymore. You're *Doctor* Williams now, a big wheel who thinks he's too high and mighty for common people."

"Jamie, don't talk to your father like that!"

"Let him finish, Lou."

"What can I say? I'm a seventeen-year-old kid living at the whim of his parents. I'll be glad when I graduate so I can live in one place without having to move every couple of years."

Calvin Williams had never seen Jamie so sullen and angry and was speechless when he stormed out of the house, started his car, and quickly drove away. He returned home late, went straight to bed, and had been cordially cold ever since.

Doctor Franklin Clark, wearing a green surgical cap, shirt, and pants, approached Calvin and Louise Williams, smiling broadly. "It went very well. I removed cartilage and repaired the ligament on the left side of Jamie's knee. His leg will be in a cast for at least three months. When the incision has healed, we'll begin therapy to strengthen his quadriceps, which should prevent damage to the joint."

"What about basketball?" Calvin Williams asked.

"That's out of the question. But with proper therapy, Jamie could play next year. We'll have to wait and see. Do you have questions?" Calvin and Louise Williams shook their heads no. "Okay. I'll see you this evening when I make rounds."

Calvin Williams hugged his wife and returned to his seat. "What do you think, Coach?"

"The doctor sounded favorable."

Twenty years of coaching told Howard Martin that the odds were against Jamie Williams. This, however, was not the time and place to express his opinion or to express his doubts. People, especially parents of injured athletes, need hope.

•   •   •

Marian tried to be positive when she stepped into Jamie's room, but seeing him, the invincible Jamie Williams, looking pale, weak, and vulnerable, broke her heart, and tears welled in her eyes. Jamie was too cocky to be lying flat on his back with a large white cast covering his leg. He had not, however, lost his sense of humor.

"You look worse than I do, Marian."

"Don't be a smartass, Jamie."

"You look like warmed over death."

"Thank you very much."

"Doctor Clark said that I may not play ball again."

"Doctor Clark is wrong. You're too cocky and determined not to make a comeback."

"You leave tomorrow, don't you?"

"Yes, Jamie, I do."

He took a deep breath. "I've got to tell you something, Marian."

"Okay."

"You can't tell a soul."

"I won't tell anyone, Jamie."

"When you come home from college, I won't be living in Kirby."

"Why?"

"Dad's been called to a church in Benton."

"That's going to hurt a lot of people."

"I know. But he has made up his mind. He'll tell the church on Sunday."

"I'm glad I'll be gone."

"Me, too."

"When are you getting out of the hospital?"

"Wednesday or Thursday. Friday at the latest." Jamie looked out the window and briefly watched the traffic move up and down West Twelfth Street. "I've been thinking, Marian.

When my knee heals up, I'm going to enroll at Texas Tech instead of the University of Arkansas."

"You can't do that, Jamie. You've always wanted to play for the Razorbacks. It wouldn't be fair for me to steal your dream. The only reason I'm going to Texas Tech is because of the scholarship. You'll receive the same thing at the University of Arkansas."

Marian gazed out the window, then slowly, almost regretfully, said, "Jamie, that man, Coach Martin, has been here since the day you hurt your knee. He loves you. It wouldn't be right for you to go anywhere but the University of Arkansas."

"But I want to be with you."

Marian sighed softly. "There's something I have to say."

"I'm not sure I want to hear it."

"There's a girl in the waiting room who has diplomatically taken a back seat to me during this entire ordeal. She clings to every word Doctor Clark says about your condition."

"Michelle?"

"Yes. And I know you have feelings for her."

"But I want you, Marian."

"Wanting me and loving me are two different things, Jamie."

From the beginning, Jamie and Marian's relationship had been physical. He had, in fact, told her many times that he loved her, but what she had said about wanting her and loving her forced him to consider a new and disturbing question: Had he told her he loved her simply because he wanted her? Suddenly, love wasn't a trite little word.

"Do you think it's possible to be in love with two girls at the same time?"

"No, Jamie, I don't. But since you'll miss a year of basketball, you'll have plenty of time to think about it. Take that time, consider the question, and decide what you're going to do."

"Are we breaking up?"

"No! I'm yours until you tell me you don't love me and that you don't want me anymore. But you can take it to the bank, Jamie. Michelle is standing in the shadows. She's confident her time will come, and when it does, she intends to take what she considers her rightful place."

"You're that sure, huh?"

"It's written in stone, Jamie. Eventually, you'll have to deal with it."

Marian reached for her purse and glanced toward the door.

"Do you have to leave now?"

"It's late, and I still have packing to do."

She leaned over Jamie's bed, kissed him softly, lingered, and then walked toward the door.

"Marian!"

She turned back and faced him.

"I love you."

"I know you do, Jamie, and I love you, too. Don't forget to write."

"I won't."

"Think about what I told you."

"I will, Marian."

CHAPTER 44

A REFLECTION

Graham Wallace
Republic Sports Editor

With the United States fighting an unpopular war in Vietnam, and with students protesting the war on college campuses throughout the country, and with racial tranquility at risk because of the assassination of Doctor Martin Luther King, an athletic injury is not newsworthy or traumatic enough to be *the* news story of 1968. However, the effects of Jamie Williams' torn ligaments will change the shape of high school basketball during 1968-69 season.

In March, Jamie led the Kirby Trojans to a State Championship. He was, in fact, named the Tournament's Most Valuable Player. But Jamie had an accident while waterskiing on Lake Greeson and cannot play his final year of high school basketball.

I have had the privilege of watching Jamie play since he began his prep career at Central

Junior High School in Hot Springs. In 1965, Jamie and Terrance Brooks led the Spartans to an undefeated championship season. In 1966, Jamie was named the Most Valuable Player on the Junior High level in Louisiana. In 1967, Jamie, Terrance Brooks, and Dalton Hilliard led the Hot Springs Trojans to an undefeated season and a state championship. And this year (1968) Jamie led Kirby High School to an undefeated season, and the Trojans became the first Class B school to accomplish that feat. When you consider the fact that Jamie Williams has never lost a basketball game, it should be obvious that his absence will change the face of high school basketball in Arkansas.

Sadly, fate chose a fine young man to pick on. Jamie maintains a 3.95 GPA, he has an outgoing personality, and he is popular statewide. This writer, a host of friends, including Howard Martin, the head basketball coach at the University of Arkansas, waited for Doctor Franklin Clark and news concerning Jamie at the Baptist Hospital in Little Rock. Jamie's torn ligaments have been repaired. Time and therapy, however, will determine if Jamie plays basketball again.

Coaches nationwide have shown a great deal of interest in Jamie. The question is, will they recruit him after he misses his final year of high school eligibility because of an untimely accident? Jamie has expressed his desire to play for the Razorbacks many times, but it does not seem fair—at least to this writer—for Jamie to miss the fanfare of recruitment because, like Terrance

Brooks this year, he would have been one of the most sought-after athletes in the country.

Finally, coaches should not consider Jamie damaged goods and write him off, thinking he cannot compete at the college level. That would be a mistake because Jamie Williams is a winner, and despite the odds, winners fight back and never give up.

Jamie, the State of Arkansas is pulling for you, and we look forward to seeing you in red, leading the Razorbacks to a national championship, because that is what you do, win championships. Get well soon, young man. Our thoughts and prayers are with you.

CHAPTER 45

"Jamie! Get up! We have a busy day ahead of us."

Louise Williams had a pleasing voice, except of a morning, when it was, Jamie thought, shrill and irritating, especially when he was in a foul mood, and he had been in a foul mood for two weeks. Angry at the world, he slipped on a pair of jeans cut to accommodate his cast, stumbled into the kitchen, and almost gagged when he smelled bacon and eggs cooking on the range. Jamie liked bacon and eggs, but since he had had surgery, nothing tasted the same, and the smell turned his stomach.

"Where's Dad?"

"He went to Glenwood to meet the movers. He should be back any minute."

"This isn't like most moves, is it?"

"No, Jamie, it isn't. Emmanuel Baptist Church is different."

"How?"

"They consider it an honor to have called a distinguished pastor like your father."

"That's great for Dad, but as for me, I don't give a shit."

"I've had enough of your foul mouth, young man." Louise Williams stared darts into Jamie's eyes, hesitated, and then said, "If you'll lose your sorry attitude, you may like Benton."

"Don't hold your breath, Mom. I'll go to Benton High School, graduate in nine months, and then I'll get the hell of Dodge. I'm not getting close to anyone."

Louise Williams slid eggs and bacon onto Jamie's plate and irritably said, "You've made that statement before. I didn't believe it then, and I don't believe it now."

Jamie ate the gooey mess and did not say another word until he heard a truck backing up to the front porch. He pointed his thumb—arrogantly, his mother thought—toward the living room. "It sounds like the distinguished pastor and his peasants have arrived."

Thirty seconds later, Calvin Williams walked into the kitchen and noticed that his wife was glaring at Jamie. He did not ask questions because he knew the answers.

"How are you feeling, son?"

"I'm fine," Jamie replied coldly.

•   •   •

Jamie grabbed his crutches, eased off the front porch, and stared at the vacant house. A southwest breeze rustled the oak trees, black Angus cattle bellowed at a nearby pond, and a tractor hummed in the distance as a neighbor bailed hay for the winter.

"Do you think it will be this peaceful in Benton?"

"No, son," Calvin Williams replied, "but I think, in time, you'll like our new home."

Jamie said, "Yeah, right," and then scooted into the Impala next to his mother. There was no way in hell he would ride in the Nova with his father. Calvin Williams had taught him all his life that a man is bound by his word, but *he* had not kept *his* word; therefore, *his* word, in Jamie's opinion, was nothing but a fart in the wind.

•   •   •

Louise Williams took the first Benton exit, crossed Interstate 30, and entered the Brownwood Subdivision. She was excited. For the first time in twenty-five years of marriage, she would not be living in a parsonage. Emmanuel Baptist Church provided a housing allowance and she and Calvin had purchased a new brown-brick home with a freshly sodded lawn. When she pulled into the driveway, she pushed a button on a rectangular gadget attached to the sun visor, smiled proudly when the garage door went up, and said, "Home sweet home, Jamie."

•   •   •

Benton High School, a sprawling campus, was larger than Kirby's elementary, junior high and high schools combined. Jamie had attended larger schools most of his life, but after a year at Kirby High School, the change was more than a little overwhelming *and* depressing.

The only familiar faces were some kids he had met at church and his brother-in-law Phil Westerman, who coached basketball and taught American History. Phil felt sorry for Jamie when he moved to Benton and intended to place him on the Panther basketball team as an inactive player, but his brother-in-law's sullen attitude and smart mouth had pissed him off, and he changed his mind. In Phil's opinion, Jamie was a sulking prima donna who needed his ass kicked. In Jamie's opinion, Phil was nothing more than a vaguely familiar face in a static crowd.

For the first time in three years, Jamie had nothing to help him open doors and tear down walls. At Bogalusa Junior High School, he had had basketball and Michelle. At Hot Springs High School, he had had basketball and lifelong friends. At Kirby High School, he had had basketball and Marian. But at Benton High School, he had nothing to fall back on and nothing to look forward to; he was stuck in a vacuum, a black-hole, an empty nothingness. Angry at the world, he opened a spiral-notebook and wrote:

I am miserable,
Not happy with the world.
How will I survive?
For the world is dark,
And I am not part of it.

Assuming he had found a klutzy bookworm to harass, Robin Jones leaned over Jamie's shoulder and tried to read what he had written. Bookworms were fair-game, and humiliating them, especially *new* bookworms, made a boring day more interesting.

"What are you writing, NUG?"

Jamie closed his notebook, looked up, and stared into Robin's eyes. "It's none of your damned business."

The brusque reply was not what Robin had expected. New students usually shivered like whipped puppies until the chosen figured out where to rank them in their time-honored caste system. Bookworms usually ranked at or near the bottom.

"You know what a NUG is, don't you?"

Jamie knew the harassment would come. He was surprised that it had not started already. Things had gone too well for too long, and it was a bitter pill to swallow.

"A NUG is a New-Unimportant-Guy," Robin continued smugly.

Jamie crossed his arms and coldly replied, "I don't care what a NUG is or isn't, so sit down and shut up. I'm not in the mood for your new guy bullshit."

Robin reached for Jamie's arm and was shocked when the crabby NUG slapped his hand away and snarled, "Touch me again and you'll pick your ass up off the floor."

NUGS were supposed to be passive and easily intimidated. *This* NUG, however, had mean eyes, and Robin knew if he did not back off, *this* NUG would whip his ass, or at least give it a valiant effort.

"If you weren't a cripple, I'd knock your teeth down your throat."

Jamie struggled to his feet. "Don't worry about the cast, asshole." The NUG, Robin noticed, was much bigger standing than sitting. "My hands and arms work just fine."

Jamie stared darts into Robin's eyes.

"You're not worth the trouble, Crip. When your wheels are fixed, I'll break your other leg."

"You're scaring the shit out of me," Jamie replied, his voice dripping with sarcasm.

Robin shook his head and walked back to his desk. Jamie sat down seething, knowing his nine months at Benton High School would be a living hell.

•　　•　　•

For years, Jamie's autumns had been filled with screaming coaches, squeaking tennis shoes, and basketballs. Now all he had to do was study, listen, and watch. Studying was not a problem—he had always been a good student—but what he heard and saw at Benton High School reminded him of Bogalusa Junior High School.

Although Benton High School was integrated, black students were nonentities, persons to look through and ignore.

They had, however, united in a cause: banning the playing of *Dixie* at pep rallies and athletic events. The song, they believed, condoned white-Arkansas' support of slavery, and they had resolved to walk out of Panther Field House when the band played *Dixie* at the next pep rally.

White students, of course, thought there was nothing wrong with playing *Dixie*. Jamie, however, knew better. He had attended the first pep rally and watched each class—sophomores, juniors, and seniors—cheer for the Panther football team. Then the drums rolled, the student body rose to its feet, clapping and stomping, and *Dixie* echoed throughout the arena. An electric atmosphere overwhelmed what had been a docile crowd. Jamie had experienced the electricity before. It was bigotry, and it was real.

•　　•　　•

The second pep rally seemed spirited and friendly, potential problems forgotten, as the student body cheered for the Panthers. Sleeping dogs, however, never rest for long. The drums rolled, and *Dixie* echoed throughout the arena. With their heads held high and their backs straight, Benton High School's black students stood, left their seats, and walked out of Panther Field House.

Determined to make a statement of their own, white students stomped harder and sang louder. Tired of the show, Jamie headed for the doors. The students who noticed thought he was probably going to the restroom. A southern white boy raised on fried chicken, pinto beans, and fried taters would never walk out on *Dixie*.

CHAPTER 46

The Saline County School Board met and banned the playing of *Dixie* at pep rallies and athletic events. Students, of course, discussed the directive in and out of class. But the discussions—some heated—were pointless because the musical relic with its chords of grace or disgrace, depending on one's point-of-view, had been shelved and would never again stir hearts and minds at Benton High School.

Hating the idea of giving up a sacred tradition, Robin Jones slapped his desk and bellowed, "If we don't stand up for what *we* believe, it won't be long until *they're* running everything."

Jamie laughed, loudly, belligerently.

The room fell silent.

"What the hell are you laughing at, Crip?"

"You."

"Why me?"

"Because you're showing your ass, as usual."

Robin leaned back, crossed his arms, and narrowed his eyes.

"When I enrolled in this school, the guidance counselor told me that Benton High School prides itself on academics. You're a senior, Robin, which means you've taken American History. Don't sit there and tell me you don't know what *Dixie* represents."

"Where were you born, Williams? Connecticut?"

"No, I was born in Arkansas, but if I had lived during the Civil War, there's no way in hell I would have fought for the Confederacy. Rich white men raised armies from people they called poor, white trash. The sad thing is, poor white trash died by the thousands so that rich white men, who didn't give a shit about them, could own slaves and hold on to their idea of a southern nobility."

Robin stood and walked stiffly across the room. Jamie did not care. If Robin wanted to fight, he would fight him. He had kept his mouth shut and had looked the other way for years. Damned if he would keep his mouth shut and look the other way now.

Red-faced and scowling, Robin leaned over Jamie's desk. Before he could yank him to his feet, however, Jamie tapped the shoulder of a black student he had met during the walkout.

"Charles, do you want to run Robin's life?"

"No. I just don't like the song. It's degrading."

Jamie looked Robin in the eyes and smiled drolly.

"Charles says say he doesn't want to run your life, Robin. He just doesn't like the song, thinks it's degrading. So, shut up, sit down, and stop making an ass of yourself."

"Who in the *hell* do you think you are, Williams?"

Jamie struggled to his feet, fists doubled, ready to parry Robin's first punch. Mr. Newcomb, the teacher supervising study hall, stepped between the red-faced boys and stopped the altercation before it amped out of control. "What you're going to do, Robin," he said, "is sit down and keep your mouth shut until the bell rings."

In a sterile classroom setting, Mr. Newcomb would have given Jamie a "B" for his simplistic assessment of southern polity in the mid-nineteenth century. But this was not a sterile setting, and although Jamie Williams was obviously a bright, young man, *he* had incited Robin Jones, *he* was the guilty party, and *he* was the one who needed to be punished.

Mr. Newcomb returned to his desk, wrote a brief note, motioned Jamie to the front of the room, handed him the note, and gruffly said, "Take this to the principal's office. Hopefully, spending the rest of the week in Detention Hall will teach you to keep your mouth shut."

Jamie took the note, smiled facetiously, and replied, "Thank you *very* much." Mr. Newcomb's eyes narrowed, and his face flushed red. Jamie grabbed his crutches and limped out of the room quickly. His sugary sarcasm had not sat well with Mr. Newcomb.

Callie Thomas had known and liked Robin Jones for years. He was a football player, hot-tempered, and she knew that when someone crossed him, he took immediate action, especially with new students who talked back and did not accept their subservient place in the pecking order. Eventually, Jamie Williams would pay for his unsolicited remarks. Callie did, however, think it was cool when Jamie Williams bristled and gave whoever invaded his personal space a go-to-hell look that said, "Mess with me and you'll pick your ass up off the floor."

Callie, of course, was a part of the ruling-clique and took part in all the in-crowd frivolities — that would never change — but a smart-mouthed nonconformist was something new and different. Jamie Williams, whoever he was, and wherever he came from, was tall, handsome, and fearless — he had bucked Robin Jones twice — and that, Callie thought, was more than a little intriguing. In fact, Callie thought in time Jamie Williams might be someone worth knowing.

CHAPTER 47

An unusually chilly northwest wind chilled Jamie as he stood outside Panther Field House. His patience was running on empty. Although he felt better and had an appointment after school to have his cast removed, he knew the road to recovery would be long, hard, and bumpy. Physical therapy would ease the stiffness in his leg and enable him to walk without crutches, but that, Jamie knew, would not be enough. He needed someone—a trainer—to help him get back on a basketball court.

He needed Phil Westerman.

Phil, however, was going to be a problem. All he had done was tell his father—sarcastically, Jamie admitted—that he hated Benton and that he would just be marking time until he graduated from high school. Phil did not like that—Jamie had noticed his icy stare—and his hard-ass brother-in-law had been cordially cold ever since.

Jamie took a deep breath and stepped into Panther Field House. Phil glanced toward the door and mumbled, "Shit." The last thing he wanted was to deal with his smart-mouthed brother-in-law.

Jamie knocked on Phil's door and stepped into his office. Irritated by the interruption, Phil leaned back in his chair, crossed his arms, and asked, "What do you want, Jamie?"

"I want to play ball."

"That's impossible and you know it."

"You don't understand. I'm not talking about this year."

Phil leaned forward. "Again, what do you want, Jamie?"

"Dad thinks all I need is physical therapy, but you know, and I know, to play ball again, I'll need a trainer. You're a certified trainer, Phil, and I need your help."

Phil had coached Jamie at Bogalusa Junior High School— even then he had been a smartass—but he had not disrespected anyone the way he had disrespected Calvin Williams at the Labor Day cookout in the Williams' backyard. To Phil, a son, even the illustrious Jamie Williams, treated his father with dignity and respect.

"I don't think you have the guts to make a comeback."

Jamie's face paled.

"Why?"

"Because you're a titty-baby and you'll have to work you ass off."

"That's not fair, Phil."

"If you haven't figured it out by now, Jamie, life isn't fair."

"Then you won't help me?"

"I said that I don't think you have the guts."

"And that means?"

"Rehab is a long process."

"How long?"

"Nine months, if you're lucky. Probably a year, maybe more."

"Well, there goes my scholarship."

Phil leaned back in his chair, took a deep breath, and exhaled loudly. "If you'll keep your smart mouth shut, I'll work with you, but I won't put up with your bullshit, Jamie, not for one second."

"I'll be a good boy, Phil."

"Lose the sarcasm, Jamie."

. . .

Jamie was shocked.

What had been a muscular and well-toned leg was now a scarred and shriveled mess. Doctor Clark, however, seemed pleased as he gently rotated Jamie's knee up and down.

"I think you're on the mend, young man."

"When will I be able to walk without crutches?"

"Not long. Why?"

"I've asked my brother-in-law—he's a certified trainer—to work with me." Jamie handed Doctor Clark a copy of Phil's certification. He read the document carefully and then dropped it on the counter next to the examining table.

"I'll let Coach Westerman work with you, but you'll still have to take physical therapy at Saline Memorial Hospital, and, of course, I'll want a weekly report on your progress."

"Thank you, Doctor Clark."

"With that settled, let's see about teaching you to walk again."

. . .

Jamie had expected his knee to be stiff and sore but being immobile frightened and depressed him. The white knee brace he had bought at the Smith-Caldwell Drug Store covered the scar adequately, but his left leg looked shriveled and mutated. Reality hit him squarely in the face as he limped around Panther Field House. He could not do it; he was through; and he would never play basketball again.

Facing the truth and accepting it, Jamie limped off the court, sat in the bleachers, and stretched his aching leg. Thirty seconds later, Phil Westerman—hands on hips—stood in front of Jamie like a pissed off drill sergeant. "No one walks off my court without asking permission. Who in the hell do you think you are, Jamie?"

"It's no use, Phil."

"What do you mean?"

"I can't do this."

"You're right...if you sit on your pampered ass and feel sorry for yourself." Jamie's eyes widened; coaches never talked to him like this. "If you want to play ball again, stop acting like a pouting prima donna and walk around the court like I told you to do."

Stiff as a board, Phil whirled, walked away, and took his usual place at mid-court. Jamie forced himself to stand, winced, and began walking around the court one painful step at a time.

•   •   •

An hour later, Jamie scooted beneath the steering-wheel of his father's Impala—he still could not clutch the standard transmission in his Nova—and inserted the key into the ignition. The engine sputtered and came to life. He pulled off the Benton High School campus cautiously—the principal was obsessed with students driving safely—and drove to Saline Memorial Hospital, where Doctor Clark had placed orders for his therapy.

He checked in with the receptionist, saw the waiting room was empty, took a seat, then leaned his head against the wall and closed his eyes. Five minutes later, a sarcastic feminine voice said, "This is a dumb place to take a nap."

Jamie opened his eyes.

Callie Thomas was standing in the doorway, smiling.

"It beats the hell out of sleeping on the street."

Callie laughed and sat down. "What are you doing here?"

"Therapy. You?"

"I volunteer three days a week after school."

"Well, aren't you sweet?"

"I'm trying to be."

Like most of his classmates, Callie treated Jamie as a non-person at school. That she would talk to him in an empty waiting room with no one around pierced a nerve. He leaned his head against the wall, closed his eyes, and ignored her.

"You don't have a lot to say, do you?"

"You haven't given me a chance."

"What do you mean?"

Jamie sat up quickly, startling Callie. There was, she noticed, fire in his eyes. "I mean, Little Miss Popularity doesn't want to be seen talking to a NUG."

"That's not fair."

"But it's the truth. And your whole damned school is just like you, nasty-nice. You know? You fake a smile, say hello, then join your little group, laugh, joke, and ignore the new guy, who sits around waiting for someone to talk to, and it never happens."

Callie bolted for the door.

"You don't want to talk anymore, Nurse-Good-Body?"

Callie turned back and faced him, her face as red as her hair.

"No, thank you. I've had enough conversation for today."

Jamie chuckled when Callie scurried through the door. If she was too good to talk to him at school, there was no way in hell he would let her talk to him in an empty waiting room with no one around. As far as he was concerned, if Little Miss Popularity did not like them apples, she could cram them up her pretty little ass.

CHAPTER 48

Jamie read Marian's letter, put it down, and thought about their last conversation. She was right. Michelle was in the back of his mind. But what difference did that make? Even if he and Michelle got back together, he would never give up Marian.

"Another letter from Marian?" Calvin Williams asked as he stepped into Jamie's room.

"Yes, sir."

"How is she?"

"Fine."

"Are things better at school?"

"No, Dad, they're not. I hate the place."

"Maybe you're not giving Benton High School a chance?"

"I told you when we moved here that I'd only be marking time until I gradate." Jamie stared into his father's eyes. "I'm not in the mood for a pep-talk, Dad."

Calvin Williams had grown tired of walking on eggshells. Jamie had been irritable and smart-mouthed for three months and encouragement had not tempered his bitterness.

"Do you want to know what your problem is?"

"You're the man with all the answers, *Doctor* Williams," Jamie replied sarcastically.

"You're wallowing in self-pity and loving every minute of it."

"How would you feel if you lived in a place you didn't like and couldn't preach or teach?"

"There's a vast difference between ministry and basketball, Jamie."

"Not really. Ministry is your life. Basketball is mine."

"If that's true, and I don't think it is, God may be teaching you a lesson."

"What can I learn from this?" Jamie asked, pointing at his knee.

"That you're human. For years, you've been like a Greek god with an incredible ability to do things other people couldn't. Now, for the first time in your life, your wings have been clipped, and you're stuck on earth with the rest of us mortals."

"That's not fair, Dad. I've never flaunted my talent."

"I'm not saying you have."

"Then what's your point?"

"That you've become one-dimensional. Think about it, Jamie! Basketball has been everything to you. Now, for a few months, you'll have to function like an earthbound mortal." Calvin Williams paused, gave Jamie time to consider his point, and then continued: "You'll make a comeback, Son, and you'll be as good as ever, but use the downtime to branch out and prove you're gifted at something besides basketball."

"That's reassuring."

"If you don't get your thinking straight, Jamie, you'll never play basketball again. Solomon, a wise man, wrote, 'As a man thinks in his heart, so is he.' You are what you think, Jamie, which means if you stay positive, eventually positive things will happen."

"That sounds too easy."

"Life doesn't have to be complicated, son."

Calvin Williams stepped into the hall, hesitated, then turned back and said, "Even if I have moved you to a town you don't like, Jamie, I still love you. Don't shut me out. Okay?"

Jamie stared at the floor, then at his father. "I won't shut you out, Dad."

CHAPTER 49

Jamie did not recognize the new, metallic-green Ford Fairlane parked behind his father's Impala. Phil had worked with him longer than usual and he was running late. Since it was the Christmas season, he decided his parents were probably entertaining church members; they usually held an open house about this time every year.

He entered the house through the garage and was surprised when he saw Horace, Nelda, and Marian Wood sitting at the kitchen table. Marian's smile lit up the room and Jamie's heart skipped a beat. "Well," she said, "look who's walking."

"And he doesn't even limp."

"I have to admit you look a lot better than you did in August."

Jamie pulled out a chair, sat next to Marian, and was not surprised when she pressed her knee against his leg. Their relationship had always been physical, and he could not wait to get her alone.

•   •   •

Jamie scooted out of his car, walked to the takeout window, and ordered two Cokes. He did not see anyone he knew and would not have spoken even if he had. Two minutes later, he handed Marian a Coke and slid beneath the steering-wheel.

"The Minute Man is a busy place," Marian observed.

"A lot different from Doc's, huh?"

"You can say that again. Why don't you like living in Benton?"

"Dad says I have a bad attitude. I hardly know anyone at school."

"I find that strange."

"Why?"

"You're so outgoing. You know? People are drawn to you."

"Not in Benton."

"It's their loss."

"The only reason you say that is because…"

"I love you." Jamie sipped his Coke and smiled. "Have you thought about our conversation in August?"

"Yes."

"And?"

"You have nothing to worry about with Michelle."

"Why?"

"I never see her."

"That really wasn't my question."

"You're asking if I've made a decision?"

"The way you sound, I don't think I want to know."

"When you smiled at me, I saw…"

"Adoration, Jamie. I adore you."

"When you smiled at me, I knew I could never give you up. Not now, not ever."

Marian laid her head against the seat, sniffled, and wiped away tears.

"You're not crying, are you?"

"Tears of joy, Jamie, and relief."

He started the Nova and shifted the transmission into reverse.

"Where are we going?"

"It's time to continue our unique relationship."

Marian reached into her purse and handed Jamie a small cellophane package. He chuckled and said, "Damn, using that will be like taking a shower in a raincoat."

"Not for me," she replied huskily.

CHAPTER 50

For three months, Phil Westerman worked to resurrect Jamie from the athletic dead. Sleeping late on Saturday morning—Jamie's norm—had been replaced by quick cups of coffee, short jogs through the neighborhood, stretching, and lifting weights. A stern taskmaster, Phil never complimented Jamie—compliments, Jamie thought, were beyond Phil—but he was feeling better, and he knew his hard-ass brother-in-law's gut-wrenching regimen was accomplishing its goal: his strength and mobility were returning.

There was, however, an unexpected bump in the road: Callie Thomas. At school, she remained distant, but three afternoons a week—during physical therapy at Saline Memorial Hospital—she was outgoing, likable, even caring. Once, when the therapist stretched Jamie's knee farther than he had expected, he groaned and winced. Callie instinctively grabbed his hand. Her eyes widened when she felt a surge of electricity pass between them and quickly released his hand.

In early February, jogging with Phil, Jamie saw Callie picking up the morning newspaper in her front yard. He did not know that she lived in his neighborhood because their conversations at Saline Memorial Hospital usually ended with an argument. Callie glanced toward the joggers, saw Jamie, smiled, and waved. Jamie waved back and decided to add more running to his regimen, but in the afternoon, and alone.

Two days later, he approached Callie's house and saw her sitting on the front porch, thumbing through a magazine. Wearing a sleeveless, sweat-soaked T-shirt and gray running shorts—the weather was unusually warm—Jamie jogged across the yard, stepped up on the porch, and flopped down in a green, metal chair.

"Don't you believe in taking a shower before you visit someone?"

"I wanted you to smell a real man."

"You're disgusting, but at least you're feeling better."

"Yep. I finish therapy next week."

"So, we won't be having our afternoon visits?"

"That's right. Won't you be glad?"

"Oh, I don't know. You're rude and obnoxious, but you make my day interesting three afternoons a week."

"I'd rather make your nights interesting."

"That will never happen."

"Why?"

"Because you're mean."

"Mean, or honest?"

"Maybe a little of both. But it doesn't matter. I'm dating someone."

"Yeah. Edwin Winfield, a skinny little jerk who can't walk and chew gum at the same time."

"You don't even know him."

"Anyone who walks around with his pants unzipped half the day can't be the brightest lightbulb in the chandelier. Commonsense says, 'Zip your pants after you take a leak.'"

Callie tried not to smile.

"Edwin's a nice guy…and he drives a Camaro."

"I bet he kisses like a mule."

"What does *that* mean?"

"Mules are sterile, Callie, so there's not a lot for them to get excited about. Edwin, and I think you already know this, will never paw the ground and chase you like a stud running after a mare in heat. A mule just doesn't have it in him."

"Does that mean what I think it means?"

"Probably."

"I don't like being compared to a mare in heat."

"All I'm saying is, when you kiss me, you won't be satisfied with a Camaro."

"Sorry. I think I'll pass."

"Well, it's your mistake, Miss Thomas."

Jamie stood and walked toward the steps.

"What's your hurry?"

"Since I don't take rejection well, I'm going home, taking a shower, and heading for Hot Springs. Who knows? I might get lucky and find a girl who likes to fool around."

Jamie stepped off the porch and jogged toward the street. Callie impulsively followed him. "If you'll give me a ride home, I'll run with you to your house."

"I really don't think my car is good enough for you."

"I try to be nice, and what do you do? Make a smartass remark."

"I'm *so* sorry."

For three months, Callie had thought about Jamie Williams. He made her laugh — and she liked that — but he was also a smart-mouthed jerk. When she grabbed his hand, the smile on his face told her he was not surprised that she had followed him. Knowing she was about to jump in over her head, Callie threw caution to the wind because there was something about Jamie Williams that she liked.

•   •   •

"I like your shoes."

Callie spent a great deal of time cleaning up after she invited Jamie to play records and listen to the stereo. She showered, slipped on a bra, stepped into a pair of white bikini panties, and wondered, as she put on her makeup and stared at herself in the mirror, if she really was a mare in heat who wanted Jamie Williams to be her stud — dangerous thoughts.

She slipped on a short beige skirt and a black pullover sweater, stood in front of the mirror, and wondered if she looked as sexy as she felt. When she opened the front door, however, and led Jamie into the den, he did not mention her clothes or her makeup. Of all things, he noticed her shoes, which surprised and pleased her. Hiding a smile, she placed the Beatle's *Abbey Road* album on the turntable.

"Thank you. You smell better, by the way."

Jamie chuckled. "You look so damned good I should have rented a tuxedo."

"You're not the tuxedo type."

"What type am I, Miss Thomas?"

"You want the truth?"

"Sure."

"You're overconfident, foulmouthed, and arrogant."

Jamie laughed.

"What's so funny?"

"Your description."

"Why?"

"The last thing I expected was for someone to think I'm confident."

"That surprises me. You come across as someone who has it all together."

"What gives you that idea?"

"The way you handle people. You know? When someone harasses you at school, you cross your arms and give them a go-to-hell look that says, 'Back off, asshole!'"

"I didn't know you paid that much attention to me."

"Don't let it go to your head. I'm still not sure I like you."

"So, you agree with me? Benton High School is full of assholes?"

"We're not assholes, Jamie. If you'd try a little harder, you'd see that."

"No one gives me a chance. You talk to me when we're by ourselves, but does little Miss I'm-Afraid-Of-What-Everyone-Will-Think talk to me at school? Hell, no! She plays the game and ignores Mr. New-And-Unimportant like the rest of her blueblood friends."

"You're mean, Jamie."

"How about honest?"

"How about judgmental, rude, obnoxious *and* mean?"

"Do you want me to leave?"

"Yes. Inviting you here was a dumb idea."

The phone rang.

Callie crossed the room, picked up the receiver, and turned her back to Jamie. He knew the impromptu date had come to a screeching halt when she said, "Edwin! What am I doing? Nothing really. Just listening to the stereo."

Jamie really did not want to leave. If he had kept his mouth shut, he probably would have already been kissing Callie by now. She had looked at him all afternoon with glistening eyes. Instead of leaving, he slipped across the room, wrapped his arms around Callie's waist, and kissed her neck. She giggled, said, "Oh, it's nothing, Edwin," then turned and faced him, protecting herself from further attacks. "Can I call you back later? Mom wants me to clean up the kitchen. Thanks, Edwin."

"Your parents aren't home, Miss Thomas."

"Edwin doesn't know that. I hope he didn't hear you."

"I hope he did. You deserve better."

"And you think you're the one?"

"Yes, I do."

"I don't."

"Fine. If you'd rather date a Camaro, go for it."

"What makes you think it's the car I like?"

"Girls in Benton go out with guys who drive new cars. Edwin has a new car, so you date him. It couldn't be his good looks, or his intelligence. Edwin is a goofball."

Callie touched Jamie's chest, looked into his eyes, then reached for his hands and led him to the sofa. He pulled her close and kissed her deeply. Jamie, Callie noticed, was not shy or inexperienced. Within minutes, her bra was loose, and his hand was beneath her panties.

Callie had been dating for two years, had kept her legs tightly clenched, and had never considered coloring outside the lines, but with Jamie's hand working beneath her panties, she was torn between brazen desire and her mother's pointed lectures about dating and sex.

Was Jamie right? Was she a mare in heat? Did she want him to be her stud? Yes! She kissed him wildly. No one had ever made her feel this way, and the intense longing surprised her. If they were parked down a secluded road, she would let him do anything he wanted, but they were not parked down a secluded road, they were on a sofa in her parents' den, and she reluctantly pushed him away.

"Who do you think you are?" she asked, trying to sound offended.

"I'm the guy your momma warned you about."

Callie had stumbled on new ground and was not sure what to say. She had never let a boy push down her panties and turn her into a moisture laden sponge. The right thing to do was send him home, but she knew it was too late for that.

"Do you want me to leave?"

"Yes, but I'm going with you."

"Where are we going?"

"I don't care. Just not here. Okay?"

She reached for his hand and led him toward the door. Why not? Her stud had pawed the ground, she wanted him, and there was no reason to make him chase her across the pasture.

CHAPTER 51

On national signing day, Coach Martin knew Jamie had been rehabbing his knee for five months and that he was running and working out every day. He also knew that Jamie's knee had not been tested in the start and stop arena of competitive basketball. According to Doctor Clark, Jamie had made remarkable progress, but he did not say when, or if, he could play basketball again.

Coach Martin did, however, think it was odd that most of the athletes he had recruited usually mentioned Jamie. In fact, Terrance Brooks had said, "When Jamie gets here, we'll have a Guard who can shoot the lights out of the gym and get me the ball." Even Graham Wallace, the de facto voice of Arkansas athletics, had mentioned Jamie. Wallace had proved himself an ally, complimentary in his articles, but Coach Martin had detected great disappointment in Wallace's eyes when he mentioned he had reservations, deep reservations, about offering Jamie a scholarship.

Graham Wallace, Coach Martin believed, wanted the Razorback basketball program to succeed. He also knew the man was opinionated, that he told it like it was, and that criticism would come if he did not produce, in time, a winning team. Coach Martin also realized that Graham Wallace had taken a personal interest in Jamie Williams.

Doesn't he realize there is no "I" in team and that one player doesn't make a team great? But just as the sun rises in the east and sets in the west, Graham Wallace thinks Jamie Williams will be the savior of Razorback basketball.

Howard Martin was willing to admit that Terrance Brooks was right. The Razorbacks were lacking—sadly lacking—at the Guard position—every position really—and his team, to put it bluntly, did not have the athletes to win consistently. Terrance Brooks had been a positive force as a sophomore, and that, Coach Martin believed, would give the Razorbacks a fighting chance, but his first two seasons as head coach had been disasters—there was no other way to describe them—because superior talent had dominated strategy and tempo.

Howard Martin shook his head, frustrated, when he thought about the many shots his inept Guards had missed during the season. And when he thought about the long-range bombs he had seen Jamie make, he wanted to offer him a scholarship. But when he reached for the telephone, a gut-feeling hit him in the pit of his stomach. Experience had taught him that any time he ignored the ole gut-feeling, disaster usually followed. And he had the ole gut-feeling about Jamie.

Howard Martin sighed, leaned back in his chair, and did not dial Jamie's number.

•   •   •

Jamie was devastated.

The University of Arkansas, or any school, large or small, had not offered him a scholarship. Phil Westerman was stunned. Phil, of course, was well-aware that his cocky, free-spirited brother-in-law had sustained a devastating, often career-ending, injury, but Jamie was an elite athlete, a former MVP, he had worked his butt off, and Phil believed he deserved a chance to prove himself, especially after Jamie had followed Phil's gut-wrenching regimen for five months.

Phil had assured Coach Martin that Jamie would be ready by August—September at the latest—but Coach Martin had been skeptical and told him that he did not think Jamie's knee would hold up under the constant stress of college basketball. Expecting an angry outburst when Jamie walked in Panther Field House for his evening workout, Phil was surprised when, looking defeated, Jamie slid into a folding metal chair, stared at the floor, and quietly asked, "What did I do wrong, Phil?"

"Nothing, Jamie."

"I had to have done something wrong."

"Coach Martin is afraid you'll re-injure your knee."

"That's not fair. I've worked my ass off."

"I told him you'd be ready by August, but he was adamant."

"Was all the pain and hard work for nothing?"

"You have options."

"Spit them out, man. I'm desperate."

"You won't like them."

"I guess I'll have to adjust."

"I talked to the head coaches at LSU and Ole Miss. If you're serious about playing for them, they'll consider offering you a scholarship when and if you visit their campuses."

"But I want to play for the Razorbacks."

"That's another option."

"What do you mean?"

"You could walk on."

"Hell, no! I'm an MVP, and an MVP doesn't walk on and pay his way."

"Don't make a hasty decision, Jamie! You're the best Point Guard in the State of Arkansas. A healthy Jamie Williams would put the Razorbacks on a championship level. Think about it! You and Terrance Brooks were impossible to stop at

Hot Springs High School. If you walked on, Coach Martin would see that you're ready, and with your talent, it wouldn't take long for him to offer you a scholarship."

Jamie weighed Phil's logic, but anger overwhelmed commonsense.

"Line me up for Ole Miss. I feel like a Rebel."

•   •   •

Jamie's sullen mood surprised Callie. They were supposed to go to a movie and then drive to their favorite parking place near the Saline River. Knowing what happened *after* the movie always put Jamie in a good mood. His scowling face, crossed arms, and stiff demeanor, she thought, were more than a little unusual.

"Who peed in your Rice Krispies?" Callie asked kiddingly.

"What do you mean?"

"It's Friday, we have a date, and you're not pawing the ground."

One night in the backseat of Jamie's Nova was all Callie needed to realize Jamie's assessment of Edwin Winfield had been right on the money: Edwin *was* a goofball, and she had dropped him so fast that his head rattled. Edwin was a gangly mule who never got excited or pawed the ground. Jamie was a thoroughbred, determined, and aggressive. When he kissed her and slid his hand between her legs, all she wanted to do was hang on and enjoy the ride.

"The University of Arkansas didn't offer me a scholarship."

Basketball, to Callie, was just a game, an excuse to get out of the house and hang out with friends twice a week during the winter. In fact, she did not think it was a big deal that the University of Arkansas had not offered Jamie an athletic scholarship. He was smart, articulate—even if he had a foul mouth—and with his GPA, all he had to do was apply and he would receive a full ride from any college he wanted to attend. Callie knew Jamie had been an exceptional basketball player, and that he had been obsessed with rehabbing his knee, but she did not know him in the context of basketball—what he had been, what he could be—and that lack of knowledge immediately placed her in the realm of the living dead.

"What did you expect, Jamie? You were All-State and an MVP, but..."

"You've never taken me seriously, have you?"

Jamie's cold voice and steely eyes chilled Callie.

"You didn't let me finish. I was going to say..."

"Just forget it."

Red-faced, Jamie jumped up and stepped off the porch.

"Where are you going?"

"Home."

"Don't leave, Jamie. We're more than just friends. You know that."

Stiff and angry, he walked across the yard, scooted into his Nova, backed out of the driveway, and drove away without looking back. Stunned, Callie stared at the empty street, walked into the house, and tossed her cookies in the bathroom. Jamie Williams had argued his way into her life, he had won her heart, and now he was gone. She washed her face, looked in the mirror, and was not surprised to see that she was crying.

•　　•　　•

"Jamie, Coach Martin called. He wants you to call him back."

"Did he mention what he wanted, Mom?"

"No, but he said it was important."

"You call him. I have nothing to say."

"But, Jamie, we've been friends with the Martins for years."

"Well, as the old saying goes, Mom, all good things must end."

CHAPTER 52

Phil Westerman thought that beneath Jamie's nonchalant demeanor lurked a rattlesnake, coiled and ready to strike. Although Phil felt sorry for Jamie—they had grown close during his rehab—he was convinced that his brother-in-law's hot temper, smart-mouth and rotten attitude had destroyed any hope he had of playing college basketball.

After the fiasco on national signing day, Callie thought Jamie's anger would eventually subside, but when he treated her as a nonperson at school and jogged by her house without a glance, she knew he had banished her into outer darkness. She wanted to tell him he had jumped to conclusions, that she never intended to insult him or hurt his feelings, but two months had passed, and Jamie had not given her the time of day.

In May, he graduated with honors from Benton High School, clueless about what he was going to do with his screwed-up life. Howard Martin had tried on several occasions to contact him, first by phone, then with a visit, but Jamie ignored his calls, was conveniently absent when he visited, and Coach Martin eventually gave up.

Hoping to improve Jamie's rotten attitude, Calvin Williams offered to buy him a new car for graduation, but Jamie told him he liked his Nova and asked for another motorcycle. Calvin

Williams did not like *that* idea at all, but finally gave in and bought the black and gold Honda Seven-Fifty-Four Jamie had been raving about.

In late May, Jamie visited Louisiana State University. He liked the LSU campus and was impressed because the school was building a new basketball arena, which he thought was exciting. Two weeks later, he visited the University of Mississippi. William Faulkner, one of his favorite authors, had been a student at Ole Miss, Oxford was a unique college town, and Jamie thought he would fit in well with the Rebel's basketball program. Once LSU and Ole Miss offered him scholarships, Jamie knew he would have a tough decision to make. To his dismay, however, neither school called nor asked him to sign a National Letter of Intent.

•   •   •

Frustrated by the pathetic direction his life had taken, Jamie turned on the radio, reached for his little red football, and stretched out on his bed. After several commercials, the disc jockey reached into his vault of golden oldies and played *Solitary Man* by Neil Diamond. The song struck a nerve and Jamie decided that was what he wanted to be—a solitary man—and that he would never get close to anyone again.

He dropped his little red football on the floor, sat down at his desk, and wrote Michelle a stinging letter, ending four years of torch-burning. Marian, he believed, deserved more. Without saying a word to his mother—Jamie considered himself an adult now—he walked through the kitchen to the garage, slung his leg over his motorcycle, and headed for Kirby. Two hours later, Marian led him to the barn to feed and water the horses, and within seconds, they were kissing. Before he lost control,

Jamie pulled away and mumbled, "There's something I have to tell you."

"I don't think I want to hear it."

"I need time to sort things out."

"What do you mean?"

"I won't be coming back."

"Why?"

"It's time to move on."

"You don't act like it's time to move on."

Marian was right. Kissing her had distracted him, and his well-rehearsed goodbye had not gone the way he had planned. It was time to put the train back on track.

"I'm an asshole. I got what I wanted for three years, and I'm moving on."

"I don't believe you, Jamie. What we feel is…"

"What *you* feel, Marian."

For the first time, he saw a flicker of doubt in her eyes. "But you said you would never give me up."

"A lot has happened since then."

"And none of it has been my fault. Why should you hold me responsible for what other people have done?"

"I've made up my mind."

"Don't do this to me, Jamie. I love you. I've always loved you."

Marian wrapped her arms around him and kissed him wildly. Jamie knew she was doing whatever she had to do to keep him from leaving. Disgusted with himself, he pulled away.

"Don't leave me, Jamie! Oh, god, please don't leave me."

"I'm not leaving."

Marian took a deep breath, closed her eyes, and sighed.

"I feel like I turned you into…"

"A whore? A desperate woman?"

"Both."

"You did, but I forgive you, because I love you."

"I didn't mean a word I said, Marian."

"Then why did you say them?"

"Because I decided to become a loner."

"That's stupid and childish. You're a people-person, Jamie, and you always have been."

"I know."

"Can you look me in the eye and tell me you don't love me and that you don't want me anymore?"

"No."

"I begged you not to leave me, Jamie, but I won't beg you again. If you hop on that pretty new motorcycle of yours and ride off into the sunset, don't come back kissing me like nothing's on your mind but a roll in the hay and then kick me in the gut like you did today. I have feelings, Jamie. Don't humiliate me again."

"I won't, Marian."

"Are you leaving or staying?"

"Staying."

"Then let's finish what we started."

•   •   •

After spending a long afternoon discussing his screwed-up life with Marian, Jamie decided to find a job, work, run, lift weights, enroll at the University of Arkansas at Little Rock, and walk on the UALR basketball team. UALR was transitioning into the University of Arkansas System, and since major universities were no longer interested in him—Phil said it was because of his piss-poor attitude—Jamie thought UALR would be a good place to settle, play ball, and earn a degree. It was not what he wanted, but there was no way in hell he would kiss

Howard Martin's ass and walk on at the University of Arkansas.

Pride would not allow him to stoop that low.

• • •

Jamie walked into the Minute Man Drive-In, stood in line, and placed his order at the serving-counter. Callie Thomas smiled at him and waved. Even if Jamie was being a stubborn ass, she wanted to correct the misunderstanding that had driven him away. That, however, did not look promising; instead of returning her smile, he nodded curtly, picked up his order, walked across the dining room, and sat down at an empty table.

Before he could dip his first French Fry in a pool of ketchup, Callie was standing by his table. "Are you still angry with me?" she asked, testing the water.

"Not at the moment."

"May I sit down?"

He nodded at an empty chair.

"I want to straighten out our misunderstanding, Jamie."

"Oh, yeah, our misunderstanding. What was it you said? 'What did you expect?' which means you think I'm nothing but a washed-up basketball player."

"I didn't mean that at all."

"Bullshit!"

Callie noticed that her friends, and several others, had heard Jamie's outburst concerning bovine excrement. She looked and felt extremely uncomfortable. "Are you afraid someone might hear our conversation, Miss Thomas?" he asked with venomous sarcasm.

"To tell you the truth, Jamie, I am."

He lowered his voice, almost to a whisper, and hissed, "Before I walk out of this blueblood shithole, I want you to know that I've hung mistletoe on my belt loop. I'm sure you know what to do with mistletoe, Callie. You kiss what's under it."

Jamie pushed his hamburger and French Fries to the middle of the table, stood, and walked stiffly out of the restaurant. There was, Callie was relieved to see, no mistletoe hanging from Jamie's jeans. Holding back tears, she nibbled a French Fry and watched him pull off the parking lot and accelerate down Military Road like a batt out of hell.

Mistletoe? Where does he come up with that stuff?

CHAPTER 53

One Year Later
August 1970

BAD BOYS AND SECOND CHANCES

Graham Wallace
Republic Sports Editor

I have been thinking lately about the movie *Boys Town*. Was Father Flannigan right when he said, "There are no bad boys. There is only bad environment, bad training, bad examples, and bad thinking?" In the movie, Spencer Tracy plays Father Flannagan, and Mickey Rooney plays bad boy Whitey Marsh. The movie, of course, has a happy ending. Bad boy Whitey Marsh learns the value of proper environment, proper training, proper example, and proper thinking. He is elected mayor of Boys Town, and the school is flooded with new donations.

You may think, "Why is Graham Wallace, a sportswriter, writing about an old, black and white movie?" The answer: I think, and I believe I am right, that Arkansas is home to a bad boy, who, like Whitey Marsh, may deserve a second chance.

His name is Jamie Williams.

Jamie was the Most Valuable Player in the 1968 State Basketball Tournament. In fact, he probably would have been named Arkansas Player of the Year during the 1968-69 season if he had not injured his knee water-skiing on Lake Greeson. Jamie underwent knee surgery prior to his senior year in high school and endured months of therapy because it was his dream to play basketball for the University of Arkansas. Unfortunately, Coach Howard Martin did not offer Jamie a scholarship.

I am not criticizing Coach Martin. From his perspective, and professional point-of-view, he did the right thing, sincerely believing that Jamie Williams was not ready for the stop, start, cut, and run arena that is college basketball. I probably would have handled Jamie's situation differently, but I am not a coach, and I have not dealt with injured athletes, or what it takes to overcome a devastating, possibly career-ending, injury.

Jamie, however, *thought* he was ready, and when Coach Martin did not offer him a scholarship, it devastated him. Devastation led to anger, and anger, of course, destroyed any chance Jamie Williams had of receiving a scholarship from any major university.

I have spoken to sources at Ole Miss and LSU—they will remain anonymous—and they told me that two overriding factors kept them from offering Jamie a scholarship: he did not respect authority, and he had a rotten attitude. This is sad when you consider Jamie's environment, his training, his examples, and his intelligence.

What environment was Arkansas' bad boy raised in? His father, Doctor Calvin Williams, is a prominent Baptist minister who heads the Evangelism Department at Mid-South Seminary in Little Rock. His mother is actively involved in women's ministries nationwide, his brother recently graduated from Baylor University and has been admitted to Baylor's prestigious School of Medicine, his sister is an elementary school teacher, and his brother-in-law is the head basketball coach at Benton High School. Obviously, Jamie was raised in an excellent environment.

What training has Arkansas' bad boy received? Jamie was raised in church, and his coaches, all disciplinarians, were, and are, fine men. He graduated with honors from Benton High School, a school that prides itself on academics, and after completing his first year of college at UALR, he was on the Dean's List both semesters. Obviously, Jamie has received excellent training.

What examples has Arkansas' bad boy followed? The men who coached Jamie in junior and senior high school have stated that they never—not one time—had a problem with him. In fact, Jamie helped coaches statewide conduct summer basketball camps, and they have emphatically stated that he set an excellent for the young athletes he worked with. Furthermore, Jamie's teachers—I interviewed them—lauded his academic achievements and said, except for a few instances, that he had been a bright, articulate, and well-behaved student. Jamie, obviously, has been mentored by people of high integrity.

What about the thinking of Arkansas' bad boy? This is where Jamie Williams has a problem. Instead of talking to Coach Martin in March 1969, Jamie shut him out—rudely—and took recruiting trips to Ole Miss and LSU. During the summer of 1969, the few coaches who recruited Jamie felt he was flippant, which is a kind way of saying they thought he had a smart-mouth and would be difficult to coach.

What changed Jamie's thinking?

What made him become a coach's nightmare?

His dream was shattered!

The first time I saw Jamie Williams play basketball, he was in the eighth grade. Even then, he dreamed of playing for the Razorbacks. During his high school career, coaches from several major universities sent letters of inquiry to Jamie, but they knew signing him would be a longshot, because he frequently said that it was his dream to play for the Razorbacks.

And that dream was shattered on National Signing Day in 1969.

In August 1969, Jamie enrolled at UALR and walked on the Trojan basketball team. Coach Happy Mahfouz told me that Jamie would have started every game on the freshman team if he had not suffered a lingering high-ankle sprain that limited his playing time. In fact, Coach

Mahfouz said that he would love to coach Jamie for three more years but thought that prospect was unlikely because he believed Jamie would eventually swallow his pride and follow his dream.

My question is, how many chances should an athlete—or any man—have before he is a lost cause? Can a person, once he has set a course in life, change? To be specific, if Jamie Williams follows his dream, should Howard Martin give him the opportunity to fulfill that dream?

Why not?

Jamie has three of Father Flannagan's principles—environment, training, and example—working for him. If he gets the fourth one—thinking—straight, there is no reason Jamie Williams cannot become the All-American this writer believes he can be.

CHAPTER 54

The job was hot, boring, and hard. A brick mason in Emmanuel Baptist Church, a basketball fan who thought Jamie had gotten a raw deal, had hired him as a summer helper. For three months, Jamie carried seventy-five-pound sacks of mortar, mixed them with sand and water, and kept the man supplied with endless piles of gray mud.

The outdoor job had toned Jamie's muscles and the summer sun had tanned him darkly. Wearing faded jeans, a light-blue, denim work shirt with the sleeves cut off at the shoulders, dark-tinted, wire-framed sunglasses, and his long, brown hair inching beneath his black and gold safety helmet, Jamie Williams, looking as ragged and rebellious as he felt, climbed on his Honda, and headed for Fayetteville.

North of Russellville, mountains shrouded in fog appeared in the distance. He exited Interstate 40 at Alma and headed north on Highway 71. An hour later, he pulled onto the campus of the University of Arkansas, stepped off his Honda, and walked into Barnhill Field House.

Coach Martin's office was protected by a receptionist talking on the telephone. A nameplate identified her as Margaret Anderson. She ignored the rough-looking young man standing impatiently in front of her desk, then finally looked over her glasses, covered the mouthpiece, and asked, "What can I do for you?"

"I'm here to see Coach Martin."

Margaret did not like the looks of the young man or his gruff attitude. "Would it trouble you too much," she asked sarcastically, "if I asked you why?"

"Yes, it would, and to tell you the truth, it's none of your business."

Margaret stood and pointed toward the door. "I think it's time for you to…"

"Lady," Jamie interrupted, "why don't you be nice and tell Coach Martin Jamie Williams is here? If you don't, I'll walk right past you, and there's not a damned thing you can do about it."

Margaret hesitated, hung up the phone, knocked on Coach Martin's door, and stepped into his office. "I hate to disturb you, Coach, but there's a rude young man outside wanting to see you."

"What's his name?"

"Williams, I think."

"Jamie?"

"Yes. Jamie Williams."

"Was he terribly uncouth, Margaret?"

"When I asked him what he wanted, he told me it was none of my business. He also said that he'd walk in uninvited if I didn't tell you he was here."

Howard Martin had grown weary of Jamie's pigheaded attitude and believed he had carried his resentment too far and too long. His friendship with Calvin Williams was strained, his players were antsy because they believed Jamie had gotten a raw deal, and, of course, there was Michelle to consider.

"Do you want to see him, Coach Martin?"

"Yes, I'll see Jamie. Send him in."

Appalled that the Head Coach of the Arkansas Razorbacks would take time to talk to the rude young man waiting outside his office, Margaret opened the door and motioned Jamie inside. Coach Martin stood, extended his hand, and said, "It's good to see you, Jamie. I read Graham Wallace's article. I've been expecting you."

Jamie ignored the extended hand. "I'm glad I didn't disappoint you, Coach."

Howard Martin slowly withdrew his hand. "You didn't. What can I do for you, Jamie?"

"I'm here to play for the Razorbacks."

Everything about Jamie irritated Howard Martin: his tone of voice, the way he was dressed, his long hair, the way he stood, and most of all, the sullen look on his face.

"Oh, really? I thought that was my decision."

"It was your mistake, Coach Martin, and I'm here to…"

"Wait a minute, Jamie! We've been friends for a long time. I've always liked you, but friend or not, I won't allow you to march into my office and lecture me. If you want to talk, we'll talk, but if you're going to be a smart-mouthed punk, there's the door."

Howard Martin glared at Jamie for ten seconds—it seemed much longer. "Are we going to discuss this like gentlemen? Or end it before you've had your say?"

Momentarily stunned, Jamie hesitated, then reluctantly said, "Like gentlemen."

"Then have a seat." Coach Martin crossed his arms, leaned back in his chair, and calmly asked, "You know why I didn't offer you a scholarship, don't you?"

"Yes, Coach Martin, I do, and I totally disagree with you. I worked my butt off because you led me to believe all the pain and work would pay off, that you would offer me a scholarship, but on National Signing Day, you didn't even have the courtesy to…"

"Wait a minute! I called, but you wouldn't talk to me."

"What were you going to say? That I was washed up? That I was no longer valuable to your program?"

"What if I had offered you a scholarship, and you found out your knee couldn't handle the stress? Or worse, what if you re-injured your knee and had to undergo another surgery?"

"Did you consider the fact that I might take up where I left off two years ago? That *is* possible, you know. Did you consider the fact that it was my decision too? That I understood what might or might not happen? That I realized I might fail? Or worse, that I might injure my knee again? Coach Martin, the only reason you didn't offer me a scholarship was because your friendship with my dad meant more to you than my life."

Jamie's words stung Howard Martin. No longer sure of his logic, he stared at the ceiling, turned his head from side to side, and tried to relieve the tension in his neck.

Is he right? Did personal feelings cloud my judgement?

"Am I right or wrong, Coach?"

"Your father and I *are* close friends, Jamie, but that doesn't mean I'm not concerned about you. You're an outstanding basketball player. I didn't want to be the man who ended your career."

"But Doctor Clark said I'd be ready."

"Doctor Clark said that you *might* be ready. As a coach, I've seen too many athletes re-injure themselves, or fail to regain their previous skills. As much as I love basketball, Jamie, there are things more important, like walking normally for the rest of your life."

"Or having to face my father if I ended up in a hospital?"

Howard Martin thew up his hands, exasperated. "You haven't listened to a word I've said."

"You haven't either, Coach," Jamie replied, holding his ground.

"Okay, you've made your point. What do you want me to do?"

"It's not what *you're* going to do. It's what *I'm* going to do."

"And what might that be?"

"When the Razorbacks practice on October 15th, I'll be there. In time, probably a very short time, you'll offer me a scholarship, because as Coach Sam Lequieu told me, if a coach can't see that I belong on a basketball court, he's nothing but a damned fool, anyway."

Howard Martin was furious. A nineteen-year-old kid had pointedly called him a fool. No! A damned fool! He slapped his desk, and with the same hand, pointed toward the door. "Jamie, this conversation is over. It's time for you to leave."

"Fine, I'll leave, Coach, but I'm a problem that won't go away. On October 15th, you'll have to deal with me."

Howard Martin wanted to grab Jamie by his long hair and pull him out of his office kicking and screaming, but commonsense prevailed. He glared at Jamie for thirty seconds — it seemed much longer — and finally said, "I'll deal with you, Jamie. You can count on that. For your edification, however, the odds are against any walk-on ever seeing the court in Barnhill Field House, and that includes you, Jamie. *I'm* the coach, and *I* decide who plays or doesn't play for the Razorbacks, not you. I have two months to think about this conversation. If you show up on October 15th, and I decide to let you in — and that, young man, may or may not happen — if I see a sullen attitude, and I hear one negative remark, you'll find yourself on the street so fast your head will swim."

Jamie stood and walked toward the door, his mind reeling. Coach Martin had tried to be cordial. He had even asked what he wanted him to do, but, as usual, he had let his big mouth destroy what could have been a golden opportunity. He considered apologizing, but when he glanced at Coach Martin and saw anger on his face, he knew the wise thing to do was walk out of the office without saying another word.

•   •   •

Jamie pulled on his safety helmet, adjusted his sunglasses, straddled his motorcycle, and glanced at the metallic-blue Firebird parked next to his Honda. He rolled his eyes when Michelle Martin stepped out of the car, frowning and shaking her head.

"You never change, do you, Jamie?"

"I don't know what you mean."

"You, or one of your girlfriends, writes me a letter. I decide to forget you, and then you ride back into my life on one of your pretty little chargers." Michelle nodded at the motorcycle. "Have you been to see my dad?"

"Yeah, and I made an ass of myself."

"You've been doing that for over a year." Jamie pulled his helmet off, shook the hair out of his eyes, and looked up at the hazy blue sky. "Dad would have offered you the scholarship if you had talked to him. But no, you let stupid male-pride stand in the way and blew it."

"There are two sides to the story, Michelle. Your dad had doubts, I understand that, but he let me get my hopes up on National Signing Day, then he left me hanging."

"Okay, he handled the situation badly, but he would never hurt you intentionally, Jamie. He did what he thought was right. Later, he had second thoughts. The scholarship was yours, but you refused to answer his calls, took recruiting trips to LSU and Ole Miss, and wrote his daughter a hateful letter. You have no one to blame but yourself."

"That's good, Michelle. Put the monkey on my back."

"Isn't that where it belongs?"

Jamie glanced toward Barnhill Field House and saw Coach Martin walking toward them. It would not have surprised him if the man told him to leave and never come back.

"I was just talking to Michelle, Coach Martin. I'm leaving now."

"An explanation isn't necessary, Jamie," he replied, seeing for the first time in months the boy he had known for years. "You and Michelle have been friends for a long time."

Coach Martin stepped into the Firebird. Michelle, obviously disgusted, shook her head, opened the door, and scooted beneath the steering wheel. Jamie had done what he had planned to do. He had told Howard Martin off, just as he had rehearsed it a thousand times. Quoting Coach Lequieu and calling Howard Martin a damned fool felt good standing in front of a mirror, but as he watched Michelle's Firebird pull off the parking lot in front of Barnhill Field House, he had a hard time accepting the fact that his well-rehearsed speech did not feel as good now.

•   •   •

Howard Martin pushed his seat back as far as it would go, glanced at Michelle, and said more than a little sarcastically, "Your boyfriend put on quite a show in my office this afternoon."

"Was he terribly rude, Dad?"

"He called me a damned fool."

"I think he regrets what he said."

"Said the daughter who is in love with the coach's problem-child."

"He told me—pardon the language—that he made an ass of himself."

"I wanted to drag him kicking and screaming out of my office."

"What are you going to do about him, Dad?"

"I haven't made up my mind. I have two months to think about it."

"Are you going to let him walk on?"

"Same answer: I haven't made up my mind. I told him that if I allowed him to walk on—and that's a big 'if,' Michelle—that I won't tolerate his sullen attitude and smart-mouth."

"What did he say?"

"Nothing. He walked out of my office without saying a word."

"You know how I feel about Jamie, Dad, and I'm not blind, so don't take what I'm about to say the wrong way. Jamie was wrong when he didn't talk to you last year, but I don't think he knew until today that you had changed your mind and were going to offer him a scholarship."

"That doesn't excuse his obnoxious behavior."

"No, it doesn't, but it's something to think about."

"How did Jamie seem when you talked to him?"

"You won't like my answer."

"I want to hear it, anyway."

"He seemed normal, Dad. He listened to what I had to say, argued back a little, and then clammed up when he saw you walking across the parking lot. Honestly, I think he's ready to take responsibility for his actions and move on."

"So, what do you think?"

"That you should give him a chance."

"Said the daughter who is in love with the coach's problem-child."

CHAPTER 55

Venus by the *Shocking Blue* was bouncing off the walls of the Student Union when Jamie walked into the building and headed for the vending machines. He dropped two quarters in the slot, reached for the red and white aluminum can, then walked across the room and sat down at a vacant table. Reflecting on what had been an all-around shitty day, he sipped his Coke and was startled when a hand touched his shoulder and a feminine voice said, "I don't see any mistletoe, Jamie."

He flinched and almost spilled his Coke. "Damn, Callie, you scared the hell of me."

"You never change, do you?"

Jamie laughed.

"What's so funny?"

"You're the second person who has asked me that today?"

"You don't change, Jamie. You're sitting in a room filled with people and you're still alone."

Callie pulled out a chair and sat down.

"I thought you were going to Henderson."

"I changed my mind."

"I didn't know that, but we haven't talked much, have we?"

"You haven't given me a chance to tell you anything."

"Yeah, I've been an ass."

"You can say that again."

Jamie rolled his eyes and grunted.

"Don't tell me I'm the second person who has told you that, too."

"You guessed it."

"I'd say you've had a bad day, Jamie."

"And, as usual, it's my own damned fault. I have this habit of talking when I would be better off keeping my mouth shut."

"But that's what makes you special. Although you hurt my feelings, I thought it was hilarious when you supposedly hung mistletoe on your jeans and walked out of the Minute Man in Benton."

"You're as crazy as I am, Callie." Jamie narrowed his eyes. "Why are you here?"

"I want to straighten out the misunderstanding we had last year."

Jamie shrugged. "I was in a bad mood."

"I know how hard you worked rehabbing your knee. I was there, Jamie, and I should have been more sympathetic. But you were such a horse's ass you didn't let me finish. What I intended to say was, 'What do you expect? You messed up a knee, but you're the most determined person I have ever met, and you're too cocky not to play college basketball.' Now, Jamie Williams, can we be friends again?"

Jamie leaned back in his chair, crossed his arms, and said, "I'll have to think about it, Callie." For a moment, she thought he was serious, until she saw him smile.

Michelle Martin tried not to stare when she saw Jamie talking to an attractive girl. In fact, she wanted to slap herself and say, "Stop it! He's fickle, bigheaded, and a smart-mouthed prima donna." But seeing him talking to a pretty, redheaded girl with glistening eyes upset her, and she wondered why she had asked her father to give him a second chance.

Faking a yawn, Michelle told her friends she was ready to leave, put on her best "I could care less" expression, said, "Hi, Jamie," as she passed his table, and walked out of the Student Union without looking back. Forgetting everything, Jamie turned and watched her leave.

"Uh-oh."

"What does that mean?"

"That there's someone else in your life you didn't tell me about. Who is she?"

"Michelle Martin."

"How long have you known her?"

"Five years."

"She must be important. All it took was one look and a 'Hi, Jamie' and you swooned. I can't believe it. The invincible Jamie Williams has a crack in his armor."

"It's that obvious, huh?"

"You turned green around the gills over a polite greeting. Tell me about her."

"Her father is Howard Martin, the head basketball coach here at the university. We were in the ninth grade together. My dad was the Martin's pastor in Louisiana."

"And Coach Martin didn't offer you a scholarship?"

"We had a gentlemen's agreement. He didn't honor it, and I'm here to prove him wrong."

"I don't want to make you angry again, Jamie, but can you really blame him?"

"No. It's too bad I didn't realize *that* until today."

"What are you going to do?"

"I'm going to walk on the team. You know? Become a non-scholarship player. I hope, when Coach Martin and his assistants see my play, that I'll earn a scholarship."

"You didn't even play basketball last year."

"I did, for the UALR freshman team, but I sprained my ankle and had to sit on the bench."

"Which means you didn't play basketball last year."

"Callie, I've played with or against every player Coach Martin has on scholarship. They're my friends. And they know, except for Terrance Brooks, I'm better than all of them."

"You're too vain, Jamie."

"I've heard that before, too."

"So, they'll welcome you with open arms?"

"They're my friends, Callie."

"Will Coach Martin give you a chance?"

"After today, I wouldn't be surprised if he placed armed guards around Barnhill Field House with orders to shoot Jamie Williams on sight. As far as giving me a chance? I don't know. Coach Martin wasn't a happy camper when I walked out of his office today."

"You've explained Coach Martin and the scholarship. Now tell me about Michelle."

"Let me put it this way: Five years ago, we made a promise to each other. She kept it, and I didn't."

"You were only fourteen years old. How could you *or* Michelle take it seriously?"

"Circumstances, I guess. My dad says Michelle was a friend when I needed one."

"And you've carried a torch all this time?"

"I've dated another girl."

"The one you kissed at the Minute Man?"

"How do you know about that?"

"I saw you kiss her."

"Really?"

"I was in the car next to yours."

"I didn't see you."

"You were preoccupied. She's prettier than Michelle, by the way."

"Her name is Marian Wood, and she's another problem."

"Your life is a soap opera, Jamie."

"I know."

"Do you want to know what your problem is?"

"No, but I think you're about to tell me."

"You're too serious about basketball and girls."

"You've never been serious?"

"To be honest, Jamie, you're the only boy I've ever wanted."

"Why? I treated you like crap."

"There's something about you I like."

"I have that effect on girls."

"You're also an egotistical asshole."

Jamie chuckled. "The difference between me and most guys is, I admit it."

"What has being serious accomplished for you, Jamie? Twenty minutes ago, you were surrounded by people and still alone. You need to loosen up and have fun just to have fun."

"You're probably right. I need to make some changes."

"You won't. I saw the look on your face when the mysterious Michelle walked by. The two of you are inevitable. I almost envy her."

"You think so, huh?"

"It's written in stone."

Jamie rolled his eyes and shook his head.

"Don't tell me you've heard that before, too?"

"Two years ago. But that's another story."

Callie glanced toward the door. "It's getting late. You want to walk me to my dorm?"

"Sure."

"Just because I said I want you doesn't mean I'll let you feel me up or anything."

"Why? You like it when I feel you up."

"Shut up, Jamie."

"You moaned when I…"

"I said shut up, Jamie."

"Your face is flushed, Callie. Are you running a fever?"

She opened her mouth, started to say something, changed her mind, then looked Jamie in the eyes, and took the plunge: "I've been running a fever since the first time you kissed me."

"You mean since the first time I..."

"Especially that, you conceited jerk."

"You want a couple of aspirins for your fever?"

"I don't need aspirins, Jamie."

"They're in my apartment."

Callie reached for her purse. "Maybe I need some aspirins after all?"

CHAPTER 56

October 15th, 1970

The University of Arkansas was ablaze with gold, yellow, and red when Jamie parked his motorcycle outside Barnhill Field House. Although he did not live in Wilson Sharpe, the athletic dorm, he had worked out with Dalton Hilliard, David Thompson, and Terrance Brooks for two months, but today that would change. It was time to step out of the shadows and face Howard Martin and the Razorback coaching staff.

He paused outside the dressing room, took a deep breath, and then opened the door. Terrance Brooks motioned him to a folding metal-chair on the front row and quietly mumbled, "You'll make the team, Jamie—you're too good not to—just keep your big mouth shut."

Jamie nodded and scanned the room as two-dozen conversations echoed off the walls. Five minutes later, Howard Martin opened the door and walked to the front of the room. Looking solemn, he kept his head down, scanning notes in a black portfolio, while his assistant coaches, also looking solemn, stood behind him with their arms crossed. Finally, he lifted his head, stared at his team, and spoke softly, almost in a whisper. "There are going to be some changes around here." Each player leaned forward. "I'm tired of losing and I won't tolerate it any longer." He let the words sink in, then raised his voice and continued: "Losing is distasteful to me. I hate it."

Coach Martin paused and stared at Jamie.

"This is a new season. All positions are open. Every player will have an opportunity to prove himself. The five young men who work the hardest and develop the fastest will start when we open the season against Southwest Missouri State in November."

Tears welled in Jamie's eyes. Coach Martin was giving him a chance.

"There are three words that will soon become your mantra: discipline, control and defense."

Again, Coach Martin stared at Jamie.

"Without discipline, wars are lost, lives become failures, and young men grow up without proper respect. Gentlemen, if you don't follow my rules, no matter how good you are, you will never play for the Razorbacks, which means, if you can't discipline yourselves and follow my rules, you might as well pack your bags and leave now."

Jamie felt very uncomfortable.

"The next word is control. If you expect to run up and down the court and shoot the ball from wherever the mood strikes you, you're in for a big surprise. Every move you make, every shot you take, will, and I stress the word *will* be made and taken with control.

"Think about it, gentlemen. If you drive a car and lose control, you'll wrap it around a tree, destroy the car, and possibly yourselves. The same principle applies to basketball: If you don't play with control, you'll wreck the team, and when you wreck the team, we lose, and as I have already stated, I'm tired of losing.

"I'm not, however, outlawing individual talents. In fact, I like a little showboating myself, and I want your personalities transcending to the court, but showmanship must be within the context of the team. So, if I see you losing control during a game, don't be surprised when I call timeout and set you on the bench next to me. Playing with control, gentlemen, is the difference between winning and losing.

"The last word is defense. What have we accomplished if we score a hundred points, and our opponent scores a hundred and one? Nothing! Therefore, every practice will be dedicated to the art of defensive basketball. This isn't high school, gentlemen. College basketball is too competitive for coaches to coddle one-dimensional players.

"Finally, before we hit the hardwood, let's end this discussion on a positive note. This is my third year as Head Coach of the Razorbacks. I've recruited most of you, so I have no excuses, and it's time to see where my leadership is taking us. Last year was disappointing, but I believe the drought is over. We're young, but we're also talented.

"How talented?

"Let me put it this way: If we put self aside and work together, we'll take the Southwest Conference by storm, and possibly experience a year that we'll cherish for the rest of our lives."

•   •   •

There was not a doubt in Howard Martin's mind that Jamie Williams considered himself the heir apparent, the anointed one, smiling, cocky, and ready to assume the throne. He could not put a finger on it, but there was something about Jamie's demeanor that said, "I'm back, I've got this. Deal with it!"

Standing at mid-court watching Jamie go through his usual ritual of circling the goal and filling the hoop from varying distances—Howard Martin remembered Jamie following the same routine at Bogalusa Junior High School—Coach Bobby Culver, smiling a little too smugly, asked what had been on his mind for five days: "Coach, when are you going to give your boy a chance?"

"Do you think he deserves one?"

"You're the boss."

"You know what I mean, Bobby. What do you think about him?"

"I like him. He's outgoing, he's fun, and I don't think he's here to cause trouble."

"Okay, work Jamie and the sophomores against Terrance Brooks and the upperclassmen." Coach Culver smiled mischievously. "You've been itching to see him work, haven't you, Bobby?"

"If Jamie Williams is half the player he was in high school, he'll be All-Conference, make Terrance Brooks an All-American, and lead the Razorbacks to a national championship."

"Wow!"

"He's that good, Howard."

"I'm not worried about Jamie's ability, just his attitude. When he gets *that* under control, he can move into Wilson Sharpe with the scholarship players. If he doesn't, he can hit the road."

"When will you know?"

"That's between Jamie and me. You just do what you always do, Bobby: work with the younger players, build their confidence, and make them believe no mountain is too high."

Coach Culver threw Coach Martin a sloppy salute and shouted, "Yes, sir."

Howard Martin laughed, walked to the bleachers, and sat down.

•   •   •

Jamie simply nodded when Coach Culver put him on the court with Dalton Hilliard, David Thompson, and two walk-ons to scrimmage against Terrance Brooks and four upperclassmen. Although he appeared calm, Jamie was more than a little nervous when a graduate assistant lofted the ball into the air. He knew, after two turbulent years, that Coach Martin was giving him an opportunity to prove his worth as a basketball player and as a man.

Terrance Brooks roamed beneath the basket, but the upperclassmen's Guard play was lacking. Jamie quickly intercepted an errant pass and took the ball to the hoop, but Terrance, arms spread wide, was standing beneath the goal, waiting to block the shot. Jamie backed off, as the coaches had taught him, and played with control.

As he passed and dribbled the ball and made cuts toward the basket, Jamie knew the months of therapy—running, stretching, and lifting weights—had paid off. His knee felt good, so good, in fact, it was as if he had never been away from the game.

Dalton flipped him a quick pass.

Jamie faked a defender out of his shoes, cut left, shot, and hit nothing but net.

Terrance Brooks raised his arms in triumph.

Jamie Williams was back.

Coach Martin was stunned as he watched Bobby Culver's sophomores make Jackie Harrell's more experienced but less talented crew look like the benchwarmers they really were. And Jamie Williams, good as ever, was the obvious leader. Looking somber, he stepped off the bleachers, walked to mid-court, and told Coach Culver, "When they hit the showers, tell Jamie I want to see him in my office."

"The kid's attitude improved in a hurry, didn't it, Coach?"

"Shut up, Bobby!"

"Howard, we're looking at a six-foot-three-inch passing and shooting machine, who, along with Terrance Brooks, is going to lead us to a national championship."

"I should have listened to you and offered Jamie a scholarship two years ago."

"Occasionally, we all suffer from tunnel-vision, Boss."

Dalton Hilliard slid across the floor on his belly, trying to control a loose ball before it rolled out of bounds. Coach Martin said, "Nice play, Dalton," then turned to Coach Culver and mumbled, "Split them up, Bobby! This is embarrassing."

•   •   •

"Coach Martin, Jamie Williams is here."

"Send him in, Margaret."

Jamie walked toward Coach Martin's office; then turned back.

"So, you're going to make him wait this time?"

"No, ma'am. I want to apologize for the way I talked to you in August."

Before Margaret could respond, Jamie walked into Coach Martin's office. Coach Martin stared at him for several seconds, and finally pointed toward a chair.

Jamie sat down.

"I never dreamed we'd get off to such a shaky start."

"It's my fault, Coach. I shouldn't have barged into your office the way I did."

"I agree." Coach Martin stared into Jamie's eyes. "Why didn't you answer my calls?"

"I've asked myself the same question a thousand times. I guess I was stupid."

"You've never been stupid, Jamie." Coach Martin leaned back in his chair and crossed his arms. "I don't know what you want. Am I supposed to eat crow or something? God knows you were impressive during practice today."

"All I want to do is play ball, Coach. Nothing more, nothing less."

"Your resentment and anger were real, Jamie. Why the change? And why so quickly?"

"I concluded I was wrong." Jamie stared briefly at his hands, then looked Coach Martin in the eyes and said, "You know I've always wanted to play for the Razorbacks."

"Yes, I do."

"My head hasn't been screwed on right for a long time, Coach. I didn't want to leave Kirby. I hated Benton High School, rehab hurt, and I couldn't play basketball. If I had talked to you—taken your calls—I could have avoided this whole situation."

"Our last conversation, although painful, told me what I already knew, that I handled your situation badly. Your father *is* my closest friend, and I didn't want to hurt him by hurting you. I was wrong."

Howard Martin stood, placed both hands on his desk, leaned forward, and stared into Jamie's eyes, obviously deciding what he intended to do. Jamie knew his future was held in the balance.

"If you ever walk in my office the way you did two months ago, I'll grab you by the hair of your head, drag you out of Barnhill Field House, and throw you on the parking lot."

"I believe you, Coach."

"You better believe me, Jamie."

"Yes, sir."

"There's a bed reserved for you in Dalton Hilliard's room. Consider yourself on scholarship."

"Thank you, Coach."

The intercom buzzed. "Coach Martin, your daughter is here."

"I'll be with her in a minute, Margaret."

He clicked the intercom off. "Jamie, we can't allow a lack of communication to destroy our relationship again. From what I saw on the court today, you're about to become the team leader. We — you and I — must be on the same page."

"We will be, Coach."

Howard Martin extended his hand. Jamie clasped it. Deep emotions passed between them as they ended their standoff. For the first time in months, Jamie felt like himself again.

•   •   •

"Hi, Michelle," Jamie mumbled when he stepped into Margaret Anderson's office and walked toward the door. Jamie, Michelle knew, did not go where he was not wanted. She also knew that if she did not take the first step, he would be too stubborn to contact her later. Jamie was, and always had been, a prima donna, but he was a sensitive prima donna. Their last conversation had not been pleasant, and she knew Jamie had not forgotten that. But enough was enough. She loved him, and she could not let him walk out the door without a confrontation.

"Wait a minute, Jamie!"

He turned and faced her.

"Did you work things out with Dad?"

"Yeah, I got tired of being an asshole."

"When are you going to work things out with me?"

Jamie glanced at Margaret Anderson, who seemed more than a little intrigued by the conversation, and hedged the question: "What things?" he asked uncomfortably.

"Don't be an evasive ass, Jamie!"

"Okay. We'll talk. But not here."

"When?"

"Anytime."

"Do you know where I live?"

"No."

Michelle pulled a small spiral-notebook from her purse, drew a simple map, and handed it to Jamie. "Our house is easy to find. I'll be waiting for you at 7:30."

.   .   .

Jamie noticed that Michelle had changed out of her jeans and was wearing a short brown skirt, black tights, and a beige sweater when she answered the door and led him through a large den to a redwood deck overlooking a ragged ravine.

"You have a beautiful home."

Michelle laughed, bitterly Jamie thought, and said, "It's probably temporary, meaning, if Dad doesn't produce a winning team soon, it's goodbye Fayetteville."

"I think this is going to be a turnaround year for Coach Martin."

Michelle rolled her eyes and sarcastically said, "That's right. Jamie Williams, the anointed one, now has a room in Wilson Sharpe, and he intends, with the flick of his magic wrist, to lead the Arkansas Razorbacks to the Promised Land."

Jamie's eyes narrowed. If Michelle intended to be a sarcastic bitch, he would hang mistletoe on his belt loop and walk out. He was a basketball player, not a miracle worker, but he had never lost a game, and damned if he intended to lose one now.

"That's what I do, Michelle, win championships."

"You've always been too arrogant, Jamie."

Struggling to control his temper, Jamie took a deep breath, leaned against the three-tiered railing, and stared at the nocturnal landscape. "Do you want to beat around the bush or shuck down the corn?"

"You lived in Kirby too long. I don't know what you're asking."

Jamie chuckled. "Do you want to make small talk? Or do you want to get down to business?"

"Let's settle it tonight, one way or the other."

"I don't think that's possible."

"Why not?"

"Because I'm different now, and so are you. We've both been through a lot—letters, an hour here, an hour there, more letters, moves to different cities—we can't settle this in one night."

"It has been one setback after another, hasn't it?"

Jamie stared at a possum scurrying down the ravine. "There is a difference, Michelle."

"Tell me, Jamie, what's different?"

"We're not kids anymore, and there's nothing to keep us apart…except us."

"So, you're saying?"

"That after five years, we're in control."

"Then what are *we* going to do?"

"Isn't that what this meeting is about?"

"You didn't answer my question."

"I'm not sure that I can give you the answer you want."

"What do you think I want, Jamie?"

"Me."

"Wow!" Michelle wilted into a white wicker-chair, looking sullen and angry. "Who do you think you are, Jamie Williams? God's gift to women? I'm not desperate, you arrogant jock. What happened to the boy I fell in love with five years ago?"

"He grew up."

"And I haven't?"

"In some ways you have, and in some ways you haven't."

"How have I not grown up?"

"You're in love with a myth."

"Give me a break."

"You *think* you know me, Michelle, but you don't. In five years, we've seen each other two or three times. I'm not soft, warm, and fuzzy. I'm not a knight in shining armor, and I don't want to be. I'm rough around the edges, I like to cuss, I say what I think, I don't take shit off anyone, I like to fool around with girls, and I'm one hell of a basketball player."

Total silence. An owl cooing in the distance was the only sound. A noise emanated from Michelle's throat—a sob or a snicker, Jamie could not tell—and then, with a credible backcountry drawl, she replied, "Well, shee-it, Jamie. I thank you just described the fourteen-year-old-boy this ole gal fell in love with five years ago."

Jamie leaned against the railing and chuckled. Michelle pushed herself out of the chair, walked to him, and placed her arms around his waist. Her eyes, he noticed, were glistening.

"Are you going to kiss me, or stand there like a knot on a log?"

The temperature was in the low fifties, but Michelle's body felt warm, almost hot, as she pressed against him. Jamie lightly brushed her lips, then kissed her deeply, her tights offering ample protection from his roaming hands and probing fingers.

Several minutes later, she broke the embrace. "That wasn't so bad, was it, Super Star?"

"No, you have a sweet ass."

"Thank God for tights and pantyhose."

"I can work around them."

"We're meant to be, Jamie. I told you that a long time ago."

"I remember. In Bogalusa. On a street corner near Brett Smithers's house."

"It's time to find out if I was right."

Damn, I don't know if I'm ready for this.

"We have three years. Do you want to fool around some more?"

"What do you think, Jamie?"

•   •   •

Callie ran across the leaf-covered lawn outside Old Main, stood on her tiptoes, kissed Jamie on the cheek, and immediately knew there was a problem. "Why the long face?" she asked, dreading the answer.

"Remember when I told you about Michelle Martin?"

"So, you've had the inevitable rendezvous with the mysterious Michelle?"

"I'm sorry, Callie."

"I knew it would happen."

"Michelle is convinced that we're supposed to be together."

"The question is, are *you* convinced?"

"When I'm with her, yes. When I'm with you, no."

"You're one screwed up guy, Jamie."

"I feel terrible, Callie. What am I supposed to do?"

"Have your fling with fate, I suppose. At least I'm not pregnant."

There was, Jamie noticed, deep bitterness in her voice. Callie left him standing with his arms at his side, her red hair floating in the wind as she walked steadily out of sight. Jamie shook his head whimsically, wondered if he had done the right thing, took a deep breath, exhaled, and then walked down a steep hill toward Wilson Sharpe Dormitory.

CHAPTER 57

Howard Martin believed his Razorbacks were the most enthusiastic and talented group of young men he had ever coached. Graham Wallace, in Fayetteville preparing an article for the opening game, thought they looked feisty.

"Who is your starting five, Howard? I know you've decided."

"Terrance Brooks, of course."

"Every school in the conference knows that, Howard."

"I like Tommy Jackson at Power Forward."

"Again, every school in the conference knows that."

"I'm leaning heavily toward the sophomores. I've never seen three more intelligent, mature, or talented young men. They're something special."

"What about Jamie Williams?"

"Your favorite player?"

"What can I say? I like Jamie."

"Jamie—I thought sportswriters were supposed to be objective—is a unique combination of power, skill, and heart. Everyone, even the coaches, love him. From day one—even before I let him on the court—everyone knew Jamie would be the team leader. The truth is, he's the glue that holds the team together."

"That's high praise for a walk-on."

"Jamie is not, and never should have been, a walk-on." Coach Martin leaned against the bleachers and placed both hands behind his neck. "Do you want to know what my assistants are saying after coaching Jamie and his friends for a month?"

"Sure."

"They think we'll win the Southwest Conference *and* the NCAA Tournament. I'm serious, Graham. Bobby Culver and Jackie Harrell believe we're going to win the National Championship."

"What do you believe, Coach?"

Howard Martin smiled drolly. "I believe whoever we play better bring their lunch."

•   •   •

"Do you have a date with Michelle tonight, Jamie?"

"We're going to Pizza Hut. Do you and Marcie want to meet us there?"

"Sounds good." Jamie nodded and walked toward the door. "Hey, wait a minute!" Dalton, Jamie thought, had been acting squirrely all day. He turned back and faced his friend. "Aren't you nervous about tomorrow night? Southwest Missouri State is a veteran team, and we're only sophomores. Do you think we're ready?"

"Coach Martin thinks we are. And to answer your question: Yeah, I'm nervous."

"You don't act it."

"Neither do you."

"I haven't felt this jittery since I thought you were going to beat me out of a starting position four years ago."

"We were a team then, and we're a team now. Relax, Dalton."

"I guess you're right."

"I know I'm right."

Jamie stepped into the hallway and shook his head. He was not at all nervous. On October 15th, when he stepped on the hardwood in Barnhill Field House, he knew he had found his way home and that he was in his element.

Excited? Yes! Nervous? Never!

CHAPTER 58

A POINT OF ORDER

Graham Wallace
Republic Sports Editor

According to experts in the Southwest Conference, the University of Arkansas is expected to finish in or near the cellar at the close of the 1970/1971 basketball season. Before the Powers-That-Be adhere to their pre-season predictions, however, this writer rises to a point of order. Namely, they, the prognosticators, have not considered the potential excellence of Jamie Williams, Dalton Hilliard, and David Thompson, and, of course, the proven excellence of Terrance Brooks.

Point Number One: This is not the same team that finished the season 15 and 16 last year. If the prognosticators think the Razorbacks have deteriorated because of graduation, they will soon be surprised. I do not want to sound critical, but the seniors who graduated last spring were not Division 1 caliber athletes. Grant it, they did an admirable job, but when the game was on the line, they did not have the horses to pull the wagon to victory.

Point Number Two: Coach Howard Martin is now working with athletes he has recruited. This will make a vast difference.

It is not a secret that during Coach Martin's first two seasons, several players left the team because of his discipline; consequently, he had to compete with less talented athletes. This Razorback team, however, thrives on discipline and plays, or shall I say practices, with intensity and control. This will win a lot of basketball games.

Point Number Three: This sophomore class comprises genuine blue-chippers. This writer unequivocally believes that there is not a coach anywhere who has had a better two years of recruiting than Howard Martin. Consider the fact that Jamie Williams has never lost a game on the junior and senior high school level. I know Jamie did not play his senior year of high school because of a knee injury, and that an ankle injury kept him out of UALR's freshman lineup last season, but to play four years without losing a game is phenomenal. Consider the fact that for two years David Thompson, Jamie's teammate at Kirby High School, did not lose a game until the finals of the State Championship against, you guessed it, Dalton Hilliard and the Hot Springs Trojans. Consider the fact that as a high school player, Dalton Hilliard lost only three times. The point is, Arkansas' sophomores do not know how to lose, and this winning tradition will carry over to the Razorbacks.

Point Number 4: Terrance Brooks. Not enough can be said or written about the Razorback's six-foot-eleven-inch Center. Terrance, in fact, provided what little respect the Razorbacks garnered last year. Mercifully, he now has a talented supporting cast to complement his potent inside play. With a potential twenty-win season on the horizon, look for Terrance Brooks to become a consensus All-American.

Back to the pre-season poll.

Burn it!

When the Razorbacks open the 1970/71 season against Southwest Missouri State University tomorrow night in Barnhill Field House, you will see a tsunami of speed, skill, and strength that will change the face of college basketball.

CHAPTER 59

Trying—unsuccessfully—to relax in his recliner, Calvin Williams sat up, stretched, and screamed at the top of his lungs. The sound echoed throughout the house. Louise Williams, more than a little startled, ran into the living room and was relieved to see that her husband was not grabbing his chest or foaming at the mouth.

"Why are you screaming like a wild banshee? You nearly gave me a heart attack."

"This house is too quiet."

"You certainly remedied that."

"I miss the sound of kids, Lou. In fact, I'm ready for Bud and Judith to move to Arkansas so that we can babysit Cal-Three. Better yet, call Sherry and tell her to get off those birth control pills. It's time for her and Phil to have a baby."

"You're losing you mind, Cal."

"I think it's called empty nest syndrome."

The phone rang.

"Well, as Jamie used to say, 'Someone is probably constipated again.'"

"Shut up and answer the phone, Cal."

"Hello."

"Calvin Williams please."

"This is he."

"Cal, this is William Hilliard."

The last person Calvin Williams expected a call from was William Hilliard. They had never been friends. In fact, they had an adversarial relationship that began when Calvin's father moved his family to Hot Springs during the Great Depression.

Before the stock market crashed in 1929, Clarence Williams was a prosperous lumberman in Caddo Gap, owning and operating a small but flourishing sawmill. Life was good. Calvin Williams, the youngest of eight children, had fond memories along the banks of the Caddo River. There was plenty of time for play, ample food, and every other Saturday an exciting trip to Glenwood with store-bought candy and ice cream at the drugstore. Clarence Williams, a happy, outgoing man, believed his life promised many years of prosperity and a comfortable retirement, but two years after Black Tuesday, he lost everything: his business, his savings, his self-esteem, and his desire.

Clarence Williams searched for a new job in Mena, but the economy was no better there, just more people in the same situation, trying to grasp the last straw of a dying way of life. The only alternative Clarence saw was to move his family to a larger city where there might be more jobs. So, he moved to Hot Springs, became a timber-estimator, and day after day walked through parcels of land, estimating the number of trees lumber companies could cut and sell on the market. Clarence Williams put food on the table, but his heart was never in it.

Hot Springs, Clarence Williams soon learned, was a city filled with bars and gambling casinos, and he made friends with both. Sadly, the successful businessman of the Twenties became an introverted, disillusioned drunk in the Thirties.

Calvin, of course, noticed that his fun-loving pop had morphed into a silent creature who spoke only when spoken to, and usually with a weak yes, no, or I don't care. He also noticed the difference in his own appearance; he no longer wore bright denim overalls and shiny new shoes, but faded hand-me-downs with patched knees and scarred leather brogans. The change in his father and his own shabby appearance, however, never bothered Calvin until he met William Hilliard, a respected attorney's son, at Ramble Elementary School in Hot Springs.

"Where'd you get them shoes?" William asked when Calvin stepped onto Ramble schoolyard for the first time. "From one of the clowns down at the circus last week?"

Calvin glanced at his shoes, then at William, and kept walking.

"Where you from, Hick?"

Calvin had been raised in a close-knit community surrounded by family and friends and had never encountered a stuck-up city-boy with a condescending attitude.

"I'm from Caddo Gap."

"Where on God's earth is that?"

Calvin shrugged his shoulders.

Tentatively, as if trying to avoid the plague, William touched one of the straps on Calvin's overalls, then jerked his hand back and shook it, like he was casting off some strange form of scum. "I haven't seen clothes this shabby since Daddy drove me to the train station and showed me the hobos. I swear, Hick, they were dressed better than you."

William glanced at his smirking friends and rubbed his chin thoughtfully.

"I think I'll call you Hobo."

"My name is Calvin Williams."

"Whoa, he's got a fancy name, boys, but I like Hobo better, don't y'all?"

William's friends nodded their heads tauntingly.

Realizing he had stumbled on an unfriendly crowd, Calvin moved on, but when he took his first step, William Hilliard tripped him, and he almost lost his balance. Angered by the unprovoked act, Calvin immediately attacked. William did not expect the charge and defended himself by pulling Calvin to the ground where the two boys flayed each other with fists and feet, accomplishing nothing but to raise dust and catch the attention of the school principal, Miss Nichols, a beagle-faced old bitty who naturally assumed a fine, upstanding student like William Hilliard had to have been provoked by the disgustingly shabby newcomer. She pulled the boys apart, glared at Calvin suspiciously, and asked, "What did this troublemaker do to incite you, William?"

"I don't know, Miss Nichols," William replied innocently. "I was just trying to get acquainted. When he walked off, he tripped, and before I knew it, he was trying to beat me up."

Calvin wiggled nervously and shriveled beneath Miss Nichol's icy stare. "Young man," she said indignantly, "we don't tolerate untoward behavior at Ramble Elementary School." She grabbed Calvin's left ear, pulled him inside the three-story, red-brick building, and gave him three hard licks with a wooden paddle.

Hearing from an old adversary was more than a little discomfiting. Calvin Williams searched his brain, trying to figure out what he had done that had provoked some anonymous person to sue him and hire William Hilliard as an attorney. Expecting a legal bombshell to ruin a perfectly boring day, he tentatively asked, "What can I do for you, William?"

"Have you heard from Jamie?"

"Not this week."

"Dalton just called. He and Jamie are starting tomorrow night."

"That's quite an accomplishment for two Hot Springs boys."

"The reason I've called is Helen and I are flying to Fayetteville for the game. We thought it would be a good idea to land in Benton, pick up you and Louise, and fly to

Fayetteville together. Jamie and Dalton are best friends, roommates in fact, and Fayetteville is only an hour and a half by air. You won't be tired when you return home, and you'll have plenty of time to rest before church on Sunday."

"I'm overwhelmed, William. What time do you want us to meet you?"

"How about eleven o'clock? We'll spend some time with the boys and then eat dinner before the game starts at seven."

"Thank you, William. You've made my day."

"No thanks are necessary, Cal."

Calvin Williams hung up the phone.

"Who is this William we're meeting at the airport?"

"You remember William Hilliard, don't you?"

"The attorney in Hot Springs?"

"That's the man. He and his wife, Helen, are flying us to Fayetteville."

"I'm *not* flying to Fayetteville."

"Dalton and Jamie are starting tomorrow night. It's a four-hour trip by car and only an hour and a half by air. Do the Math, Lou, it makes sense."

Louise Williams weakened quickly. "What time are we leaving?"

"Eleven o'clock."

"I wonder what I should wear?"

"Something red, my dear, something very, very red."

CHAPTER 60

"The University of Arkansas Razorbacks are on the air. This is Bob Barnes, along with my colleague Dave Winder, tipping off another exciting year of Razorback basketball on the Arkansas Sports Network. This promises to be an interesting year. We'll be seeing a lot of new faces, won't we, Dave?"

"That's right, Bob. Coach Martin hasn't officially named a starting five, but the State's leading newspaper strongly hinted that we'll see three sophomores and two juniors starting for the Hogs."

"The sophomores are exceptional athletes, but athleticism and experience are two different animals. As a former coach, Dave, do you think it's wise to field such a young team?"

"I never liked starting sophomores, but this could be a special class. First, there's Dalton Hilliard, the State MVP in 1969; he plays great defense and has a soft touch. Then there's David Thompson, who always seems to be in the right place at the right time. The wildcard for this team, however, is Jamie Williams. In 1968, Jamie was the State Tournament's MVP, but he injured his knee and didn't play his senior year in high school."

"Jamie Williams is an interesting story, Dave. After his injury, Coach Martin didn't offer him a scholarship, so he walked on at UALR, injured his ankle, completed his freshman year, transferred to the University of Arkansas, and immediately impressed the coaches."

"I watched Jamie Williams play in the 1968 State Tournament, Bob. If the young man plays for the Razorbacks as well as he played for the Kirby Trojans, Razorback fans may be in for an unexpected treat."

"And don't forget about the man, Terrance Brooks, the Hogs six-foot-eleven-inch Center. If his supporting cast pans out, this Razorback team could make some waves."

•   •   •

Howard Martin wondered how well his young Razorbacks would wear the collars he had placed around their necks. When the pressure hit, would they choke? And if they choked, would he be able to control them when he pulled in the reins? In a matter of minutes, he would know. He cleared his throat, smiled, and calmly told his team, "I'm a teacher. Mentally, physically, and tactically, you're prepared. Hit the court and show me what you've learned."

•   •   •

"Here they come," Bob Barnes observed as the Razorbacks took the court inside Barnhill Field House. "The Sports Information Director just handed me the starting lineup, and as we discussed at the top of the broadcast, Coach Martin is starting the sophomores."

"That's interesting, Bob. Southwest Missouri State is a veteran team. Howard Martin's young and inexperienced Razorbacks may have their hands full tonight."

"At least we'll know, when the dust settles in Barnhill, if the sophomores are as good as Coach Martin thinks they are, and if the confidence he has in them is merited."

•   •   •

The crowd was subdued and small. Jamie had expected a larger turnout, but he understood that four losing seasons had dampened the fans' enthusiasm toward Razorback basketball. Winning, he believed, would bring them back, and he intended to reestablish that winning tradition by beating the dog out of the Southwest Missouri State University Bears.

Except for Terrance Brooks, the fans had little to cheer about. The new players, all with unfamiliar names, had never played a varsity game. Despite the small crowd and empty seats, Jamie's spine tingled when the public address announcer called out his name for the first time in Barnhill Field House. He clenched his right hand, raised a fist into the air, then ran to mid-court and stood next to Terrance Brooks.

The small crowd cheered when Terrance tipped the ball to Jamie, then roared when Dalton received a pinpoint pass down court and laid the ball in for an easy two points. The Bears, a patient offensive team, passed the ball repeatedly, overloading one side of the Arkansas matchup zone and then the other. The Hogs responded by applying tight defensive pressure, forcing the ball away from the goal. Finally, an impatient Guard put up an ill-advised jumper from downtown Fayetteville and missed badly.

Jamie grabbed the ball, ran down court, and surveyed the zone defense packed tightly beneath the goal. Southwest Missouri's approach to the game, as Coach Martin had expected, was box in Terrance Brooks and beat the Arkansas Razorbacks.

Not this year.

Jamie shot the ball from the top of the key and hit nothing but net.

Trying to counter the lucky shot, Southwest Missouri State ran the ball down court, but Terrance Brooks, filling the lane, raised his arms and blocked an easy chip-shot. David Thompson chased down the loose ball and passed the ball to Jamie on the left wing. Jamie faked a pass to Dalton, then threaded the needle and hit Terrance Brooks with a pinpoint pass. Terrance responded with a bone-crushing slam.

The crowd jumped to its feet and roared.

Stunned, Southwest Missouri State called timeout but could not adjust to the Razorback's up-tempo style of play. Something new was going on in Arkansas and the Bears could not stop it. When the first half ended with the Razorbacks holding a comfortable eighteen-point lead, Howard Martin glanced at the scoreboard, headed for the dressing room, and asked Coach Culver, "Bobby, how good are these guys?"

"They *will* be National Champions, Howard."

•　　•　　•

Jamie and Dalton drove their parents to Drake Field and watched the Cessna accelerate down the runway, reach for the sky, and then disappear into the darkness. It had been a relaxed and fun evening. Old animosities that Jamie and Dalton knew nothing about had given way to a new camaraderie between two proud fathers who relished watching their sons play as Razorbacks.

As Jamie pulled off the Drake Field parking lot onto Highway 71 and headed back to Fayetteville, Dalton said, "I think we played a hell of a game tonight."

"Coach Martin seemed pleased."

"Do you think Southwest Missouri is any good?"

"I don't know. But even if they aren't, the game was never close."

"Did you feel comfortable? You know? Like you belonged out there?"

"I was a little tight at first. I haven't played in two years."

"It didn't show, man."

"You don't think I looked rusty?"

"Hell no! Your passing was right on the money. And the fakes! I had to keep my eyes on you constantly. I was afraid you'd flip me a quick pass and I wouldn't be ready."

"Terrance was amazing tonight, and the way he dominated the middle was incredible. After a few tries, the Fuzzy-Wuzzy Bears backed off and settled for long-range jump shots. They had enough of Terrance the first five minutes of the game."

"Terrance Brooks is the best Center in the country, Jamie."

"Take it to the bank, Dalton. This team is going to be something special."

•   •   •

The Razorback coaching staff was ecstatic following the game. The Hogs had shot 64 percent from the field, had out rebounded Southwest Missouri by ten, and committed only six turnovers.

"How can we top this, Boss?" Bobby Culver asked jokingly.

Howard Martin scanned the stat sheet and replied, "I just hope they didn't play their best game of the year on opening night."

Coach Harrell leaned back in his chair, then abruptly sat up and said, "Howard, you have to feel good. Southwest Missouri made us look like dogs last year. Tonight, *we* schooled *them*. I know it's only the first game, but like I've said all along, these kids can go all the way. They're quick, they're strong, they're disciplined, and their team chemistry is phenomenal."

"You may be right, Jackie, but the season is young and so are they. Eventually, a team will come along that has their number. It's easy to play loose when you have a big lead. The question is, how will they play when the game gets tight?"

"Personally," Coach Harrell replied, "I believe they'll display the same discipline and character they showed tonight. But you're right, Howard. A close game will tell the tale."

"Tonight was fun, gentlemen. Let's go home and savor it. The next game may not be as enjoyable."

"Good idea," Coach Culver agreed. "But think about! If we win our first five games, we'll be undefeated when we go to Atlanta for the Dixie Classic. If we win the Dixie Classic, we may crack the Top Twenty."

Howard Martin laughed and said, "Good thought, Bobby, but we have four games facing us, and once we're in Atlanta, we'll face two of the top teams in the country."

"And we'll beat them, too," Coach Culver confidently replied.

CHAPTER 61

The predominately University of Georgia crowd reacted with intense enthusiasm when the eleventh ranked Bulldogs took the floor inside Atlanta's Omni Arena. Jamie leaned toward Dalton and nodded at the stands. "Hostile bunch, huh?"

Dalton laughed and said, "I don't think they like us very much." Then he lowered his voice—he was good at impersonating Coach Martin—and added, "They won't like it when we school their precious Bulldogs on the art of offensive and defensive basketball."

Jamie chuckled and turned to Terrance Brooks. "Are you ready to send the Puppy Dogs home with their tails tucked between their legs?"

"You get me the ball, Jamie, and I'll make them eat it."

Jamie walked to the Razorback's bench and sat down. The game was televised and, for the first time in his collegiate career, a sportscaster had interviewed him. Jamie frowned as he recalled how amused the prominent know-it-all had been when he told him that the Razorbacks would defeat Georgia convincingly.

•   •   •

Surprised to see the Bulldogs packed in a tight zone, Jamie passed the ball to Dalton on the left wing and rotated to the top of the key. Seeing Jamie lightly guarded, Dalton passed him the ball. Jamie confidently ripped the net for an easy two.

Georgia in-bounded quickly, ran down court, and tried to force the ball inside, but the Bulldog's Center, athletic but surprisingly skinny, could not handle Terrance Brooks. Like previous opponents the Hogs had faced, the Bulldogs became impatient and forced an ill-advised shot that Terrance rebounded, swinging his body from side to side, defying anyone to tie him up or steal the ball.

Despite Jamie's lucky first shot, Georgia continued to box in Terrance Brooks. It was blatantly obvious that the Bulldogs did not respect the Razorback's perimeter game. Again, lightly guarded, Jamie took the open shot and hit nothing but net.

Georgia called timeout.

The pressure came, but instead of being pushed around, Jamie spun, penetrated the lane, and passed the ball to Terrance Brooks, who slammed it home. The partisan crowd mumbled discontentedly.

Georgia finally scored, but Arkansas' quick hands, quick feet and quick tempo had confused and surprised them. The Bulldogs did not recover, folded their tent in the second half, and lost the game by sixteen points.

The final game with the fifth ranked LSU Tigers was a totally different experience. The Tigers were one of the more physical teams in college basketball and it took the Razorbacks time to adjust to their style of play. Arkansas trailed by four points at halftime.

The second half, however, was a different story. The Razorbacks gradually took control of the game, won by eight points, and in the process opened a few eyes concerning Howard Martin and his undefeated Razorbacks.

.   .   .

Lulled by the monotonous hum of jet engines, Jamie reclined his seat and closed his eyes. He was tired and wanted to sleep on the flight back to Fayetteville. Dalton, too excited to sleep, elbowed Jamie in the ribs and asked, "Since we won the Dixie Classic and beat two ranked teams, do you think we'll crack the Top-Twenty this week?"

"I think we deserve it."

"If we're not, rankings are a joke."

"According to Coach Martin, the only poll that counts is the one at the end of the season."

"That's bullshit and you know it." Jamie chuckled. "All I'm asking for is a little respect."

"Respect will come, Dalton."

"When?"

"In March when we win the National Championship."

"You think we're *that* good?"

"We just beat two of the best teams in the country, Terrance Brooks is the best Center in the country, you, David and Tommy are great players, I've never lost a basketball game, and I don't intend to lose one now."

Dalton had known Jamie for years, both as a friend and as an adversary, and he had never heard him make a statement he could not back up. "You're serious, aren't you?"

"Yep."

"You lied to me before the Southwest Missouri State game, didn't you?"

"Yes, I did."

"You're never nervous, are you, Jamie?"

"No."

"Why?"

"I know what I'm supposed to do, and I do it."

"That's too simple."

"I don't see giants when I take the court, Dalton."

"What *do* you see, Jamie?"

"I see five guys who are about to get their asses kicked." Dalton chuckled. "When I was rehabbing my knee two years ago, Dad quoted a scripture that said you are what you think." Jamie tapped his head. "It's all in here, Dalton."

"So, you *think* you're the best Point Guard in the country?"

"I *know* I'm the best Point Guard in the country."

"You're crazy as hell, Jamie."

"There's a thin line between genius and insanity, Dalton, and if you haven't figured it out by now, I walk that line. I always have, and I always will. I don't want anyone, especially teams I play against, to figure me out. I like to keep people guessing."

CHAPTER 62

The Arkansas Razorbacks' perfect fourteen and zero record had little effect on national coaches and media. Going into conference play, the Hogs still were not ranked in the polls. The Razorbacks had not played a cupcake schedule, but the preseason favorites were having banner years, and the upstart Hogs were largely ignored.

The media's cold-shoulder, however, was having a positive effect on Howard Martin's team. In fact, the Razorbacks believed the only way to prove themselves was by winning. Polls, Coach Martin believed, were—to a degree—political, but admitted that they were usually accurate. Despite what he told his players—focus on games, not polls—he believed his Razorbacks were one of the best teams in the country and that his feisty young Hogs belonged in the AP Top-Twenty.

Following Monday's practice, he tuned in a local sports station, smiled when he heard the latest AP poll, and then walked down the concrete-block corridor to the Razorback dressing room. Coach Martin usually left his players with the trainers when practice concluded. When he walked into the dressing room, they sensed something unusual had happened and immediately stopped talking.

"Not that it means anything, gentlemen, but according to the Associated Press, we're ranked Number-Nineteen this week." Cheers echoed off the walls. "Which means we have lost the element of surprise and that the target is now on our backs. I'm confident, however, that you'll handle being the favorite as well you've handled being the underdog."

Coach Martin returned to his office, picked up the newspaper he had not taken time to read earlier in the day, and frowned when he read a well-known reporter's interview with Coach Warren Billingsley, the head coach at Texas A & M. When asked about the recent success of the Arkansas Razorbacks, Coach Billingsley said, "The Razorbacks are playing above their heads. There's no way three sophomores and two juniors can maintain that kind of intensity. They just sneaked up on Georgia and LSU."

When asked about the emergence of Jamie Williams, Coach Billingsley said, "He's too young and too fragile to have a long-term impact on the league." The article closed with Coach Billingsley saying, "Hogs are dirty, they smell bad, and when conference play is complete, the Razorbacks will wallow in the mud where they belong."

Howard Martin knew Coach Billingsley was just being witty—he was known for his off-the-cuff remarks—but he thought the statement about Jamie being fragile was a low blow. He dropped the newspaper on his desk, leaned back in his chair, and smiled, knowing a transfer of power was about to take place; the Arkansas Razorbacks were going to win the Southwest Conference championship —there was not a doubt in his mind—and Texas A & M would be the first to fall.

•   •   •

A cold northwest wind greeted Jamie and Michelle when they exited Barnhill Field House. The sky was dark, gray, and spitting occasional snowflakes. The Nova's engine sputtered, then came to life, reluctantly warming against the unusually cold weather.

Jamie pulled out of the parking lot, headed downtown, and stopped at the Pizza Hut on College Avenue. Forty-five minutes later, it was snowing harder when he parked the Nova in the Martin's driveway and followed Michelle into the house.

A fire was blazing in the den. Jamie walked to the fireplace, briefly warmed his hands, then sat next to Michelle on the sofa and dove into the pizza. Twenty minutes later, full and contented, he stretched and laid his head against the sofa.

"Are you tired?"

"It's been a hard week. You know? Getting ready for the conference opener and all."

"Do you ever get tired of basketball, Jamie? You hardly have time for anything else."

"Yes, and no."

"What do you mean?"

"I love the game, but basketball and school are demanding."

"Have you ever thought of giving it up?"

"When I hurt my knee, I hated not playing."

"I've read, if you keep it up, that you'll probably be drafted and earn a big salary in the pros."

"With three years of college ahead of me, that seems a long way off."

"If you do make it big, Jamie, what would you do with the money?"

"Buy some property near Kirby, build a house with a gigantic fireplace and windows overlooking the mountains, drink coffee, ride dirt bikes, and write the great American novel."

Michelle frowned. "You'd become a hermit?" she asked incredulously. "That's insane."

"One man's trash is another man's treasure, Michelle."

"I want to live in a big city: Houston, Memphis, or Dallas. I thought you wanted that, too."

"Why?"

"Because you're so outgoing. You know? Like after the Dixie Classic? You were in your element when that television guy interviewed you after the LSU game."

"I like the attention, Michelle, but to be honest, I can live without it. It's no big deal to me."

"Are you telling me you could walk away from the newspaper articles, television interviews, and having your picture in the paper with no regrets?"

"Probably."

"I don't think you could."

"Why?"

"Because you like it too much."

Jamie's eyes narrowed. A sign, Michelle knew, that anger, always simmering beneath the surface, was about to explode like a gaseous, pressure-filled volcano. She had forgotten how quickly Jamie could lose his powder-keg temper.

"I like what playing basketball does for me," Jamie replied calmly and deliberately. Another sign, Michelle knew, that he, like a startled rattlesnake, was coiled and ready to strike, "but I don't know what the future holds. I may earn a million dollars or die a pauper. You may become a lawyer or do something else. Right now, I'm playing for the Razorbacks and getting some attention. The only thing I'm sure of is, I have now, this moment, and I intend to enjoy every minute."

Determined not to lose his temper and say something he would regret later, Jamie took a deep breath, stretched, and calmly said, "I guess we're not as much alike as we thought."

"But don't you think we're good for each other?" Michelle asked.

"Most of the time," Jamie replied matter-of-factly.

• • •

G. Rolly White Coliseum was jampacked, loud and rowdy when the Razorbacks entered the raucous arena. Coach Warren Billingsley's off-the-cuff remarks had not bothered Jamie at all—the Aggie's head coach had recruited him in 1968 and he liked the man—but borrowing Coach Martin's terminology, he intended to teach the Aggies, emphatically and on their home-court, the art of offensive and defensive basketball.

On the first possession, Jamie made a quick move to the basket, challenged the Aggie Center, was fouled, and smiled smugly when the ball fell through the net. The crowd booed rudely, but that was okay—Jamie had faced many raucous crowds. He stepped to the charity stripe and completed the three-point play.

From that point on, the first half belonged to the Razorbacks. The defending Southwest Conference Champions, out of sync, fell behind and were down by twelve points at intermission. But in the second half, the Aggies employed a new strategy: get physical and manhandle Jamie Williams. In fact, the first attack caught Jamie by surprise when two slapping, double-teaming Aggies stripped the ball and knocked him to the floor. With no foul called, an A & M Guard took the ball to the hoop for an easy two points.

As the game became more physical, the Aggie press became vicious. Three minutes into the second half, Jamie caught an in-bounds pass from Dalton and was again knocked to the floor. On hands and knees, he scrambled for the ball, but it rolled out of bounds and the Aggies gained possession. Jamie slapped the floor in frustration.

Coach Martin jumped to his feet and yelled, "Hey, Ref! Is your whistle broke?" The referee turned his back and ignored him. Coach Martin stormed the court and continued his tirade.

"We may be the only non-Texas school in the Southwest Conference, but that doesn't mean you have to call the game one-sided. Where are you from? College Station?"

Red-faced, the referee called a technical foul and put the Aggies on the free-throw line. Then, when A & M converted an awesome slam, Coach Martin called timeout. The crowd yelled boisterously as the Razorbacks gathered around their coach.

Following the timeout, the Razorbacks maintained their lead, but the physical approach continued. With ten minutes left in the game, and the contest still up for grabs, Jamie made a quick move to the basket, was pushed from behind, and fell awkwardly to the floor. He could not believe the official had not called a foul. Frustrated, he jumped up, fronted the guilty player, and scowled tauntingly.

A referee stepped between the two smirking players and sent both teams to their benches. When play resumed, skilled passing, precise shooting, powerful rebounding, solid defense, and an enraged six-foot-eleven-inch Center overwhelmed the Aggies and gave the Razorbacks their first victory in the Southwest Conference round robin.

When the final seconds ticked off the clock and the buzzer sounded, Howard Martin walked to mid-court and shook Warren Billingsley's hand. Not surprising him, the A & M coach smiled warmly and said, "You have a hell of a team, Howard."

"Thanks, Warren. For a herd of smelly hogs, they play some pretty good basketball."

Both coaches laughed and headed for their dressing rooms.

CHAPTER 63

Followers of Southwest Conference basketball were shocked when the University of Arkansas defeated Texas A & M, Baylor, Texas Tech, Rice, Texas Christian University, Southern Methodist University, and the University of Texas convincingly and that midway through the conference round robin the Hogs were in sole possession of first place with a pristine 22 & 0 record. The Razorbacks had risen to Number Ten in the polls, a lofty ranking, but not complimentary since the University of Maryland Terrapins, the only other undefeated team, was ranked Number One.

Since the Razorbacks had breezed through the first half of the season, Coach Martin thought opposing coaches would know what to expect and be more adept at stopping it. Coach Martin, however, was wrong. The conference race never heated up, and with one road-game remaining, the Texas Tech Red Raiders at Lubbock, the Razorbacks seemed, to some observers, invincible.

The pressure was intense and mounting weekly, but Coach Martin believed his young Razorbacks had proved they were more than capable of handling the heat. A victory over Texas

Tech would give them a perfect 29 & 0 record, and five post-season victories would earn them a national championship.

For the first time in his coaching career, Howard Martin thought a national championship was within reach, but quickly chased the thought from his mind. It was too early to think about the NCAA Tournament. As always, it was one game at a time.

•   •   •

"Marian, this is Jamie."

"I thought you'd probably call."

"I didn't know if you'd want me to. How are things going?"

"Scholastically or sexually?"

Marian's natural bluntness shocked Jamie. Without a second thought, she usually said the first thing that popped into her mind. "Things in general, Marian," Jamie answered dryly.

"In general, everything's fine. Sexually, it's rather slow. You're the one I want."

"Marian, you know…"

"I'm not a fool, Jamie. Your letters always came like clockwork. When you stopped writing in October, I suspected that you and Michelle had gotten back together."

"I didn't want to hurt you, Marian."

"But you *did* hurt me, Jamie. I thought we settled everything between us. Then you sent me a bullshit letter filled with flowery regrets. After the initial shock, I felt jilted, even used. But do you want to hear something stupid?"

"What, Marian?"

"I still love you."

Jamie groaned.

"I even thought about transferring to the University of Arkansas, but logic prevailed, and I stayed at Texas Tech. To be honest, though, if circumstances were different, your darling Michelle would have some stiff competition because I'm convinced that in less than five minutes I could have you scratching on my panties again."

"You know I loved you, Marian?"

"Loved, Jamie? You still love me. Sure, Michelle was in the back of your mind, but if you'll practice the honesty you're always preaching, you'll find that I'm there now." Jamie took a deep breath and didn't respond. "Do you remember what I told you?"

"That I have to tell you I don't love and want you anymore?"

"You never told me, Jamie."

"Wouldn't that be cruel?"

"In the long run, wouldn't it be kinder?" Marian took a deep breath, then asked, "Are you ready to tell me, Jamie?"

"Tell you what?"

"Don't be an evasive ass! Are you ready to tell me you don't love me and that you don't want me anymore?" Jamie took a deep breath, exhaled loudly, and did not answer the question. "Just as I thought. There's no way you can tell me that."

"I'm not enjoying this conversation."

"I didn't enjoy your bullshit letter."

"Damn, Marian! I thought I finally had my shit together."

"If you had your shit together, Jamie, you wouldn't have called me. You had to know if I'm putting out for someone else. Well, I'm not, and I won't, until I know there's absolutely no hope for us."

Jamie sighed deeply. "I'd like to see you, Marian."

"I'll be at the game tonight."

"I'd meet you for lunch, but Coach Martin won't let us out of his sight."

"I'll be at the coliseum early. We can talk then."

"I want to do more than talk."

"What am I going to do with you, Jamie?"

"What you always do."

"You're a two-timing jerk."

"I know."

"Goodbye, Jamie. I'll see you tonight."

"Goodbye, Marian."

•   •   •

Jamie and Marian sat in the bleachers and talked until his teammates began filtering into the arena. Uncomfortable with their suspicious stares, he knew it was time to leave. Marian laughed. "Are you afraid your little friends will tattle?"

"No, but Coach Martin will pitch a shit-fit if he sees me sitting in the stands."

Marian draped her arms over Jamie's shoulders, kissed him, lingered, then pulled away. He watched her leave and then stepped onto the glistening hardwood floor. The brief time he had spent with Marian confirmed what he already knew: he was in love with two women.

Jamie stood motionless at the top of the key, lost in his thoughts. Dalton passed him a basketball. He caught it, squared up to the goal, shot, and hit nothing but net.

Dalton laughed. "What's so funny?"

"You."

"Me? Why?"

"One second you're thinking about your X-girlfriend, who is the best-looking girl I've ever seen, and the next second I flip you a basketball and you rip the net like there's nothing on your mind by the Texas Tech Red Raiders."

Jamie smiled facetiously. "What can I say?"

"Did you dump her?"

"Hell, no!"

"Are you going to dump, Michelle?"

"Hell, no!"

"You're insane, Jamie."

"What else is new?"

Jamie grabbed a loose ball, drove to the basket, and laid it in. The one thing he was sure of was basketball. He was a greedy, two-timing jerk, but when it came to basketball, he had no doubts. He understood the game, and he knew how to win.

The contest with the Texas Tech Red Raiders was never in doubt, as the Razorbacks built their usual first-half lead. Unfortunately, the Red Raider's second-half strategy failed miserably. Hoping to gain a rebound and two points, they fouled repeatedly. Howard Martin, however, opted to keep the ball in Jamie's hands — he *was* the leading free-throw shooter in the country. With ice-water running through his veins, Jamie hit the one-in-ones repeatedly. As the final seconds ticked off the clock, Coach Martin relaxed and shook hands with the losing coach, knowing his Southwest Conference Champions had earned a berth in the NCAA Tournament. After a brief interview, he walked into the Razorback dressing room, raised five fingers into the air, and exuberantly yelled, "Five more wins, gentlemen."

The Hogs exploded, uniting in a cause. They had to win it all. Nothing else would suffice.

CHAPTER 64

"Mrs. Martin, Coach has given us a couple of days off before the tournament. Is it okay if Michelle spends the weekend in Benton with my parents and me?"

Pamela Martin had grown accustomed to Michelle and Jamie being inseparable—he often slept on the sofa in the den—and she did not have a problem with Michelle staying with the Williams, good friends she knew and trusted.

"That's fine, Jamie," she replied. "Just be careful driving to Benton."

Ten minutes later, he loaded Michelle's suitcase in the trunk and headed south out of Fayetteville on the Pig Trail—a crooked and steep road students and fans occasionally drove instead of the heavily traveled Highway 71—to Interstate 40 near Ozark. Two hours later, he pulled into the Brownwood Subdivision and parked in his parent's driveway.

That evening, after watching a movie at the Royal Theater, he and Michelle pulled onto the Minute Man parking lot, where, to his surprise, he received a hero's welcome. Jamie had not forgotten the lonely months he had spent at Benton High School but quickly decided that being an asshole would get him in trouble—Coach Martin told his players repeatedly that they were ambassadors for the university *and* the State of Arkansas—so he smiled at the friendly greetings, accepted the warm handshakes, then scooted into the Nova and handed Michelle a Coke.

"For someone who hates Benton, you have a lot of friends."

"The only reason they're talking to me is because I play for the Razorbacks."

"You love it, don't you, Jamie?"

"It's better than being an outcast."

Michelle shook her head and laughed.

"What's so funny?"

"You."

"Why me?"

"Not long ago, on a snowy night in Fayetteville, you told me you didn't need the publicity *or* the popularity, that you wanted to build a house in the woods and get away from it all."

"In time, I could, but since I play for the Razorbacks, why not enjoy the benefits?"

"I've known you for five years, Jamie. You've never been stuck-up, but there's one thing you've always loved." He stared darts into Michelle's eyes, knowing he would not like her assessment. "The spotlight. You know? Center court."

"I never said that I don't like what basketball does for me." Michelle saw fire in Jamie's eyes. They reminded her of the day he challenged the first-period English class to a fight at Bogalusa Junior High School. "Two years ago, my leg was in a cast, and I couldn't play basketball. Guess what? The sun came up every morning. For a while, I was so depressed I had to reach up to scratch bottom. Dad told me I was like a Greek god who had had his wings clipped, that I had to learn to live in the real world like every mortal. That pissed me off at first, then I thought about it, and it made sense, so I applied myself to other things—my schoolwork, my writing—and I found that Jamie Williams is more than a basketball player, that he is a guy who can do a lot of things. So, don't think I can't live without the cheering crowds and the newspaper articles. I can, I have."

"I understand what you're saying, Jamie. You *are* a good student, and you have a way with words. All I'm saying is, you shouldn't bury your personality down a dirt road."

"You want to know what *your* problem is?"

Michelle stiffened. "I don't have a problem."

"You worry too much about five or ten years down the road and are always thinking about what might or might not happen. Why worry about tomorrow when all we have is today? You're right. I like the attention—I always have and I always will—and I enjoy being with you...when you're not obsessing about the future."

"Do you ever think about the future, Jamie?"

"I'm too damned busy with the present."

"You never think about a pro-contract and making money."

"I can't do that."

"Why?"

Jamie hesitated, then mumbled, "I don't know how long my knee will hold up."

"It's not hurting you, is it?"

"No, but I'm living on borrowed time."

"I hadn't thought about that."

"Coach Lequieu told me there would come a day when an education would mean more than basketball. For me, that day arrived two years ago on Lake Greeson. Three months later, limping around Panther Field House on a shriveled-up-leg that hurt like hell and doubting that I would ever play basketball again, I realized Coach Lequieu was right. That's why I bust my ass at school. I graduated with honors from Benton High School, and I'll graduate with honors from the University of Arkansas simply because I know the odds are against me making it to the pros."

"So, the invincible Jamie Williams is a realist, after all."

"Hell, yes! I have no idea what I'll be when I grow up."

"Don't be a smartass, Jamie."

"I've always been a smartass, Michelle — you know that — but there's one thing I'll never be."

"What will you never be, Jamie?"

"A washed-up jock wondering what the hell to do with his life when he can't play basketball anymore."

•   •   •

As the morning sun filtered through the window, Jamie looked around his bedroom, momentarily lost, and then remembered he was home. A lawnmower hummed monotonously, as a meticulous, early rising neighbor got a head start on the early spring grass.

Jamie slipped out of bed, pulled on a pair of jeans, stepped outside, picked up the Sunday paper, then walked back into the house and put on a pot of coffee. When the water started gurgling through the filter, he eased into the living room, sat in his father's recliner, and began reading the sports section, eager to see what teams had won their conference tournaments, when an article by Graham Wallace caught his eye:

In Retrospect

Graham Wallace

Republic Sports Editor

For the first time in years, the Arkansas Razorbacks men's basketball team will be competing in the NCAA Tournament with a legitimate shot at winning the National Championship. Considering the recent lack of success in men's basketball, what is it that makes this team different? Why the turnaround?

In retrospect, this very successful season started five years ago at Central Junior High School in Hot Springs. I had the privilege of watching the Spartans win a conference title with Terrance Brooks and Jamie Williams leading the way. As I watched Jamie Williams play, it occurred to me I had never witnessed such an outstanding display of shooting in my life. The way Jamie shot the ball, and the way it sailed through the net, was almost eerie.

I spoke with Coach Jim Johnson after the game about the Williams kid, and all he said was, "He could shoot the ball when I met him." Naturally, I pressed a little harder, and according to the notes I still possess, Coach Johnson said, "Jamie played basketball with older kids and from the fifth grade on he could shoot." Coach Johnson then said, "I talked to his brother, and he says, and don't quote me on this, Graham, that Jamie has a gift, and that he just can't miss."

Pure fantasy?

Think about this: Jamie Williams started playing organized basketball five years ago and has never lost a game. In his career, Jamie has won 186 games. In 1965 and 1966, he earned two MVP awards in Louisiana. In 1967, he was named Arkansas Newcomer of the Year. In 1968, he was named the MVP of the Overall State Basketball Tournament. A knee injury kept Jamie from becoming the Player of the Year in 1969. Currently, he leads the nation in field goal and free-throw percentages.

Coincidence?

Fantasy?

Back to the interview five years ago.

After Coach Johnson told me Jamie's brother believed he had a special gift, I asked, rather sarcastically I might add, "Do you believe that, Jim?" Coach Johnson, looking rather sheepish, replied, "No, of course not. But I will admit I've never seen anyone shoot a basketball like Jamie Williams."

Later that evening, I could not sleep, so I went to my study, looked over my notes, and asked myself, "Does God look down from Heaven and say, "Here's a good kid. I'm going to give him the gift of shooting a basketball. Go out and get 'em, son?"

Although I laughed at the prospect, at the ridiculousness of such an absurd thought, deep inside I had a gnawing feeling that said, "There may be something to it."

Now, after seeing the turnaround the Razorbacks have made this year, the same gnawing question has returned: Does Jamie Williams have a special gift that others do not have? When the ball leaves his hand, and it goes in more often than not, is there a supernatural force leading it to the basket?

Commonsense says, "No," because no one believes in such hocus-pocus, especially an old and battered sportswriter. Yet, if I was a betting man, I would place my money on Jamie Williams and the Arkansas Razorbacks to win the National Championship.

Why?

Call it fate, call it luck, call it skill, call it what you want. Against all odds the cards have fallen the Hog's way this year, and the NCAA Tournament will be no different.

Woo — Pig — Sooie!

After Jamie finished reading the article, his thoughts drifted back to a conversation he had had with Coach Sam Lequieu at Bogalusa Junior High School. Coach Sam had asked him, "Has anyone ever told you why you're such a good basketball player?" and then pointed out that other players could not do what he did on a basketball court because they were not as talented as he was. Then he corrected himself and said, "No, as gifted as you are." Jamie remembered telling Coach Sam the moment his brother put a basketball in his hands, he knew he was born to play the game. Coach Lequieu then advised him about playing with "mere mortals," as he had called them.

Jamie had not paid a great deal of attention to everything Coach Sam said that day. He had taken his advice about not acting or feeling superior. He was an excellent student, and he was not a ball hog. But what Coach Sam said about being gifted simply went in one ear and out the other.

Jamie thought about his basketball savvy for a few seconds, wondered briefly if he had a special gift, then shook his head, folded the paper, and laughed. "What's so funny?" Michelle asked as she walked into the den and leaned over the back of the recliner.

"In today's article, Graham Wallace insinuates that I have some kind of supernatural gift."

"He's just written what everyone already knows. Dad says there'll…"

"Go ahead, Michelle. Finish your statement."

"I don't think I'm supposed to."

"Don't keep me hanging. What did Coach Martin say?"

"He said there'll never be another player like you, that you have *something* he's never seen before: an uncanny ability to put the ball through the hole when there's no way—humanly speaking—to do it."

Jamie chuckled and said, "I guess that means I'm out of this world, doesn't it?"

Michelle rolled her eyes. "Don't let it go to your head, superstar. Achilles had his heel and Superman has his Krypton, so I'm sure you have your weakness, too."

"Yeah, my left knee."

"I didn't mean that the way it sounded, Jamie."

He smiled smugly. "Other than that, I don't have any weaknesses."

Michelle rolled her eyes. "You really *are* an arrogant prima donna."

Jamie stood and headed toward the freshly brewed coffee. "Graham Wallace's article may be funny, but I guarantee the rest of the team won't let me live it down. They're going to ride me high over this one. You can take *that* to the bank."

CHAPTER 65

"Good evening. I am Vern Holloway, and this is my colleague, Stan Attwood, coming to you live from Norman Oklahoma for first round action in the Mid-West Region of the NCAA Tournament. Stan, what do you think of this evening's matchup between the Arkansas Razorbacks and the Kansas Jayhawks?"

"This will be an interesting game, Vern. First, tournament action is not new to Kansas. The Jayhawks are a veteran team and have had an outstanding season. Personally, I feel the Jayhawks may be dark horse contenders for the Final Four. But the University of Arkansas Razorbacks may have something to say about that, as they play the role of Cinderella this year. Coach Howard Martin, coming off two disappointing seasons, has led the Razorbacks to a perfect 29 and 0 record."

"The question is, Stan, are the Razorbacks for real?"

"Obviously, to go undefeated and to be ranked Number Ten in the nation, Arkansas is a good team. But are they experienced enough? And what caliber of competition have they played?"

"They won the Dixie Classic," Stan Attwood interjected.

"That was early in the season and doesn't carry a great deal of weight now. The Razorbacks compete in the Southwest Conference, which, as you know, isn't a basketball league."

"That's a valid point, Vern—football is king in the Southwest Conference—but since the Razorbacks have an unblemished record, let's look at their personnel and see how they match up with the University of Kansas."

"Stan, the Razorbacks have Terrance Brooks, an outstanding Center. If the Hogs were a little less obscure, I believe he would be an All-American. The only upperclassman who gets much playing time is Tommy Jackson, a tough defensive player who is dangerous close to the basket. The rest of the Razorbacks starters are sophomores."

"Are the young Hogs as good as we've been told?" Stan Attwood asked.

"They're outstanding. David Thompson crashes the boards with reckless abandon. Dalton Hilliard, the Off-Guard, is an outstanding defensive player. And, of course, there's Jamie Williams."

"Oh, yes, the gifted one. An article in Arkansas' leading newspaper has received a lot of national attention. It seems Jamie Williams is such a good shooter that some folks think he's blessed. You know? The Good Lord watches over him and gives him a little help from time to time. What do you think, Vern?"

"Gift or no gift, Jamie Williams may need divine intervention tonight. Kansas is a physical team. They've been here before, and even if the Jayhawks are a higher seed, their physicality and experience may overwhelm the Razorback's youth and inexperience."

"What do you think Arkansas' primary weakness is, Vern?"

"Depth. Grant it, the Razorbacks have a great starting-five, but they don't have a bench. In this, and every game during the tournament, fatigue will be a factor."

Stan Attwood turned toward the camera, smiled, and said, "The Arkansas Razorbacks are a good team, but they are new to tournament action, which may be their greatest weakness.

After a commercial break, we'll discuss the Kansas Jayhawks, a team that will not sail silently into the night."

•   •   •

Because of Graham Wallace's article, the week had not been easy for Jamie. He was, it seemed, the one player in the Tournament who received the most attention. Everything from his *miraculous*, as they were calling it, recovery from knee surgery to his free-spirited personality were open for scrutiny. One reporter even credited his father's ministry as the reason for Jamie's *supernatural* ability to shoot a basketball.

Jamie struggled with how to handle his elevated status. Coach Martin told him that the Sports Information Director would handle the reporters. Jamie's teammates, however, had urged him to take advantage of the situation by dropping subtle hints, bringing all the publicity he could to the Razorback program.

When the Razorbacks arrived in Oklahoma City — according to the predetermined agenda — the team had to meet with the press for pregame pictures and interviews. Surprisingly, nothing was said about Graham Wallace's article or Jamie's so-called gift. But as the session concluded, one reporter smugly asked, "Hey, Jamie, do you really have a gift?"

There was a moment of tense silence. A few snickers filtered through the arena. The same reporter then asked, "Are you going to use witchcraft against the Jayhawks?"

Coach Martin stepped toward the podium, but before he could intervene, Jamie smiled mischievously and replied, "I'm going to use anything I can to beat Kansas."

Relaxed laughter quickly replaced the tension. Small groups of reporters turned to one another and whispered, "What did he mean? Is he admitting that he has a special gift?"

Cameras flashed, reporters reached for their pads, and Jamie realized worrying about Graham Wallace's article had been a waste of time. He was just a story, nothing more, nothing less.

•   •   •

Vern Holloway was stunned. The Arkansas Razorbacks had literally destroyed the Kansas Jayhawks and were leading by twenty-two points at the half. He turned to his colleague during a commercial break and asked, "How about them Hogs, Stan?"

"They're a hell of a team. I've watched a lot of basketball this year, and honestly, I haven't seen a better inside-outside combination than Brooks and Williams."

"To tell you the truth, Stan, I'm tempted to believe the hocus-pocus about Jamie Williams. He's one *hell* of a basketball player."

Stan Attwood laughed. "We both know it takes five games to win the championship, but gift or no gift, the Razorbacks have a chance to go all the way."

"Maryland is the Number-One seed, and they are a great team, but when, and I mean *when*, the Terrapins face the Razorbacks in the finals, they had better bring breakfast, lunch *and* dinner."

•   •   •

After the Razorback's convincing win, Stan Attwood, microphone in hand, approached Howard Martin. "Coach, how does it feel to have that first tournament win under your belt?"

"It feels good, Stan. The young men did everything I asked. They're phenomenal."

"Vern Holloway and I were impressed with the inside-outside combination of Williams and Brooks. Can the rest of the field expect the same strategy?"

"That's been our approach all year. No changes now. We'll stick with what got us here."

Attwood said, "Thanks, Coach," then turned to Terrance Brooks. "You looked like a man on a mission tonight, Terrance. How did you get open so easily against a tough Kansas defense?"

"Like most teams, the Jayhawks tried to box me in with a tight zone, but when Jamie hit a couple from downtown, they had to respect the perimeter. That opened things up."

"So, Williams' outside shooting is the key to the Razorback's offense?"

"If Jamie—we have more than one great shooter, by the way—doesn't drop the ball in from outside, whoever we're playing tries to box me in, but as you saw tonight, that won't happen."

"Well, it certainly worked this evening, Terrance, and you played a great game."

Attwood turned to Jamie. "Young man, how do you shoot the ball so well?"

Jamie winked. "Haven't you been reading the papers, Mr. Attwood? I have a gift."

The sportscaster laughed good-naturedly. "After the exhibition you put on tonight, I almost believe it." Attwood glanced at his clipboard. "Unofficially, we have you scoring thirty-one points, leading all scorers. That's not a bad evening's work for a Point-Guard.

"Kansas surprised me by staying in a zone. That helped a lot."

"In the booth, it looked as if the Razorbacks played a near perfect game. Was it just one of those nights? Or can we expect more of the same throughout the tournament?"

"I'd look for more of the same."

Stan Attwood turned and faced the camera.

"There are several outstanding teams in the NCAA Tournament this year, but from what I've seen tonight, the Arkansas Razorbacks are going to make some waves. From Norman, Oklahoma, this is Stan Attwood, wishing you a pleasant evening."

CHAPTER 66

"A penny for your thoughts."

Howard Martin closed his suitcase and sat next to his wife on the bed.

"I was thinking about what the next few days will bring."

"A National Championship, of course."

Howard Martin smiled drolly and rubbed his wife's knee in an aimless circular motion. "It's odd, Pam, how quickly things change. Last year, I didn't think I could keep this job. Now I'm coaching in the Final Four. Do you realize how few men reach this point in their careers?"

"You're one of the few," she replied, a touch of pride in her voice. "Speaking of odd, you know how nervous I am when you're about to play a big game?"

"You're like a cat on a hot tin roof."

"You're facing the two biggest games of your life and I'm not nervous at all. I feel as if it's already in the bag. You know? Like it's inevitable. Arkansas will win the championship."

"You sound like Graham Wallace."

"What does *that* mean?"

"It means you believe Jamie has a special gift."

"And you don't?" Pamela asked incredulously.

"Jamie is a thoroughbred—high-spirited and crazy—who won't stop running until his heart bursts. I think he's the most competitive person I've ever met. What Jamie does during a game seems effortless, but it is the result of hours of repetitive preparation. I think he demands more than I do."

"How?"

"Last week, for example, Jamie lofted a high, arching pass to Terrance. That pass was right on target, but Terrance fumbled it. Jamie never said a word, just talked to Terrance with his eyes. When Terrance ran back down court, he patted Jamie on the butt and told him it wouldn't happen again."

"Then there are Dalton, David, and Tommy. They're all talented athletes, but the glue that holds them together is Jamie Williams. They keep their eyes on him constantly. If their play becomes sloppy, Jamie makes eye contact, and then they go all out, trying desperately, and I mean *desperately,* to pick up their game. It's uncanny."

"Isn't that what you drum into your players? To give their best every time they take the court?"

"Yes, but Jamie's different. He has…"

"A gift?"

"No! He has a way of getting the best out of people, bringing them up to his level. Another example: During the second half of the conference round-robin, the team was flat during practice. The next day Jamie showed up with a tape by Johnny Rivers, plugged it in Barnhill's sound system, and the team practiced in sync with *Memphis* and *Maybelline.* Then when this crazy song, *The Seventh Son,* started playing, Jamie went wild. It was as if his adrenaline had erupted and had lifted him to another level. It rubbed off on the rest of the team, too. We ended up having the best practice of the year."

"Then you *do* think Jamie has a special gift?"

"Not the way the newspapers are saying. Jamie's greatest gift is his knack for getting others to put out and play as a team. If he never played another game for the Razorbacks, I'd hire him as a coach. Jamie is *that* good at motivating and forcing his will."

"That, to me, sounds incredible because Jamie is such a good-natured young man."

"Good-natured? Have you forgotten how he acted when I didn't offer him a scholarship?

"He was upset."

"Whether you're willing to admit it or not, Pam, beneath Jamie's calm demeanor, is a dark side. When I was thinking about offering him a scholarship, Coach Johnson—he's the Head Coach at Hot Springs High School—told me that there are two sides to Jamie, the calm and the angry, that he'd seen the latter in action, that it is quick, decisive, and that Jamie has a touch of Dr. Jekyll and Mr. Hyde. Coach Johnson is right. There are two sides to Jamie Williams. You've seen it, and I've seen it."

"But he seems like such a nice young man. And our daughter loves him."

"All I'm saying is, there's another side to Jamie Williams. To tell you the truth, I believe his dark side, as Coach Johnson called it, is what makes Jamie such a great basketball player."

"Dark side? You make it sound like he is possessed by the devil."

Howard Martin chuckled. "Oh, there's nothing Satanic about Jamie—unless you're trying to guard him—that's when you wish he'd go to hell and play for the devil."

• • •

Jamie placed his suitcase on the floor and stretched out on his bed. He had enjoyed the NCAA tournament, and had, he thought, handled the probing-reporters well, so well, in fact, that he had developed a squeaky-clean persona. Jamie liked the idea of people thinking well of him, but to be honest, he felt like a hypocrite. The media had, in fact, made a big deal out of him being a preacher's son, and had, to a degree, set him up as the epitome of what a young man with character could accomplish without compromising his morals. And that bothered him.

His father *was* a moral man, and Calvin Williams had taught him the morals *he* lived by, the morals *he* based his ministry on, but Jamie knew he was not like his father, never had been, and probably never would be. In fact, Calvin Williams would have a dying calf in a hailstorm if he knew his baby boy had made love to three beautiful young women. Jamie had, in fact, spent three days with Marian during Spring Break. He had lied to Michelle and told her he would be helping his brother-in-law prepare the Benton Panthers for the State Tournament. He helped Phil and the Panthers, but each day after practice he rode his motorcycle to Kirby and an hour after he pulled into Marian's driveway, they were making the beast with two backs in the barn like there was no tomorrow.

Jamie reached for his little red football—he always had one with him—and threw it at the ceiling. Old habits die hard. He had been throwing little, red footballs at ceilings for as long as he could remember, and, as usual, the senseless and repetitious act relaxed him.

Do I want to set the right example? Do I want to be a role model? Hell, no! I like the way Marian wiggles her ass when she pulls down her jeans. I like the way she slithers out of her panties. I like the little moan she makes when I push it in, and come hell or high water, I'm not giving that up.

He threw the little red football across the room and it hit the wall next to Dalton's bed.

So what if I have a few skeletons in my closet? That doesn't make me a bad person. It just means I like girls, and that I need to work on being…moral, or at least being faithful to one girl.

Jamie laughed cynically.

And that will last until summer break when I park my Honda in Marian's front yard. An hour later, she'll take me to the barn, wiggle her ass when she pulls down her jeans, my pecker will jump to attention, and I'll screw her toenails off.

Enough of this shit! What Michelle doesn't know won't hurt her, and Marian has come to grips with the situation. Time will straighten everything out. Until then, I'm the luckiest guy in the world. Two beautiful girls love me. I'm about to win a national championship, and life doesn't get much better than that.

CHAPTER 67

The University of Michigan kept the game close in the first half, but the Wolverine's physical style of play proved ineffective in the second half. Arkansas, an outstanding free-throw shooting team, gradually pulled away and won the game by twelve points.

The University of Maryland, however, had a tougher time with the University of Indiana, but the Terrapins' superior depth eventually prevailed. The Atlantic Coast Conference champions controlled the last five minutes of the game, won by five points, and set up a battle between two undefeated teams for the National Championship in Memphis, Tennessee.

•   •   •

"There isn't a doubt in my mind this is the best team I've ever coached. You've won thirty-three games in a row. Think about it, gentlemen. Thirty-three teams have tried to take you down and those teams are sitting at home watching *you* on television."

Jamie stared intently at Coach Martin and admired his composure. The man was facing the biggest game of his life, but he seemed relaxed and unfazed by the pressure.

"What can I say that I haven't said before? You're mentally, physically, and tactically prepared." Coach Martin smiled confidently and pointed toward the door. "Hit the court like you own the place, take Maryland's best shot, and make it thirty-four in a row."

Jamie caught glimpses of the crowd as he walked down the narrow corridor leading into Mid-South Coliseum. Coach Martin paused briefly, then raised his right fist and led the Razorbacks into the jampacked arena. The crowd erupted, and the roar was deafening. Jamie's spine tingled. He had never felt such electricity, such emotion in his life.

Maryland fans tried to emulate the Razorback's boisterous welcome, but Arkansas was just across the Mississippi River and Hog fans, by the thousands, had bought tickets, streamed into Mid-South Coliseum, and were giving the good folks from Maryland a down home, country welcome.

Suddenly, Mid-South Coliseum became eerily quiet when the Razorback cheerleaders spread the length of the court, raised their arms, leaned right, and led the Hog call.

Woo, Pig, Sooie echoed through the arena.

Jamie stood erect, pumped, wanting to cry.

•   •   •

"That's some cheer, isn't in Vern?" Stan Attwood asked his colleague.

"It's almost spooky. Look at the Maryland team. They've never heard anything like it."

"Before we go on the air, Vern, what's your prediction?"

"Maryland is a second half team. If Arkansas has a twelve-point lead at the half, which is their norm, the Razorbacks will win. If the game is close, the Terrapins, with their superior depth, will win. The Razorbacks are fun to watch, but my bet is on the Terrapins."

"Arkansas is a tremendous young team, but you're right, fatigue will be a factor in this game. Since the Razorbacks don't have a bench, they won't be able to stop Maryland in the closing minutes of each half."

"I agree, Stan, but stranger things have happened. Ten seconds. Let's go to work."

•   •   •

Terrance Brooks out-jumped Maryland's All-American Center and slapped the opening tip down court. Jamie caught up with the ball, saw a brief opening, popped the net, and drew first blood.

The Terrapins walked the ball down court and patiently passed it around the Arkansas matchup zone, their plan obvious: work the Hogs on defense and systematically wear them down throughout the game. If they fell behind, no big deal. It was all part of the plan.

Lightning quick and red-hot, Jamie repeatedly faked defenders out of their shoes and released quick, smooth bombs that found their target with ease. Throughout the season, Jamie had taken each game in stride, almost stoically, a businesslike approach, talking with his eyes. But this was a unique atmosphere. Each shot produced an excited jump, or a high-five, as the Razorbacks, on schedule, built their usual lead.

The Terrapins, however, did not panic. It was business as usual, nothing fancy, just a continual working of the ball, a methodical and tiring approach, fresh players sitting at the scorer's table, oblivious to the score, having one objective: work the Hogs on defense, wear them down, and destroy their potent offense.

Coach Marvin Adams, however, was doubting his strategy. The Arkansas team was unreal. The quick onslaught had been stopped, but the fourteen-point lead seemed carved in stone. Then, at the seven-minute mark, the incoming tide of players washed it away, subtly at first, then more dramatically, as the Razorback's quick feet became a step slower, and their crisp passes sailed high and off target. When the buzzer sounded ending the first half, Coach Adams glanced at the scoreboard, smiled, and clapped his hands. Down by six, he had found and exploited the Razorbacks' Achilles heel: they were human and capable of tiring.

•   •   •

Jamie knew the Razorbacks had played a near perfect thirteen minutes of basketball, but he also knew the final seven minutes had been a living hell, as the Terrapins, without mercy, worked the Hogs from side to side and systematically wore them out.

Jamie glanced around the room. Except for Terrance Brooks — who was obviously disgusted — his teammates looked spent, out of gas, and exhausted. For the first time all year, a feeling of hopelessness had enveloped the Razorbacks, a feeling that said, "We're going to lose, and there's not a damned thing we can do to stop it."

Jamie stood, stretched, and smiled drolly at Terrance Brooks. Terrance winked, nodded his head, and elbowed Dalton Hilliard. Both young men scrambled to their feet. Within seconds, everyone was standing, giving Coach Martin their undivided attention.

Howard Martin was awed.

The gentle arrogance of Jamie Williams had once again impacted his team. An ability to draw from some inner force, to reach deep inside themselves and stand, had taken place because Jamie Williams had willed it. Jamie was cocky — in many ways a prima donna — but he was a leader of men, and this game belonged to him.

•   •   •

Neutral observers loved the 1971 National Championship game, but for fans on both sides, it was a gut-wrenching ordeal. Maryland could not take the lead, and Arkansas could not pull away. To those privileged to watch the two elite teams compete in Mid-South Coliseum, there was no doubt the game would go down to the wire.

Playing the best game of his career, Jamie changed roles with each possession. On one possession, he was a scorer, putting up a long jumper or penetrating the lane. On the next possession, he was a quarterback, attacking, faking, passing, finding open men, giving them opportunities to score, keeping the Maryland defense off guard and uncertain.

Despite Jamie's soft touch and Terrance Brook's explosive power, the Terrapins followed their exhausting strategy and attacked the Razorbacks with an endless tide of fresh players. With less than a minute to play, Maryland was down by one-point and poised to take the lead.

Coach Adams called timeout and instructed his team to work the clock. There was no way in hell that he would allow Jamie Williams—he *was* a freak—to shoot the basketball again, because as sure as the sun rose in the east and sat in the west, he knew it would go in. Coach Adams decided to win or lose the game with one shot.

Following the timeout, the Terrapins in-bounded the ball and worked it around the perimeter. Uncharacteristically—it may have been fatigue—Jamie lost his footing and fell to the floor. The Terrapin's All-American Guard dribbled toward the basket, sank a ten-foot rainbow over Terrance Brook's outstretched hands, and gave Maryland a one-point lead with eleven seconds left in the game.

Jamie jumped up, formed a "T," and ran to the Razorback bench, disgusted with himself. Coach Martin said, "Forget about it. We have plenty of time." He glanced at the scoreboard, and then said, "Jamie, when you receive the in-bounds pass, push the ball up court, cross the timeline, and call timeout. There'll be some light pressure, but not enough to put you on the free-throw line."

The Terrapins did not make it easy for the Razorbacks by fouling the leading free-throw shooter in the country. They pressured Jamie just enough to eat up the clock. When he crossed the timeline, he called timeout, and walked quickly to the Arkansas bench.

00.07 left.
Maryland 73 – Arkansas 72

The crowd was loud, almost deafening, as Coach Martin, exuding confidence, addressed his team. "Terrance, set up under the goal for a tip-in. Dalton, inbound the ball to Jamie between the circle and mid-court and then head for the corner. Jamie, dribble to the top of the key. If you're double-teamed, pass the ball to Dalton. Make quick, sound decisions, put the ball in the hole, then we'll go home and celebrate."

For a split second, Jamie broke free, but was immediately sandwiched between two defenders. He saw Dalton wide-open in the corner and passed him the ball. Dalton did not hesitate, squared up, and took the shot, but a fast-charging Terrapin tipped the ball as it left his hands.

Jamie chased the loose ball, grabbed it before it rolled out of bounds, turned, faced the goal, and took the shot. The release felt good, but feelings, he knew, were often deceptive. He watched the orange globe, seemingly in slow motion, spiral toward the cylinder. He leaned right, using body-English to help the ball through the hoop, and then took a quick look at the clock. The buzzer sounded and zeroes appeared on the scoreboard. Milliseconds later, the ball sailed through the hoop, hitting nothing but net. An official near the play clenched his fist, raised his hand into the air, and emphatically pressed it down, signaling the shot was good.

Momentarily stunned, Jamie did not move. He just stared at the ball as it bounced harmlessly out of bounds. His teammates, with hands held high, jumped, and formed the number one.

Suddenly, they were upon him, burying him in a mausoleum of flesh. Dead to six years of hard work, rehab and intense pressure, Jamie was raised as the Most Valuable Player in the NCAA Tournament, and a hero of mythical proportions to the people of Arkansas.

Nonplussed, Jamie loved it.

CHAPTER 68

A stiff south wind mussed Michelle's auburn hair as she stood next to Jamie on the front porch of the Martin's sprawling home. There were no "For Sale" signs planted in the yard as there had been the year before. After winning the National Championship, Howard Martin was now the most revered man in Arkansas.

"Do you have to go home today?" Michelle asked.

"Mom would pitch a fit if I didn't show up. The whole family will be there, including Bud, Judith, and Cal-Three. I'll be back in a couple of weeks to start the summer weight program."

"I know you need to spend time with your family."

"It'll go by fast." They held hands, stepped off the porch, and walked to Jamie's Nova. He opened the door, rested his right arm on top of the car, and said, "This has been a special year, hasn't it?"

"The best."

Jamie stared at the cloudless blue sky and shook his head whimsically. "What's left, Michelle?"

"Two years of college and the rest of our lives."

"But how can it get any better?"

"It may not."

"What do you mean?"

"I'm not trying to be clairvoyant, Jamie, but this year was meant to be. After six years of turmoil—wishing, hoping, and waiting—everything came together. You know? Like someone or something said, 'You've had enough setbacks. Make your dreams come true.'"

"It seems that way, doesn't it?"

Jamie scooted beneath the steering wheel, closed the door, and placed his hand on the ignition. Michelle eased her head through the window, kissed him softly, and then pulled away. "Be careful driving home and call me when you get to Benton."

Jamie nodded and turned the ignition. The Nova's dual exhausts roared briefly, then settled to a smooth, resonant idle when he shifted into reverse. "I'll see you in a couple of weeks, Michelle."

"I'll be here."

Jamie backed down the Martin's driveway, feeling ecstatic. The day was warm and the wind blowing through the car felt good as he negotiated the hilly streets of Fayetteville. Ten minutes later, he passed Drake Field on Highway 71, and his exuberance moved to his foot. He pressed the accelerator to the floor, quickly hit eighty-five miles per hour, then let off the gas and listened to the pipes rumble and pop.

Jamie did not think a State Trooper would give him a ticket—he was, after all, a hero of mythical proportions—but he slowed to a sensible speed, laughed at his wit, and smiled with modest conceit.

Michelle is right. This year was meant to be.

He pressed the accelerator to the floor again, passed an old gray-headed man and woman in a battered pickup truck loaded with chickens, then reached for his Johnny Rivers tape, and flew low down Highway 71 toward Mountainburg, a look of satisfaction on his face.

No basketball and no workouts for two weeks.

I can't wait to see Marian.

About the Author

Personal experience and stories from his father and grandfather compelled Frank Heller to write *Gentle Arrogance*. Holding degrees from several schools, including a doctorate, Frank captures the essence of living in the South during the volatile sixties. *Gentle Arrogance* is a must read for every generation.

Note from Frank Heller

Word-of-mouth is crucial for any author to succeed. If you enjoyed *Gentle Arrogance*, please leave a review online—anywhere you are able. Even if it's just a sentence or two. It would make all the difference and would be very much appreciated.

Thanks!
Frank Heller

We hope you enjoyed reading this title from:

www.blackrosewriting.com

Subscribe to our mailing list – *The Rosevine* – and receive **FREE** books, daily
deals, and stay current with news about upcoming
releases and our hottest authors.
Scan the QR code below to sign up.

Already a subscriber? Please accept a sincere thank you for being a fan of
Black Rose Writing authors.

View other Black Rose Writing titles at
www.blackrosewriting.com/books and use promo code
PRINT to receive a **20% discount** when purchasing.